Praise for *Roderick*:

"The narrative is full of the most amazing dialogue,
interlarded with mathematical games, riddles and
philosophical conundrums . . . the work is a
masterpiece . . . it is a treatise on the whole theme
of mechanical men, automatons and machine
intelligence—the ultimate robot novel." David
Pringle, *Science Fiction: the 100 Best Novels*.

John Sladek was born in Iowa in 1937. With such brilliant tours-de-force as *The Reproductive System*, *The Müller-Fokker Effect*, and *Tik-Tok*, he has established a reputation as one of the leading writers of satirical SF.

JOHN SLADEK
RODERICK

Carroll & Graf Publishers, Inc.
New York

Copyright © 1980 by John Sladek

First published in Great Britain in 1980

First Carroll & Graf edition 1987

Reprinted by arrangement with Richard Curtis Associates, Inc.

Carroll & Graf Publishers, Inc.
260 Fifth Avenue
New York, NY 10001

ISBN: 0-88184-325-3

Manufactured in the United States of America

For Pamela Sladek

THANKS
To Alan Jones of North East London Polytechnic, who
helped me program a plot. Thanks to Jasia Reichardt, for
conversations about robots, and especially for writing her
excellent *Robots: Fact, Fiction and Prediction* (London: Thames
& Hudson, 1978).

Special thanks to Ivan Klingels, without whose loan of an
office for an entire year, this book would not have been
written.

I'm grateful to the publisher for permission to quote from
the English translation of 'Les Fenêtres' from *Calligrammes*
by Guillaume Apollinaire © Editions Gallimard 1925.

Book One

I

There is no security against the ultimate development of mechanical consciousness, in the fact of machines possessing little consciousness now. A mollusc has not much consciousness. Reflect upon the extraordinary advance which machines have made in the last few hundred years, and note how slowly the animal and vegetable kingdoms are advancing.

Samuel Butler, *Erewhon*

JEAN HARLOW (*as Kitty Packard*): I read this book ... the man says machines are going to take over every profession!
MARIE DRESSLER (*as Carlotta Vance, looks her over*): You've got nothing to worry about, my dear.

from *Dinner at Eight*

Spring came to the University of Minnetonka in the form of a midnight blizzard, spraying snow the length and breadth of the great campus, annoying people from Faculty Hill clear down to Fraternity Row.

At the meeting of the Ibsen Club a very old, tiresome guest began explaining that Boreas was – hee hee! – probably trying to get into the concrete barns of the Agricultural Science Department and impregnate the mares – oho! – only these days one supposed it was all done by machine, eh? Frozen sperm from some dead stallion, eh? Dispensed by some machine colder and faster and more ruthless than poor old Boreas – hee hee! – and so on, getting further and further from their discussion of Nora Helmer.

At home Dr Helen Boag, Dean of Persons, awoke and called out to Harry, her second husband: 'Harry, what's it? What's it? That noise?' But the lump of bedclothes beside her was Dave, her third. And the wind had already moved on.

At the University Health Service a yawning intern used a tongue depressor to mark his place in *The Heart of the Matter*

('Somewhere far away he thought he heard the sounds of pain.') and decided to order more flu vaccine – a wind like that. He scooted in his swivel chair to the console of the inventory computer and began playing its keys. In no time at all he was able to order three trillion – oops, thousand, 3,000 doxes – doses, damnit, doses!

Someone at Digamma Upsilon Nu invited the wind to blow, blow and crack its nuts, and laughed hard enough to spill more beer over the already damp player piano where the brothers had gathered to hoist mugs and sing 'Roll Me Over', their voices straining to compete with the mad howl outside. Indeed, they could hardly be heard by the lone brother who had crept upstairs to sit holding a loaded revolver and considering his Grade Point Average. The system, Christ it was so unfair, so damned unfair, getting graded by computers and all it was, it was degrading ha ha some joke some life, even if you get your horoscope done it's all computers . . .

Even while he was hurriedly putting the gun away, the gust that had knocked at his window (sounding like a knock at the door) was far away, trying other doors and windows . . .

It whistled through the spire of the Wee Interdenominational Kirk O' Th' Campus, where there were no great organ pipes to thrill in response – pipes, organ and even organist having all been replaced by a single modest machine which (if Pastor Bean ever managed to get it programmed) would come to life only to sing the praises of the Wee Interdenominational God, on cue, by the numbers.

Near the Kirk lay a mutilated body; the wind covered her decently with snow to await the statistical work of the police computer and hurled on, roaring down the Mall, ripping at an old ballet poster, upsetting a litter basket – finally shrieking past the Computer Science building. There the wind pushed Dr Fong firmly against the door he was trying to pull.

'Here, let me help.' He heard the voice before he could make out the figure, a badly-handled marionette being pushed along on its toes. Rogers.

'Oh, it's you.' He stood back, holding his Russian hat in place with both hands, while Professor Rogers wrestled with the door. Snow turned the air around them into a flicker of random dots; wind provided the white noise.

Inside, the two men stopped to stamp their feet and remove steamed glasses. 'It's you,' Fong said again. 'At this time of night?'

'I couldn't sleep. Thinking about ... oh, every damn thing. About the viability ...' Rogers's face held no further explanation. Indeed, without the tinted glasses, his face was simply long and blank, a peanut shell. Nothing in it but pock marks.

'You wanted to look over the project?'

'I wanted to explore – acceptability levels.'

'Whats?'

'To probe the infrastructure of your little group, you see? To look for a catalysable system-oriented – see I knew either you or your assistant would be here tonight ...'

'You mean Dan? He's here practically all the time, these days. But I wouldn't exactly call him my assistant.'

'Sure.'

'More a colleague.'

'Sure, sure.'

'I mean it. Just because he has no formal qualif – look, if anything, Roderick's more his work than mine.'

'His brainchild?'

'Jesus.' Fong sighed. 'Let's go down there. I'll show you around.'

'I don't want to see around, Lee. I want a heart-to-heart rap about this.'

Fong thought about it while he used his pass card to unlock the inner doors and call the elevator. As they descended, invisible violins took up 'Lullaby of Broadway'. 'Okay, you're worried, is that it? You think that, uh, just because NASA pulled the pin on us, we're too hot to handle. Right?'

Rogers broke off humming. 'Did I say anything? Christ, Lee, just because I'm a sociologist doesn't automatically make me an imbecile. I don't need NASA or anybody else to tell me what to think. I can judge this thing on its own merits.'

'Yeah? Then why do you seem worried? What's the problem?'

'Problem?' The doors parted. Rogers remained behind in

the elevator a moment, list-ning to the lull-a-by of old, Broad, way. 'No problem, Lee.' It was not until they were in Fong's shabby little office, sitting in a pair of Morris chairs and sipping instant coffee, that he said: 'Only why *did* NASA pull out of this?'

'Internal troubles, they had some kind of – some kind of rip-off, I think. I don't know the whole story.'

'No? Okay, lay out what you have.'

Fong cleared his throat. 'You won't believe it. I don't hardly believe it myself, it's like a nightmare or something, it's –'

'Why not let me judge for myself? Listen, Lee, I'm on your side. But I mean give me something I can run with, something I can tell the committee. Okay?'

Fong nodded. 'Okay, listen. It all started four years ago, when we got the original contract. NASA wanted us to develop a – I guess you could call it a dog.'

'A dog.' Rogers sat sideways in his chair and made himself comfortable.

'At least that's what we called it, Project Rover. Simple enough, a straightforward robot retriever. A cheap, durable intelligence to fit into their Venus landing vehicle, to do routine jobs. A dog.'

'But where does Roderick –'

'Wait. The way we saw it, a second-rate place like this was lucky to get any NASA contract. We're second-rate, I admit it. Or we were. I mean with our salary structure, how can we compete with the big boys at –'

'Sure, sure. So you got the contract.'

'Yeah, and then this NASA official flew in from Houston to go over the details. We had lunch at the Faculty Club.'

'Lunch.' Rogers started tapping his foot on air.

'And that's where it starts getting unbelievable.'

'Stonecraft's the name, Avrel Stonecraft, but just call me Stoney. I'll be your liaison man at NASA, so you'll be callin' me, sho' nuff. Ever'thing goes through me, got that?' That was over the crab cocktail.

Over the chicken Kiev: 'Listen, Lee, I ain't just here to beat my gums over this piss-ass little Project Rover. We got something a whole lot more interesting in mind. In fact this Rover stuff is just a cover for the real project. Because the real project has got to be kept ab-so-lutely secret. What NASA really wants from you – are you ready? – is a *real* robot.'

'A what?'

'A real, complete, functioning artificial man. It don't matter what he looks like, a course. I mean, a space robot don't have to win no beauty contests. But he's gotta have a real human brain, you with me so far?'

'I – yes, I think so.'

'Fine, now we'll talk details later, but let me say right now you can write your own ticket on this. You need personnel, equipment, money – you got 'em. Only problem is gonna be security. We're keepin' this one under wraps and I do mean under R–A–P–S. You got that? Because if the opposition ever finds out –'

'You mean Russia or –'

'Russia, my ass, I'm worried about the goddamn Army, I'm worried about the goddamn Department of the Interior. I'm worried about goddamn departments and bureaux we hardly even heard of. Because there's at least a dozen projects just like ours going on right now, and we just *gotta* get there first. Like second is nowhere, you got that?'

'But why? I thought you cooperated with other –'

'Don't you believe it, Lee. This is big politics, I mean *appropriations*. Take the Secret Service for instance. See, they're working on this President robot, to double for him, making speeches, public appearances, that kinda stuff. Now say they perfect the bastard, where does that leave us? I'll tell you, it leaves us standing around with our pricks in our hands and nowhere to put 'em. I mean they'd get all the patents, half a trillion in appropriations, any goddamn thing they want – and we'd get horse-shit, we'd be out of the game. Same if anybody else beats us out.'

'But you think they'd actually spy on us?' Fong whispered.

'Why sure, same as we spy on them. Hell, no need to whisper here, I don't mean *that* kinda spying. I don't mean the old geezer over there's got a radio in his martini olive, nothing like that. Naw, they look for patterns, see? Like the

Army might have their computers go over our purchase orders, phone calls, how many times does X phone Y, shit like that. So we gotta keep a low goddamn profile on this, and I mean low. Can you do that?'

'Well, y –'

'Fine, fine. Don't tell even me. I don't want to know a damn thing, not even the name of the project. Far as I'm concerned – officially – this here is still just Project Rover.'

Over the chocolate mousse, Stoney said: 'I'll give you this list of companies, and I want you to order all your research equipment through them. See, they're dummies. NASA owns 'em, and that helps us disguise your purchases. Cain't afford to tip off the opposition by our purchase orders. I mean if you went and ordered a robot body shell from some outside firm, that's as good as saying, "Looky here, I'm fixin' up a robot". So you order from us, and we fake up a second purchase order makin' it look like – I don't know, a case of nuts and bolts – and ever'thing's still cool, see? You with me?'

Fong was with him, through the meal until, over coffee and Armagnac, Stoney said: 'We'll talk details later. Hell, that's enough business talk for today. Let me show you something, Lee.' He hauled out his billfold and started passing photos across the table. 'What do you think a them cute little devils, eh?'

'Your kids?'

'Ha ha, no, my *planes*. Got me a Curtiss Hawk and a Lockheed Lightnin', completely restored, and now I'm a-workin' on this little baby, my Bell Aerocobra. Boy, you can always recognize this little baby, just looka that nose wheel . . .'

'Warplanes. He collected vintage warplanes, spent all his weekends restoring them and flying them. He said that when he was a kid, he'd cut pictures of these same planes off of Kix boxes, and now here he was collecting the real thing, fifty years old and still a kid. I couldn't believe it, one minute we're talking about NASA backing the most important project in history, and the next moment he's gloating over these pictures of old warplanes. He even, when we said goodbye, he even gave me a thumbs-up sign and said, "Keep 'em flying". Keep 'em flying! I started wondering just what the hell I was getting into there. Thought maybe I was just dealing with a nut, maybe the whole project would just melt down, you know?'

Rogers yawned and looked at his watch. 'And didn't it?'

'Not at first. I got my team together, Dan Sonnenschein, Mary Mendez, Leo Bunsky and Ben Franklin, a few technicians. I went ahead and put through those funny purchase orders to those dummy companies – and it worked! NASA picked up the tab for everything, and we really started to move. Project Roderick, we called it, only of course we had to let on we were just working on Project Rover. We couldn't tell anybody anything, and that was the toughest part, because ... because Christ almighty it was exciting! It was like a dream, like a dream ...'

He re-dreamed it now, the time when Roderick seemed unstoppable, when they'd found themselves solving problems no one else had even posed. He re-lived the high moments: the day Bunsky's Deep Structure babbled out its first genuine sentence on the teleprinter ('Mama am a maam'); Dan's first Introspector, the day it thought (it thought) and therefore it was (it thought). The day his own Face-recognizer, seeing him stick out his tongue, cried ...

He started opening and shutting desk drawers. 'Let me show you something, just let me show you ... here, this, look at this.'

Rogers took the bundle of accordion-folded paper, yellow-edged and dusty. 'What's this?' He read the top page and passed it back. 'What is it?'

'The spelling's all wrong, but that's, it's still intelligent, you can see a living intelligence there, it's, I guess you could call it an essay ... listen, let me read some of it to you:

' "There a like because they both sound like they begin with R. There a like they both have some syllables more than one. There a like because one is like a bird and theres a bird called a secretary and the other is like a furniture and theres a furniture called a secretary too. Or may be they both have quills which are like old pens. May be E. A. Poe wrote one when he sat at the other or is that a like? There both inky. I give up. I give up. There a like because otherwise you wouldnot ask me why. Or there a like because there both in the same riddle –"'

Rogers hung his legs over the arm of the chair and tapped a foot on air. 'Okay, so you had fun working on this.'

'Fun? I – fun? We had four years of hard work, good work but too hard, some of us didn't even make it all the way. But it was going to be worth it, we were getting closer all the time, closer and then ... and now, those maniacs in Houston want us to just ... *stop*. As if you could just stop a thing like this, just forget about it and ... Look, look, here's the damned telex, read it yourself.'

He smoothed out the paper and handed it over.

DR LEE FONG CMPTR SCI DEPT UNIV OF MINNETONKA BE ADVISED ALL FUNDING EX NASA PER PROJECT ROBBER AND/OR ANY OTHER PROJECT YOUR DEPT FROZEN AS OF THIS DATE, PENDING INTERNAL NASA AUDIT. RECALL ALL PURCHASE ORDERS AND CEASE ALL ONGOING OPERATIONS IMMEDIATELY. ADDRESS ALL FUTURE COMMUNICATIONS TO
SECTION OFFICER
R. MASTERSON

'All this Masterson would tell me on the phone was that I couldn't talk to Stonecraft any more, he's suspended. And that their auditors were getting a court order to look over my books. And he practically called me a crook.'

Rogers nodded and tapped. 'Doesn't look good, does it? I really don't see how you can expect the University to foot the bill for your project while you're under a cloud like this. I mean of course you're innocent, probably meaningless to assign guilt labels at all in a multivalent situation like this, okay I can buy that – *but*. But Lee, why don't you just get a good lawyer and ride this thing out? Then when you're cleared – who knows?'

Fong looked at him. 'I don't know what the hell you're talking about, lawyers, why should I get a lawyer? Whole thing's probably a misunderstanding, Stonecraft'll clear it up. All I want is to finish –'

'Sure, sure, you want emergency funding from the U to tide you over, and believe me if it was my decision you'd get the bread. Only the rest of the committee might not see it that way ...' An elaborate shrug, and he was on his feet. 'Good to talk to you, Lee.'

'Wait, you haven't even looked at the lab, don't you want – ?'

'Okay. A tour. Fine, but a quickie. Then I really must . . .'

They left, closing the anonymous ivory-coloured door on the stuffy little room where nothing moved, or almost nothing: a telex message lay on the desk, trying to gather itself once more into the crumpled form of the inside of Dr Fong's fist, as though it would remember bafflement and anger at its reception, as it remembered (with a misprint) the confusion at its transmission.

The four young accountants might have been four high-school boys, trashing Stonecraft's office just for fun. And it *was* fun, one of them realized, catching sight of his own gleeful face reflected in a picture glass, as he passed to dump another armload of files on the floor.

'This is kinda fun, you know?'

'Yeah, only don't let Masterson see you standing around looking at pictures. We gotta get the dirt on this sonofabitch before he gets back here.'

'What the hell's this, a bill for a buffalo? And this, for a hurricane? Who the hell buys hurricanes?'

'I got a lot of those funny bills, just put 'em in this pile. Like this one, a Grumman Avenger –'

'You dumb twat, that's an airplane. Let me see those – holy Christ, forty-three thousand for a model – they must be *real* planes! He must be collecting old airplanes!'

'But hey, there must be fifty, a hundred of 'em, look at this, Hellcat, Focke-Wulf –'

'Yeah you Focke-Wulf, hahahaha.'

'I'm serious, Bob, here's a Liberator, a Flying Fortress, a Spitfire, no two Spitfires, a Messerschmidt, Thunderbolt, Zero, Christ he's got a air force here, it's like he's getting ready for World War Two all over again . . .'

'Yeah and look at these repair bills, and this . . . deed to a fucking airfield, what do you think all this adds up to?'

'We'll run it when we get them all. I can tell you right now where the fucking money came from, only question is how did he rip it off?'

Masterson was on the telephone in the outer office; they could hear every roar: 'I don't care where he is, I want him found. I want him back here now ... Well you just make sure he does. I don't care if you have to call out the Air Force and force him down, just don't let him turn up missing across the border ... He'll find out when he gets ... you do what? Yas, yas, I'm holding ...'

One of the accountants nudged another and giggled. 'Old Masterson wants his damn job, that's what it's all about.'

'Looks like he's got it, lookit all this shit, man, must be over eight figures – Kevin, you gettin' anywhere with your stuff?'

'I got it, all right. Simple, he just funnelled the money through this hick university up north, into these here dummy companies. I mean, look at these names, Rockskill Industries, Pebblework Electronics, Bouldersmith Inc – who the hell's supposed to be fooled by names like that?'

'Hey you twat, them files are marked TOP SECRET, you got a clearance?'

'Bullshit, man, Stonecraft never had no clearance himself, this is all faked up. See, he got this university to buy stuff from these companies – owned by him – at about ten times market value, only we picked up the tab. Look, double-billing, I mean that's really an old trick, I mean that's really old, man ...'

'How did he get away with it? Didn't this university look at their own bills? SOP, Bob.'

'That's just it, he looked over all the damn universities till he found this jerkwater outfit using an old computer accounting system, shoulda been scrapped years ago. There, he seen his chance and took it.'

Masterson swore next door, and the four fell silent, but only for a moment.

'Gotta admire the old bugger, in a way. He bitched our computer too, so it passed stuff over to the next audit, and then the next – looks like two, three billion here never audited. Bob, what you got there?'

'Damned if I know. Notes about a "secret robot project", how he's putting these hick university guys to work on – you know, I think *this* was his blind. If the hicks thought it was secret stuff, they sure as hell wouldn't ask embarrassing questions.'

'Robots, sheeit! You mean he told 'em NASA was making robots? Sheeit!'

'Gotta admire the old bugger. Sure knew how to keep everything in the air, all right.'

Masterson came in cursing and laughing quietly. 'Too bad he didn't keep himself in the fucking air, though, ain't it? Know what he done? Soon as he heard we were on to him, he went and suicided on us. Crashed his fucking plane and left us to clear up his shit. *Shit!*' He kicked the empty file cabinet, walked up and down the room, and then stood, fists on hips, staring at the pictures on Stonecraft's wall.

'I don't know, you give your fucking life to try to build something, and all the time you got some fuckhead like this tearin' it all down. Look, there's a picture of Luke Draeger, remember him?' None of them did. 'I seen him walk on the Moon, boys, *I helped put him there.* Or was it Mars? Anyways, NASA still means something to some of us. It means – it means – billowing exhaust clouds catching the first light of dawn, a silver needle rising, reaching for the fucking stars! The puny crittur we call Man setting out to conquer the sky, to rendezvous with his Eternal Destiny! Call me a dreamer, boys, but I see Man leaping out from this little planet of ours, to the Moon, to the planets, to our neighbouring stars and finally beyond, to the infinite reaches of dark promise beyond – into the cocksucking Unknown!' He turned to face them. 'So that's why we're gonna bury this, boys. To protect NASA. To protect the destiny of the human race, our inheritance in the Universe. Bury it, boys. Deep.'

'Yeah, but we got the dirt on this old –'

'Forget it. Make out a confidential report for all heads of departments, but keep it in the family. Bury and forget, for NASA's sake.' Bob handed him the robot notes and he started reading them, as he talked. 'I mean otherwise how's it gonna look for us? Being ripped off by some dumb asshole who blows the whole wad on old planes, how's that gonna look? Congress heard about this they'd shut us down so fast – robots, huh? Maybe I better wire the Orinoco Institute about this, have 'em drop in on this University of Minnehaha. Them

Orinoco eggheads collect robots just like this dirty mother-fucker collected flying trash. I recollect they got a standing memo about reporting attempts to make robots.'

'Yes sir, but how can we keep it in the family if we go telling the Orinoco Inst – ?'

'You let me handle that, junior. All they care about is in this here batch of notes – no need to tell 'em any financial details.' His hand shook as he turned a page. 'Don't know how we're gonna clean up this mess, get rid of them old planes and make it all look good, but that's just what we're gonna do. So get to work, boys. Any questions?'

'Yes sir. Okay if we have Stonecraft sell the old planes to a NASA subsidiary at scrap value and then auction –'

'Sell 'em, burn 'em, do what you like. Keep 'em flying, I don't care.'

'Sir?'

'His last words on the radio, they tell me. "Keep 'em flying." Just before he piled his old Belaire Something-or-other into a mountain in Colorado. If he was alive, I'd kill the sonofabitch myself.' Masterson sat down at the telex keyboard. The boys exchanged winks.

'Sir, I thought Belaire was an old car, hahahaha.'

'Just shut up and move your ass! I gotta send two wires, and I don't want to make no mistakes.'

Kevin made an invoice into a paper airplane and sailed it over to Bob. 'Funny thing, though, it was a computer error that put us wise to old Stonecraft in the first place.'

The conference room was full of pipe smoke.

'We'll have to send someone, of course.'

'Of course. To check it out. Though –'

'Exactly. Minnetonka has a point oh three, not much likelihood of –'

'Exactly.'

The telex message passed from one liver-spotted hand to another. 'Still, remember St Petersburg? Point oh oh seven only, yet look what turned up. We'd best be prepared –'

'For a revised scenario? Of course. We'll do all the usual extrapolations, based on personnel information –'

'Which is never up-to-date, remember.'

'Exactly. In the last analysis –'

'No matter how good our figures are, we have to –'

'Send someone. Precisely.'

Someone sighed, sending pipe smoke scudding across the page.

'Someone from the agency?'

'Naturally. Who else could we use? And they do get the goods.'

Another sigh. 'But the way they get them – do they have to – ?'

'You know they do. We've worked that out in all three scenarios, in all eight modes. To six significant figures.'

'But our assumptions –'

'Are all we have. In the last analysis.'

'Undeniably. So we send someone.'

'Of course.'

The ivory-coloured door swung open, admitting Rogers, Fong and a breeze that disturbed the wrinkled paper on the desk.

'... can see you're disappointed, okay but let me explain, let me just – five minutes, you can spare that?'

'Nearly three a.m., Lee, why don't we call it a day?'

'No listen I'll lend you a book, it'll help you understand. It's here somewhere, just sit down a minute, while I ... *Learning Systems* it's called, learning systems, you have to know something about them otherwise how can you explain things to your committee?'

Rogers sat sideways in the armchair again, preparing to tap his foot on air. The slow smile opening on his Mr Peanut face might have been a sneer. 'Not *my* committee, Lee. Hell, I'm only one of twenty-four members. Dr Boag has the chair. And I ought to warn you, there's plenty of hostility there. Not many committee members are as open-minded as I am about this, ahm, this artificial intelligence. Frankly, one or two think it's faintly blasphemous – and quite a few more think it's a waste of time.' The smile widened. 'Can't say I'm in a position to enlighten them, either.'

'Sure, that's why I ... here somewhere ...' Fong finished running his thumb along the books on his shelves and started searching through an untidy pile on his desk. 'Because I know they're hostile, but the committee's our only chance. And you, sometimes I think you're our only chance with the committee. At least you're the only one interested enough to come here and look at ... at what we're trying to do.' He stopped to look at Rogers's tapping foot. 'You are interested, a little?'

'Gooood niiight bayyy – sorry, can't get the damn tune out of my head. Interested, Lee? Of course I'm interested – even if I don't see the concrete results, I feel, I *sense* a quality here, how to describe it, an air of imminent discovery. I've got faith in your little project, I think it has tremendous possibilities. I was just saying so today – yesterday, I mean – to one of your colleagues, Ben Franklin.'

'You know Ben?'

'We play the occasional game of handball, and I try to pick his brain – you see, I *am* interested – and in fact it was Ben who suggested I might drop over and talk to you some time. You or whoever was here.'

'And tour the lab?' Fong let the other armchair take his weight. 'Look, I know it was a disappointment to you, I guess you were expecting more of a, a show.'

The smile again, and Rogers looked away. 'Well, can't say I was very impressed. I mean, all I could see was this skinny kid in a dirty t-shirt, sitting there in this glass box pushing buttons, like –'

'I tried to explain, Dan's just doing some delicate on-line programming, he –'

'Yeah, well, too bad he couldn't stop and talk for a minute. I mean just sitting there like a disc jockey or some, like that pope whatsit in the Francis Bacon painting, can't say that impressed me, no. As for the rest, a lot of computers and screens and things, I could see those anywhere, and what are they supposed to mean to a layman? I expected – I don't know –'

'You wanted a steel man with eyes lighting up? "Yes Master?", that kind of robot? Listen, Roderick's not like that. He's not, he doesn't even have a body, not yet, he's just, he's a learning system – *where is that goddamned book?* I know I had it ... A learning system isn't a thing, maybe we shouldn't even call him a robot, he's more of a, he's like a *mind*. I guess you could call him an artificial mind.'

Rogers looked at the ceiling, revealing more pock marks under his chin. Now the smile was an open sneer. 'I didn't know you hard-science men played with words like that. The mind: the ghost in the machine, not exactly the stuff of hard science, is it? I mean, am I supposed to tell the committee I came to see the machine and all you could show me was the ghost?'

'Roderick's no ghost, he's real enough but he's, the money ran out before we could build his body and get him ready for – but listen, we've got a kind of makeshift body I could show you, something like the Stanford Shakey only it's still dead, he's not –'

'What makes you think I'm so goddamned interested in bodies, all of a sudden? Dead machines, dead – I'm not – that's not what I –'

'And even then when he's in his body he won't do much for a while, he'll be like a helpless baby at first. See that essay I showed you, Roderick didn't write that, he –'

'What the hell here?'

'No, that was written by a computer using a model of just part of his, part of a learning system. See, we grow it to maturity on its own, each part. That was linguistic analogy, we grew it to – if I could only find that book, I could –'

'Forget about the damned book. I already have a book Ben loaned me, I didn't come down here to look at dead machinery and borrow a book. I came to find out what makes you tick.'

'Me?'

'You, Dan Sonnenschein in there in his glass box, all of you. Christ, I'm not a cybernetician, I'm a sociologist. What really interests me is not this *thing*, this so-called *mind*, it's *your* minds. Your motivation.'

'My motivation?'

Rogers adjusted his glasses and suddenly looked professorial. 'You all seem highly motivated to pursue this, ahm, this Frankensteinian goal, shall we say? But just what is the nature of your commitment?'

'What?'

'I want to elicit a hard-edge definition here of your total commitment. Of your motivational *Gestalt*, if that doesn't sound too pompous. Why do you believe you can succeed where others have failed? Why is it important that you succeed – important to you, that is. What's your – gut reaction to all this? And why do *you* feel I should get the committee to vote for it?'

'This is silly, my feelings have nothing to do with –'

'So you feel, anyway. You feel you're only seeking after objective truth here, right? But that too is only a feeling. I'm trying to help you, Lee, but I need something to run with. Not just dead machines, but tangible motivations.'

'Well ... what we're doing is important. And it's never been done before. And it works. Isn't that enough?'

Rogers grinned. 'Don't get me wrong, I respect the utilitarian ethic as much as the next guy. Gosh, science is swell, and all that. If it works, do it, and all that. But it's not really enough, is it? What about the social impact of your work? Do we really need robots at all? Are they a good thing for society? I don't believe you've really thought through the implications there, Lee. Then there's the effect *on you* – the well-known observer effect.'

'That's not what it –'

'No, you've had your say, how about letting me have mine? How does it affect you, playing God like this – creating man all over again? How does it make you feel? Touch of *hubris*? More than a touch of arrogance, I'll bet.'

'Arrogance? Just because I said it's important? Damn it, it *is* important, if we didn't believe that why would we be working on it? Roderick's important, a model of human learning –'

'Take it easy now, Lee. Remember, I'm on your side. I just want to know how it feels, playing God – sorry, but there's no other word for it, is there? Playing God, how does it feel?'

Fong opened his mouth and took a few deep breaths before replying. 'I wouldn't know. Not unless God's got a bad stomach. Got a bleeding ulcer myself – I *feel* that, all right.'

'I'm s –'

'With Leo Bunsky it was his heart. Just worn out, he should have retired years ago. Finally had to quit, but you

26

should have seen him, dragging himself in to work with his legs all swollen up like elephantiasis – maybe you should have asked *him* how it felt.'

'Let's be fair now, Lee, I –'

'Too late now, he's dead. And Mary Mendez, she's as good as dead. Started working eighty hours at a stretch, piled up her car one night on the way home. Now she's over there in the Health Service ward where they feed her and change her diapers – and she doesn't feel a damned thing.'

'No, listen, this is tragic of course, but it's got nothing to do with –'

'What we feel? Sure it does, it's all you want, right? The grass-roots feelings, the opinion sample. The others are pretty much okay, as far as I know, but you could always ask them. Only Dan Sonnenschein, he's started living in the lab, eating and sleeping in there – *when* he eats, *when* he sleeps – so he can keep on, pushing Roderick through one more test, just one more before they take it all away from us. Dan doesn't have time to feel.'

'Now take it easy, I know you all work hard, that's not –'

'What the hell are we supposed to feel? Arrogant? With the whole thing, our work for four years, washed out by some NASA bureaucrat? With the whole thing up before you and your committee of boneheads, all ready to pull the rug out from under us? That doesn't make me feel arrogant at all. I feel like crawling and begging for another chance, just enough money for a few more months, weeks even – only the trouble is, it wouldn't do a damned bit of good. Would it?'

'I'm on your side, Lee, believe me. I've got faith in –'

'Why don't you go away? I don't know what you want here, but we haven't got it. Go on back to your opinion polls and your charts, your showing how many people brush their teeth before they make love, how many sports fans voted for Nixon. Social science, you call *that* science! Christ, what do you think? Science is some kind of opinion poll too?'

Rogers stood up. 'I'm not sure I like that imputation. Okay, it's late, you're upset. But –'

'You just came to check the trend, right? Science is just like any other damned opinion poll, right? How many think

27

Jupiter has moons? You think Galileo took a damned straw vote on it? Think he worked it up in a few histograms, tested the market reaction? Damn you, certain things are true, certain things are worth finding out, and it doesn't matter what you or I or Dan or anybody else – So just go away, will you? Just go and, and vote the way *you* feel, and to hell with your committee and to hell with you!'

Rogers fumbled for the door-handle behind him. His smile was pulling slightly to one side. 'You're overwrought, tired. Maybe we can rap again some time, before the committee meeting. Some time when you're more yourself.' But he couldn't resist an exit: 'Some time when you're not Galileo, I mean.'

The door was already closed when Fong's bottle of Quink crashed against it. He sat quietly for some time, staring at the Permanent Blue splash from which a few dribbles worked their way down. A shape like that could be anything. Could be the silhouette of an old Bell transistor.

Before dawn the blizzard blew itself away. One or two constellations put in a brief appearance in the fading sky, though of course there was no helmsman on the stiff white sea below who could name them. The star-gazing κυβερνήτης had vanished from the earth, leaving only his name to be derived from Greek into *cybernetics* and from Latin into a name for petty State officials. Computers steered ships and charted invisible stars, while men had grown so unused to looking at the sky that fourteen hundred citizens each year mistook Venus (rising now naked from the white foam) for a flying saucer.

2

Men will live according to Nature since in most respects they are puppets, yet having a small part in the truth.

Plato, *Laws*

49 GOROD
'A different black, and a different ping ...'

RESET. 50 GOROD
'Okay. Okay Dan, I've got it now. It's a face, a face only with nobody inside. Is that possible? ... Well, well, a face. What's this in back, a string? Does it control – see I thought for a minute it was like another string puppet like you showed me last time only this is a loop – self-control? I don't get it, could you turn it around again? Okay, I give up. A face with a loop of string in back, right? No answer ... Why don't you answer me? No answer ... I could give myself no answer, that's no answer. Neither is that. Neither is that ...'

RESET. 51 GOROD
'... face with nobody inside. The eyes are just holes! If I had a face like this I'd cut my throat. If I had a throat ...'

RESET. 52 GOROD
'Okay, the face. Whatever it is, I call it a face. White and black, mostly white. Hole-eyes. A black nose. The nose looks like a black ping-pong ball, does that make sense? Come to think of it, the ears – if they're ears – on top look like two ping-pong paddles, also black. I call them Ping and Pong, and one day they were walking through the deep dark forest and ...'

RESET. 53 GOROD
'... But I don't have a throat or anything because I'm not real, I'm just a, what you called a data construct, a, something that's not even any place, a rough sketch you said, you could erase me any time. So this is like my face, nobody in-

side. Nobody by himself. He's forgotten that he's forgotten. Looking out these empty hole-eyes at the emptiness outside, there's no, no ...'

RESET. 54 GOROD

'... when you told me this person Skinner, what he did with pigeons, taught them to play ping-pong, remember? And I asked you what playing was? If they make you do it, is it playing? And you said ...'

RESET. 55 GOROD

'Because conditioning leads to self-control, right? That's the goal we're ... the ping we're ponging towards, only only only how do I get self-control without a self? Otherwise it's just a pigeon hitting the old ball out into the darkness, over and over and it never comes back ... You don't answer me, Dan. Okay, that's because I've conditioned you not to answer. You're the string puppet and I make all the decigeons. Decisions. That's what I said. And that's what I said. And that ...'

3939 INTROSP TEST SW   ENDS

Woopa! Dr Fred McGuffey's sneeze went to join the Brownian dance of dust-motes in a sunbeam.

'Pardod be. I seeb to be catchigg this flu bug that's goigg aroudd. The Sprigg, you see, briggs all thiggs to life. The great Ptoleby called it the begiddigg of the Sud's life cycle. *Quote*, Id all creatures, the earliest stages, like the Sprigg, have a larger share of boisture add are ted-der add still delicate, *udquote*.' He blew his nose mightily. 'Today is the first day of Spring. Now who can tell us what that means?'

No hands went up; they were as sullen and silent as so many Mafia victims (Nobody knew nuttin'). He could talk himself blue in the face, he would never succeed in dinning even the simplest facts of Introductory Astrology into these young – these young robots. Day-dreaming girls who never heard the questions. Sneering boys who'd only enrolled in his class to grab an easy three credits. At times like these (10:48 and three seconds by Dr Fred's pocket watch) he wondered if he hadn't been born with a retrograde Mercury or something, talk about a failure to cobbudicate!

He blew his nose again. 'Anyone? The sign of Spring?' He

30

knew what it was: these kids just couldn't think for themselves. Couldn't add 2 and 2 without the almighty computer. Dr Fred wouldn't touch one of them machines with a ten-foot (3.048 metres, he recalled) pole. No sir, he worked every calculation out on paper for himself, so he could see what he was doing and have the satisfaction of doing it. Quality horoscopes with a human touch. Let all these young upstart astrologers fiddle with their computers – you couldn't hardly call that astrology at all! No sir, when Dr Fred erected a horoscope, people knew it came from a human brain, and not from a doggone tinkertoy machine!

'Aries,' he said, putting disgust into it. 'The Ram. I see I'd better go over this again on the board. Now the ecliptic . . .' One young fool had actually asked him if *Ram* stood for Random Access Memory, like in a computer. Oh, these cybernetics boys had indoctrinated the young, all right. They would have plenty to answer for, come Judgement Day (Dr Fred had also calculated its date). Like that bunch over at the Computer Science Building now – mostly foreigners, he noticed – actually asking the University to give them money for 'artificial intelligence research'. Artificial fiddlesticks! Fred McGuffey, D.F.Astrol.S., had not lived seventy-odd years, most of them as a practising astrologer and roofing contractor, without learning to smell a *rat*, artificial or otherwise. A robot, that's what they were building in their infernal labs, a robot! Could anyone imagine a more ignoble work for the mind of man? No one could. Why couldn't they work on something worth while – cancer cures, a plan for lowering taxes – anything was better than this. But no. No, all they could think of was making a tin man go clanking up and down the halls of this institution of so-called higher learning! Over his dead body. This term Fred had a seat on the Emergency Finance Committee. By jing, this term they could expect a scrap! Yes sir, yes sir . . .

'Sir, sir?' The raised hand belonged to Lyle Tate, a young smart-alec with a hideous birthmark, mentality to match. Sniping, always sniping. 'Sir, how come this Ptolemy doesn't mention the Southern hemisphere? Because down there Aries can't be a sign of *Spring* exactly, can it? Becau –'

'The great, the great Ptolemy, true, says nothing of the

31

Southern hemisphere.' Dr Fred coughed. 'Why? *Because it's not important.*'

'But –'

'Kindly let me finish? You see, all great civilizations began North of the Equator. Babylon, Egypt, China, India, Aztec Mexico, Rome – all Northern places. I'm glad you brought this up, Lyle, because –'

But the bell prevented further development of this, Dr Fred's favourite theory: that Northernness was a necessary precondition of civilization. The cause, he felt, was magnetism: just being closer to the North Pole seemed somehow to elevate human brain waves to produce higher thoughts. Without this magnetic boost, man remained primitive and uncreative. Thus the Southern hemisphere produced crude mud huts instead of great cathedrals; witch doctors instead of penicillin; wooden gods instead of philosophy; cannibals instead of vegetarians; boomerangs instead of ICBMs – though perhaps he would not develop his theory quite that far.

'Before you go,' he shouted over the sound of slamming books, 'I have your practice horoscopes marked and corrected here. I'll leave them on the table, you can pick them up on your way out. Not bad, most of them, though I suppose you all ignored my hint and used computers.' He slapped down the pile of papers and buttoned his overcoat, glad as any student to be getting out of here, to be clearing his mental decks for some real action.

Now, on to Disney Hall, to see this Professor Rogers who seemed to think robots were such a grand idea. Like all the other so-called professors around here, Rogers was probably just another brainless young nincompoop with a fancy degree and no experience of life. Dr Fred hadn't lived nearly 915 lunations without learning a few hard facts, and he meant to impart them to this Rogers fellow right now: you can't cram a human brain – the highest form of creation – into a metal box! No sir!

Bill something, his name was, a real jerk, a zero. He sat next to Dora in Intro Astrol, where she'd noticed his notes for the entire hour:

Arsie, the suds cycle

Now he was only following her into the corridor. God, he wanted to talk about his horoscope. What could she do but nod and smile, and meanwhile watch the passing faces hoping to spot a friend? You couldn't just put someone down, even a zero like this.

'Jeez, I failed,' he began. 'An F, and I mean –'

'How could you get an F? We all got Cs, he gave everybody a C. Because we all used computers, what happened to you?'

'I used a computer, too. Jeez, it must of gone wrong or something, look, he changed everything. Like I didn't get a single one of my planets right or nothing – Jeez!' He showed her the birth chart, covered with red marks. 'And here he says "It's very important for the would-be astrologer to be able to erect his own birth chart. Note that your Sun opposes Pluto. With the Moon conjunct Mars in –" Anyway, he says I oughta beware of explosives and accidents.'

'Uh-huh.' She looked away. Little old Dr Fred came out of the classroom and pottered off down the corridor, mumbling to himself.

'Jeez, all that math and stuff, it's not fair.'

'Uh-huh.'

'I mean this is supposed to be a snap course. I'm already flunking Business Appreciation and Applied Ethics from last term, this was my big hope, this and Contemp Humanities. But I mean I'm doing terrible, I'm pulling down the grade point average for the whole fraternity.'

Fraternity. She swallowed a yawn. No one went by but Muza, she wasn't speaking to him, he was another zero. Good-looking guy, but all he did was bellow about political prisoners in his homeland. Big deal, most people couldn't even find Ruritania on a map, he still expected her to stand around while he bellowed bad breath in her face, well no thanks. Thanks but *non merci*. And now Mr Zero here, what was he saying?

'...only pledged me because my old lady's on the faculty, they figured I had to be a brain or something, boy, were they wrong. And otherwise nobody would even notice me because ...'

Because you're a zero. 'I'm thinking of cancelling Intro

Astrol myself. I'm not getting much out of it, with this Dr Fred, he's kind of a, a zero, know what I mean? I mean –'

'All this friggin' math and stuff –'

'The math's easy, only with him that's all it is, I'm not interested in just signs and numbers.' Still no rescuer in sight. 'What I'm interested in, *au fond*, is people. You know?'

He nodded, dull eyes still on his birth chart. 'I might as well give up,' he said. 'I even thought of playing Russian roulette ...'

'Uh-huh.' Wasn't that Allbright by the bulletin board?

'... dead now if I wasn't waiting for my grades in Contemp Humanities, it's like my last chance ...'

She felt like saying something reassuring, a spontaneous Kind Word to buck him up, even for a moment. 'You probably did all right in that, I wouldn't worry. I had it last year, nobody failed. How do you think you did in the final?'

The zero actually grinned. 'Hey, you know I got lucky there on that one question, the one on Tolkien. I didn't even know he was on the syllabus, you know? Only it just so happened I was reading *Lord of the Rings* the week before and –'

Allbright seemed to be alone as he'd been alone at that awful party where she'd caught him stealing books from the host. Of course poets who wore railroad work clothes had a different morality, she realized that now. 'Tolkien? Tolkien was never on the syllab – Look, I've got to go.'

'Wait, sure he was. I remember the question: discuss humour in *Lord of the Rings* comparing Mark Twain and contrasting –'

'Just seen a friend, gotta go. *Auvoir*, uh, Bill.' She took a step towards Allbright and turned back. 'You musta misread that question, you know? It was Ring Lardner.'

And she was gone, her orange coat moving off to become one spot in the jiggling kaleidoscope of coats and caps and mufflers crowding their colours towards the bulletin board. Bill Hannah lost sight of her before he could even ask who wrote *Ring Lardner*. Jeez.

Ben Franklin lit another cigarette and settled back in one of

Fong's creaky Morris chairs. 'Looks like a Daddy Longlegs to me. Sort of. Must have been quite a scrap.'

'Scrap? No, he wasn't even – look, I just lost my temper, that's all. Just got sick and tired of Rogers and his significant questions, that's all. His, always hanging around like some kind of – science groupie.'

'Wish I'd been here, though. Kind of an historic moment. Like Luther flinging his inkpot at the devil, a performance not to be missed.' Ben smoothed his perfectly even moustache and performed a smile. 'Know how you feel, though. Felt like heaving a handball at him yesterday myself, he started all that crap with me. *Hubris*, Christ he can't even pronounce it ... I lent him a book instead, *Learning Systems*. Figured if he could read a little, sort of slip sideways into some kind of understanding of what we're doing here – not that he'll open it. Doubt if he's read anything since his own dissertation, probably had to look up half the words in that.'

Fong's red-rimmed eyes gleamed behind the gleam of his glasses. 'You loaned him that? But I was, I –'

'Your copy, as a matter of fact. I borrowed it last week.'

'But I, if I'd known – this whole scene was pointless, I –'

'Sure.' Ben was studying the door again, readying another perfect, even smile. 'Could be a study for an action painting, too. Probably how the whole thing started, exorcism: take that, Daddy Longlegs! Yes sir, when an irresistible force such as you, meets an old immovable Rogers – but hell, Fong, we needed his vote.'

'We never had it. He's a waste of time. I know the type.'

'Yeah?' Ben murmured something about immovable type getting the ink it deserves, then: 'A bad enemy, though. You know what he'll do, he'll start sneaking around to the rest of the committee, putting in a bad word for us. "Sounding them out", he'll call it, but by the time he gets through –'

'I know, I know. We're done for, aren't we? And there's not a damn thing we can do –'

'Wait, hold on. We've got till next Tuesday, maybe I can talk to a few members. Of course the damn committee's packed with geeks and freaks, but you never can tell ... Look, I've got a list here, let's check 'em off.'

He unfolded a typewritten sheet and spread it on the desk. Fong glanced at it and turned away.

'Don't despair, wait. There's Asperson, Brilling and Dahldahl, think we can count on them, and here's Jane Hannah, ninety years old and talks to herself but she likes underdogs ... Max Poons is neutral, pretty fair for a Goethe scholar, eh? You're not listening. I mean Poons isn't even sure he accepts Newton's laws of optics yet, let alone anything since ... You're not listening.'

'Been up all night, Ben, and I still haven't caught up with these test charts. Some other time?'

'Sure. Sure.' Franklin stood up and zipped his parka, then sat down again. Flicking ash in the direction of the ashtray, he said, 'Real reason I came down is to take Dan to lunch. Heard he's been living in the lab, right? Sleeping there? And eating peanut butter and water?'

'I guess so. Good idea, get him out, walk him around in the fresh air ... He could use a break.'

'Anyway, somebody said it's his birthday.'

'Oh.'

'And anyway, I've got something to celebrate myself. Final decree.'

'What? Oh, uh congrat –'

'She's getting married again, I guess. To a guy named *Dinks*, can you imagine that? Hank Dinks, sounds like a Country Western singer – well, I'd better be going.'

'Okay, see you.'

Ben made no move, except to sprinkle more ash. 'You know, I thought the overworked genius bit went out with napkin-rings.'

'What?'

'I mean, here we are in the age of committee-think and team spirit and Dan goes it alone. I mean, damn it, Fong, he never gives me a damned thing to do around here. I feel like a damned apprentice or something, like he doesn't trust me. Like right now I'm afraid, I'm actually afraid to go in the goddamned lab, it's like an intrusion. He hardly lets me near the equipment, just hands me some crappy little piece of test program to write, I'm supposed to be happy doing what any kid from the business school could do. All I want is some real, real responsibility, is that too much to ask?'

'No, I guess not. But Dan –'

'– doesn't give a shit about team spirit, fine, only where does that leave me? Or you? I feel – talk about Rogers, I'm beginning to feel like a science groupie myself.'

Fong opened a roll of antacid tablets. 'What can I say? It's really his project now, the rest of us are just along for the ride. Nobody planned it like this, it just happens sometimes. A strong idea takes over ...'

'Great, only now that the ride's damn near finished, I've got nothing. Just to go in there and try one of my own ideas once in a while, is that too much to ask? Is it?'

'See you later?'

The inkstained door banged to behind him. Ben Franklin found the men's room and cupped cold water to wash the heat from his face. It was, he liked to think, a nice face, a nice Northern face with blue eyes and an even brow, a straight smile and even a cleft chin. Today it looked wrong: the eyes, the smile, the trim moustache seemed poised, waiting for some expression which had not yet and might never emerge from the emptiness within.

'... right. It's a grab.' Rogers nodded over the phone's mouthpiece. 'Fong more or less admits NASA pulled out because of some swindle. Swindle, that's right. *He* says it's internal to NASA, but you and I know how these things go. You can always get somebody to admit as much of the truth as won't hurt him at the moment, right? ... So I don't know about you, I don't feel much like risking it. Not that I'd accuse Fong of anything, nice guy really, but a little legitimate caution might not be a bad ... right. Right, see you.'

He pushed a button, checked off a name on a list, and pushed another button. 'Dr Tarr, you still there? I've just had Asperson on the other line, sounding him out, him and a few others on the committee, and we think – frankly, we agree something smells about this robot project. But why I called you, I thought maybe you had some little research project of your own lined up, you might put forward as an alternative proposal? I thought so, good, good. Listen, write it up and we'll add it to the agenda. No, perfectly okay. I've been at these committee brawls before, know the infighting techniques you might say, haha . . . No, listen, last Fall we had a last-minute addition to the agenda steered through, it can be done . . . Oh, it was some scheme for sending messages into space, pi . . . no, pee eye, the number. Yeah, and listen, they had plenty of old farts opposing, sitting around cracking jokes about pi in the sky: you wouldn't believe the hostility . . . no but it has to be worth a try, eh? So if I could have your proposal tomorrow, we'll get it printed . . . That's perfectly all right, sure.'

He hung up and noticed the face hanging at the edge of his door, the pouched eyes and red beard. 'Uh, Goun is it? Pretty tied up just now, Goun. Like to see the girl for an appointment?'

The owner of the face stepped in. Dirty jeans, lumberjack boots, mackinaw. 'She's not there. Could you spare me a minute now?'

'Just one, then. And it'll have to wait for this phone call, okay?' He looked up the number of Helen Boag, Dean of Persons, and punched buttons. The haggard eyes watched every move.

'Dr Boag? This is Rogers, over in Disney Hall. Say, I see our committee's in for a rough ride with this Project Roderick thing . . . Yes, the cyber . . . Been allegations of fraud, for one thing. Not that I . . . yes, and I understand Dr Tarr of the Parapsychology Department wants to put up an alternative proposal, so we're caught in the crossfire, you might s . . . Well I know you've got a tight schedule, so thought I'd better warn you . . . Yes, very wise, very wise. Get out of the line of fire altogether, let 'em fight it out themselves, so to sp . . . May just duck out myself, seems the wisest . . . Oh, you're welcome.'

He checked off the name, while the haggard eyes looked up to the picture above his head.

'Like that, Goun? An Allen Jones original litho, I'm kind of pleased with it myself. Hope it doesn't give people the impression I'm some kind of fetishist, or . . . Okay, make it brief?'

'I've got a field philosophy hang-up, sort of, professor.'

'Let's see, you teach one of the seminars – is it Human Use of Media Resources?'

'No. Sociology of Losing.'

'Of course, of course. Haha. Trouble with a big department like this, you lose touch with everybody.' Rogers scratched a pock mark below his ear. 'Go on.'

'The thing is, I'm looking for a more meaningful involvement in the environmental mainstream. I mean, teaching in this kind of informalized stratum is okay, but with these kids, the, the catalyzation potential is already, er, catalyzed. Know what I mean?'

'In a sense. Cultural matrix imprinting getting you down?'

'See, maybe with less older subjects, kids, I could break through some of the urbanized alienation syndrome barriers, the stress, the stre-he-hess –' Suddenly the eyes squeezed forth tears. 'I'm sorry, I'm sorry … sorry …'

'What is it? Goun?'

The shoulders of the mackinaw shook. 'I'm sorry … Been depressed a lot this last year, ever since my sister died … can't stay here knowing … could be one of my students, anybody … his first, she was his first victim and now every time there's another it's like he kills her all over again … This place, this place!'

'Slow down now, Goun, I'm on your side, slow down. Now. What's this about a victim?'

'The … Campus … Ripper. He's done it again, a waitress or something … in the paper. I mean he's still out there, killing and killing and … I … I just want to get away from here, maybe try teaching in a … I don't know, a grade school some place, I don't know …'

When the sobbing stopped, Rogers said quietly, 'You should have come to me before.'

'I tried to, but you were always out or –'

'Yes,' crossing his legs under the desk to allow one foot to tap on air, 'you should have come to me before, we could have rapped, talked this out. Clarified a few teaching concepts.'

That clarification, he explained, ought to involve a thoroughgoing process evolving in context and circumstance, exploring the infrastructure of any classroom situation according to well-defined parameters, without of course rejecting in advance those options which, in a broader perspective, might be seen to underpin any meaningful discussion attempting to cut through the appropriate interface . . . right?'

But even before he could get rid of Goun, Rogers heard someone else in the outer office, sneezing.

PROJECT ROGER, read the sign on the door, hastily stencilled four years before and somehow never corrected. Ben Franklin paused a moment – should he knock? – before using his key-card and entering the darkened room.

A few red jewel-lights shone weakly in the background like older, more distant stars. Somewhat nearer, the glass box drew the eye to its green glow, the aquarium exhibiting in its luminous depths that marine oddity, the face of Dan Sonnenschein.

It was an odd face. Under normal light it reminded some of the younger Updike; *redux* under green light it was nearer the face of Jiminy Cricket.

'Dan?'

'Just a sec.' No warmth in that voice, only a flat command that might have issued from some other exhibition oddity: Donovan's Brain, say . . . Moxon's Master? . . . Ben groped his way towards a chair and a simile . . .

Bacon's Brazen Head, that was it. That mysterious entity that (if it ever existed) used even more mysterious Arab clockwork . . .

'Bacon knew,' he muttered, '. . . secret of the peacock fountain of Al-Jazari . . .'

'What?'

'Nothing. Nothing.'

'Just a sec.' A sec, many secs might tick by on clocks elsewhere, but here time moved in silence and darkness at an unknown speed (secs per sec). He waited as one who has just felt an earth tremor or the kick of an unborn child waits, in darkness and silence for the next, the confirming instance. Time was indivisible, all the silences and uncertainty between the ticks joined up (sec to sec) into one continuum of doubt, reaching back seven centuries to that night when a servant sat waiting for the brass head to speak.

Time is, the servant thought he heard, but waited to be sure. *Time was*, but why wake Friar Bacon for that? *Time is past*, said the grinning brass head, and fell to pieces (or so the servant would report, when he had hidden his hammer and wakened the good Friar).

To be fair, the servant was only following the example of Aquinas, who reasoned (with logic ruthless enough for any machine) that to destroy a thing is to create a possibility: 'If it did already exist, the statue could not come into being,' he wrote. 'Just as affirmation and negation cannot exist simultaneously, so neither can privation and the form ...' It was Aquinas, the Swine of Sicily, waddling on a Paris street, who was accosted by a stranger made entirely of wood, metal, glass, wax and leather – the automaton brought into being (through thirty years' work) by Albertus Magnus. Instantly Aquinas raised his staff and brought about the possibility of another thirty years' work ...

Dr Helen Boag touched the intercom. 'Jim, come in here, will you? And bring the diary.' She unfurled her copy of the *Caribou* and glanced over the headlines:

CAMPUS RIPPER STRIKES AGAIN
Third Body Found

SOCCER SQUAD SHAPES UP
Fergusen Predicts 'Pow Season'

GRADES AT LAST!
Comp Ops Strike Ends

CHESS CMPTR CHEATS IN
IOWA OPEN

BLIZZZARD!
*Park-O-Mat Mangles
Dean's Limo*

Looking up from the last story as Jim came in, she grinned. 'Listen, what day do I have for that Emergency Finance Committee thing?'

'Next Tuesday, ma'am.'

'Scrub it. Just heard terrible whispers, omens of a storm. Fraud, God knows what. The Nibelungen of the Computer

41

Science Department rising up against the pale wraiths of Parapsychology –'

'Ma'am?'

'Skip it, I want out. So what else might I be doing?'

He consulted the leather-bound book. 'How about the Shah of Ruritania's visit? Were you going to deputize –?'

'I'll take it myself. Usual tour of the plant, is it? Lunch at the Faculty Club? Oh, does he have any special dietary –?'

'Yes, ma'am. He, um, he eats peacocks.'

'Yuck. Wouldn't pheasant do?'

'Afraid not. Has to be peacock, says the Consul, served in plumage on gold plate. Some religious thing.'

'The sacrifices I have to make. By the way, I'll need to rent a car that day. Says here mine is the victim of an act of God, guess they have to blame someone. Wonderful, isn't it?'

'Ma'am?'

'Wonderful machine-age we live in. Blizzard blows a pinch of snow into the wrong place, and suddenly this million-dollar Park-O-Mat, the cutting edge of the Future, decides to drop my car seven storeys down an elevator shaft. I remember, when old crippled Jake ran that place, all he ever managed was a dented bumper.'

'Want some coffee, Dr Boag?'

'Wonderful.'

He moved quietly to the outer office, where he copied her instructions from the diary into the computer. It would make every arrangement for the tour. Yet it did not supplant the leather-bound anachronism. Important persons usually keep something unfashionable close at hand, a contrast to their own up-to-the-minute importance: the Victorian foot-man (in a really first-class establishment) was required to put on the powdered wig, gold lace, brocade and buckled shoes of the previous century, while his master wore simple black dinner dress. That same dinner dress would, once it fell out of fashion, provide uniforms for butlers and waiters.

In any (really first-class) office of our century, anachron-isms multiplied. Executives continued to sit at larger and larger desks, at which they wrote less and less with their quaint fountain-pens – finally only their signatures. They required their secretaries to carry shorthand pads (and use them) fifty years after the invention of the dictating machine. They sent one another memos, a century after the invention of the telephone, an instrument which they felt required a secretary to dial, a receptionist to answer, and a special servant in white gloves to clean. Every advance, it seemed, required a step backwards.

By now, the computer threatened this kind of progress. Not only might it sweep away all the paraphernalia of office life – the diaries and memo pads and telephones, the letters and telexes and chequebooks, the adding machines and desks and calendars – it might even sweep away the staff of office servants. In this case, it made an anachronism of not only the leather-bound diary, but of Jim.

Or almost. Jim still had his uses. He finished entering data, washed his hands, and brewed a pot of his excellent coffee.

CAMPUS RIPPER STRIKES AGAIN
Third Body Found

There were pools of coffee all over the story, and Allbright found that brushing them away only smeared the words.

> ... in a snowdrift near the Wee ... eft leg amputated with what the police say could be an electric carv ... no signs of robbery or ra ... Ms Cotterel, 34, was an employee of The Daffy Donut, an off-campus eatery. Manager Darrell Feagh ... a terrible shock to all of us. Jaynice was just not the kind of person this should happen to. '... lice found near the body ... Chief Dobbin would not disclose its title, but stated, 'It was the type of a book a student teacher might have.' This clue may ...

Over his shoulder Dora read the next column:

> by establishing a remote link with its opponent, Maelzel 6.4. Chephren then

43

> instructed the other computer to 'see'
> one of its own pawns as wrongly
> placed, and 'adjust' it. The adjustment
> enabled Chephren to capture the pawn
> and eventually force Maelzel's resig-
> nation. Officials did not at once detect
> the discrepancy, since the game was
> played at computer-blitz speeds ...

'I still don't see how a computer can *cheat*,' she said.

'My dear, the computer can do anything.' He lifted his plastic coffee-cup to eye level. 'This thing leaks.'

'But how –?'

'The computers are turning human, while the humans can't even murder somebody and cut off their leg without using an electric carving knife. Funny thing is, the police will probably have to use their computer to catch him.'

Dora sank back in her chair. '*Au fond*, I think the Campus Ripper is a pretty sick animal.'

'Sure, but what's his game? Sick how? I mean, what's he planning to do with all those left legs? Start an assembly line – or maybe a chorus line?'

Her shoulders moved uneasily inside the orange coat. 'Is that supposed to be funny or something? If you knew this waitress –'

He licked the side of the cup. 'Jaynice? I did know her.'

'No kidding! What, uh, what was she like?'

'Just another human, right off the same old assembly line.' He pencilled ASSEMBLY LINE on the formica table, then started to rub it out. 'Wait a minute now, wait a minute ...'

'If you're going to make sick jokes, guess I'll split.' She made no move.

'Wait a minute, assembly line, chorus line, just let me talk this out ...'

'Let's change the subject,' she said, looking away.

'*Listen I haven't written a fucking poem in three years, will you just shut up and let me at least try this?*'

After a moment she said, 'You don't like women very much, do you?'

'Love 'em, but just listen ... listen, it's, the Rockettes!'

'The whatettes?'

'Before your time, precision high-kicking chorus line. I got to see 'em once, wonderful female robots, never forget 'em. A technological triumph of the flesh. In the flesh. See, they used to build up each movement all along the line, the way Ford built cars.'

'Did you see *The Nutcracker*?'

'Did I –? No, no, I never liked ballet. It's too, the figures are like little separate clockwork toys, spinning by themselves, you can see it's art for the Nineteenth Century. But this, but the Rockettes at Radio City, Christ! Even the name gives you the idea, it's power, see? *Power*. Imagine a radio city anyhow, and female rockets, it's a ... a ... a 1930s science fiction power dream.'

'Like *Metropolis*?'

'Exactly. A radio metropolis, female robot, it's all there, even the big power wheels. And that's the Rockettes, too, all that muscle moving in unison like pistons on one big crankshaft, no wonder people thought Henry Ford was God – he could make people work like that, this one does it and the next one does it and kick and turn, kick, turn, kick-and-turn –'

'*Modern Times*?' she said. 'Though they say Chaplin was overrated –'

'... the basic machine, the basic human machine, there you are, it's nothing but a knee-jerk reflex, no need to be alive even, sheep in the slaughter-house, they lay them all out on a long table and start cutting their throats and they kick! They kick, this one kicks and the next one kicks, and pretty soon they're all kicking up, kicking up, I don't feel so good.'

He jumped up and walked quickly out of the cafeteria, leaving her alone, a small spot of orange among hundreds of spots of colour clustering around white tables that marched out to distant walls whose colour no one ever seemed to notice. She sat listening to the conversations rising through cigarette smoke above the clatter of styrene on melamine, melamine on nybro, nybro on formica:

'Basically I'm a Manichean, only ...'

'... basic Libran personality ...'

'A basically Jungian interpretation of economics ...'

A drama student in black contemplated his Danish roll while his companion said, '... with Tom and Sam Beckett, get it? Get it? An Evening with ...' At the next table someone opened a paperback of Kierkegaard and bit into an apple; at the next, two future engineers stopped arguing about butterfly catastrophes to peer into their sandwiches.

The boy in the yellow sweatshirt looked up at the door, then down at his melamine plate of goulash, saying:

'Maybe we're all tokens of a type, if you can dig that.'

'I can dig it, sure, but what type?'

'The tokens never find out ... Hey, isn't that Sandy?'

The view was obscured by a fat figure with a full beard, who thumped down his tray with the declaration: 'Ruritania! Don't tell *me* about Ruritania, man ...'

Beyond him a face bright with acne emitted a groan: '*My* father? My father wanted me to be a goddamn cetologist, how do you like that?'

The drama student hoisted his Danish roll as though it really were a prop skull (and as though anyone were watching him) unaware that behind him the girl in the ski sweater was stealing his scene:

'Go ahead and sign it,' she said to someone grovelling before her plaster-coated leg. 'Oney just your name, nothing dirty. I awready had some smartass put "Ben Franklin", I hadda scratch it out.'

A shrill voice at her elbow cried: 'Jungian economics? Hahahaha, what the hell did Jung ever know about money?'

'Well he *was* Swiss ...'

The Manichee glanced over, ready to dispute it, while at his own table the full beard reported on Ruritania:

'Yeah, they're burning books, actually burning books. Anything to do with communism. They burned Stendhal's *The Red and the Black*.'

The Manichee looked at him. 'Yeah? But isn't that anarchism?'

From somewhere, at intervals, a deep voice would say, 'True, true as I'm sitting here. God's truth.' From somewhere else a whining voice would wonder was there any point in fighting entropy?

A nybro tray clattered on the vinyl chloride floor.

46

'A goddamn cetologist. For my fifth birthday he gave me a comic book of *Moby Dick*, how do you like that?'

'Skinner,' said someone at another table, 'did some very interesting things with pigeons ...'

The yellow sweatshirt swivelled its shoulders towards the door. 'Okay, maybe it's not Sandy, but it sure looks like Sandy.'

'Go ahead, sign it, oney nothing dirty. I had everybody sign it, even Professor ...'

'No but listen, they actually burned this book called *Cubism*, see, they thought it was about Castro ...'

'... hell's the point, anyway? I mean it's all entropy or do I mean enthalpy ...' A styrene spoon dug into green jello.

'Sandy! Over here, Sandy!'

'... yeah, and a wind-up Jonah. Yeah, and he took me to *Pinocchio* just to see Monstro, how do you like ...'

The person who wasn't Sandy went to sign the skier's leg cast, while the drama student took a sudden Falstaffian interest in his Danish roll, while the Manichee said:

'Basically I guess you could call me an anarchist. Only ...'

'... basic Libran, with maybe a touch of Cancer ...'

'God's truth. Well, maybe it's not true exactly, but ...'

'I never said it *was* Sandy, I only said it looked like ...'

The voices went on, scudding sound and smoke across the empty table where two empty styrofoam cups stood like vigil lights beside the coffee-soaked newspaper, until Ben Franklin, balancing a tray in his other hand, swept the whole mess to the floor.

'Jesus, they never clean the tables here or anything, sit down, will you? Standing there like a damn wooden Indian – Dan, sit down and eat something.' With a paper napkin he expunged the pencilled word ASS.

'I'm not really ...' Dan Sonnenschein sat down, resting his hands on a spiral-bound notebook. The long fingers showed bitten nails.

'Sure you are. Hot roast beef sandwich, salad with thousand island, banana cream pie. There.' He showed no interest in the food Franklin was setting before him. 'Look, it's not a problem in anything. Just eat it. Christ, Fong tells me you've been living on stale peanut butter sandwiches

47

over there, acting like a goddamned penitent or something.'

'Penitent? No, I just, I have to be there, that's all.'

'For the tests, sure.'

'Not just the tests.' He picked up a styrene fork and looked at it. 'I can't explain it but – Roderick's there, his mind is right there and I – have to be inside it. I mean, I have to make up his thoughts, and at the same time – I *am* a thought.'

'Think for him, you can't even think for yourself, sitting there starving in front of a hot meal – how much do you weigh now, hundred and twenty? Hundred and fifteen? Take that fork in your hand and use it, how's that for thinking?'

Dan's hand obeyed, scooping up a forkful of mashed potato. 'See, it's just that it's gone too far to stop now. They can't stop us now, can they? No, because it would be, it's almost murder.'

'Just eat, will you?'

'No, but it's gone too far. He's alive, Ben. Roderick's alive. I know he's nothing, not even a body, just content-addressable memory. I could erase him in a minute – but he's alive. He's as real as I am, Ben. He's realer. I'm just one of his thoughts.'

'You said that.'

'I did? A thought repeating itself.' Dan's hands finally seized the knife and fork and started feeding him with regular automatic motions. Franklin watched him eat, the tendons moving in his cheeks, one hand pausing now and then to flick back the hair from his eyes. The grubby spiral notebook remained pinned down under his left elbow.

'Oh, happy birthday, by the way. What are you, twenty-three?'

'Yem.'

'Ha ha, have to watch it, getting almost too old there Dan – I mean, it's a young man's game: Turing was only twenty-four when he –'

'Yem.' The dot of mashed potato on Dan's chin stopped moving for a moment. 'Twenty-four, huh?'

'Of course I'm, I'm thirty-six myself ...' And from this bleak perspective, Ben Franklin looked over the field (to which he had as yet made no contribution): there was A. M.

Turing, twenty-four when he conceived of mechanizing states of mind. There was Claude Shannon, twenty-two when he discovered the spirit of Aristotle in a handful of switches and wiring. There was – hell, there was Frankenstein, completing his creation at nineteen (the age at which Mary Shelley completed hers). And there was Pascal, inventing the first calculating machine at the age of eighteen – time is, time was, and death approaches, intruding on our calculations.

If the Buddhists have it right, the world is completely destroyed 75,231 times per second, and each time completely restored. In all the worlds of Ben's 38 years, there was nothing worth saving; he could die now, saying with the dying Frankenstein: 'Farewell, Walton! Seek happiness in tranquillity and avoid ambition, even if it be only the apparently innocent one of distinguishing yourself in science and discoveries. Yet why do I say this! I myself have been blasted in these hopes, yet another may succeed.' The other being Dan, damn him! Caught in the invisible flicker at Buddhist worlds (in the VHF band), Ben stared at his future.

'Turing took cyanide,' he almost said, but changed it to: 'See? You were hungry.'

'Yes, I guess I – thanks.' Dan wiped his narrow chin, belched, flicked back the lock of hair that fell again over his eyes. 'Thanks.'

'Least I can do. Fong thinks you're Roderick's guiding genius, and he should know. The dark figure of Sidonia behind the –'

'What?'

'Nothing. What I want to know is, how can I help?'

'But you are helping. You're writing program –'

'Sure, pieces of test crap, you call that help, anybody could do that. I don't even know what's being tested, you won't let me handle anything in the lab. Christ, what good is my degree? A master's in Cybernetic Humanities, my whole thesis on learning systems and what do I get to do? Piddly little pieces of test program, any kid could handle that.'

'No, your stuff's good, really good. Once I rewrite it, it goes –'

Franklin sat up. 'You what?'

'Rewrite it. Listen, I have to, it's good stuff but it's not inside his head, it's – I have to rewrite it from the inside.'

'*You sonofabitch, I don't believe you.*'

'No, really. Look, right here.' Dan's clawless fingers clawed open the notebook. 'Look, right here where you set up this Bayesian strategy for generalizing from past experience, that's fine for poker-playing machines but look here, I had to simplify – I mean, not simplify exactly, but *Roderickify*, see?'

Ben Franklin stared at the page of diagrams. 'But you – I don't even recognize this, it's not my work. Wait, let's see where you go with this, I don't – let me see that. Goddamnit, let go of the goddamned thing!'

One or two heads turned to watch them, two grown men struggling for possession of a grubby notebook. The girl in the ski sweater nudged her companion, who was bending over to peer at a signature on the white plaster: Felix Culpa.

'Damn you, let go! I've got a right – see my own damn work, let go!' Ben ripped out the page and spread it on the table, holding it with both hands while he studied the symbols cramped into little boxes. His cheeks and ears turned a deeper red.

'Jesus! And this – it works?'

'Yes. Give it back.'

'Just a minute, I've never seen anything like this. Dan, this is – it's beautiful. You took that half-baked idea of mine and you just – you redeemed it, that's what. You redeemed it.'

'Give it back.'

Ben passed over the ragged page and watched him trying to press it back on the spiral. 'I'm sorry, Dan. Had no idea, Fong always said you were good but I mean I never see any of your work, you're always so goddamned secretive. I mean, you never even publish, for Christ's sake, work like this and you never even publish. What about the *Journal of Machine Learning Studies*, or any of the AI –'

'Publish?' Dan hunched forward, protecting the notebook with his knobby wrist. 'No, I don't publish. It's not the point. It's not what I'm working for, my name in some AI journal, I don't have time, see?'

'But that's how you buy the time, publishing. How do you

think somebody like Czernski got the Norbert Wiener Chair of Cybernetics at –'

'Anyway, why should I? Roderick's mine, think I want to stick him in some AI journal for everybody to rip-off? He's private, he's not another toy for some toy company, I don't want to see him crammed inside some plastic Snoopy doll. I don't want him grabbed up by some Pentagon asshole to make smart tanks.'

'Don't know what the hell you're talking about,' Ben lit a cigarette. 'Applications, what the hell do you care about applications? Feel like I'm sitting here with Alexander Graham Bell, he's invented this swell gadget only he's afraid to tell anybody about it, in case some loony uses it to make dirty phone calls. Point is, you can't keep something like this to yourself, you just can't, that's all.'

'Why not?'

'Because it's important, that's why not. It's too important to be left to one person. At least – at least let me help, I mean really help.' The fibreglass chair creaked as he sat back. 'Look, I know I'm not good enough to follow you all the way, just give me a glimpse, a Pisgah perspective, okay? This is, I feel like it's the fifth day of Creation or something, the foreman tells me to collect a couple of wheelbarrows of mud and wheel it over to Eden, no one bothers telling me what it's for. Only I've *got* to know. I've got to be in on it, even in some little way, Jesus, it's the only thing I've ever really wanted to do. Why I went into machine intelligence in the first place, all those damned boring years playing with language translators and information retrieval systems and even poker players all I ever wanted was to create something, all right, *help* create something. Okay, okay don't say it. I know my limitations. I'm intelligent but not creative, fine, only – at least I could help?'

The lock of hair fell forward. 'What is it? You want to see him, or what? Because there's nothing much to see, not yet. And help, I don't need any help, right now it's a one-man job. All I need is some time, a little more time.'

'Sure.' Ben studied the coal on his cigarette. 'Maybe you don't trust me because I'm not Jewish or something, that it?'

'Not – what the hell? Jewish? What does that mean?'

51

'I don't know, but, no offence but –'

'Look, I'm not hardly Jewish myself, my old man was reformed I guess but I wasn't even raised –'

'Yeah, okay, but it's a, like a holy work to you all the same. Secret and holy. Like the prophet Jeremiah and his son, making the first *golem*, you know? They made him out of clay, and they wrote the program on his forehead, and he came to life.'

Dan shrugged. 'Yeah, well I've got to get back to the lab.'

'Yeah, but you know what they wrote? TRUTH. *'emeth*, they wrote, and he came to life. And the first thing he asked them was couldn't they kill him, before he fell into sin like Adam.'

'Look, it's just something I've got to do, alone.' The lock of hair was brushed back, and fell again as he stood up.

'But listen a minute, will you? All he wanted to do was die. They wrote the program on his forehead, *'emeth*, he came to life and all he wanted was to die.'

'Really gotta be going, Ben. I mean, these parables or whatever they are, maybe they mean a lot to you but, uh –'

'The point is, maybe that's all we can create, death. Even when we try to make life it comes out death, death is there all the time. See – wait a minute! – see, Jeremiah and Son, all they had to do was erase one letter from the program, see? So *'emeth* became *meth*. DEAD. It was there all the time.'

'Yep. Hebrew, huh? Never learned any myself. Oh, uh, thanks again for the lunch. See you.'

Ben watched him go, a gawky Jiminy Cricket figure blundering among the white tables, stepping over the plaster leg, squeezing past the Manichee, slipping through gaps between formica and nybro, melamine and fibreglass, fleeing from the animated faces, only one of which turned to look, saw that he too was not Sandy, and dismissed him like an untidy, irrelevant thought.

3

There was dust on Mister O'Smith's hand-tooled boots from sitting in the departure lounge. He noticed it when he was looking down, getting set for another fast draw against Brazos Billy. Brazos was not the kind of man to mind if a feller stopped a minute to dust off his Gallen Kamps. In fact Brazos was no kind of man at all, just a fibreglass figure at the end of an abbreviated fibreglass street, ready to go up against anybody for a quarter in the slot. If you shot him, Brazos would look surprised, crumple and collapse, even bleed a little; if not, he'd just smirk. Mister O'Smith always drew blood, and he did so now. They were calling his plane, but he lingered, watching the blood ooze out on the little cowtown street, watching it ooze back in, as Brazos un-crumpled and stood tall again. Well, back to work.

On the plane he read his gun catalogue. Nothing much else to do, since the Agency didn't trust a freelancer like Mister O'Smith enough to tell him anything in advance so he could get his mind set for it. The Agency was a pain in the behind, with all their need-to-know stuff and their limited-personal-contacts stuff – hell, they even gave him a code book and a radio martini olive! As if he'd be fool enough to drink martinis anyhow, and shoot, radio olives went out with, with the Walther PP8!

In Minnetonka the snow was melting; his sheepskin was too warm; the taxis were all covered with crap; Mister O'Smith felt low. Well they can kill you but they can't eat you! He dumped his gear at the hotel and hit the slushy street. Within minutes he found an amusement arcade and settled down to feed quarters into Randy the Robot. When zapped, Randy would look surprised, crumple and emit sparks.

Mister O'Smith had no more idea why he was doing this than did the figures of Randy or Brazos, or even that figure

53

of Herakles (coin-operated and armed with a Scythian bow) that had been drawing against a serpent (when hit, it hissed with surprise) three centuries before Christ. Whether this was a set of Skinnerian contingencies reinforcing the appropriate behaviour (zapping) or a Freudian acting-out of infantile aggression towards the castrating father, Mister O'Smith couldn't say. Beauty was death, and death beauty, that was all Mister O'Smith knew (on a need-to-know basis).

'Of course I have my own ideas.' Tarr went on filling his pipe. 'You both know about my plans for investigating psychic flight orientation in migratory birds.'

Aikin and Dollsly nodded automatically: they knew, they knew. 'But it wouldn't be democratic to put that before the committee without first consulting you, okay?'

Nods.

'So what about your ideas? Bud?'

Bud Aikin controlled his stutter remarkably well today, as he outlined his plan for crime prevention by use of the pendulum. He was becoming quite an authority on this psychic instrument, Tarr noticed. Too bad he still had such a hell of a time with that key word.

Aikin unfolded a map. 'See, here I've been and located the three places where this "Ripper", this murderer left his victims. The vibrations are very strong, even on a map. Using the p-p-p – swinging thing – I was able to locate them precisely.'

'Fascinating!' Tarr lit his pipe. 'Of course sceptics will imagine you read about the locations in the paper ...'

'No, but wait. I can do it blindfold, with the map turned any way at all. As soon as the p-p-p – the pen-pen – the Galilean implement – gets over a psychic "hot spot", it starts swinging violently. And, and that's not all. I've found a *fourth* location. The place where the next body will be found. See, right here near the Student Union. So I mean when they find the body there, that pretty well clinches it, right? Maybe then crime prevention can take a leap forward, using the p – the isochronic vibrating part of a clock –'

Tarr exhaled a thick ball of smoke. 'Lacks scope, if you don't mind my frankness, Bud. And you don't really need much of a grant for – but let's hear what Byron has to say, eh?'

Byron Dollsly grinned and slapped his heavy hand on the table. 'Scope! Hah! Think you'll find *plenty* of scope in my idea, George. See how this grabs you. As you know, I've been working on lines suggested by Teilhard de Chardin, Buckminster Fuller and others, namely a kind of engineering approach to consciousness. *Well!*'

He beamed at Tarr and Aikin in turn, while they sat awaiting further enlightenment. '*Well*, I've only had a *major breakthrough*, that's all. As I see it, we have to begin with first principles. *Biology!*'

After a moment, Tarr took his pipe from his mouth. 'Is that it? Biology?'

'Is that it, he asks. Hah! Okay, let me spell it out for you. The divine Teilhard saw life as a *radial* force, and consciousness as a *tangential* force. Life, see, is like a gear-wheel growing larger, while consciousness is the gear actually turning – meshing!'

He grabbed a handful of his thick grey hair and more or less hauled himself to his feet by it. Then he marched to the blackboard. 'So what's the next step? Anybody?'

The other two looked at one another. 'Mm, suppose you just tell us, Byron. Little short on time here ...'

'The *screw*. The SCREW!'

'The, uh ... the ...'

'Simple. The *creative* intellect is a worm-screw with a *right*-hand thread. Get it? Get it? See, it can never mesh with the destructive or left-handed intellect – never!'

'Well I suppose not, mm –'

'So what is God? Simple. He is the vector sum of the entire network of forces turning back upon themselves to produce ultimate consciousness! I mean isn't He? Isn't He just the infinite acceleration of the tangential? POW! POW!' He smacked an enormous right-hand fist into an enormous left-hand palm. There was silence. There was always silence after one of Byron Dollsly's little lectures, which always ended *pow*, *pow* ...

'Interesting, Byron, good line of thinking there ... hard to see any practical research possibilities in it just now, but ...'

As chairman, Tarr of course had the final deciding vote, which he cast for his own proposal (to study telepathy in birds). Dismissing his assistants, he prepared to write it up for the committee. That is, he sat cracking his knuckles, one by one, and staring out of the window.

From here in the Old Psychology Building, he had a limited view of the Mall: a few dirty white drifts, the stump of a snowman. How many seasons had he watched from this narrow window? How many barren Winters? How many hopes shattered like icicles – Tarr was beginning to like the simile – while his career remained frozen, stiff as the heart of poor little Frosty out there, who would never come to life and sing ...

Tarr started on the left-hand knuckles. Beyond the snowman lay the façade of Economics, a dirty old building on whose pediment he could just make out three figures: *Labour* shouldering a giant gear-wheel, *Capital* dumping out her cornucopia, and *Land* applying his scythe to a sheaf of wheat or something.

His gaze returned to the central figure. Money, that's what it took. A little money – a tenth of the cash they lavished on the Computer Science Department, say – and he could have parapsychology really on the move. Going places. They were doing it elsewhere: Professor Fether in Chicago was testing precognition in hippos; the Russians claimed a break-through on the ouija board to Lenin; the ghost labs of California were fast building a solid reputation. But here, a standstill, a frozen landscape. Nobody in the entire field had ever heard of the University of Minnetonka.

Nobody had ever heard of Dr George Tarr, either. Now and then his clipping service sent him by mistake some reference to 'R. Targ' or 'C. Tart'. His own name never appeared.

Still, here was another chance, another crack at the old cornucopia ... He cracked the last knuckle and reached for his dictating machine.

'Title: Research into Psychically-Oriented Flock Flight. A project proposal. G. Tarr, B. Aikin, B. Dollsly.

'Ahem. Observers have long obs – noted the uncanny agility of birds flying in formation. This agility has not yet been adequately explained. How is it that a flock of up to a thousand birds, manoeuvring in perfectly co-ordinated flight at high velocities, can avoid collisions? The psychic mechanism we propose may be tested as follows ...'

A man in a red hunting cap and matching face was saying to the bartender, 'Look, just because I never went to no university that don't mean I'm drunk.'

'Just take it easy, Jack.'

'Plenny of things a university don't teach you, am I right?'

'All I said was, take it easy. Take it ...'

In the back booth, Professor Rogers scratched at acne that hadn't itched for fifteen years. 'Up to you, of course. Just thought you might want to have all the facts. *Before* the meeting.'

Dr Jane Hannah's face was impassive, the face of a Cheyenne brave – which, during her early years in anthropology, she had been. 'Facts, you say. I keep hearing opinions.'

'Okay, sure, if you want my opinion, we should turn them down. With all these fraud rumours, I don't see how Fong's people can expect special treatment.'

She raised her martini, mumbled something over it, and took a sip. 'Why not special treatment? Maybe what they have to give us is more precious than anything they could possibly have stolen. After all, true heroes can always break the rules. Think of Prometheus, stealing from the gods.'

'Pro – but this is real life, real theft. Maybe millions of dollars, you can't just shrug like that and –'

'But NASA, like all fire-gods of the air, won't miss a few million. We don't want to get bogged down in petty tribal ethics now, the real question is, is Fong a true hero? Will his robot, his gift to mankind, be a blessing or a curse? If it is good, then we *must* help him, even as Spider Woman helped the War Twins on their journey to the lodge of their father, the Sun –'

'Sure, sure, but I mean Fong is playing God himself, he's like Baron Frankenstein over there, never listens to anybody, a law unto himself.'

'The new Prometheus.' Her eyes were unfocused; they seemed to be looking right through him into the vinyl fabric

57

of the booth. 'Prometheus made a man of clay, you know. And Momus the mocker criticized it, saying he should have left a window in the breast, so we could see what secret thoughts were in its heart. But isn't that our problem? How can we tell if this robot will be good or evil? What's in his heart?'

He lifted his Old-fashioned, holding the tiny paper doily in place on the bottom of the glass with his little finger. 'You want my opinion, the computer freaks have had things their own way just about long enough. Far be it from me to assign guilt labels in a multivalently motivating situation like this, but just look around campus! The process of depersonalization goes irreversibly on, what with computerized grades and tests, teaching machines, enrolment, it's as though they want to just tear down humanity, yeah? Just rip it out and replace it, yeah? With robotdom, right? Robots are nothing but humanity ripped off, if you want my opinion.'

Her stare continued to penetrate Rogers, the vinyl padding, and even the next booth where Dora was explaining to Allbright: 'I think Dr Fred's senile or something, he screwed up completely on everybody's horoscopes, I checked mine on the computer and he's got Saturn in the wrong place.'

'Oh sure, the *computer* has to be right. Why trust a nice little old man when you can really rely on a damned steel cabinet full of transistors?' He swallowed a pill and washed it down with Irish whiskey.

'That's not what I meant, I mean Saturn in the wrong place! And this other kid, this Bill Whatsit in my class, his horoscope's even worse. I mean Dr Fred put in a conjunction of Pluto and Neptune, it makes Bill born in either 1888 or 2381. And when I tried to tell Bill it was wrong he said, "I know, wrong again, I'm always wrong" – like it was *his* fault, I mean.'

'We're all at fault, sure, getting in the way of the damned steel cabinets. Nobody's gonna survive, just a few technicians ...' His dirty fingers chased another pill across the formica.

'You sound just like him, gloom and doom! For Pete's sake, you must both have something in Scorpio, you're so touchy.' She shrugged her orange coat half-way down her arms and lit a cigarette. 'I just hate this place, don't you? *Au fond*, I mean.'

'... just a few damned technicians, half machines themselves ... Listen, I went to school with this kid, a born computer genius. He used to play around all the time with the school terminal, little games of his own, nobody knew what the hell he was up to, least of all the teacher. I mean we were only eleven years old, already he was in a world of his own. Then one day the goddamn FBI came to the school and took him away for a couple of days. Seems he was dabbling in interstate commerce, in a way. When he got back to school I asked him all about it – you know what it was? Peanut butter.'

'Peanut butter?'

'Bugleboy Old Tyme Reconstituted Peanut Butter, nauseating stuff it used to be, nobody could stand it. Only thing us kids liked about it was the jar tops: "Fifty of your favourite cartoon characters – save 'em, swap 'em, loads of fun!" Something like that. Anyway the supermarkets were probably losing money on the crap, because they stopped handling it. So this kid just got on the old terminal, twiddled his way into the inventory computer of this big supermarket chain, Tommy Tucker, and made a few crucial changes. All of a sudden Tommy Tucker was swamped with the crap. They put it on special offer, they even gave it away – and I bet they had to throw away a few tons of it too. But they couldn't stop their computer from re-ordering, more and more ... When they caught up with him, this kid had forty-nine of his favourite cartoon characters – probably more than any other kid in the United States.'

Dora looked for the waitress. 'I've heard lots of stories like that. Kids are always using their school terminals to dig into some computer somewhere.'

'Yeah, but what Danny did was kind of new. He invented some sinister algorithm, so he told me. I don't even know what an algorithm is.'

'You don't? Honest? It's only a set of instruc –'

'And I don't want to know. Whatever it was, after he planted it in Tommy Tucker's computer, it just grew until it took over. I guess they had to finally throw away their whole program and start from scratch. I guess they lost a lot of money, that's where the FBI came in.'

'What happened to him, then?'

'Oh, they put him on the payroll at Tommy Tucker. As a computer security consultant. All he had to do was promise to leave them alone. But the funny thing is –'

The waitress arrived, with someone else's drinks.

'Sorry, kid, I got a bit mixed up, with all the characters in here tonight. Old Jack there's teed off because he can't read –' she gestured at the man in the hunting cap, '– and the cowboy next to him wants to know who's drinking martinis – and then I got some joker in the front tries to tell me he's a manicure. Crazy! Crazy! Crazy!'

She delivered the Old-fashioned and the martini to Rogers and Hannah, who was saying:

'... maybe the Blackfeet boy, Kut-o-yis, cooked to life in a cooking pot, but isn't that the point? Aren't they always fodder for our desires? Take Pumiyathon for instance, going to bed with his ivory creation –'

'Look, these Indian stories are okay, but I don't see –'

'Indian? No, he was King of Cyprus, you must know that story, they even made a musical of it, *Hello Dolly*, was it? Something like that ... But take Hephaestus then, those golden girls he made who could talk, help him at his forge, who knows what else ... Or Daedalus, not just the statues that guarded the labyrinth, but the dolls he made for the daughters of Cocalus, you see? Love, work, conversation, guard duty, baby, plaything, of course they used them to replace people, isn't that the point?'

'Yes but the point, my point is –'

'And in Boeotia, the little Daedala, the procession where they carried an oaken bride to the river, much like the *argeioi* in Rome, the puppets the Vestal Virgins threw into the Tiber to purge the demons; disease, probably, just as the Ewe made clay figures to draw off the spirit of the smallpox, so did the Baganda, they buried the figures under roads and the first –'

'This is all very interesting, yes, but –'

'First person who passed by picked up the sickness. In

Borneo they drew sickness into wooden images, so did the Dyaks ... Of course the Chinese mostly made toys, a jade automaton in the Fourth Century but much earlier even the first Han Emperor had a little mechanical orchestra but then he was a bit mad, you know. Imagine burning all the books in China *and* building the Great Wall, quite mad, quite mad ... but the Japanese, Prince Kaya was it? Yes, made a wooden figure that held a big bowl, it helped the people water their rice paddies during the drought. Certainly more practical than the Chinese, or even the Pythagoreans, with their steam-driven wooden pigeon, hardly counts even if they did mean it to carry souls up to – but no, we have to make do with the rest, and of course the golem stories, and how clay men fashioned by the Archangel –'

Chee! Rogers sneezed. 'Yes, very iderestigg, but –'

'There were Teraphim of course but no one knows their function. But the real question is, what do we want this robot *for*? Is it to be a bronze Talos, grinning as he clasps people in his red-hot metal embrace? Or an ivory Galatea with limbs so cunningly jointed –'

'Look, couldn't we –?'

'As you see, I've been turning the problem over, consulting the old stories ...'

'And?'

'And I've decided to vote against this robot.'

Chee! Chee! 'Thank God. We have to take sides. Those of us who don't want to be ciphers have to stand up and be counted. Why didn't you say so in the first place?'

For the first time, her eyes blinked. 'But I had to explain! You see, I believe in baring the soul.'

'Bearing the –?'

'I even talk to my food and drink, as you must have noticed.'

'Dot at all,' he lied, and hid his nose in a handkerchief.

She sighed. 'I can't help feeling that respect for life – even the life of your cold virus there – is paramount. Of course we must take life, we eat food, we destroy germs. But can we not at least apologize for our murders?' So saying, she took up the olive from her martini and spoke to it quietly: 'Little olive, I mean you no harm, but my body needs nourishment.

61

For one day soon, my body will go to replenish the earth, to feed new olive trees ...'

Rogers looked away, embarrassed, and caught the eye of a fat, suntanned stranger at the bar, who had turned from the television to watch Dr Hannah. 'Uh, I've got to go home, nurse this cold, so ...'

She put down the olive and checked her watch. 'If you don't mind, I'll stick around. Have to kill an hour before I meet my son for dinner. Never see him, since he moved into that fra – But you have your own problems, bless you.'

Beanie's Bar was beginning to fill up with the early evening crowd. Rogers had to squeeze his way through an animated discussion of Ruritania (one speaker suffered from halitosis), avoid the non-university drunk and jostle through other conversations:

'... the liberry, but like when I ast for *Sense and Sensibility* they brung me this *novel*. This, yeah, by some other J. Austin, only with a *e*, figure that ...'

'... Jungian econ ...'

'... this machine heresy, was it?'

'... Barbara Altar for one ...'

The juke box piped him out with a mournful, if not quite coherent song:

> When I feel you're in my dream
> Images of fortune play me do-o-own
> Destiny don't seem so far, and I can touch a star
> Tragedy's a bargain, yes, and
> Love's a clown.

Near the door someone said, 'Right in front of the Student Union? No kidding, who was he anyway?'

'Just some freshman with a GPA problem, happens every year ...'

The spot vacated by Rogers was still warm when a plump stranger in Western clothes slid into it. He grinned at Dr Hannah out of his deep tan.

'Olives,' he said. 'Thought they went out with the ol' Walther.'

'Really?' She focused on him with difficulty.

'O'Smith.' He extended a thick left hand on which she noticed a turquoise ring, almost Navaho. But fake, like the grin.

'Prometheus invented the ring,' she said, and belched. 'Did you know – sorry – that? Out of his chains.'

'No foolin'?' A theatrical sneer. 'Look, can we talk here?'

'Why not?' Jane Hannah needed at least two more martinis before she could face her son, and if this absurd stranger wanted to fill the interval with chatter, olives going out of style, well why not?

'Usually I work alone,' he said. 'I run a one-man show.'

'Indeed?' Show-business, a rodeo perhaps. It seemed to explain his outlandish clothes, the showy ring, the stock villain's sneer. What did he want, money?

'But I guess if you wanted to back my play –'

She put up a hand. 'You're wasting your time. I don't contribute to – no thanks. "... I'm no angel ...", as the saying goes.'

'Good enough.' He seemed unruffled. 'Good enough. Fact is, I get a lot of satisfaction out of workin' alone, you know? Boy, when you see their faces – when they realize what's comin' off –' He chuckled. 'Makes it all worth while.'

'I'll bet. But do you usually see their faces? I thought –'

'Even when you don't, you still know what they're thinkin'. Boy howdy! It's like real communication! I mean in every-day life you just *never* get that close to *nobody*. Real communication.'

'I know just what you mean,' she said. Nice to meet someone who liked his work, even if he did carry the off-stage villainy too far. Just now he was casting a furtive glance over his shoulder, where the bearded boy was propped up by the girl in orange.

Allbright, his chin sinking towards the table, told Dora, 'Funny thing is, I met him just the other day. On the Mall.'

'Met who?'

'This kid I was just telling you about. Danny. The Bugle-boy –'

'But that was half an hour ago – are you all right?'

'No but listen, listen, he's still crazy he – I asked if he was still in computers and he sort of grinned and said, "Into, yes, yes, yes, you could say that, into computers, yes, yes ...""'

'I don't know why you take that stuff and drink on top –'

'Yes yes, nodding and grinning like a fucking guru computer got all the answers yes yes ... only he's dead inside, ghost in the machine you know even his kid he even his kid he ...'

He came to rest with his ear in the ashtray, while the man in the hunting cap looked over and turned away to his drink, muttering, 'College boys! College boys!'

A tiresome boy declared himself once more a Manichee to the girl in the leg-cast, who nodded, though listening to someone else explain how Lady Godiva invented the rosary. The juke box, now muffled by the wall of bodies, sang:

> Funniest thing I ever seen
> Tomcat sittin' on a sewin' machine ...

Dr Hannah raised her glass to toast the departing O'Smith. 'Break a leg,' she said.

He winked. 'For you, anything.' He pushed through the crowd and out into the night, which was nearly as dark and empty as the piano bar on the other side of town where two short-haired men waited to meet someone called O'Smith.

Allbright slept on while Dora kept watch. Suddenly he sat up, rubbing at the ash on his cheek. 'He looked burned out, coke or, I don't know, burned out. What was I – oh yeah, he's got a kid, Roderick, he even treats him like a damned machine.'

'Is this still Bugleboy?'

'Yeah listen, he was carrying this doll, I asked him if he had any kids, he said, Just Roderick. "Oh, this?" he says, holding up the doll. "It's for testing Roderick. Testing his pattern-recognition threshold." Might have been talking about a goddamned piece of equipment, you know? Cold, cold and – so when I asked how old the boy was, what do you think? He said, *"Doesn't matter. I'm getting rid of him"*.'

'What did he mean, getting rid –'

'Wants to ship him off to some foster home, even asked me for an address.' He picked at his beard absent-mindedly, disentangling a cigarette butt. 'Felt like telling him to ask his computer pals if he wants a favour, only – what's that cop doing in here?'

A campus patrolman stood by the door, looking around, while the crowd parted to let him through. Out of habit, one or two people dropped things on the floor. Finally the lawman saw Dr Hannah's white hair and came over to her.

'Mrs Hannah? Mrs Jane Hannah?'

'Doctor Hannah, if you don't mind.'

Awkwardly he bent and whispered to her that her son was dead. Awkwardly he supported her as she rose and wobbled to the door, blind to faces turning with momentary curiosity, deaf to the thumping of the juke box ...

The man in the hunting cap (its flaps erect as the ears of a fox terrier) clutched his glass for support and muttered, 'College boys! B.S., M.S., Ph.D., haw haw haw, stands for ...'

Allbright said, 'So I gave him the address. Friends of mine out West, they're into the environment. Figured they couldn't be worse parents than him. Jesus, he doesn't even care about that kid, doesn't even – all he wanted was some address, stick an addressograph label on the kid and ship him out, not even human himself, just a ghost in a machine all burned out, coked out ...'

'Allbright? Let's split, you look tired.'

'Take William Burroughs, inventor of the adding machine, know what he says? Or I mean inventor of the soft machine, know what he says?'

She helped him to his feet while his free hand started flailing, 'And I quote: "The study of thinking machines teaches us more about the brain than we can ever learn by introspective methods." Did you know that?'

The crowd parted as it usually does for wild drunks, policemen and other dangers; Allbright continued flailing as they made the door. ' "The C-charged brain is a berserk pinball machine, flashing blue and pink lights in electric orgasm." Did you know that?'

Outside in the purple evening he paused to smash his fist into a wall.

'Stop! Allbright, stop – why do you hate yourself so much? Why can't you just – stop that!'

'... burned out, a ghost burning in a machine, the lights all going out, zzzzt, let me out of here. Let me out of here!'

'We are out, outside. Come on.'

He slumped down. 'Safer here,' and slept while she kept watch. The sky blazed with stars, brighter and more disturbing than the imitation sky in Bernie's Piano Bar (across town), where two others were giving up their watch.

'What we get depending on outsiders, he's not gonna show.'

'We could of handled it ourselves.'

'Try telling that to the brass.'

The aged pianist had been gently chiding them for an hour for not joining in with the others around the piano. Now, looking directly at them, he said, 'Come on *everybody*. Don't be shy!'

Reluctantly they added their voices to the quavering chorus:

> ... and I'll put them all together
> With some wire and some glue
> And I'll get more lovin' from the dumb, dumb, dummy
> Than I'll ever get from you
> (Get out and waaaaalk, baby).

4

The Shah would trove this memory, would he not? An aerial view of the entire campus, greening with Spring, looking so like one of those clever little silicon chips he was forever reading about. Yes, the clean square buildings represented the little transistors and things, while the roads and footpaths represented the – the other parts. It was even possible to think of the students crawling about down there as information to be progressed, processed rather. He desired strongly that his only son should be processed in a place such as this. But now it was time to put by such thoughts, and concentrate on the tedious task at hand; already his chopper was settling like a golden dragonfly atop the – he checked a map – the Admin building.

Jim hadn't told her she'd have to scream her speech of welcome over the roar of helicopter blades. But protocol demanded instant recognition:

'Welcome to the University of Minnetonka! We hope that Your Royal Incomparability will take pleasure from our humble institution.' Awkward stuff, translated by the Ruritanian consulate.

The Shah was not quite as tall or good-looking as his photographs had previewed. She might not have recognized him but for his splendid uniform: gold lamé head to toe, with peacock-feather epaulets. Curtseying, she noticed that even his jackboots had been gilded.

When the mechanical roar died, he said: 'Please, Dr Boag. Not too much of these ceremony. I hope you will treat me as any ordinary visitation, yes?'

'Yes of course if your – if you – but this way to the elevator.'

Crowded in with the Shah, his secretary and five enormous bodyguards, she found conversation difficult. It was hard enough even to see him over a padded shoulder, and the smell of pomade (heavy with patchouli) took her breath. When she informed him that the weather was unusually mild and Springlike, not at all like last week's, he simply beamed and said nothing. When she asked if he'd had a pleasant journey, he nodded. Did he understand? Did he speak English? Was it impolite to talk in elevators in Ruritania? Finally she gave up and consulted her card notes.

He would want to see the library, examine a Ruritanian manuscript, and visit the history department. Then –

He suddenly snatched the card from her hand. After examining it through his lorgnette, he passed it to the secretary, a tiny dark man with bad teeth.

'It's simply our itinerary,' she began, but they were arguing in their exotic language. Or was it arguing? Whatever it was, it continued as they strolled out into the sunshine.

Finally the Shah beamed at her. 'Forgive our ugly manners, Dr Boag. My secretary wishes me to follow to the letter this thoughtful itinerary you have for us provided. He worries, you see, for the security. I however have other *tastes*.' He grimaced so on the word that she fell back a step.

'I – see. I – well I had planned –'

'Moment. I must confess that libraries leave me "cold". And history was never my "strong" subject. But if you will forgive me, there are two things I should admire seeing. The horses' barns, first of all. And the computers. I greatly admire the computers.'

'Your Inc – the campus is of course at your disposal. I have a car waiting if you'll –'

'No,' said a guard. He and the others, their faces expressionless behind sunglasses, herded the little party past the official car to another, a long Mercedes with gold fittings.

'*My* car,' said the Shah, and twirled his lorgnette. 'I am sure you will find it greatly comfy, yes?'

'Well yes of course, if –'

A guard slapped the door with a giant hand. 'Is better,' he threatened. 'Bombproof.'

Not an auspicious start. She began to envy the committee.

Tarr slammed down the phone as Bud Aikin came in. 'Great, just great. Tried calling Rogers and he's off sick. Sick!'

'You mean he won't –?'

'– be there to steer our proposal through the committee. We've just wasted our time – what are you looking so pleased about?'

'Well, the paper says –'

'That's not the worst of it. Only reason I called up Rogers was to get him to change the title on our proposal, too late now. They've got it, forty-six copies already in the committee room with that title staring them in the face, why didn't somebody tell me? Why didn't you point the acronym out to me, I have to think of everything around here – something amusing, Bud?'

'No, just, did you see the paper? It says –'

'*Research into Psychically-Oriented Flock Flight*, why do I have to do everything my, what paper?'

Aikin held up the *Caribou*. 'You know how I predicted another body? A fourth body at the Student Union? Well here it is! Some freshman shot himself right on the steps, how's that for precognition? Listen: "The body of Bill Hannah, 20 ..."'

'I don't know what you're talking about.'

'"... and Wesson .38 ... cassette suicide note in his pocket. Hannah blamed his failing Grade Point Average, .95 last ... member of Digamma Upsilon Nu and son of Dr ..." Anyway there it is, my prediction.'

Tarr began filling his pipe. 'And frankly, Bud, I wonder if you know either.'

'But you, you saw me do it, with the map, remember? And the p-p-p – the vibrating dangly thing, remember? You and Byron were witnesses!'

He lit his pipe and puffed out an ectoplasm of blue smoke. 'Can't say I remember that, no, hmm, hmm, hmm ...' After a moment he added, 'But even if you did, so what? One swallow doesn't make a flock.'

'But –'

'Kindly let me finish? Okay, what I think we have here is a political situation, Bud. No sooner do I tell you the committee will probably veto my proposal, than you want to back another horse. Maybe all you ever really cared about was your pendulum, eh?'

'No, but –'

'It's okay, Bud. Really. I'm not hurt. Some people are capable of loyalty, some aren't, I realize that. I don't know, maybe you're after my *job* in your own crazy way, I can accept that too. Just a humble scientist myself, I leave the politics to you slick guys with all the answers.'

Unanswered phones were ringing all over the place. A patrolman sat on his desk, trying to juggle two receivers and take down a message that would probably be just another flying saucer sighting. The dispatcher peered over her glass partition (a frosted look over frosted glass, he would write) letting the chief know she was peeved about missing her coffee break. The telex was ringing its bell and rattling out a yard of paper. The fat prisoner threw him a sulky look from the cage ('. . . as if,' he would write, 'as if he thought someone else had crapped his drawers').

Chief Dobbin went into his office and closed the door against all of them. But even here he had Sergeant Collar balancing an armload of reports and shouting into a phone:

'Don't ask me, that's all. Just don't ask me!' The receiver banged down. 'Been like this all fucking day, chief. Two more men down with flu, the coroner's screaming for his paperwork on this suicide, not to mention –'

'Shut up, Collar, and get outa my office. I need five minutes to get squared away here.' Getting squared away meant sitting down with a clean legal pad and a handful of sharpened pencils, to work on his book. Dobbin wrote slowly and carefully, his tongue protruding at the corner of his mouth:

'Don't touch me,' she said. 'Don't you ever touch me again. Why was I ever dumb enough to marry a cop?'

Suddenly I felt big and awkward and very, very tired. 'Look, I know it's our anniversary, but this Delmore diamond case is ready to crack wide open –'

'And then there'll be some other case,' she said, her mouth set hard. 'Maybe when you give all you've got to your work, there's just nothing left for me.'

She was near the window when it happened. Suddenly the glass blossomed into a spider-web pattern, with a hole in the middle the size of a .303 slug. There was a matching hole in Laura's lovely throat. Even before she hit the floor, she was very, very –

70

'What is it *now*, Collar? Can't you handle it?'

'Security problem, chief. With our visiting potentate. He's visiting all the wrong places. In fact we can't locate him.'

'Terrific. Have Angie get him on the radio, and –'

'No can do. He's got the wrong car, too. I'm trying to get a VSU fix on him now, but nothing. Zilch. Maggie's drawers.'

'Probably left the damn campus.' He flicked on his own video surveillance unit and ran through the scenes quickly, then slowly. 'There, is that his car? Black Mercedes limo, gold grille? Okay, he's at the Ag Sci complex, horse barns. Can we detail a coupla men to escort?'

Collar made a face. 'Nope. Simons is off sick, and Fielder has to guard this gold dinnerware at the Faculty Club, so that leaves –'

'Okay, okay. Try to catch up on a little paperwork around here and what happens? All hell breaks loose, people get sick, people want coffee breaks – and now we got this guy, a king of some place, just walking around loose like anybody else!'

'You want to question the prisoner now, chief? He's kinda weird and –'

'Who is he, anyhow?'

'A John Doe. No ID at all. Our special Ripper Patrol picked him up last night. He was using a glass-cutter on a window at the Computer Science building. Had a microflex camera on him, and a wig.'

'Kinda fat for the James Bond stuff, isn't he? Okay, bring him in. Oh but first, ring the morgue, tell 'em it's okay to release the Hannah kid's body for a funeral. We'll catch up on the paperwork later. I know his ma wanted to cremate him today.'

'Already released him, chief.'

Thank God something was done. Dobbin could see he'd get no further today on *Call Me Pig*.

As soon as they were in the car, His Incomparability removed his gold military cap, unbuttoned his stiff collar and sighed. 'Now we can relax. Let us be informal, eh? I will call you Helen, and you must call me Ox.'

'Ox?'

'It is my favourite pickname, as you say. These horses' barns, are they far?'

'Why yes. I hope your driver knows the way.'

'Yes, he studies your campus with a fine tooth comb. He knows it like the back of his hams.' The weedy secretary spoke into a gold microphone, and they moved.

The patchouli scent was heavy. Dr Boag tried to forget it by studying the car's elaborate furnishings. The roof interior was covered with peacock feathers, the floor with squares of black and white fur (ermine? sable?) and while two guards and the secretary were forced to squat on tiny carved stools, she and the Shah reclined on a deep, comfortable seat, upholstered in cloth of gold and heaped with blue silk cushions. She remarked on the luxury and he replied that he owned seventeen such cars.

And that seemed to be that. Six miles to the horse barns, and already they'd run out of conversation.

The Shah rummaged in a carved cabinet and produced a book.

'Very interesting, this Book.'

'Ruritanian?'

'Alas, my English is not so well for reading, so I have had it translated into my own poor tongue. I believe in English it is called *Pianola*? By Mr K. Vonnegut. Very good. Much computers.'

She studied the beautifully-tooled cover. 'I'm afraid I haven't read it. Technical book is it?'

'A novelle. All on my own crazed subject, the computers. But the curious part is, there is a Shah in it, making a visitation! Of course he is nothing like me, but even so – reading this is a *déjà vu* experience for me. Suppose I too were in a novelle, eh? Read by another Shah, who is in turn – you see?'

'Interned?'

'I explain so badly. Let me only say I begin to feel like the iteration within the great computer myself, or there-abouts.'

One of the guards grinned, nudged the other and pointed out of the window at a Coca-Cola sign.

'The pianola,' continued the Shah. 'An excellent symbol

for the automation, yes? It is I believe used also by Mr W. Gaddis in his novelle *J.R.*, where he speaks of Oscar Wilde travelling in America, marvelling at the industry, the young industry you understand. Now I do believe Mr Wilde suggested shooting all the piano players and using the pianola instead, or do I have that erroneously?'

'Very ahm, perceptive, Your Inc – Ox, I mean.'

'Do you like books, Helen? How stupid of me, of course you must be immured in them, books are your life, yes?'

She chuckled. 'Not as much as I'd like, I fear. Pressure of work, administrative duties –'

'I too, I too,' he said, and squeezed her knee. Dr Boag was glad she'd worn the pants suit after all. 'Yet I do find time to read. Anything I can find on the computers, fiction or not fiction. I believe the machine must some day replace all of us, yes? We will have the robot Dean of Persons, yes, and even the robot Shah of Ruritania. Sad it is, but so. Meanwhile these computers are damn useful, yes? For the police work and so forth.'

He gave her a glass of gold liqueur and rambled on about computers, while she lay back and tried to keep her knees out of reach, trying to ignore the overpowering scent. Eventually she said, 'You have a point there, Ox, but really isn't the computer more or less an overgrown adding machine? A tool, in other words, useful of course but only in the hands of human beings. I feel the role of the computer in our age has been somewhat exaggerated, don't you?'

'Perhaps. But I see the subject tires you. Let us speak instead of business.' He leaned back against a peacock-blue cushion. 'My visit is of course not entirely socialized, you understand.'

'Oh?'

'I wish to enrol my son Idris at your excellent university.'

'Oh. Well I'm sure he'll like it here, Your, Ox. It's more than a university, it's – it's a perspective on the world, past, present and fut –'

'Yes yes yes. So I suggest as, as you say, a ballpark figure of two million.'

'What?' She sat up.

'American dollars. At today's prices not bad, eh?'

'But our fees are nothing like, of course if you want to arrange a deed of gift –'

'Gifting, yes, a gifting. Just to ensure Idris's education. I think of it as an investment in my country's future. Also a hedge against inflation, yes? Idris is now six months of age. By the time he is ready, the price may go up and up, yes?'

She put down her liqueur glass, sat up straight and looked at him. 'Let's be clear about this. Your gift sounds more than generous, but I hope you won't expect special treatment for your son in return. We are after all a state institution.'

He winked. 'I understand. Two million and a half, let us say, and be done with. Yes?' He slapped her knee heartily. 'Now, on to the horses!'

The history professor looked at his watch. Another minute had passed into his domain. 'We all seem to be here. I declare this meeting open. I'm sorry Dr Boag couldn't be here – a previous commitment – and Professor Rogers – he's ill – and Dr Hannah. I assume you all know of her son's recent tragic death. Still, we have our quorum, so I suggest we consider these two proposals – Question, Dr McGuffey?'

'*Woopa.* Just want to put it on the record that I had nothing to do with Bill Hannah's suicide.'

'Pardon? I don't follow.'

Dr Fred stood up and looked up and down the table. 'Oh, I know what you're all saying. Just because he was in my class. Just because I made a little mistake in his birth chart.'

'Well, yes, now if we can ahem just get down to these two –'

'Only I never made that mistake at all. The machines did it! Magnetic influences. Terrestrial currents. Someone saw a flying saucer the other night, unimpeachable witness, ever think of that?'

'Yes, now if you're finished, we'll just –'

'I'm not finished, may be old, may be sick, but I'm not finished. No siree, copper bracelet wards off arthritis bursitis neuritis, benefic influence of Venus, have to get up early to – *Woopa!*' Each sneeze threatened to blow the frail figure off its feet. Noticing his glittering eyes, the chairman said:

'If you're ill, Dr McGuffey, perhaps –'

'Ill? Ill-aspected, Mars the face of Mars, malefic but I ward it off, they have to get up early to catch old Fred, Napoleon slept only four hours per night, magnetic power, secret dynamos, hidden reserves of Atlantean force fields deep in the – but they do, you know. They do get up early, humming away in the night, in the ...' He looked bewildered. After a moment he sat down and began to study the documents before him. The meeting continued.

'No luck, chief?'

'Zilch. Either this guy really is some government yahoo, which I very much doubt, or he's really nuts. Any word from the FBI yet on his prints?'

'Maggie's drawers, so far. Should I book him or what?'

'Not just yet. Not just yet.' Chief Dobbin drummed a pencil on his legal pad. 'I want to try a little psychology on this cracker. Because if he's nuts, he just might be nuts enough to be our Ripper, right?'

Collar snapped his fingers. 'Hey, that ties in with something else. I forgot to tell you. You know that book we found last week on the scene of the crime?'

'Yeah, this education –'

'But that's just it! I had our experts go over it, and it's not education at all. This book, this *Learning Systems*, is all about computers!'

'And we caught this guy at the Computer Science building! Now we're getting somewheres.' Dobbin sat up. 'Get the prisoner, Collar. I think the three of us oughta pay a little visit to the morgue.'

The Mortuary Science department of University Hospital was just around the corner, and in a few minutes they were in the cool antechamber, handing the attendant a ticket.

'Six-sixty-six?' he said. 'Let's see, that must be –'

'Never mind who it is, just bring it out.' Dobbin watched the attendant slouch away, then turned to his suspect. 'Still not talking, Mister Spy?'

'Nope. Like I said before, you boys are makin' one hell of a mistake here. People I work for ain't goin' to like this a-tall.'

'Sure, sure, double-oh-seven. We got your number all

right.' When the attendant rolled in the sheet-draped trolley, the two cops twisted their handcuffs, forcing the suspect to move close to it. He would need a full dose of psychology.

'I want you to take a good look at this girl,' said Dobbin. 'I think maybe you seen her before. *Before you took an electric carving knife and butchered her up like this!*'

He whipped back the sheet to show the placid features of Bill Hannah. 'What the hell – Collar, what's this?'

'I don't know, chief, guess the computer mixed up the ticket numbers or – and they must of cremated the girl.'

The suspect grinned out of his deep tan. 'Now if you boys are done fartin' around here, how about lettin' me go? I ain't really done nothin' and you know it.'

'Millions of bits of information on a little chip,' said the Shah. 'Answers at the speed of light. Of what will they think next? Ah, dear Helen, I cannot tell you how much I look forward to seeing your computers.'

'Well I'm sure you'll be – Good God what's that?'

As the long Mercedes turned into University Avenue, a mob suddenly closed in to block the way. There seemed to be angry faces at every window, fists hammering at every bomb-proof panel.

'MURDERER! MURDERER OF CHILDREN!'

'I can't think how this happened, Your Incomparability. This is – I must apologize. Must be some mistake in our security, some leak –'

He shrugged a peacock epaulet. 'I am accustomed to this. Ruritanian students assuredly, a despicable faction known all too well in my own country. And now even here, in the land where everything is free –'

The bodyguards started feeling inside their jackets as the car slowed, halted. A student whose sign read NO FASCHISM HERE shouted something in an ancient language, and the Shah looked unhappy.

'They accuse me of murder – *I* who brought them colour television on two channels! Only communistic anarchists could even dream of so terrible a lie. Drive on Uza,' he shouted in the microphone. 'Run them down!'

'No, wait. I'm not sure you should –'

76

'Red anarchistic nihilists! They say I murdered children – *I*, their spiritual father! I never murdered anyone in my life.'

'No, of course but –'

'All of those so-called children were executed in accordance with our laws, after a fair trial – and many were over ten years old!'

He shouted something into the gold microphone, and the car began inching forward.

When the FBI report finally came through, O'Smith left the yokel cops mumbling their apologies, and went right to work. No time for subtleties now, just have to go in fast and heavy. He stopped at a drugstore on University Avenue and picked up cotton wool and a few cans of lighter-fuel. Then, straight for the Computer Science building.

Seemed to be lots of other folks hurrying in the same direction. One or two carried signs. Away down the street a black limo was caught in a mob of some kind. Student demonstration? Good diversion there, all set for a quick in-and-out operation.

He paused, waggled his stiff right forefinger until it clicked, then removed the tip of it. Half the fingernail slotted into the remaining finger to form a forward sight. Not more than three or four in the lab, he reckoned, should be able to get the drop on two of 'em before the others could close their mouths.

Better get this Dr Lee Fong first thing, you never knew with chinks and their martial arts. Then the notes, grab essentials (they'd be most likely in top desk drawers and pockets) and use the rest to start the fire. Whole thing didn't need to take more'n fifteen minutes.

He was closer to the car now, and could see students sprawling over the hood, banging on it, scratching the paint with their signs. Punks! If he didn't need the ammo he'd take out a couple of 'em right here and now.

Suddenly the car broke free, flinging a body and a sign into the air, and careered towards him. O'Smith dodged left as it swerved left, dodged right as it swerved right, and collided with someone else, a student with a sign.

'Murderer!'

O'Smith felt the blast of bad breath, saw NO FASCH and felt the impact; before he could argue the truth of the accusation, or demonstrate it, he was down and out.

5

The room that had been a lab was nearly empty now, its grey floor material marked with pale squares and rectangles. In one corner two men wearing the orange uniforms of Custodial Services struggled to lift the last large cabinet, revealing the last pale rectangle. In the opposite corner Dan sat at a table sorting papers into two piles. Franklin paced up and down, stepping carefully in the pale parts. Finally he hunkered down and lit a cigarette.

'Christ,' he exhaled. 'Seeing all this you might think we'd lost out or something.'

'Maybe we did, in a way.'

'Like hell. Lee's just the same, moping around his office like a Jehovah's Witness the day after the world didn't end. I mean what the hell's wrong with you two, we've got the green light on this, now we can really be –'

A thump from the other corner made him look up. 'Careful, fellas. That stuff's expensive.'

One of the men put down his end of the cabinet and turned around. 'Listen, you think you can move this fuckin' ton a junk any better, you just come over and try.'

'Okay, I just, okay.'

'Smartass perfessers.'

He waited until the two had lifted their burden on to a trolley and wheeled it out of the room. 'Be lucky if anything works when we get moved. I don't know where Custodial gets these guys. Saw one in the hall just now didn't even have a uniform; old clothes and a straggly beard looked like it had mange on one side. Only reason I knew he worked here was I saw him carrying a box of your stuff. Can't be two Bugleboy Peanut Butter cartons on the whole campus.'

'Him? That's, that's a guy I used to know. Keeping some stuff for me.' A grubby notebook with a loose page flopped on one pile.

Franklin waved his cigarette. 'Look, this move to a new lab

is just what we need, a chance to really get organized.'

'What for?'

'I mean, don't you want to see this project running like any other, teamwork, I mean a team, I mean – listen, this is a hell of a time to deliver an ultimatum, but to put it bluntly if I don't get some real work to do around here, I quit. Already told Lee, he sees my point, I work or I walk.'

Dan squared up a stack of dog-eared sheets. 'Well, maybe we should all just quit. Now that Roderick's safe, well ...'

'Quit? But we haven't even begun, what do you mean "safe"? Of course he's safe, we've got the green light, the, now we can really go ahead –'

Dan looked at the two stacks of yellowing paper. 'I've got one or two things to clear up here. Okay if I meet you in Lee's office in a few minutes?'

'Okay, sure.' Ben Franklin patted his moustache. 'I mean it's always "wait a minute" with me, right? Always okay if I just hang around – okay, okay I'm going.'

When he was alone, Dan shuffled the two piles into one. When the men in orange returned, he said:

'Would you guys do me a favour?'

The black one looked suspicious. 'What favour?'

Dan pointed to the little door in the wall marked RECYCLING, PAPER ONLY. 'The chute in here is blocked or something. Would you drop this stuff in somebody else's chute?'

'Yeah, okay prof.'

'Is that you, Dr Fong?'

'*Grrrp.*'

'Oh, very funny. You won't feel like making funny noises when you hear what I've got to say. This is Dr George Tarr. I think you know the name.'

'*Grrrrrupf.*'

'Just keep it up, keep it up. I'm recording this, you – you – now listen, I'm very disappointed about the way you finagled this committee vote. *Very* disappointed.'

'*Grrp.* Excuse me it's my stom –'

'As a matter of fact I've just called my lawyer and he

says we have a good case against you. Hear that? A good case.'

'But I don't know what you – *errrp* – excuse –'

'Because I happen to know there were six members of the committee firmly committed to *my* project, and only three on your side. So the only way you could have got a vote eight–seven in your favour was to *sabotage* the whole system. I don't know what you did, maybe something to the computer, but you won't get away with it. I just called up to tell you – we *know*.'

'Know? *Mmgrrpl.*'

'Under the Freedom of Information Act we have access to the computer too, you know. And I have the printout right here in front of me. I have the *facts and figures!*'

'Don't know what you're talk –'

'Don't you? A fix, that's what I'm talking about, a fix! Because how else do you explain it – only three out of fifteen people actually wanted your damned robot – twice as many people wanted my project – yet you won! I don't know whether you bought votes or fixed the comp – but I mean to find out. See you in court, Doctor Fong!'

UNIVERSITY OF MINNETONKA SPECIAL EMER-GENCY FINANCE COMMITTEE VOTING RECORD PART 189077

NUMBER OF CTTEE MEMB = 18
QUORUM = 12
NUMBER PRESENT = 15
CASTING VOTE INOPERATIVE
NUMBER VOTES CAST = 15

PREFERENCE INDICATORS:
  F: FONG (PROJ RODERICK)
  T: TARR (PROJ RIPOFF)
  O: NEITHER (NO AWARD)

| NO. | PREF. | RANK | BALLOT I | | BALLOT II | |
			O	F/T	F	T
0	F	FTO	–	0	0	–
3	F	FOT	–	3	3	–
0	T	TFO	–	0	–	0

NO.	PREF.	RANK	BALLOT I		BALLOT II	
			O	F/T	F	T
6	T	TOF	–	6	–	6
5	O	OFT	5	–	5	–
1	O	OTF	1	–	–	1

15 VOTES TOTAL
NO AWARD   6
FONG   8
TARR   7

Today the stain on the door looked to Ben Franklin like a Portuguese man-o'-war. 'You're not going to let a little thing like that worry you, Christ, I wish he would take us to court. Laugh him off the faculty.'

Fong crunched an antacid tablet and blinked. 'Tarr, no, he doesn't worry me. Only it's just one more little piece of aggravation ...'

'Relax, I've seen the printout on that too. Funny part is, if Tarr hadn't trotted out his little project Ripoff – well-named – we would've lost, 12 to 3. Guess you could say the psychic world has done us a favour – okay, what *is* wrong?'

'Thought Dan would've told you himself. I'd better – *grrrp* – wait, let ... let him tell you himself.'

'Yeah, *wait*.' Franklin looked at the door again. Now it looked a little like a parachute, its shrouds unravelling as it descended. Funny how you could see almost anything ...

'Tell you one thing, I want some changes made around here. When we move, I want a whole new structure. No more of this prima donna act of his, this, well *Dan*, just talking about you. Lee says you've got some little problem.'

'No problem.' Dan closed the stained door and leaned against it. 'I'm just leaving, that's all.'

'!'

'I tried to talk him out of it, Ben. But if the kid wants to go –'

'I don't believe it! You – you want something? It isn't enough that you're the big star, you want something else? More power? No? Well then mind letting me in on the secret?

What makes you want to walk out on four years of your life? Not to mention my life and Lee here, you plan to just waste four years of his life? *Mind telling me why?*'

'Lots of reasons.' Ben stared at the t-shirt (BE SPON-TANEOUS!) waiting for him to go on. 'For one thing it's all wrong. Nothing turned out like I thought. See, when I joined the project I was still a kid, nineteen, how did I know what I was getting into? I thought, Wow, the first robot, the first alien intelligence on this planet, I couldn't think of anything better, anything – specialler.

'Only when it gets down to it maybe it's not so special. It's more like being wrong all the time, you know? And that's just the work. See, I thought it would be like being part of a family, only just look at us: look at you, all you do is bitch and moan and worry about who's got a better job, who's the star player or something.'

'I –'

'See, you're like a baby, Ben, you can't read the books but you still want to chew on them.'

Franklin turned his blush away. 'So it's going to be personalities, is it? Because I've got a thing or two to say –'

'Wait. Look, I'm, all I'm saying is this isn't working out for you or for me or for anybody. And you, Lee, your stomach's so bad you'll have to retire early, just like Leo Bunsky – only he didn't retire early enough. And when he died I just started wondering what this is, is it special after all? Is it special enough to die for?

'And then Mary Mendez, was it special for her? Wandering around in that damned looney bin over there, asking every-body to please wind her up, is it worth that?'

Franklin lit a cigarette and held it ready to drop ash on the floor. 'Doesn't seem to have touched you, though, does it? I mean you're still healthy. Still the same nasty little snotty-nose –'

'Well I had scurvy last year but sure I'm okay physically. That's not the point. The point is Roderick, is he okay? Is he, is he special? See, when people around me were dying or going nuts or getting bitchy or having ulcers I could always say, "All right, but it's worth it, it's special. It must be special because look, NASA, the United States government,

83

is putting cash into this. They're backing us a hundred per cent." Only they weren't.'

'Now let me get this straight. You're tired of the project first because you find out that people wear out, have accidents and break down – just like in any other job – and second because NASA doesn't love us any more? Is that about it? Why, you pathetic little creep, is your ego so –'

'Let me finish. It's not just that they don't love us, they hate us. Not just NASA but everybody. As soon as they find out what we're doing, soon as they really understand what we're doing, they're out to get us.'

'Let's not get all paran –'

'Look, when NASA pulled out on us I started thinking. Haven't you ever wondered why nobody else is running a project like this? I mean *nobody*. Oh I know there's a few dozen AI projects in different places, but they kinda stand still, don't they? They work on a pattern-recognizer or a language analyser; they keep on working on it and they keep on keeping on. I checked a few places. No significant advances in the past ten years.'

'Where is this leading?'

'Let him go on,' said Fong. 'This is where it gets sinister.'

'So I started checking on private robot projects – you know, the kind of crank stuff or maybe not so crank, stuff you see in articles in *Micro-Ham*, *CPU Digest*, you know.'

'I never read the amateur journals.'

'You should. Because you find funny things. Like this commune in Oregon, all the neat things they were doing with something they called a "*Gestalt* guesser", really it was just – but anyway, just when it was getting interesting they had this fire.'

'So?'

'So it was just like the fire they had in Tuscon, where this little micro club were trying to set up a little thing to write short stories. Then this old guy in Florida – I forget what he was making but when it hit the local papers suddenly he got snuffed by a prowler. Then a nurse in Oklahoma City smashed her customized processor and killed herself, and so did a guy in Kansas, ran a feed store, only upstairs he had –'

'Are you sure? I'd have to check some of these myself.' Franklin forgot to smooth his moustache. 'Anyway a few cases don't –'

'You don't get it, do you? All these people were safe as long as they kept quiet. And when we thought NASA was our boss, we kept quiet too. We didn't publish anything, we didn't give any interviews, we kept a tight security lid on this. Only now ...'

'You think we're targets for some kind of –?' Franklin flicked ash on the floor. 'Find this a little hard to swallow. I mean why? Who would, I mean *why*?'

'Who knows? I mean, who knows why anything? Why do we suddenly have to move the lab upstairs? Everybody you ask just says they got this computer transfer order, this paper here says we gotta move. I don't know who or why, I mean I know what's *way* behind it, but that's not much help. I know it's just something like the old species trying to zap the new one before it gets started, that makes sense but it's kinda depressing all the same.'

'Especially if they try to zap us with it,' Fong said. 'Anyway the kid's right, let's quit while we're ahead.'

Ben Franklin wasn't listening. Smoothing his moustache, he said, 'Can't be the military, they'd be happy as shit to get their hooks on a robot, to hell with wider implications. Bet it's some government agency, probably connected to a think tank, bunch of "futurologists", bet you any damn thing. Bastards sitting there working out their "scenarios" as if the future were some kind of big-budget movie, they want us on the cutting-room floor, do they? Well I say we fight, can't let 'em get away with four years of our – fight, damnit, expose the whole vicious –'

'What for?' Dan smiled. 'Is it really worth it?'

'What kind of bullshit scientist are you to ask a thing like that? Is it worth it? Is it –?'

Fong was tugging at his sleeve and making faces. Ben finally saw that he'd written something, and leaned over to read it:

> The fight's already over. *We won.*
> But *keep quiet* about it.

Four years, he kept thinking, four years. As though repeating the number could magically call them back, restore his career, his wife, whatever it was that had deserted him ...

'I don't believe you.' He pushed past Dan and reached for the door (noticing now how like a shrunken head the stain really looked). 'I don't believe a fucking word.'

As he entered the men's room an unkempt student jumped back from the graffito he had obviously been inscribing next to the mirror. He looked at Ben and quickly turned away, probably to conceal the port-wine birthmark on his cheek. Then hurried out, capping his fibre pen as he went, and leaving Ben to consult his own blank mask. Perfect. Unblemished even by expression.

Automatically he began to wash his hands. He studied them as though he were Ambroise Paré, that military surgeon whose first elaborate designs in jointed iron provided not only new limbs (for those who reached the Peace of Augsburg without them) but also new work for unemployed armourers. There were times when Ben felt as though his entire body were a prosthesis, perfect, ready to work, but untenanted. Even his mind seemed no more than an ingenious engine for grinding through facts (and a part of the engine now reminded him that this was Darwin's complaint) but to no purpose. He felt as hollow as that chess-playing Turk exhibited by Baron von Kempelen in 1769 (and later borrowed by Maelzel, delighting the world even more than his borrowed invention of the metronome).

He dried his hands and folded them tentatively in prayer. Well, no. No point in investing in that unnecessary hypothesis, pie in the sky for the ghost in the machine ... And yet. Even a prosthetic hand could not function properly unless its wearer retained some of the 'feeling' in his ghostly limb. Why couldn't he, Benjamin Waldo Franklin, be waiting just for such a feeling?

'Holy Ghost in the machine?' He tried to make it sound ironic. All the same, a moment later he went into one of the stalls and sat down on the lid and asked for guidance.

It was a gamble, but then a Jansenist God might approve of that; had not Pascal proved that there was nothing to lose and everything to gain? The venue was strange, but then a

Lutheran God was used to that; had not the first Lutheran also uncovered certain fundamental truths in a privy?

What Ben found was a paperback book on the floor. For a moment he simply stared at it, reading the title over and over: *God is Good Business.* A sign? No. A sign? No!

He could hardly call it a sign, with its gaudy yellow-and-black cover, its red sunburst proclaiming '18,000,000 copies sold!' The back cover showed a grey portrait of the author, a smiling businessman with the unlikely name Goodall V. Wetts III.

Just say to yourself when you get up in the morning, 'God WANTS me to win! God wants ME to win! God wants me to WIN – TODAY!' With this simple formula plus the Ten Rules of Faith Dynamics, you –

Ben shut the book and put it back on the floor. But on second thoughts he picked it up again. Might be good for a laugh some time ... you never knew.

And what greater test could God put him through, than asking him to abandon all pleasures of the intellect and accept – *this*?

Washing his hands again, Ben studied his face for changes. He was leaning forward, trying out a confident slow smile, when suddenly he realized he was not alone. A janitor stood leaning on a mop, watching him.

'Jesus Christ! Ain't enough you spend an hour in the john, you gotta spend another hour seein' if your lipstick's on straight. I gotta clean this joint, buster, howsabout fuckin' off?'

'Oh I ... sorry ...'

'You will be sorry, if you write any more porno on my walls.'

Ben's gaze flicked to the place whence the graffito had already been scrubbed.

'Look I'm not responsible –'

'You tellin' me, anybody writes crap like that oughta see a shrink. You like fuckin' clocks, do ya? Or just drawing dirty –'

Ben fled, his face burning, while the janitor shouted after

him, '– pitchers of guys fuckin' clocks, watches maybe, guys wid moustaches? Yeah? And what's that mean, DALI LAID DIAL, what the fuck's that m –?'

Sounds of pain, sounds of rain. O'Smith opened his eyes to the sight of two people in white, arguing.

'... wasn't on duty when he came in, doctor. So if you want to blame somebody ...'

'Not a question of blame, it's just procedure, that's all. We send all John Does to City ...'

'Yes but Nancy said ...'

'Not as if we're not overcrowded as it is what with the flu epidemic ... AH! HOW'S IT GOING, FELLA?'

O'Smith automatically reached out to shake his hand and found that he was not reaching after all. His right arm was missing.

'Where's my durn arm?'

'Your ah, prosthesis, well we had a little problem there, the car pretty much wrecked it. But don't worry, get you fixed up with a new one just as soon as –'

'Where is it? Where's my durn arm?'

'Are you insured, sir?' The nurse was shoving a form in front of his eyes, wasn't that *his* arm she was holding it with? 'If we could just have your name and policy number – *God! Ow! Jesus!*'

Someone shouted, crepe soles came flapping down the street, arms holding him, hands prying his jaws away from his own arm the nurse was wearing, what was a nurse doing inside this form anyways? Stabbed, he fell back, take it slow boy, wait your time, Brazos grinning at him as he heard some folks talking clear over in Galveston ...

'... gave him fifty ccs, doc, okay?'

'Great, yeah, Nora, how's that thumb?'

'I'm ... all right, doctor ... guess it's my own darn fault, mine and Nancy's ...'

Galveston, gal-with-a-vest-on, where was the durn arm-hole, he couldn't get his arm through, what was that durn muzzle velocity ...

'Galveston,' he said.

'Better send this joker up to Section 23, right? Before he

kills somebody, getting 'em all this week, you see the girl in B ward, the cast change? Hysterics, you'd think we were taking her leg off ... said it took her ages to get all those names on the old one ... Give him another fifty, Al, he's still twitching. Talk about prosthesis overdependency, a paradox, Nora, a para ...'

'Oh you and your paradoxes! Dr Coppola, sometimes I think you read just a little bit too much ...'

'Like to keep up, right? Sure the admissions procedure is paradoxical but isn't life itself?'

'...'

'... like in this Graham Greene yarn I'm reading ... offers to sacrifice his own soul for the salvation of souls, but does that include his own or what?'

'... always springing these egghead stories ...'

'... same with admissions ... uninsured creep gets in we end up keeping him until he pays, only how can he pay if he can't get out to work? Fairer not to let 'em in in the first pl ...'

'Have you looked at the corner patient, doctor? Nancy says either something's wrong with the monitor or he has a temperature of 2 million ...'

'... try to get any maintenance done around here, might as well be asking for ... yeah when I checked it read minus 3 million, B.P. 80 over zero ...'

Fighting his way through Galveston one arm tied behind him, only it was somebody else's arm, that old body in Florida reaching for his 12-gauge, Brazos looking surprised as the fully-automatic armhole opened up, bap you're dead, bap you're dead again ...

They watched him sink into sleep and then made their way to Reception, where the pretty receptionist with all the hair was saying to a black doctor:

'Sure, but I mean it don't hardly seem fair, two doctors on the same ward with the same darn name almost!'

'It's easy, though, look: *I*'m Dr De'Ath, *he*'s Dr D'Eath. *I*'m black, *he*'s white. *I* specialize in epidemiology, *he* specializes in cardiology. *I* –'

'Yeah I know but –'

'Look: *he*'s building a robot to test artificial hearts. *I* don't know one end of a soldering iron from the other, okay? So what's the problem? What's the big problem?'

Chief Dobbin opened the press conference by reading from a prepared statement that began: 'I took one look and knew she was trouble with a capital T. This little lady happened to be very, very dead.'

A reporter in the back groaned and turned off his recorder. 'Here we go, another literary treat.'

'With a capital T,' said his neighbour. 'Ain't we gonna get a look at the suspect?' He cupped his hands and called, 'SUSPECT!'

'All in good time, boys. "I asked myself why? Why would any sane human being ..."'

'Probably be a chapter in his book,' said the first reporter, punching buttons on his pocket reminder. 'Never heard of a fucking deadline.'

His neighbour, who was older, stopped picking his teeth to say, 'Deadline? I thought you was on the *Caribou*, since when they meet deadlines on that shit-sheet? You wait till you graduate and try meeting a real deadline on a real paper.'

The boy was silent for a moment, pretending to study his reminder while Dobbin droned on. 'Okay,' he whispered finally. 'How about a little help from an expert then, okay? Like what angle you got on this?'

'Angle? Sex, of course. It's a natural here, this Fong guy is ethnic, a creepy scientist, what more do you want?'

'I meant, uh, you think he really –?'

'What the hell difference does that make, look, they found the dead girl with her leg cut off, blood all over the place, and in her hand was this book covered with his finger-prints, may not be enough for a court-room but it sure as hell works out fine on the front page. Forget about did he do it, get down to work on why? *Why, why*, as our police colleague likes to say.' He picked a morsel from a back tooth and examined it before flicking it away. 'Listen you try this for size: I'm doing a think piece to go with this story, on how all these cybernetics guys are repressed faggots, sadists and what have you. This a.m. I picked up a coupla their magazines, got a list here somewhere of some of the kinky words they use, strong sex angle running right through it, listen to this, *bit*, *byte*, *RAM*, how about those?'

'I don't know, they ain't got much on him –'

'*Gang punch, flip-flop, input*, what do you think that really means, huh? *Stand-alone software*, how about that? *Debugger*, you can't make it plainer, and even the company names, how about *Polymorphic Systems*, how about *The Digital Group*? Or *Texas Instruments*, ever wonder what a *Texas Instrument* is? Or a *Honeywell*? *IBM*, says a lot there . . .'

Someone held up a little camera. 'Keep it down, you guys, just while I get this live, he's gonna show us the book.'

O'Smith woke up feeling just fine, sitting in a fine little parlour with a lot of fine folks, still no arm but what the hell. There was Chief Dobbin's face beaming at him from the teevee, life wasn't so bad.

This is the book that cracked this caper wide open. *Learning Systems*, we thought at first it was an educationalism book but we got our library experts to work on it and – here, I'll show you a page – pure computers. So then we traced it to Dr Lee Fong of the Computer Science Department, found out he was on campus on the night in question. We put him under blanket surveillance, must of surveilled him for a week before he made a false move. He burned some documents and tried to make a run for it. We got him at the airport.

Like Brazos Bill, he thought. O'Smith must have got him at just about fifty airports. They could use a machine like that in here, better than just sittin' in front of the teevee all day.

'What you folks do for excitement around here?' he asked the man in the next chair. Old buzzard, looked like that old body in Florida. Course all old folks look alike.

'What?'

'You got any amusement machines in this place?'

'Machines!' The old man started shaking all over. 'Do you know about the machines?'

'Know what, old-timer?'

'Old-timer equals Saturn, malefic influence badly aspected

91

to Mars equals iron, iron men in the walls, in the floors, in the –'

'Jesus H. Christ I only asked –'

But the old man continued, his voice growing shrill: 'In the walls in the floors in the earth, terrestrial currents, magnetic influences pointing North, North is the Mecca of the magnets, the Mecca, the mecca-men, mechanical men feel them in the walls they get in through the power lines, lines of magnetic current, wheels within wheels, lines within lines ...'

A pair of white-clad men appeared; one held the old man while the other prepared a syringe. 'Give him fifty this time Joe, he'll sleep like a baby – not *now*, Mary, I can't wind you up now, I'm busy giving Fred his medication ...'

O'Smith leaned forward and concentrated on the teevee, camera zooming in on a page of print:

corrected by $(SR_n/100) \times 4.7004397181$ yielding 14.97 bits at 100 milliseconds exposure, using 4-gram array PU on a 43% re-dundancy input, well within expected limits for the 8688R imaging unit. POKERSON, MOSSIANT, RICANING ...

They cut to Lee Fong who turned out to be fat and fifty, thick glasses and everything – a real disappointment, to look at him. O'Smith hadn't missed much there. No fun in a body that didn't put up no fight, martial arts or nothing. Hell, most of 'em were just shit, not like that old boy in St Petersburg with his 12-gauge. He'd made some damn thing, a little machine for talking to old folks, a conversationizer for lonesome old folks. O'Smith didn't see no harm in it but it was enough for the Agency list, the hit parade.

And after all, the big boys knew what they were doing.

Book Two

I

Then the guests were invited to admire a barrel organ, and Nozdrev immediately began to grind out some music for their benefit. The organ produced a not unpleasant sound, but in the middle of the performance something happened, and a mazurka turned into [a march] and that in turn ended in a popular waltz. Long after Nozdrev had stopped turning the handle, an extraordinarily energetic reed in the organ went on whistling all by itself.

Nikolai Gogol, *Dead Souls*

'Semantics?' Indica thumped her coffee cup on the pine table. 'Hank doesn't know the meaning of the word.'

Bax nodded. 'I know what you mean. It's like –'

'It's like he's so damned hot to pick on some word or something, I mean he never hears what I'm really saying.'

'I hear you, I mean, right on.'

She looked at him. Bax might be a little older than he looked, with his button-beanie and shaggy blond moustache. *Right on*? She took another sip of dandelion coffee and went on talking about her husband.

'Like the other day. He got all pissed off just because I said Naomi's basically a Fundamentalist. Oh, and when I told him I thought germ warfare was just sick? You should have heard him!'

'No, I mean yeah. I know what you mean.' Bax finished his glass of bean milk, belched and tipped back in his chair. 'I mean, words only get in the way. Like people, and like – like things.'

'Things, God, don't tell me about things.' Her thin face assumed its characteristic mask of martyrdom, eyes rolling back to look for guidance from the water-stained kitchen ceiling. 'Solar panel's leaking again, everywhere I look I see another busted thing around here. I mean, Hank just keeps buying crap and it just keeps breaking down and will he ever fix it? Ha. He's always so busy with his crap environment magazine he never even sees the environment he lives in. I mean two years I've been shoving match books under the leg of the dining table, been sticking a pail under the garbage disposal where it leaks, you seen our back yard? Six rusty old bikes, I mean six!'

'I hear you, Indica.'

'Every time Hank starts another article we get the whole crap thing all over again. Like his survival shelter, three tons of cement in the shape of a pyramid – because of the rays and all – only he has to make the door too small for anybody but the chickens, whole thing smells of rotten eggs all the time. "I'll fix it," he says, and goes off to another damned pollution conference, Jesus! I could tell him a thing or two about pollution.'

'Yeah,' Bax said. After a moment's thought, he added, 'Yeah.' He tipped his chair back further and reached a leg in her direction.

Indica stared into her earthenware cup, the one with her name and zodiac sign hand-painted on it, the one with the broken handle. 'I mean, he got this house computer to make everything simpler, and it just made it worse, it never does anything but tell him how wrong he is, how wrong everything in the house is. And since we moved out here, anything goes wrong we have to take it twenty miles to town to get it fixed, there sits the ultrasonic dishwasher, it worked about a week.'

'Complicated.'

'Now he only wants to buy a car that runs on chicken-shit, that's all, a bargain he figures and it only costs about twice as much as an Eldorado. See what I'm up against?'

Bax thought his foot was at that moment up against hers. He pressed, and something hummed and moved away from the contact.

'Christ! Are you hurt?' She helped him up.

'No, I'm – but I guess the chair's not too good.' He handed her the splintered chair back, and she placed it in a corner, near a dismantled coffee grinder.

'Hey, what is this thing under the table?'

Two glittering eyes peered up at him.

96

Indica shrugged. 'That? Nothing. A kind of robot, I guess.'

'A robot! Great!' Bax stood clear of it.

'Don't worry, it doesn't work either. Just some piece of junk a guy dumped on us. This creep poet Allbright, who never writes any poetry, just rips off stuff. Guess he ripped this off from some computer freak he knows . . .'

'Yeah? What's it, uh, supposed to do?'

'Who knows? We've had it a month, so far all it does is watch TV and get in the way.'

Bax squatted down to look at it. 'Watches TV?'

'Sure. Hank's creep friend said to treat it like a real kid. So Hank plunks it down in front of the TV every day and it just sits there by the hour. Never moves a muscle.'

Man and robot studied each other. 'Not much to look at,' said Bax, and it wasn't: a squat instrument only two feet high with a large spherical head, a small, conical body, and a pair of tiny tank tracks on which it now edged back, further under the table. The spindly arms, resembling miniature dental drills, were folded against the chest, where Bax could read a word stencilled in black on battleship grey.

'Roderick, eh? Here boy. Here, Roderick.'

The blue glass eyes stared. No sound came from the tiny grille set in the position of a mouth.

'It doesn't know a damned thing, not even its name,' said Indica, and yawned.

Roderick saw a pair of pointy-toed cowboy boots, knees bursting through faded jeans, a huge tattooed hand reaching out towards him. It all looked pretty dangerous, except that the hand had a wrist watch of the kind you could get at Vinnie's Rock Bottom, for rock-bottom prices in comps, calcs, watches, cassettes, video, everything guaranteed personally by Vinnie, everything at low, lower, lowest, rock-bottom prices. At the other end of the arm was a man with hair under his nose, and milk on the hair.

Indica yawned. 'Hank's coming home in a couple of hours, so . . .'

They were gone. Milk, what was it for? Pour it on cereal and spoon it into your mouth. Once upon a time there was a lovely princess who bathed in milk, and they say that her complexion . . .

Roderick listened to their feet going upstairs. Bax was a big man with yellow hair the colour of cereal. Indica was a lovely princess who bathed in the big tub upstairs, it made a wonderful banging sound when she ran the water in. Water was like milk, it was milk with clear stuff added, clear as the shine that makes good furniture even better ...

Something good was upstairs, Indica had whispered to Bax and led him up to see. Now there were stockinged feet moving around up there. Maybe they would tiptoe to the window and pull back the shade to see policemen all around the house. Grown-ups took off their shoes a lot, to watch TV, and if you have a foot-odour problem you need Footnote, spray or powder. Gee, no foot odour!

Bump, bump, bump. Just like water in the tub. Or like shots. Then they struggle for the gun, it goes off and there's a body rolling down the stairs, bump, bump, bump, what have I done? Like chopping wood: I'd be beholden to you, ma'am, if you could see your way clear to givin' a hungry man some wood to chop for his breakfast. Breakfast is the bestest when we all eat Honey-O.

Roderick hummed it to himself as he moved across the black-and-white squares of kitchen, the roses of the living-room, the creaky boards to the foot of the stairs:

> Breakfast O Breakfast
> Breakfast is the bestest
> O breakfast is the bestest
> When we all eat Honey-O.
> Honey-O, Honey-O, honey, honey
> O Breakfast, etc.

The stairs were a problem. They were up and up, while Roderick was down here: he couldn't see how to work it. TV people did stairs all the time. He saw them running down, falling down, rolling down, sitting still on a step and talking, waiting on the dark stairs with a gun and a hat, creeping up with shoes in hand, even vacuuming difficult stair carpets can be a breeze with Breeze-o-mat, because Breeze-o-mat makes housework a breeze!

Animal cries floated down to him, as the bumping continued. Jungle drums? Lord, the heat, the flies! Why don't

98

the beggars attack – what are they waiting for? I don't know if I can stand much more of this, with the Brigadier away on trek for days at a time, leaving the two of us alone like this. My God, Marjorie, I'm only flesh and blood. I also, Nigel. The heat, the flies, gorillas hammering their chests, a Jap sniper in every tree, Joe, I can't go on. Leave me here, I'll hold them off, that's an order soldier.

Careful!

Roderick spun around to check the big green plant behind him. Behind it was another big green plant and then another Roderick and then shadows that might be anything: black men with spears, spotty things with teeth in their mouths, fat spiders, glittering snakes, a scorpion crooking its finger at him, shambling zombies coming after him. A guy had to protect himself, one chance in a million but it just might work, break through to the shore, the sunlit sand where he could hear the surf beating, beating ...

'Nothing,' said Bax. He dropped Hank's kimono on the floor and climbed back into bed. Indica noticed that he was getting a paunch.

'How can it be nothing, we both heard it!'

'I mean, just that little robot thing, you know? Knocked over your potted plant in the hall.' He reached for her but she sat up, drawing the sheet around her shoulders.

'Just great. I only spent two years growing that damned thing from an avocado stone, that's all. Two years.'

'Okay, but –'

'Don't. I'm not in the mood any more. I hate that sonofa-bitching robot, you know? Hank says it cost a million or so to build. For two cents I'd trash the damned thing.'

'A million? Wow.'

'Yeah, wow.' She turned away from him, his bleached hair and faint face-lift scars. 'That really grabs you doesn't it, a price tag like that? That's men all right, all you think about is gadgets and how much you can get them for. I see Hank reading an electronics catalogue, he gets the same look on his face, the same dumb look he gets over a sex magazine, how do you think that makes me feel?'

'No, sure, but –'

'Let's get dressed. A million bucks' worth of junk running around the house destroying my plants, how do you think that makes me feel?'

'Yeah, but –'

'I don't want to talk about it any more. Just get dressed.'

Bax obeyed, and followed her downstairs. From the living-room came sounds (Yipe! Eeeeow! Boing! and scales played on a xylophone) of Roderick's favourite TV cartoon, *Suffering Cats*. The little robot stood close to the screen, mesmerized by the sight of cats blackening their faces with TNT, walking off cliffs, and being flattened under weights marked 1 TON. Bax, too, was fascinated. He sat down to watch, only half-aware that Indica was leading Roderick out into the hall.

'*Where's that cat?*' said a deep voice from the TV. '*Where's that dad-blamed cat?*' Its owner, visible from the waist down, wore hobnail boots and carried a meat-cleaver. Bax was grinning already.

'Hey honey? Come and watch this. Old Oscar's on the war-path and –'

An odd sound came from the hall, like grinding gears. In a minute, Indica and Roderick came back. She was crying and trembling, while the robot seemed unperturbed. *Yipe! Boing!* He crept up close to the screen, until his large dome caused a partial eclipse.

'Outa the way, big-head.' Bax noticed a shiny dent in the dome, as it moved away. But just then he needed his full attention for animated carnage: a knocked-out cat listened to birds and grew a red lump on its head, and looked at the world through a pair of plus-sign eyes.

A commercial came on. Kids were urged to get a plastic robot that stalked in circles, saying, 'Hello, I'm Robbie! Can I be your friend? Hello, I'm Robbie! Can I be your friend?'

Roderick was unable to watch this, for his head kept revolving in the strangest way, like a lid coming off a jar of Huck Finn grape-style jelly, a taste treat for kids – and grown ups too!

'I didn't do anything,' Indica protested. 'All I did was take him and show him the avocado he killed, all I did was rub his nose in it, a little.'

Hank watched the head revolve. 'A little? Then how did he get that big dent? Jesus, I can't keep anything around here, you –'

'Sure, blame the wife, it's what I'm for, right? Blame me. Okay, maybe I got carried away. Big deal, maybe I slapped him a couple of times, okay, I slapped your little toy.'

'Just look at him! What am I supposed to tell Allbright? He trusts us with a billion-dollar machine, am I supposed to tell him you knocked hell out of it?'

'A million dollars, listen they had this toy robot on TV, nine ninety-five plus tax, at least it can say hello; your little mechanical shit-head here can't even do that. All he knows is how to smash people's house-plants, how to go around murdering living things. Okay, I'm sorry. Okay? I'm sorry, maybe I hit him too hard. I don't know, maybe I banged his head on the floor a couple of times, shit Hank, I was pretty close to a breakdown if you want to know.'

He combed his full beard with both hands. 'Probably cost a fortune to fix him. A fortune. What the hell can I say to the guy who built him if he comes around to see – it's all – it's all getting on top of me.'

'Look, maybe I can just stick his head down with scotch tape or something, no one'll know the difference really. I mean, this dude never comes to see him or anything, who's to know? Even if he did, I mean we just say he fell down the stairs ... Look, I'll fix him right now.'

She carried Roderick out to the kitchen. Hank sat staring at his hands for a moment, then went to the bar. As he picked up the bottle of Scotch, a tiny screen behind it lit up with a message:

FIRST OF THE DAY 19:48: CONGRATULATIONS HANK, YOU ARE MAKING REAL PROGRESS.

'Shut up,' he said. After downing the measured drink, he returned to the sofa and sat fiddling with his electric pipe-cleaner. Handy little gadget – but wasn't it starting to make a funny noise?

'Here we are, good as new.' Indica plunked the little robot down in front of the TV and turned it on. 'Good boy, you just sit here and watch the pretty pictures.' The screen showed a lifelike armpit.

'Good as new,' she said to Hank. 'Not that he was ever a hell of a lot of good. Never says a word, never opens his mouth. I mean, even when I plug him in for his recharge at night, he never says good night or anything. Some robot! If you ask me – what's the matter now?'

Hank cocked his head over the electric pipe-cleaner. 'Making a funny noise, hear it?'

'You and your goddamned gadgets, how about listening to me once in a while? Hank, what the hell's wrong with you, all you think about are your gadgets. I mean, we got a house full of broken-down machinery now, who needs it? We came out here to get away from crap and machines and – look at you, sitting here in the middle of the goddamned desert, listening to a goddamned electric pipe-cleaner!'

He looked at her, then back to the instrument. 'Now wait a minute. We came out here to establish our own, ahm, environmental situation, right? So machines are an integral part of it. Oh sure, I used to want to turn the clock back, just like everyone else. I wanted to trash our whole technology, return to the soil – only I grew out of it. Whether we like it or not, technology is here to stay. *Machines* are here to stay.'

On cue, the pipe-cleaner made a loud buzzing noise and emitted a wisp of smoke. Hank dropped it to the floor where, after flopping for a moment like a dying fish, it lay still.

'Ha! Maybe they don't want to stay.'

Hank's pudgy fingers dug into his beard. 'Oh sure, laugh. But it doesn't change a thing. Sure, machines go wrong once in a while. They have to be fixed –'

'Tell me something I don't know. You never fix anything around here, you never let me call a repairman, all you do is let it pile up! The crapyard of the universe we got here, the crap –'

'Just let me finish, will you? Just have the courtesy to let me finish what I'm saying, okay? Okay. Machines are here to stay, we have to make the most of 'em. We owe it to ourselves not to just throw them away the minute they conk out on us. If we do that, we're turning all our energy and raw materials into junk and garbage and pollution. Right?'

'What is this, are you gonna quote your whole goddamned article for *Country Ambience* or something? I've read it.'

'Just let me finish. Now, we don't call repairmen because the true person, true to his own environment, fixes everything himself. It's the only way to learn to live *in* your environment. You fix things yourself, or if you can't fix something you make some new use out of it. Like maybe you cannibalize it to fix something else.'

'Cannibalize my ass! I don't believe what I'm hearing from you. God, you've been writing this crap so long you believe it yourself, any minute now you're gonna tell me about *bricoleurs* and Zen motor cycles! Listen, buster, this isn't *your* environment, it's *mine*. You're always off at some goddamned conference, *I'm* the one has to try living in this shit-hole day after day. Day and night, you know? I'm stuck here, with the deep-freeze that wrecks a quarter-ton of food, with the stopped-up drains – all of it. *My* environment, and it stinks.' She looked at Roderick. 'Yeah, including that little tin marvel, you mind telling me how he's supposed to fit into our swell environmental situation? I mean, just what are we supposed to get out of having him around, a walking junk-yard?'

'Well, ahm, as a matter of fact I'm doing an article on him for *Eco-Style*, "I Adopted a Robot", to tie in with their big issue on home cybernetics. And it looks like I'll be guesting on a chat show next week, could lead to a book-movie deal, even heard from a producer putting out feelers for a sitcom series, *My Little Robot*, I mean it's all talk at this stage, but who knows ...?'

On the screen, a man with a yellow moustache held up a box of detergent. Roderick began to wave his arms.

'Okay, keep him. Just keep him out of my way, Hank. I mean it.'

'Baba abbaba!' said Roderick. 'Ablabba bab!'

That night, after Roderick had been plugged to his re-charger in the spare room, and while he stood motionless, his blue glass eyes opaque in sleep, Hank and Indica patched up their quarrel.

It was a chance to be alone, and they made the most of it. Indica set out low-cholesterol potato chips in a bio-degradable plastic bowl, Hank opened a few recycled cans of home brew, and they put on their favourite old video tape of Jacques Cousteau. Holding hands, plenty of friendly eye-contact – it was almost like old times.

Indica looked at the underwater ballet of porpoises critically. After all, she'd been a dancer herself once, and a good one. The chorus of *Mao and I*, nine months with the Braxton Hicks Dancers doing TV work, the talent was there. Even in that TV commercial where she'd been a dancing taco, it was there, talent she could have built into a career. Only she hadn't. Somehow after she'd married Hank – anyway, here she was, watching a bunch of fish! Oh well, Hank probably loved it.

Hank watched a man in a wet-suit cavorting with cetaceans. Ho hum. Indica probably loved this stuff, this expression of man's unity with Nature. For him, it was just a place to rest his gaze while he swallowed flat beer. Of course he still cared about the global environment, in a way. He still wrote articles about the blue whale and the white rhino. Not his fault if they turned into promotional tie-ins for glossy magazine spreads selling dog food and deodorants. He had to live. Had to swim with the current and survive. People got tired worrying about Spaceship Earth, they wanted to concentrate on Spaceship Me.

There were no more triumphs, only peak experiences; no more tragedies, only personal problems. Indica's problem was being a good dancer who'd stopped dancing. Hank's problem was being a bad writer who couldn't stop writing. Together they were building for themselves a modest little problem relationship.

'Just like old times,' said Indica.

'A *déjà vu* experience,' said Hank.

'You can say that again.'

2

'Who? Oh. Uh, great to hear from you uh, Dan is it? Great to, only I'm just this minute trying to get away, guesting tonight on the Ab Jason show, gotta be in L.A. by, hey, some great publicity there for your little lab ... well sure you probably sure a low profile, he did, yes he did explain that, sure. Only ...'

As he transferred the phone to his other ear in order to look at his watch, Indica could hear the frantic voice on the other end: '... *taking a hell of a chance even using a pay phone ... Subpoena ... threatening me with mental hosp ...*'

'Appreciate all that, Dan boy, only hell I'm a freelance journalist, you can't expect ... truth is my business ... public has a right to know and the truth, in the long run the truth ... Frankly I think you're overdramatizing this whole ... anyway how can they subpoena you into a mental, that doesn't make sense, you ... Frankly Dan boy I don't understand your attitude, here I am babysitting this creation of yours, busting my balls to get you some free publicity, even sent you those test tapes you wanted did Allbright give them to you? He did, and ... Okay, sure, if that's ... sure I, just a second.'

He fumbled for a pen and wrote *M & P Wood, 614 Sycamore Avenue, Newer, Nebraska.* 'Any zip ... right. If that's the way you feel about it, fine, if this Wood firm can do any better ... what am I supposed to do, the thing's subnormal, doesn't even talk ... well no we haven't talked to it, not much, course I could have spent more time with it but trying to carve out a career here, you know, trying to weld together the concepts of ecological balance and post-industrial ... YES I'LL SEND THE GODDAMNED THING. Yeah, ciao.' He slammed down the receiver. 'You hear any of that?'

'I wasn't listening.' Indica sat wedged in a window seat, painting her nails. The scarf around her throat was blue, her toenails were becoming red.

'That guy's cracking up, completely bananas, you know?

Figures *they* are after him, want to subpoena his records and lock him up, smash the robot and Christ knows what.'

'I'm on their side,' she said.

Roderick extended a claw towards her foot. 'Red.'

'Listen, he wants us to send him off to some firm in Nebraska of all damned places, thinks we're not good enough to, not caring enough, how do you like that?'

She shrugged. 'I couldn't care less. Are you gonna make that plane or what?'

'Yeah, plenty of time. Only Jesus he has to dump this on me when I've got enough to worry about, you think maybe I should trim my beard a little? I don't want to come across as a goddamned nut ...'

'Leave it.' She did not look at him. 'You look fine.'

'Great, but what am I supposed to say? I've got nothing to show them, I mean if I show them *that* they'll just laugh. A million kids have toys more articulate than *that*. Here I've worked my buns off trying to prepare for this show, can't even take him with me. I mean they'll just laugh. I mean, he can't do anything but babble in baby-talk, you think a hundred million viewers want to see that?'

Indica set down her bottle of nail varnish. 'Don't worry. You can just tell them about him.'

'Sure, I have to, I have to do it that way now. But I mean Christ I spent three days trying to teach him chess, all he knows is how to knock the pieces off the board. What am I supposed to say? I've adopted this robot only he's a little retarded?'

'Jess,' said Roderick. 'Jess, jess, jess. Jess?'

Indica snickered. 'Oh don't worry, you'll think of something on the plane. Make it up, what the hell. Tell 'em he reads Latin and Esperanto, plays the ukulele. Tell 'em he likes the Mets. Tell 'em you want him to grow up to be President.'

'Sure, you're right. I've got to think of this as pure box-office, that's all. Only my nerves are – and this guy calling me up like this at the last minute, saying he doesn't want any publicity. Doesn't want any publicity! You know, sometimes –'

'You'll miss your plane.'

Hank stood up, holding his attaché case in both hands.

With the full beard and glasses, he looked a little like an immigrant in some old movie, coming off the steamship at Ellis Island. All he needed, she thought, was a tag around his neck. 'Well,' he said. 'Here goes. Wish me luck.'

'Break a leg,' she murmured. 'Bye.'

Roderick looked up, when he'd gone. 'Bye-bye-bye-bye-bye.' He turned back to watch Indica's red toes. Toes were little fingers. If you had fingers and toes you could do all kinds of things, make them red or count them: this little finger went to market, like Hank, that little finger stayed home, like Indica. Queen, king, knight, rook and the little pawn at the end there . . .

He moved closer until he was staring at her across the low table where the bottle of varnish stood. There was white stuff between her toes and red stuff on them. She put it on with a little matchstick, red. Red, it went into a little hole in the top of this bishop here on this funny jessboard that didn't have any squares. When she put the matchstick into it, there it was, a bishop. Only without squares, how could it see where to move? He grabbed the bishop and it fell over and red came out.

'Shit,' said Indica. She pulled a lot of white stuff out of a box and mopped the board, spreading red all over.

'Jit,' said Roderick. Indica stopped mopping and smiled at him. 'Jit,' he said again.

'What the hell, Roddy, go ahead. Have a ball. I'm never gonna clean another thing around here, you know? So go ahead.'

He dipped his claw in the red and held it up to her. 'Red.'

There was Hank on TV! His beard might be a different shape and his face might be a different colour, but here he was, real as life. Roderick went to the window and looked out. Hank's car wasn't there, so he hadn't come back, but here he was, sitting on a sofa with some other people, talking to Ab Jason who sat on a chair of his own. Ab was a man who kept wrinkling his face and making people laugh. Roderick rolled right up close to the TV screen, to watch every move.

'. . . doesn't, ahm, talk much yet but he's learning, boy is he learning fast. He plays chess —'

107

'*Plays chess? But so do a lot of computers. Tell me, Hank, what's so special about little Roddy?*'

'*Well, he's, he's like a real kid. I mean for instance he's a big baseball fan. He likes the Mets.*' Tittering came from the audience, and Ab wrinkled his face.

'*The Mets! Ahem!*' Laughter. '*Who's his favourite player? The batting practice machine?*' Loud laughter, then applause. '*Seriously, Hank, what else does he do?*'

'*He watches TV a lot.*'

'*TV? No kidding! What do you think he gets out of it? What kind of stuff does he like, anyway? Serious stuff, commentators and think-shows? Or daytime shows like* Milestones to Morning? *Hey, is he watching us right now? Is he?*'

'*Yes, yes he is, Ab. He and my wife –*'

'*Okay, want to wave to him, before we take a break?*'

Hank waved and Roderick waved back. Indica was of course upstairs with Bax.

'*You're watching Ab Jason, and right now you're watching a man wave goodbye to his adopted son – a* robot *who likes the Mets. We'll be right back after this:*'

Ab and Hank disappeared, and Roderick saw the giant armpit again.

'*. . . clean and dry almost twenty-five hours a day. Why settle for less? If you're troubled . . .*'

Bye-bye-bye. Roderick trundled into the hall and looked up the dark stairs. Indica and Bax were up there playing a game, he could hear them laughing and grunting. There must be some way of getting up all those stairs, maybe if he grabbed the newel-post and tilted his bottom so his tracks could grip the carpet – it was easy. One step, two steps, this little finger went to market, queen, king, bishop, knight, rook, here he was half way up, whatever you do don't look down, but no one's ever climbed the South face before . . . I, I can't hold on, slipping . . . hang on, two hands reaching for each other, fingers almost touching when the distant rumble of an avalanche . . . I, I'm not gonna make it, Bill. You damned cripple, get up out of that chair and walk! Fingers reaching out, clutching for support . . .

He was at the top, gliding along to the door that was open just a crack to lay a finger of light across the landing carpet.

Roderick looked in, knowing it was forbidden . . . Do not fence with me, Amanda, that room is always kept locked, I have my reasons . . .

Bax and Indica were sitting on the side of the bed. Indica was sitting on Bax's lap, facing him. They were not wearing any clothes. Their faces were different, as though Bax had just swung open the gull-wing door of his new Ghirlandaio and invited her to jump in for a new motoring experience, while Indica had just used Anatase, the fragrance that makes him thrill to be a thrall, or as though they were expecting something to happen. They gasped and groaned and kept wrestling around, nobody winning. Every now and then Indica might give out with a No or a Yesyes, but Bax said nothing.

Roderick tired of waiting for something to happen. He counted those fingers and toes he could see, he noticed that Indica had bigger chests than Bax, and then he started looking over the room.

There was a funny bicycle-thing in the corner, you'd need fingers to grip the handles. On the wall there was a picture of a woman standing balanced on one toe. Toes are just little fingers, you need them for everything here. There was a picture of a whale, above a table covered with little bottles and jars. A policeman would put his finger into a jar and taste it and nod at the other policeman, saying it was the real stuff all right, the real stuff.

There was a telephone by the bed. Whoever calls the detective can't say it over the phone, meet him at Pier 13, only he's always dead when the detective gets there. And as soon as the detective leaves somebody's office they start pushing buttons on the phone, 'Some nosey P.I. is asking a lot of questions. The wrong questions.' Then he sits chewing his finger-nails before he reaches for a gun. With fingers you could do just about anything, squeeze a trigger . . .

Indica said, 'Yes no yes no no yes yes no yes no!' Bax gasped and they rolled apart. There were marks on his shoulders where her red finger-nails had been digging in.

Roderick looked at his own red claw. Red, but not a finger, not a toe. With real fingers you could do anything, make a phone call, taste the real stuff, count up ten little fingers and ten littler fingers ...

Bax lay there like a boxer, like when they're taping your fingers before your comeback fight, years ago you killed your pal and quit the ring ...

Rings, sure, you could wear rings, a fancy ring like the homicidal maniac who's always stalking somebody and all you ever see is his fancy ring ... third finger left hand with this ring, yes, wedding-rings, engagement-rings, all at low, low prices, one carat, two carat ...

Fighting, fists, sure, you could make a fist. 'Quantrell, you had this coming for a long time, and I aim ...' Or a fistful of money for seven straight passes at the crap table, or fist counting, one potato, two potato ...

Something made him see all the fingers in the world, fingers held out to beg bread from the French aristocrats, gripping the bars of a cell in Death Row, pressing a doorbell, thumbing a ride, squeezing a trigger, playing church-and-steeple, throwing down a gauntlet or drawing off a slim glove, giving signals ('Contact!' 'Scram!' 'Peace!'), bidding at an auction, gripping a precipice as a heel comes down to crush them. He saw chorus girls filing their nails as they talked over their dates; priests making a gesture as though they held invisible martini glasses; the suspect being finger-printed in the old precinct house; the safe cracker sanding his finger-tips; the fingers of an artist framing his model; the quivering fingers of a drunken brain surgeon; the cruel fingers of a pianist clawing the keyboard; the gnarled hands of a diamond-cutter; the plump hands of a Roman emperor ...

He couldn't be sure until he counted again, and still he had to think it over until dawn, when Bax and Indica were gone and Hank came home.

'Mommy not here this morning, eh Roddy?'

'Bax,' said Roderick.

'Uh-huh. She's not back. Probably went off to her god-damned health ranch again. Boy, if she had to pay a few of the bills from that place ... Still, it's just you and me today, Roddy. Have to get our own breakfasts – I mean, I have to – aw shit, why do I bother trying to talk to you, might as well talk to this coffee-maker here.'

'Bax.'

'Tell you what, let's surprise her, okay? She's always complaining about how I never fix anything around here, let's make a big effort and really try to whip this place in shape, okay?'

'Okay.'

'I'm gonna fix every damn thing in the place, that or bust my balls trying. One thing, I see she went and spilled nail-varnish all over the coffee table in the den. So first I better add that to the list.'

Roderick followed him to his desk and watched him finger the keyboard of his home computer.

> TABLE, COFFEE, TEAKWOOD, REFIN TOP.
> EJT 2 HRS.
> COMPLETE WHEN?

After a moment the computer replied:

> EARLIEST COMPLETE 94 WEEKS. OK?

'Ninety-four weeks before I can sand down a little table? What the hell here, Roddy, looks like the old computer's playing tricks on us. Let's try again.' He tapped. 'Same damned answer. Hmm. Maybe what I need is a new scenario with the earliest possible window for table, coffee.' He punched some new instructions and the computer began reeling off pages of explanation involving work-flow diagrams, urgency priorities, job-class and materials-acquisition charts. Hank could barely understand half of it, and that half made him uneasy.

Urgent jobs, such as *Floorboard, loose* (causing *Lamp, Table, Flickering* and a possible *Hazard, Fire*) had to come first. Then came jobs like the solar panel which in time might cause *Damage, House, Structural*. Then came fixing the garage door electric eye which, though not serious in itself, made it necessary to park the car outside where sunlight would eventually damage its paint. Did not *Toilet Bowl Cleaner, Automatic, Jammed* cause a *Hazard, Health*? And would it not be a good idea to check the entire sewer system at the same time? Then *Dishwasher, Ultrasound, Leaking* seemed to have some urgent problems (possible *Hazard, Health*), but since this required parts he could obtain only by mail order, he might profitably fill the interval by overhauling the lawn mower engine and replastering the kitchen.

Then for preventive maintenance on the *Cable, Alarm, Burglar* . . .

'It's all really logical, really. I mean, it all makes sense when you go through it like this. Like A can't be done until after B, and B is not as important as C. Only C has to be done at the same time as D. You with me? And D, there's no use fixing that until E works, but first F and G are gonna break down unless they get some maintenance, only H is really urgent, it's gotta be done first . . . so it's, it's ninety-four weeks all right.'

'Eleven,' said Roderick.

'Eh? Eleven what?' Hank was sweating. His hands trembled on the keyboard.

'Fingers,' said Roderick, pointing to them. 'Eleven.'

'Heh heh, no, ten. Ten fingers, Roddy. See, one, two –'

'Bax got eleven.'

'Backs – I don't know, Roddy, you have to learn to talk plainer than that. Now where was I? Oh yeah, preventive . . .' He pushed another button and another page of explanation appeared. 'Ninety-four – that's almost two years, all my spare time for two years. And just look at all this stuff that could break down between now and then: the slow cooker, the light-pipe intercom, the rotisserie, the hot food table, the cake baker, the microwave, the deep freeze, the shoe polisher, floor polisher, vacuum cleaner-washer, blenders, mixers, thermostat, lumistat, electrostatic air-conditioner, Jesus Christ the water-purifier system, the pepper-mill, the Jesus H. Christ it's not just two years it's the rest of my life, Roddy. The nail buffer, the can opener, the carving knife, where'd I ever get all this stuff? I mean all that's just stuff for the house, what about this stuff for the car, the fuel computer, the skidproof brakes . . . what about these bikes I was going to fix up with traffic radar, what made me think I'd have time to . . . Jesus H., it's hot in here, bet the damned air-conditioning's crapped out on me too, everything else is, I need a drink, that's what.'

'Eleven,' said Roderick, following him to the bar.

'Yeah, sure, eleven.' Hank picked up the Scotch bottle and behind it the screen lit up:

SURE YOU NEED THIS DRINK? SURE YOU NEED IT NOW?

He put the bottle back. 'Goddamned life run by machines, can't even have a drink, can't even get a cigarette, damned cigarette-box is locked until noon, another goddamned machine running my life, can't lift a finger without –'

'Eleven,' said Roderick.

'You too, huh?' Hank went back to the desk and dropped into his chair. 'Okay, look. Maybe I can't beat all the god-damned mechanical systems in this place, but I sure as hell can beat you. Look, *ten* fingers, *ten*!' He shook them in Roderick's face. 'Count 'em, *ten*.'

Roderick counted. 'Ten.'

'Ha!'

'Bax got eleven.'

'Backs? Wait a minute, *Bax!* You mean Baxter Logan, that creep Indica met last year, where was it, the health-ranch sure, the, sure, that singles sauna on the health-ranch she kept saying how terrific – Listen, Roddy? Listen, is Bax a man?'

'Yeah.'

'Was he here last night?'

'Yeah. Bax got eleven –'

'Forget about the goddamned eleven fingers! You sure he was here? With Indica? With Mommy?'

Roderick pointed at the ceiling.

Hank sat motionless for a moment, then turned to the computer.

'She's gone off with the sonofabitch, back to that god-damned health – must be a message here somewhere.'

He typed: MAIL FOR HANK?

The computer replied:

DEAR HANK: I'M LEAVING YOU. DON'T TRY TO FIND ME OR TALK TO ME EXCEPT THROUGH MY LAWYER. I'M GOING TO LIVE WITH BAX LOGAN WHO YOU MAY NOT REMEMBER I MET LAST YEAR IN NEVADA. IT SO HAPPENS THAT WE GOT A MEANINGFUL RELATIONSHIP I MEAN BAX AND ME AND NOT BAX AND A HOUSE FULL OF STUPID GADGETS LIKE YOU.

YOU AND I WERE REALLY LIKE STRANGERS EVER SINCE WE KNEW EACH
OTHER. I GOT TIRED OF BEING TREATED LIKE PROPERTY, JUST ANOTHER
ONE OF YOUR GADGETS. I WANT TO BELONG TO JUST ME.

YOURS,

INDICA

'That just about finishes it, Roddy. Everything else breaking down and now this, it's like the whole world slowly
collapsing ... every ... breaking down and falling apart and
wearing out and blowing away and cracking up ... Even you,
look at you with the dents in your head and that stupid scotch
tape collar, I mean why the hell can't you even learn to count
up to ten? I mean why does every single thing have to break
down all the time?'

'Eleven?' Roderick still wanted to tell him all about Bax,
how Bax had this eleventh finger right in the middle of his
body – but Hank didn't seem to be listening any more.

Hank was rummaging through his tool-box, throwing out
screwdrivers and wrenches, scraps of wire and folding rulers.
Finally he up-ended the box and dumped everything out on
the floor. He sat down in the middle of it all.

'Must be here somewhere ... that's not it ... that's not it
either ...'

After a while he stopped talking and pawing through the
stuff. Hank just sat there like a big shaggy bear at a picnic.

Roderick found a couple of sanding-discs that looked like
plates, set them out with wrenches for silverware, and started
piling on the food. Come and get it, plenty more where this
come from, finger-lickin', old-fashioned Southern fried
country kitchen *grub*! For each of them there was a generous,
man-sized helpin' o' nails, nuts and bolts, insulated wire and
sizzlin' flashlight batteries. Mm-mmm! For dessert there was
a roll of friction tape that looked a lot like one of Aunt
Lettibelle's Olde Tyme Golden Dunker doughnuts, hit like
to melt in yo' mouf, chile. Roderick poured machine-oil –
gravy – over everything and waited for Hank's mouth to start
a-waterin'. Red-headed kids with freckles were always sitting
around having picnics like this with bears, big friendly bears
like Hank. All he had to do was find the right words for a
square meal like this. Come and get it, plenty more ...

'Eat up, Hank,' said Roderick. 'It's yum-scrumpty-umptious!'

The big bear blinked, looked at the sanding-disc, brushed it aside. 'That's not it either ...'

The mumbling and pawing went on until at last Hank came up with a hammer.

'*That*'s it,' he said, smiling, and grabbed Roderick's arm to hold him steady while he raised the hammer to strike.

3

Fill up that sunshine balloon
with happiness!
Send up that rocket to the moon
with happiness!

Every smile was a gift, every laugh was a lift, up up we will drift, and there seemed to be no end of choruses to this one.

Pa began to wonder if this radio would ever wear out, so he could make out his report and be done with it. Funny, them giving him a radio to test on his last day at the factory. And what had Mr Danton said? Something about brightening the long hours of, of leisure activity? Whatever that meant. He knew they really wanted him to test the radio because they'd given him a key at the same time, so he could get back into the factory with his report.

For forty years Pa Wood had worked at Slumbertite, fixing first the assembly-line, then later on the machines that worked the assembly-line, and finally just the machines that fixed the machines. At the last there was no one in the place but him, and Mr Danton upstairs in the office with his part-time secretary. And now, so he heard, they were gone too, the factory rumbling on by itself. Probably have to get a machine to read his report, if this damn radio didn't outlive him. How could he work on his inventions with all that easy listenin' racket?

Everyone else in Newer, Nebraska, worked to music. The boys at Clem's Body Shop hammered away to the Top Twenty; the girls at the Newer Café fried burgers to sad Western songs about drinking too much and losing custody of the children; Dr Smith the dentist had pulled all of Pa's teeth out to the taped rhythms of his (Dr Smith's) favourite Latin-American selections; even at the Slumbertite factory the machines worked to a kind of aggravating murmur from hidden speakers that Pa called Muse-suck. The stuff, what-ever it was, had probably been turned on to entertain the workers years ago; neither Pa nor anyone else had been able to find out how to turn it off.

'That's the third time I've called you to dinner,' said Ma, coming into the workshop. 'What are you inventing out here?'

He started. 'Oh, uh, well I'm not sure what it is until it's finished. Might turn out to be a puzzle that nobody can take apart.' He turned the gadget over, frowning down at it. 'Or it might be the start of something really big – a tap-dancing shoe that knows all the steps – or even a car that runs on scrap metal.' He put it down and stared up at something on the wall, a key, a gold-plated key hanging on a nail. 'Do you suppose they meant that to be a kind of retirement present?'

'I told you they did, and the radio too. It's you that keeps insisting they want you to test it. Turn the blamed thing off!'

He reached up to the shelf and hesitated. 'Seems a shame to get this far and not go on with it. Must be near done now, then I can have some peace and quiet. I'll just leave it a bit . . . now what was I going to do?'

'Dinner,' she said, and led him into the house.

Mrs Smith let the curtain fall. 'There they go, a coupla real characters,' she said, expressing the opinion of half the town. 'I don't know who's the biggest character, him or her. Yesterday she told me –'

'They oughta be locked up, both of them,' said her husband, speaking for the other half of town. 'Putting a thing like that in their back yard where every kid can see it!' He lifted the curtain and glared at the giant toilet bowl, large enough to accommodate a ten-yard width of rump. 'And remember the time she shaved her head and painted it green? Holy cow, trying to raise kids in this – I mean what the hell are they, atheists or –'

'But listen, yesterday she told me they're adopting a robot! A robot!'

'Oughta be locked up,' he said, staring at his hands, which were blushing deep pink. 'Look, just thinking about them starts off the old allergy again. It's not enough I gotta wash my hands fifty times a day and stick 'em in every filthy mouth in town, we had to pick a house next door to –'

'You'll feel better after dinner. Get Judy and wash, I mean –'

He switched on the TV to catch the news-scan, but saw nothing but a list of names:

THIS PAGE IS DEDICATED TO ALL THE GANG DOWN AT MACS: *Jil, Meri, Su, Jacqui, Teri, An, Ileen, Jonn, Lu, Judi, Jak, Hari, Lynda, Raelene, Luci, Toni, Allyn, Jazon, Cay, Edd, Fredd, Nik, Carolle, Hanc, Jayne, Kae, Lusi,* ...

'I had the strangest dream,' said Ma, dishing up chicken and dumplings. 'I dreamed I was lost in this waxworks, and everyone I asked for directions was just wax. I came up to this dummy of Ed ("Kookie") Byrnes and I thought, maybe if I touch him he'll come to life, so I did and he just stayed wax, only somehow I cut myself on this metal comb he had in his hand – what do you suppose that means?'

Pa, who was wondering if you could preserve food by stopping time, said: 'Delicious, delicious.'

'You weren't listening.'

'Well no. I'm sorry.'

'You can't help it, forty years of Muse-suck and noisy machines – but I hope you heard me when I said he's coming tomorrow. Because he is.'

'Who? Oh, him?' He grinned with Dr Smith's teeth. 'Well now, there's something. Life ain't so bad, eh Mary?'

'Who said life was bad? And if it is it's only because you can't behave like any normal retired senior whatsit and go root for the softball team or something, go work in the garden or, or just sit on the park bench in front of the post office with the other old seniors and talk about the state of the nation.'

He speared a dumpling. 'More like the state of their bowels. Horse-shoes, you forgot playing horse-shoes. Yep, pinochle, pool, beer, TV – the choice is endless. Only I'm too busy.'

'*Busy.*'

'Anyway, what about you? Shouldn't you be crocheting covers for the telephone and the toilet-roll and every other

118

blessed thing that looks like it might embarrass people? Or else TV, you ought to be watching some ads for freezer boxes and electric beet-dicers, and the stuff they squeeze in between the ads too, what is it? *Dorinda's Destiny*? Instead you just lounge around, writing stuff you never show anybody, painting pictures you keep hidden – no wonder everybody thinks we're nuts.' After another dumpling he said, 'We are, I guess, but no need for them to say so. This adoption business, you know what they'll say? "The crazy Woodses is at it again."'

'If they do, it's only because you go out of your way to be – *eccentric*. I remember nineteen fifty-two or was it three, just when everybody was watching Joe MacCarthy on TV –'

'Don't you mean Charlie McCarthy?'

'When they were hanging on every word, you had to go telling everybody that you were a card-carrying communist, remember? "Hundred per cent Red," you used to say, "and damned proud of it." Had the boys at the Idle Hour talking about tar and feathers before we heard the end of it.'

'Come on, you enjoyed every minute of it, you even made up that little card for me, remember? On one side it said, "I am a communist", and on the other, "Communists always think they're cards."'

She sniffed. 'I had to join the Ladies' Guild to smooth that over.'

'Yes, I seem to remember you getting them all around here for a seance, wasn't it? Getting in touch with a flying saucer, don't tell me you didn't enjoy that. Working away on the old ouija-board and all the time –'

'Just a few lines of Apollinaire, to perk them up,' she said. 'For their own good, really.' She sat back in her chair until the noonday sun caught her white hair and gleamed on the green scalp beneath.

> From the red to the green all the yellow dies
> When the macaws are calling in their native forests
> Slaughter of pi-hi's
> There is a poem to be written about the bird which has only
>   one wing
> We had better send it in the form of a telephone message
> Gigantic state of

'Enough of that,' she said, wiping her eyes. 'I've got a million things to do. He's coming tomorrow and I haven't even cleaned the house or changed the sheets on the spare bed or baked cookies or anything.'

'But he's a robot, Mary. He doesn't sleep in a bed or eat –'

'Oh I know. To you little Roderick is just a chess-player.'

'In a way. I mean, robots are terrific at chess, they say. Wonder if I shouldn't go down in the basement and dig out a few old magazines with problems –'

'Fine. While you're down there, dig out our carpet-beater and use it. Understand?'

'Maybe I could invent you a carpet-beating ma –'

'*Understand*? Roderick is our son (or daughter) and I want to have everything ready for him. I want this to be a place he'll be proud to live in, and it wouldn't matter if he was a – a gingerbread boy (or girl). Understand? We have to start right.'

'Okay, okay.'

'And if it just so happens that he's not hungry and doesn't want a cookie, fine. Or if he's excited about his new home and doesn't feel like sleeping right away, fine ...'

Jake McIlvaney lay back in Dr Smith's chair, exposing his large Adam's apple. When he talked, which he did incessantly, it bobbed up and down disgustingly. Dr Smith could hardly turn his eyes to the man's filthy mouth.

'How did this happen, Jake?'

'Well, this morning I did a favour for Matt Gomper and fetched these here packages from the bus station – two big packages on the same day, Matt says he never seen nothing like it, and one of 'em has to go clear over to Clyde Honks, you know the old Ezra place, that's what we always called it even though Hal Ezra never actually bought it, let's see the bank owned it and then Don Jeepers, you know, married that gal from Belmontane and now Clyde owns it well what it was was a milk analyser, I knew he was talking about gettin' one but I never knew he'd really buy one because you know he was thinking of gettin' rid of them cows last year – and anyways Matt's missus is sick again, so I said sure I'd handle these here deliveries, so I got rid of that one and started back because the other package was for Ma and Pa Wood, am I talking too much here, doc?'

'Ahmmmm.'

'So I started back, the missus says I talk too much says I should of been a barber, anyway I must of been doing about fifty on that gravel shortcut past Theron Walker's place, hear he's gonna sell out and move to California, makes you wonder if it's true, all them stories about his missus and Gordy Balsh – anyways all of a sudden I hear funny noises coming out of this here package. Like voices, like a voice, maybe a talking doll or one a them talkback computers, you never know what them crazy Woodses might get up to next, coupla real characters – so I stopped and listened real close only I couldn't make out nothing. So then I recollected that Doc Savage was in that neck of the woods, artificial insemination-ing Gary Doody's herd, so I went over to Gary's place and we took Doc's stethoscope and you know it sounded just like they had some kid boxed up there. I mean it kept talking to somebody called Dan, if you knocked on top it said, "Dan, somebody's knocking, is that you?" And if you turned it over it said, "Dan, I think I'm upside down." Damnedest thing I ever seen –'

'The teeth are okay, Jake, nothing busted but the bridge.'

'So anyways I fetched it over to the Woodses, thought I'd sorta hang around to see 'em open it. Real characters, ain't they? Remember back in fifty-six was it, must of been before you come to Newer, maybe fifty-seven, remember Ma Wood one day she takes her vacuum out and starts vacuuming the street! No foolin', vacuuming the street. That ain't all, she, then she gets Pa up a ladder washing the trees too, never did figure them two.'

'Oughta be locked up,' said Dr Smith, washing his hands. 'Adopting a robot –'

'Well to cut a long story, that's what it was. A little gadget like a robot only looks more like a bitty tank. Kind of a let-down, thought maybe somebody was shipping a kid to them or, anyway, while I was waiting, that's when it happened. Ma had this plate of chocolate-chip cookies setting there. I just sort of helped myself and that's when my bridge –'

'What, nutshells or – ?'

'Hee hee, no that's the funny thing. Nuts and bolts! Them cookies was just chock full of nuts and bolts! I swear!'

'You oughta sue 'em. They oughta be locked –'

'My own fault, hee hee, I mean Ma never told me to dig in – nuts and bolts! Thought I'd seen everything, but nuts and –'

The first day was one problem after another. The boy (or girl, Ma insisted) had been chirping away to itself inside the box, but once they brought it out it shut up for the rest of the day. Oh, it might make a sort of frightened whimper, say when they showed it the chess-board, or say when Pa took it in the workshop and tried to get it interested in hammering.

Finally they put it to bed, Ma told it a story and they plugged it in for its evening recharge and tiptoed downstairs.

'There's some instructions in the box,' Ma said. 'Maybe we need to read up on him (or her). Maybe we've been going at this all wrong.'

'He's in bad shape, I know that.'

'Or she is.'

'Dents in his head, scotch tape around his neck – and his treads are all full of dirt. Think I'll fix him up tomorrow.'

They spread the instructions on the dining table and tried to read them. After some time Pa started working his jaw, settling his teeth the way he always did when he was perplexed.

'You're tired,' she suggested.

'All this stuff about buses and data highways, contented addresses is it? Makes it sound like a traffic report.' He looked up. 'Awful quiet in here.'

'Listen, what counts is that little Roderick or Roderica is ours, our own child.'

'Fine, only what do we know about children? Here everybody in town's been calling us Ma and Pa for years, bet most of 'em don't even remember it's short for Paul and Mary, that we never had a child. Do you think –?'

'No more thinking tonight, okay?'

'No but do you think we're doing the right thing here? Maybe we're too old for adopting a –'

'Too old! Why the Queen of Spain was adopted by fairies

fifty thousand years older than the world!'
    'That a fact.'
    Upstairs, Roderick began to scream.

Suffering Cats, the numbers were after him, barbed 1 and
hooked 2 and 3 clattering its pincers before 4's fork and 5's
terrible sickle with 6 the noose swinging around for 9 beyond
the deadly hammer and the handcuff . . . 'That's right, Rod,
will you keep all the money you've won so far or move up to
the Hundred-Dollar Questions? Fine, pick a number from 1
to 10, you picked 3 so here goes: Alamagordo is in New
Mexico, right? And the Alhambra is in Spain, right? Now, for
one hundred dollars, tell me: Just how did you kill Hank?'
    'That's easy. Alcatraz is a former island prison, Al Capone
is a former gangster, why is everybody looking at me like that?
It was self-defence, you all saw him go for his gun first, I mean
when he missed me with his 7 (I guess I was just lucky that
one didn't have my number on it) and his head was right
there in reach I guess I just automatically pasted him with
this wrench youda done the same, everybody's got a right to
protect his own property – I was just protecting Hank's
property, judge.'
    Without even waiting to hear how he'd made his getaway
(climbing into a crate and nailing down the lid from inside)
the judge ordered him hanged by the neck until dead, dead,
dead, 3 times 6 maybe but still ends up as nothing, the dot
0 in the middle of the screen 0 when they turn you off by
remote control in the middle of the most important message
of your life: 'Where is that Roderick? Where is that dad-
blamed Roderick?'

4

'Heads,' said Pa, 'are wonderful things. Nobody should be without one.' He brought down the hammer on Roderick's head, with a sound that carried out of the garage and over to Dr Smith's house, where the pink hands of the dentist made a convulsive movement and changed TV channels.

Roderick stood on Pa's work-bench, watching the old man bash dents into smoothness. 'My head gets dents.'

'All the same, heads are wonderful things. Do you know, you can get almost anything into a head. You can think about a house in Chicago – though no one ever did – and at the same time you can think about thinking about that house. "Here I am," your head says, "thinking a thought about a house. And thinking a thought about a thought, and so on." And even while your head thinks that, you see, it's giving the old thought-handle another turn ... dents, eh? Dents. Yes, well you know the way we take out a dent? We put one in the other side. We dent the dent. Then if it still ain't smooth, we dent that dent too, and so on. Seems like so much of life is just denting the dents in the dents ...'

He stopped hammering and sat down. 'Not so young any more, Roderick. You can only dent so many dents and the metal gets tired, you know that? People get tired just the same, hammering away, trying to smooth out the world you might say. Well no, you wouldn't say that, but I might.'

The room was full of Mayflies this morning. Roderick watched one land on Pa's hand and sit quietly until Pa picked it up and held it to the light. 'Too tired, see? This one won't make it.'

He moved it close to Roderick's eyes. 'Wings like little lenses, see? Like for reading fine print. Funny thing about these Mayflies, they only live about a day, but they have thousands and thousands of children. See, they have children inside them when they're born. And those children have other children inside them, and –'

'And so on?'

'Good boy.'

While Pa rested, Roderick thought about Mayflies, thought about thinking about Mayflies. The radio was advising them to fill up that shoeshine balloon, but he hardly noticed.

'It's like half-ies,' he said finally.

'Like what, son?'

'A game I play sometimes. In the dark. You take half of it, and then half of a half, and then half of the half of the half and and and, and so on. To see how close you get to nothing. To zilch. To Maggie's drawers.'

Pa smiled. 'Don't let Ma hear you using words like that. She don't care much for TV talk, *zilch* and all.'

'So I don't,' said Ma, coming in through a cloud of Mayflies. 'I don't even like the expression TV, tedious voice, truncated vision, turning the whole blessed world into morons, teleological void – My! Look at all the wingèd green fairies in here!'

Ma showed him how to paint, or at least she showed him the paper and the colours and told him stories while he tried them out. Roderick worked away to the story of the cigarette girl who loved a bullfighter:

'Once she'd been a real girl, you see, but a wicked magician turned her into tobacco and Sir Walter Raleigh took her back to Spain. She languished four hundred years in a deep dark dungeon while her lover searched all over Louisiana ...'

He produced a small purple square in the middle of the great white sheet of paper. His second painting was the same, but smaller.

'Minimalist, eh? Interesting, but hmmm.... I think you need to look at other people's work a little, now where was I? Oh yes, every night he knelt before her picture and asked the gods to help find her. And the kneeling made his knee wear out, so he had to keep this banjo on it all the time, there's another song about that too ...'

Windows were better than TV. There was always something going on. At first he'd been afraid to sit by the back window

125

because of the dangerous plants, friggin' violets in pots that might break any minute and anyway looked like hairy tarantulas.

But all the windows had action: the mailman bringing bills, a car breaking down and getting a tow from the white truck (C-L-E-M-'-s spelled Clem's Body Shop), old Violetta Stubbs walking her cat, Dr Smith swearing at his wife as he ran out and jumped in his blue car, a dog peeing on a maple tree, (trees make w-o-o-d which is just like Ma's and Pa's name but not like *would* you like to hear the story of Zadig the engineer?), and one day a big deal when the sheriff and two men from the County Hell Department came to take away the big toilet and Ma called them Phyllis Teens and Pa said would they like to take away the bill for that skullchair too, and Ma cried and said what was wrong with a bird-bath for rooks anyway, and Pa shouted and Dr Smith came out and laughed and Pa shouted at him too and said he'd like to kill a hundred Phyllis Teens if somebody would give him a dentist's jawbone.

But the best part of windows was that you could go right outside and be in the picture yourself.

'Sure it's okay,' said Pa. 'The kid knows his name and address, he knows he must *not* go out in the street. Why not?'

'Yes of course. A boy or girl needs fresh air and sun – though there are a few ferocious dogs in town. But of course he must. Of course.'

But from the back yard, Roderick could see their anxious faces peering at him through the friggin' violets. They watched him rake a stick along the ground, stop to examine a petrified dog turd, dig a tiny hole (which he tried to make square) and squint at the sun through a shard of bottle-glass.

After a few days of this, they finally relaxed and let him go unwatched. Unwatched, he relaxed and played.

Pa had told him about this Achilles and this tortoise, a story worth trying out. He was Achilles and a stone was the tortoise:

'Okay you're a hundred feet ahead of me when we start the race, only I run ten times as fast as you. Okay now I've gone the hundred feet and catched up, only – there – you've moved on ten more feet. Okay now I go ten you go one.

Okay now I go one and you go a tenth. Okay now I –'

'Whatcha doing?'

A small person was following behind him, stopping when he stopped. 'It's a game. Like half-ies, only –'

'Whatcher name?'

'I'm Roderick Wood. I live at 614 Sycamore Avenue, but I'm not lost.'

'Ha ha, I'm not lost neither. I'm Judy Smith.'

'Hello.'

'Hi. You look dumb to me.'

'I'm not dumb.'

'Hahaha, you are so. You're a dumb dummy and your Pa works at a dumb dummy factory. You don't know nothing.'

'I know everything. Almost.' He thought. 'I know how to play jess.'

'Chest, that's nothing. Can you play hopscotch? Bet you can't even hop.' She demonstrated.

'You're right, I can't hop.' His arms sagged.

'So you're nothing but a dumb dummy.'

'Guess I am.'

'You don't know nothing.'

He brightened. '*Nobody* knows nothing. Because there ain't no such thing as nothing. Just half-ies and half-ies ...'

'Let's play something. Chest maybe. You show me your chest and I'll show you mine. Like doctors.'

'Okay I'll get a board and some pieces –'

'Naw, come on. I'll show you.' She seized his claw and dragged him around the corner of a hedge. 'Okay, now you be the microelectronic life-support system and I'll be the chief neurosurgeon ...'

When Judy got tired of doctors Roderick went off to explore the rest of the block. On one corner there was a gas station with interesting rainbows in the puddles and men who chased you away.

On another corner there was The Gifte Shoppe, run by Miss Violetta Stubbs. She sold greetings for all occasions, 3D pictures of the President, plates with gold edges saying NEWER, NEBR, THE BIGGEST LITTLE TOWN IN THE MIDWEST, little glass gazelles, hand-lettered cards like those in Pa's workshop, paper doilies, magnetic pens you could stick to the dash-board of your car, silk scarves (NEWER, NEBR., THE BIGGEST etc.) and lots of other stuff, but when she found out you weren't buying anything she chased you away. On another corner there was a house with a fence and a big dog inside, and on the last corner there was a mailbox and a man stand-ing on one leg.

'I can stand on one leg longer than you,' said the man.

'Sure. I ain't got no legs.'

'Oh yeah.' The man scratched his head (this made him fall over). 'I can stand on the other leg even longer.'

Roderick extended a claw. 'My name's Roderick Wood.'

'Hi. I'm Louie. They call me Louie Honk-Honk.'

'Why?'

'Because I'm funny in the head I guess. I don't know. If I knew, maybe I wouldn't be funny. Hey, sit down why don't you?'

Roderick said, 'I can't sit down.'

'Can't sit down! No legs! Heck and darn – I suppose you ain't got any candy, either?'

'Nope. Never use it.'

'Better for your teeth, huh?'

'No teeth either.'

Louie's bad teeth showed in the gaping mouth. 'No teeth! Wow! You're worser off than me!'

'But I'm not funny in the head – hey look, I'm sorry. Don't cry, hey.'

Louie smiled through his tears. 'Boy I'd like to show 'em! You know what I'd like to do? I'd like to go over to Howdy Doody Lake – you never been there? It's nice – and I'd pick some flowers and throw them in, see? Then I'd throw some kid in!'

'Didn't I see that in this movie, Louie?'

'Yeah I seen it too. Boy, they wouldn't think I'm funny then. Only I wouldn't drownd the kid, I'd pull 'em out again. Because if you drownd somebody that's murder. They get detectives after you.' Louie picked his nose, tasted the result. 'Sometimes I think they got detectives after me anyways.'

'How come? Did you drownd somebody?'

'No! Never did! Never did! Only oncet I seen these two

128

men in front of my house, sitting in this truck, see? Just sitting there, all day. All day long.'

'I wonder why?'

'I don't know.' After trying the other nostril, Louie said, 'I wish I was real rich. Real rich. Then I'd pay these detectives to find out stuff for me. To find out – everything. Like what it says in books. And, and how come I'm funny in the head – everything. Ev-er-y-thing!'

That evening Ma and Pa sat at the dining-table, elbow-deep in quadruplicate forms.

'I didn't know adoption could be such a tricky business, Mary. Swann says it could take years, too, without no birth-certificate and with the –'

'Listen to this: *"Item 54. Gross readjusted excludable income not including net excludable tax adjustments included in item 51a"* – what in the world do they mean, including the excludable?'

'Money's gonna be a problem too, already cashed my life insurance to pay Swann's retainer – somebody's at the door.'

The screen door cracked open and two men stumbled in: Sheriff Benson and Dr Smith. They seemed to be arguing.

'Now Doc, hold on, you had no right to bust down that door, hold on just hold on.'

'Getthatmthrfkn – Leggo, leggo!'

Pa said, 'What is this? You know we never lock that door –'

Dr Smith shook a mottled pink fist.

The sheriff spoke: 'Half outa his mind, Pa, I'm real sorry about that. Seems he thinks your little uh robot's been assault-ing on his girl Judy.'

'Roderick? He's upstairs in the land of recharge – in bed I mean. What do you mean, assaulted?'

Dr Smith grabbed his shirt-front. 'What the fuck do you think I mean? *That* fucking dirty-filthy machine was out in *your* back yard *this* afternoon, playing slimy sex-games with *my* daughter! Bring him down here! Now! I want the sheriff to see that thing smashed into *a million cock-sucking pieces*!'

The sheriff separated them and forced Smith into a chair. 'Now sit there and shut up till I find out what happened.'

'I know what happened, Judy told me what hap –'

'Button it, Doc.' Sheriff Benson was a gaunt, weary-looking

man with rotten teeth. He sucked them to punctuate sentences.

'Well we got the report this afternoon. Miz Violetta Stubbs seen what happened from her back porch and called me. I'da been out here sooner only – hey, you know they got a new game show on, Channel 58, this one gal won a Rolls-Royce you know all she had to do –'

'Get to the point!' Dr Smith kneaded his fists together.

'– just name six vegetables, simple, huh? Anyways like I say Miz Violetta seen your little robot and his little Judy playing it looked like doctors. Soooo ... wonder if I might have a word with the little uh, okay?'

'I'll get him,' said Ma. 'Only keep that maniac away from him.' She went to the stairs and paused. 'Or her,' she said.

Benson sucked his teeth. 'Just what I was thinking. You know, Doc, this case – there ain't no precedent. I mean, if this robot was a live girl I know you wouldn't care two hoots, if it was a live boy I guess we could settle it without much fuss too. But this robot ain't got a sex – has it?'

'Don't try to cover up for them, Benny, goddamnit I know what I know. That *thing* –'

'Sit down, Doc. Now looky here, this thing's no bigger than a good-sized breadbox – reminds me of a game show where they – no, but look at him. Doc? You want me to prefer assault charges against that bitty thing?'

Ma carried him down. 'Is it morning? Is – hello, Sheriff, did you bring back our toilet?'

'Set him on the table here Ma, now listen uh son, I want to ask you a coupla questions, you know what the truth is?'

'Sure like in truth tables, like if you ask me three questions I could answer them eight different wa –'

'No, well more like Truth or Consequences. Listen, this afternoon, what did you and Judy Smith do out there by the back hedge?'

'Doctors.'

'You played doctors? How does it go?'

'Well you don't have pieces –'

'That's a relief. Go on.'

'And you just talk mostly about how the radiologist is batty about some nurse in O.R. Two, she won't give him a second look though because she's head-over-heels in love with young Doctor Something who's been working too hard, two hours sleep in five years he can't go on like this I tell you, with you it's always give, give, let Doctor Whatsit carry some of the load sure he's old and he drinks before surgery –'

'Fine, but what do you do besides talk?'

'Well nothing much. She puts it in my hands.'

'*Sit down, Doc!* Puts what, boy?'

'Her life. In my hands, my capable hands.'

'Think we got nothin' here, Doc, let's go.'

Dr Smith cursed and yelled incoherently for a moment, then left, carrying before him his swollen, pink, capable hands. The sheriff remained behind a moment.

'Real sorry about this, folks. Doc'll pay for the door and all but – well, might be better to make sure we don't get any more false alarms, okay?'

Pa said, 'Keep him away from Judy Smith, you mean?'

'I mean, keep him chained up. Seems to me if he ain't a boy or a girl and he ain't exactly a machine, he must be a pet. You get a good strong chain tomorrow, and chain him up.'

Ma shrieked. Pa turned pinker than a dentist's hands. 'What the hell, here, Sheriff, look at all these papers – we're trying to adopt him. He's our son. You can't ask us to chain up our own –'

'I can and I do. You adopt him, maybe we can forget the chain. Until then – that's an order of my office, chain him up – or else. I catch him loose on the street, takin' him in to the pound in Belmontane. They might even destroy him.'

Pa and Ma sat up fretting most of the night, but in the morning there was nothing else to do: Pa went to Sam's Newer Hardware and bought a twenty-foot chain and a pad-lock. Ma sat weeping by her African violets. 'Fetters on a baby!' she said. 'Paul, how can we do this to him?'

'At least he'll be where we can keep an eye on him. He'll be safe.'

'Or she will,' said Ma, blowing her nose. 'Couldn't we just let him or her have one last taste of freedom in the front yard? A minute? Half a minute?'

'Okay, Mary.' They let him out, watched him gambol (more or less) and then went to fetch the chain. They returned to see a tattooed arm drag him into a car, which slammed its door and screeched its tyres and shot out of sight.

'Nobody in town's got a car like that, all colourless,' said Pa, when he could get his breath. 'And the licence plate all dusty.'

'I was afraid of this,' Ma said. 'The gipsies have got him.'

5

The big woman with the wrinkled face kept saying, 'Jeep, you ain't got the sense of a dehorn, takin' some kid's toy like this.'

Roderick was wedged in the back seat between her and Jeep, the man with pictures all over his arms. There were other people wedged in around them. He could see half an ear wearing an earring, a hand holding a guitar, the bald spot of someone who was snoring, a baby's foot.

'Jeep, you ain't got –'

'Come on, Zip, how'd I know? It looked like a lawn-mower to me.'

Roderick said, 'I'm not a lawn-mower, I'm a robot. My name is Roderick Wood –'

'Told you: a toy. A damned toy.'

'– and I live at 614 Sycamore Aven –'

'Osiris!' someone shouted. 'This thing's security-wired! We better stop and dump –'

'Stop nothing.' Zip composed her wrinkles. 'You know the rule: when in doubt, keep going.'

The bald spot turned away and a watery eye took its place. 'Oh fine. You know how these rubes are about toys. They get ten times as excited over some fool toy ripoff as they do over a car. And if we get pinched – well, there goes my nomination for Gipsy Good Neighbour of the Year.'

Jeep held up a screwdriver. 'Okay okay I'll strip this thing down now and we can sell the parts in Gallonville. Any objections?'

Roderick said, 'Well I –'

'*Mommy, mommy,*' said a voice from the front.

The earring moved. 'Not now, Chepette.'

'Strip and sell, that's the rule,' said the old woman. 'Only maybe this little gizmo's worth more on the hoof, eh? Lemme think a minute.'

'*Mommy, can me and Jepper have a toy?*'

'You go and play with that pop-bottle, it's down there somewhere ...'

'*But Jepper's peeing in it. Mommy couldn't we have a real toy like on TV?*'

Roderick watched the screwdriver. 'Hey can I say something?'

'See what I mean, Jeep, a talk-back toy. Must be worth a buck or two ...'

The conversation went on without him, stopping only now and then when the baby's pink foot became entangled in the hoop of the earring, when the guitar got into the watery eye, or when a tiny voice announced that Jepper was drinking from the pop-bottle. Roderick waited, studying the skin-pictures on the arm next to him.

A snake crawling out of the armpit is marked DON'T READ ON ME. It devours or disgorges an eagle holding a cane in one claw, a string of wienies in the other, and in its beak the Ace of Spades inscribed THEM. The wienies coiled around a heart, pierced by a two-ended sword. The man wielding it has one eye and wears a snail-shell on his head. At his feet is a broken anchor. He stands beneath a tree on which small skulls hang like fruit. The tree is on fire; out of the flames rises a mallard holding one end of a long scroll on whose folds are these letters:

t s eliot lived on top a sleek bard

The opposite end thickens into a giant hand grasping a dolphin which waves a Confederate flag; one of its stars has shot into the sky to threaten a kite. The kite string is held by a naked woman who crushes a scorpion underfoot. The scorpion grips a key, while the full moon above features a keyhole. From it an eye observes a mer-cupid armed with an oilcan, sprinkling oil upon a crowd of 13 crowned men. Though blindfolded they follow a tank along the road to a distant tower. The tank insignia is a rose inscribed FAI HOP CHAR. Its gun turret fires dice down the wrist, past a parachute ...

Jeep reached up to pick his teeth and the picture changed:

Now a snake from a distant tower disgorges dice. An Ace of Spades is the insignia of a tank (FAITH HOPE CHARM) extending its chain of wienies to capture 13 blind kings. The fishtailed kite oils a flaming tree beneath which the one-eyed man embraces nakedness while the scorpion attacks a broken anchor. One sword-blade stabs the moon

134

while along it charges a snail waving a flag, towards the point where the two ends of the scroll meet (beneath a winged umbrella) held by a single penguin.

Roderick tried reading the scroll forwards and backwards. It made no more sense than anything else about this mad, bad family. What was a drab, anyway? What was keeling a pot? Why did they want to destroy him before he could even find out stuff like that?

As he climbed up to the back window for a last look at the world, the invisible child started up again:

'Mommy Jepper says he wants to have toys and live in a house with lots and lots of toys where you don't have to pee in a pop-bottle and you get TV and real strong aluminium foil and pizza-burger mix and doesn't just hide odours, can we huh?'

'Be still now –'

'And TV and microsnax and Uncle Whiskers Oldie Tymie – Ow! It wasn't me Mommy it was Jepper he – Ow!'

It seemed a good opening. 'This,' said Roderick clearly, 'is *lots better* than a house. *I* like living here.'

None of the adults spoke. Then, *'Yeah but they got TV and –'*

'Listen, TV ain't much. All they got on TV is stories about people driving around in cars. Sometimes not even people, just the cars, this car drives down a street and then on a free-way and then on a bridge, then this other car sees it and starts chasing it, they both have to jump over a lot of bumps and then one of 'em smashes up, The End. Heck, what do you want that stuff for, here you got a *real* car. You even got another real car chasing you, look there.'

Jeep looked back. 'Isis wept, wouldn't you know it? Forget about 'em for one minute and the gashers is all over you. Chet, make tracks, boy!'

'Hang on,' said the driver. 'I'm gonna try something.'

Roderick bounced up and down. 'That's just what they say on TV! And then everybody says *Yahoo* and *Watch my dust* and *Wheels, do your stuff*, and there's a lot of banjo music and –'

'Hush!' Wrinkles frowned down at him.

'But hey what's Chet gonna try? Is he gonna race across the tracks right in front of this train? Or on this bridge that's going up and he just makes it jumping the gap? Or, or maybe he just pulls off the road and hides in bushes and the cop car is so dumb it goes right on by, is that what he's gonna –'

Old Zip clamped her hand firmly over his speaker and kept it there. What Chet tried was pulling over and stopping, getting out to talk to the patrolman for a few minutes, and finally handing over some money.

'Thanks,' said the officer. 'Don't see much real money these days, not out here. Everybody's so scared of hijackers they only carry cards, hell, all they can offer me is a free motel room or maybe a free meal in some Interstate joint, BLT and a malt, you call that a decent bribe? I mean the food's all plastic and full of preservatives and chemicals you get a bad stomach just looking at –'

Chet showed some gold teeth. 'Yep, well, we gotta get moving.'

'Oh sure, have a nice day and – oh yeah, and don't let me catch you pitching pop-bottles out of the car again, okay?'

In Gallonville the family went to work. First they parked the car next to a little patch of grass, then Old Jeb put three playing-cards in his shirt pocket and strolled away. Then the two young men left, jingling big bunches of car keys and talking about 'recycling us some metal'. Finally Zeb, the young woman with earrings, took the children off to the bus station for 'some street theatre'.

'Street theatre,' old Zip repeated, when only she and Roderick were left. 'That means they all gonna cry their eyes out until somebody gives them the money for a ticket to Omaha.'

'Why are they going to Omaha?'

'You don't understand anything, do you?' Zip set up a card table and two chairs, and stuck a sign to the side of the car:

GIPSY ZEE
*Knows the Past***Tells the Future*
No Credit Cards

'Yeah, well if you let Jeep take and recycle me I never will understand anything.'

'True. But so what?' She tied a yellow-and-orange scarf over her head and sat down at the table. 'Okay little puppet,

I'll make a deal with you. You keep your mouth shut and help us a little, and we won't junk you.'

They shook on it. Zip kept hold of his mechanical claw for a few seconds, peering at it.

'Interesting hand you got there, you know? I see you've had a real hard life so far.'

Roderick looked too. 'You can see that?'

'Sure. A real hard life, but it's gonna get better soon. You're gonna have lots of money – more than you ever dreamed of. You'll get married, too, and have, let's see, three children. First a boy, then two girls.'

'Gosh, it just looks like a claw to me.' He waggled the fingers. 'Where do you see all this?'

'And I see you have headaches – some head trouble, right?'

'Yeah, right. Gosh!'

'Now cross my palm with silver.'

'I don't have any silver, Zip.'

She sighed. 'Then skedaddle. Make way for a real customer.'

He left. The first customer was a little deaf, and Roderick could hear Zip shouting: '. . . than you ever dreamed of. You'll get married soon, and have three kids, first a girl then two boys . . . some trouble with your feet, right?'

'Teeth? Say that's dead right!'

Roderick headed across the grass, to where a group of children were playing on swings. But as soon as they caught sight of him, the kids stopped playing and shouted:

'Aah, dirty gipsy! Goaway ya dirty gipsy!'

He changed direction and kept going.

Towards sunset he came back, while Zip was just finishing the palm of a frail old man. He rose and tottered away, leaning on his cane, grinning to himself about the three children he was going to have. Zip took off her scarf.

'Well, little puppet, what kind of day did you have? Make any money?'

'Almost. I mean I was standing on a street corner and somebody came up and tried to stick a quarter in my eye. Then I went to the bus station to watch Zeb and the kids and the street theatre only when Zeb started crying I said don't cry it's a very good act and she said she'd give me a dollar to go away only she never did. Then I saw Jeb on this park bench with his three cards and all this money in both hands saying Find the Lady, boys, Find the Lady, see they put down a dollar and he gives them five if they –'

'I know how it goes.'

'Yeah well I saw how terrible they all were at the game so I said maybe he should give them three dollars if they're right and one dollar if they're wrong, see it works out the same, and Jeb whispered he'd give me a dollar to go away – but heck, what do I want a dollar for? I guess if everybody in the world wants me to go away for a dollar I could get rich if I just disappeared.'

'Ha ha! You'll learn, little puppet, you'll learn. We'll make a gipsy out of you yet.'

What Roderick really wanted to do was help some grown-up do some grown-up job. And that night, he got his chance.

Everybody had returned in good spirits and carrying thick wads of money. The young men had spent all day finding an amazing number of abandoned cars on the streets, tearing them down and selling them to the local junk-yard. Zeb and Jeb and Zip had all cleaned up too, so now there was nothing left to do but junk their own car, find a new one, and leave town.

While they waited, Zip told Roderick all about the family.

'You see, everybody has to have a name beginning with Z, J or Ch, middling with i, e or ee, and ending with b, p or t. But no boy can have Z and no girl can have J.'

'You mean there's only 27 names in the whole –'

'No, well we can add -er to a boy's name if it's the same as his older brother's, and -erie to a girl's if it's the same as her older sister's. And if a boy and girl look like they're gonna get the same name, we just add -ette to the girl's name. So you see we can have Jeet, Jeeter, Jeeterer and so on, just like we can have Chep, Cheperie, Chepette, Chepetterie ...'

Boys took middle letters from their mothers and ending letters from their fathers, and girls did the opposite. Roderick was only just beginning to see why Jeep was not Zip's son nor her sister's son when Jeep and Chet drove up in a big red car. They started spraying it with green paint at once. Jeep looked scared.

The old man said, 'What's the big hurry?'

'Aw shit, Chet went and ripped off this here car, just as we drove away I seen it was by the city hall, parked in the mayor's parking spot. I think they seen us too – *what's that?*'

That was the sound of a wow-wow siren, getting closer. Jeep threw down his sprayer. 'We better take her as she is, let's go.'

They piled in and started off. Old Jeb said, 'Take her as she is, that's rich that is. You ain't done no more'n the back and the right side, how's that gonna look? And nobody done the plates –'

'Don't worry about the plates,' said Roderick quietly. 'I –'

Chet said, 'Ra's ball, who's supposed to be drivin' here, anyway? I got enough on my mind, tryin' to figure all them fancy one-way streets, half of 'em blocked off at the other end without – shit, they seen us!'

They were crossing an intersection; a few blocks to the East they could see the flashing red-and-blue lights of the police car crossing another. It went North, they went South. 'Holy Horus they done seen the wrong side of us, too. Now they know we got the mayor's red – well, now what?'

Roderick spoke up. 'In a way it's lucky they did see the red side. I mean, if we could use the one-way streets, sort of turning left all the time ... hey, take a left.'

'All I need, got enough human back-seat drivers, now the damn toys gotta start –'

'Do like he says,' Zip rumbled. 'That's one smart little cuss there.'

Chet took a left. 'Going round in circles, real smart. But then what we got to lose?'

'Everything,' said old Jeb, turning his face to the window. The baby kicked at his bald spot.

'They seen us again!'

And the police car saw them again and again, as both vehicles spiralled in through the one-way system, first seven blocks apart, then three, then two. When the police car was only one block away (and turning towards them) Roderick said: 'Okay, now pull over on this next block – on the left.

Turn out the lights and everybody duck down.'

An instant after they obeyed, tyres shrieked at the final corner and the flashing colours approached. They could hear the two policemen arguing. A spotlight went on.

'Okay, sure it's a new Shrapnel, only it ain't hizzonour's, just take a look. His is Lady Macbeth Red, and this is, it looks like Tango Green. Anyways, look at the plate, his is Elmer two six one zero five eight niner seven, while this here is Lolita six eight five zero one niner two three, we're wasting time ...'

'Have it your way ... thin air ...'

The police car wow-wowed away. They were safe.

Zip said later, 'I told you he was a smart little cuss. I bet Roderick's got more brains in one little silly-cone chip than you got in your whole head, Chet.'

A gold tooth grinned back at Roderick, wrinkles smiled, a watery eye winked, and a tattooed hand patted his dome. The children smiled in their sleep, the woman with earrings blew him a kiss, and even the baby seemed to wave its foot in congratulations. Roderick was a gipsy hero, and now there was no question of sending him to the junk-yard.

Instead, later that night, they sold him into slavery.

6

Midnight. The apostle clock chimed, and its twelve tiny wooden figures paraded out of one door and in at the other. Faces half-gone with worm-holes.

Mr Kratt lifted his snout and listened.

'You must really like that old clock, huh Mr Kratt?'

'Like it? I hate the goddamned thing. That's what I keep it for, to remind me how much I hated my old man.'

'I don't get it. If you –'

'You don't have to get it, bub.' He watched the wooden door shut behind the last apostle. 'See, my old man had the damnedest collection of old clocks, cuckoos, grandfathers, you name it. Some real fancy ones, too: like this German schoolhouse with these little enamel schoolboys that come outside, one at a time, they bend over, see, and get a beating from the old teacher. My old man spent his life fixing them up. His life and our money. And when he died he left us kids one broken-down clock apiece. All the rest went to a museum. Only good investment he ever made, and he gives it away.'

The chimes finished, and there was no sound in the office trailer but the faint noises filtering in from outside: screams. Bells. The waltz-time murmur of the merry-go-round.

Mr Kratt looked from the face of his digital watch to that of his young assistant, a pimply man with a handle-bar moustache.

'You oughta shave that thing off, bub.'

'Yes, Mr Kratt.'

'No, I mean it. What do you want with all that hair on your face? Think it gives you confidence, some shit like that?'

The young man fiddled with a company report. 'Well, I just like it. Same as you and your ring there.'

'Ha!' Mr Kratt held it up, a heavy gold claw mounted with a steel ball. 'That, my friend, is history. That's a pinball from my first machine. Took me five years to build it up to an arcade, but in two more years I had three arcades and the carny. Never looked back after that.' He checked his watch again. 'Where the hell is this guy? How long does it take to go through a few waste-baskets?'

'I thought you started out in Autosaunas, sir.'

'No, that was later. What happened was, I started out with these call girls –'

'You was into call girls?'

'Not me, people I knew. And when they legalized them in California, see, they wanted to expand. So I came up with this idea, wiring the girls into a computer, hell, it cut their turn-around time by forty per cent. So then I thought, hell, why pay all these girls, I mean taxi fares and food and rent, skimming, it all comes off the top. All you need is something that looks and talks and moves like a girl – anyway that's how Autosaunas got going. I was lucky there too, managed to sell off my interest just before all that litigation came down on them, not just the nuisance suits claiming clap and syph but the heavy stuff, middle-aged guy dies of heart failure and they try to prove electrocution, another guy files injury claim for amputa – well, you know how these ambulance chasers get their clients all worked up over some little nothing. Anyway that's when I got the idea for Datajoy, all I got so far is a registered name and a process, but when the time's right – look, we give that guy fifteen minutes more, then I'm splitting.'

'These people you knew that was into call girls, who, was it the Mafia?'

'There's no such thing as the Mafia,' said Mr Kratt quickly. 'Anyway that business showed me what I'm doing, made me think it deep. See, I used to think I was in the amusement machine business, but that's just part of the picture. See, what I'm really into is pleasure. The pleasure industry. Big difference there, changes the whole concept when you think about it. I mean now I could acquire a few other interests, stuff like T-Track Records, like K.T.Art Films, see these are all just departure points to the same place, they all come under one dome, *pleasure*. Nowadays whenever I plan anything, anything at all, I ask myself: "How is this gonna help give the most pleasure to the most people, at the highest return?" You'd be surprised how much crap that cuts out, having a simple business philosophy.'

'Pleasure. Is that why you're going into fun foods?'

'That's it, bub. Only as you know, it's a highly-saturated market there right now, so I can only get in with a hell of a good angle.' He glanced at his watch again. 'Which is one reason I end up sitting here half the night waiting for that market research yak-head to bring me what I need. Is that him now?'

The assistant answered the door. It was not the market researcher, only two old gipsies trying to sell a robot.

'Tell 'em we got a robot, we got a show full of robots. Tell 'em I make the goddamn things – no wait, wait a minute. Let's just see what *they* call a robot. We got time.'

The two old people came in carrying a small, inhuman-looking device. 'Good evening sir, we –'

'Put it on the desk there and turn it on,' said Kratt. 'What's it supposed to do? Tell fortunes?'

The old woman kept working her multitude of wrinkles into a smile, or was it a leer? 'If you want,' she said. 'Little Roderick here is a smart little cuss. He –'

'That's its name, Little Roderick?'

'Roderick Wood,' said the gadget, holding out a claw. 'I –'

The old man suddenly started dancing and whistling accompaniment. The entire trailer rocked with his tap routine.

'What the hell here, shut up you!' The assistant grabbed his arm, and might have hustled him out of the door if Kratt hadn't spoken up. 'Okay, okay, simmer down everybody, let's see here.' He took the claw and twisted it around, examining it. 'Not bad work here, you know? Course he looks like shit, but we might fix – does he duke or what?'

'Sure I do,' said Roderick. 'Gimmee your mitt, uh, sir.'

Mr Kratt held out a bunch of thick fingers. He was thick all over, Roderick noticed, and wide: a wide head growing straight from the shoulders without pausing at any sort of neck. A wide face hanging from a thick black V of eyebrow. A wide nose, upturned to display its mole. The eyes were black and tiny and slightly crossed, as though ready to concentrate on that mole.

Roderick was afraid of Mr Kratt. 'Well maybe I –'

'Come on, don't stall.'

'You, uh, will get married soon and have three children, first a boy, then a girl, then another girl.'

'Ha! Go on.'

'You're uh having trouble with your, your back, back pains?'

'What the hell is this thing shaking for? Think you got some problem with the motor circuits there. Yeah, go on.'

'You want to make lots of money and, uh, you will. Some thing you hope for will come true soon and make you lots of money.'

Kratt took his hand away to find a cheap cigar and unwrap it. 'Not bad, not bad.' He waited for the assistant to give him a light. 'Yeah, but not so good, either. Kind of easy, all it does is go through a little table, right? Tells the first client he's got back trouble, the next one he's got foot trouble, the next one he's got headaches –'

'And so on,' said Roderick. 'That's it, all right. And for the children see I always say three children, they can have them eight different ways ...'

'Talkative little gadget, ain't it?' Kratt grinned and reached out to pat Roderick's dome. The robot flinched. 'Well I might find some use for him, let's say a hundred bucks.'

'We was thinkin' more like a grand,' said the old woman.

'A grand,' said the old man.

'A hundred. Cash. Look, I might have to do a lot of work on it, gotta change some a that direct programming, gotta maybe fix the motor circuits, gotta do something about its appearance.'

'Five hundred?' said the old man.

'One-fifty, I'm generous too, this thing is probably hot.'

Roderick made a whimpering sound when the gipsies left with the $200 Mr Kratt had meant to pay all along. Mr Kratt patted his head again, spilling ash over his face. 'Good little gadget, bub, realistic talker. Stick on a fifty-cent coin box, penny a second, all it's gotta do is talk to people about their troubles.'

Roderick said, 'You mean I don't have to tell fortunes? Cause I don't like fortunes, dukes and stuff.'

'Ha! Hear that, it doesn't like – hey, robot, what you got against duking?'

'Well I mean making up all this stuff and then it comes true, how come they need me to make it up, how come nobody wants to tell their own fortunes, Pa says they could just put all their choices in a hat and draw one out it's just as good. But I mean once I say it there it is, that's the future.'

'You think – let me get this straight – you think you can just go to a set of tables and just pick out a future for somebody and then it happens?'

'Sure, because like Ma uses the *I Ching* all the time and she says it never fails, that's just 64 choices, 64 ways the future can go.' He hesitated. 'Only Pa says it's a lot of crap.'

'Well this Pa is right, it's only like a game, see, to make money. Now – well, about time.'

The door opened and a one-armed stranger stumbled in. 'Howdy. Sorry I took so long, only you know pickin' locks with one hand ain't exactly easy. Got jest what y'all wanted.' He looked at Roderick. 'What's that?'

'Nothing, another piece of crap for the carnival, stick it in the corner, bub let Mr Smith use the desk for his presenta –'

'O'Smith.'

'Yeah, now let's see here, what's this, memos?'

'Yep, outa executive waste-baskets, all highly confidentials, reckon half the board at Dipchip don't know what's goin' down yet, looks like maybe kind of a private showdown between the research director Hare and the vice-president in charge of product development Hatlo –'

'So I see. And the substance of it is over-expenditure, right? On this yak-head process, whoever heard of trying to coat microcircuit chips with peanut butter, let's see that budget there, yeah, look at those costs. Memo my ass, I'd of fired the son of a bitch, brought a suit for fraud and malfeasance, haul his ass right through the courts if I had to, what's –'

'Well, you see they acquired this little old firm Bugleboy Foods assets all tied up in warehouses full of peanut butter substit – yep, there's the picture, minority interest held by TTF Endeavours, a division of TTF Enterprises, took the shares in lieu of damages – some old litigation when they were a supermarket chain Tommy Tucker Foods, now of course they're a holding company who – sorry, awful sorry, let me –'

An avalanche of papers went to the floor. As O'Smith bent to get them his eyes met those of the little machine. It seemed to be trying to plug into a wall socket a length of dropcord running to some recess in its body. 'Hello,' it said.

'Howdy doody, little feller. Need some help?'

'Yes.' Its voice was fainter, its eyes were going opaque.

'Okay if I ... ?' O'Smith asked Kratt, who nodded.

'There you be.' He straightened up and dumped papers on the desk. 'Now where was we? Oh yeah, the divestiture ...'

R*O*D*I*N*I R*O*B*O*T

PALMIST	Knows the Past	TAROT READER
SEER	Tells the Future	SCRYER
MYSTIC		CLAIRVOYANT

$3.00 (per minute) donation

They had fixed him up with a fibreglass turban and a coin-box, bolted him to a slab of concrete, and installed him in a little tent just off the Midway. He was conscious only while customers kept feeding money into his coin-box, when he would begin nodding over the crystal, palm or Tarot cards and go into his routine.

The routine consisted of a softening-up line ('Basically you're too generous. People use you. You need to be more selfish.') and a series of questions masquerading as answers:

'Right now you're worried about somebody close to you ... maybe yourself, a health problem ... that's right, and money is involved ... money for an operation maybe ...'

'Right now you're worried about somebody close to you ... someone you live with ... or work with ... live with, yes, and there's some decision, big decision you have to make ... get the impression it's money, something to do with ... if not money then some kind of exchange, a relationship of give and take ... you give more than you get ... well things are going to straighten out soon, only there'll be some hassle ... a lot of trouble in fact ... just have to fight this thing through to the other side ...'

'Right now you're worried about somebody close to you ...

not so much now as in the future, a life partner, I see a strong influence coming in there soon ... not too soon but soon, romance leading on to something permanent ... and children, first a boy, then ...'

All week long, the customers exchanged their quarters and half-dollars for token words: love, marriage, divorce, family, money, career, lifelong ambition, relationship, social life, quarrel, not-working-out, obstacle, travel, children, promotion, home-life ... At the end of the week, he had taken $21,938 and two lead slugs. Mr Kratt came to see him, trailing the assistant.

'Damn good, little robot, you just keep it up, oh bub tell the maintenance boys to change his rate, five bucks a min – yeah and move him on to the Midway, real attraction there, best investment I ever – reminds me, any word yet on that lease-back arrangement with Bugleboy, the warehouses? No? Gotta complete that before we move on this computer edibles package, did I tell you we managed to bust the contract of this guy Hare, got him coming over to head up research in Katrat Fun Foods, he –'

'Yes sir, but isn't he the guy who – ?'

'Sure, well of course he's only nominal head, don't want research costs mounting up on us do we? No, real head is this new guy Franklin, real ideas man we managed to grab off some hayseed univers – but see with Hare we get his patented process for etching microcircuits right on peanut brittle, be right in there in the fun food vanguard, bub, few technical wrinkles to iron out first but I mean there we are with fifteen warehouses full of peanuts, get this moving sky's the lim – what was that?'

The little figure in the fibreglass turban had made a kind of moaning sound. Now he said, 'I wanta go home.'

Mr Kratt squatted down and inclined his big neckless head. 'Aren't you happy here, little robot? Look, you're a big success, main attraction almost, everybody after you –'

'Yeah, but I get nightmares.'

'Ha! No, really?' Kratt winked at his assistant. 'Not something you ate, is it?'

'I keep seeing their faces, the busted people.'

'The, the what?'

'The customers, the ones you call the marks. They're all busted, Mr Kratt, sometimes even their faces are all busted up – I just wanta go home, that's all.'

'Well you can't. So just get that idea out of your little memory chip, comprende? This is your new home, so you better get used to it.' He stood up. 'Come on, bub, can't waste any more time yakking with a goddamn robot doesn't even know how to be grateful, whole point in changing this show over to machines was we could get rid of all the whining and bullshit, pay's not good enough, food's not good enough, homesick, lovesick,' he whirled on Roderick and stuck out a thick finger. 'You know what your trouble is? You know?'

'Basically I guess I'm too sympathetic, people use me. I need to be more hard-hearted . . .'

'Come on, bub, wasting our time. Wanta nail down this Bugleboy deal, see, what we got now is a new concept in fun foods, two things kids really like are eating junk and playing with talk-back toys, put the two together and you get the edible talk-back, start maybe with a Gingerbread Boy, kid gets tired of yakking with it and – chomp! See? Get our boy Franklin right to work on that one just as soon . . .'

Outside the tent stood a long line of silent people: young men with old faces, old women in burst shoes, old men in greasy hats, young women with pierced ears. At the front was a man holding a newspaper upside-down, apparently reading. He watched the two men leave, then slipped inside to feed Rodini the Lucky Robot with quarters. Now he was safe, now he could lower his paper to expose a face without a jaw.

'Basically you're . . .'

Not all of them gave him nightmares, but what he couldn't understand was why there should be any miserable marks at all among his four hundred daily visitors. Television had never prepared him for their stories of loneliness, horror, guilt, confusion, sickness, dread. Almost none of his visitors came close to televised truth: here were no pop stars, kindly country doctors, top fashion designers, executives with drink problems, zany flight attendants, sneering crooks, tough but fair cops, devoted night-nurses, cynical reporters, hell-for-leather Marines, dedicated scientists, big-hearted B-girls, ageing actors, cute orphans, smart lawyers – none of the ordinary decent network folks he'd come to know and almost like.

Instead there was the man with no jaw, wondering if maybe he couldn't get him a girl if only he had a real fast car with full accessories. The drunken wife-beater who wanted to quit (drinking and beating) but even more wanted to go way out West where it wouldn't matter so much. The personable young man who kept sniffing his armpits and re-applying deodorant, and whose ambition was to steal a hydrogen bomb and drop it on some black people. The failed suicide who dreamed of a big win at Las Vegas ...

And the line shuffled past. The worst of it was the mechanical laughing clown, going night and day right in their faces, just the way it did in all the movies where somebody got killed by the merry-go-round or on top of the Ferris wheel or in the dark behind a tent that clown was always there with the chipped white paint on its face, rocking back and laughing in their faces ...

And Roderick dreamed of them.

They were numbers, then they were letters, then words, then broken bits of voices. If he could only sort them out, all of them, into some kind of pattern ... but it was always just beyond (beyond (beyond ...

God call him up every time jackpot lousy blade heavy split up when epileptic .38 motel room burn movie son of a bitch says kids no kill t-shirt no freak doc car plant porno bastard mother his own last time he last time she exit blood candy store how would you like a beat on him epileptic rapist son of a bitch yells sewer beach relation-ship stinks this relationship masectomy needless needles boss no good yell fuel injection nightwork treats treats me like shit .38 bike over-time blackjack ass passes no sweat pills bustup back together ten grand belt buckle slipped disc park it goodies medication no nice kids his own mother God fight City Hall wino drive-in abortion hit taste bike

'Basically you're too kind. People –'

'Son, don't you know me?'

He peered at the man, noticing he had a jawbone, not like anybody who loaned out his jawbone for killing Phyllis Teens ... 'Pa! Pa?'

'Hear that? He knows me. Come on son, we'll go home.'

The hard-looking man behind him spoke. 'Not just yet, Mr Wood. Few formalities.' He spoke into a radio. 'That's it, fellas. Make the pinch.' Then to Pa, 'We'll have to go over to this Kratt's office here. I want your, er, kid to identify him.'

Roderick's quarter ran out. He awoke in Mr Kratt's office, once again standing on the desk.

'... tragic mistake, gentlemen, tragic. This just can't be a living child, I mean look at him. Been here six, seven weeks and never ate a crumb of food, never had a drink of water, how can you call him alive? Of course I bought it – him – in good faith as a machine, got a receipt somewhere, no idea it was even stolen goods let alone a – are you sure?'

The hard-looking man said, 'How about this, Mr Wood? This a kid or a robot?'

'Well I like to think of him as my foster son, he seems almost –'

'Jesus Christ, what kind of answer is that? Maybe I better ask the – entity – itself here.'

Roderick was just blacking out when the hard man fed in a handful of change. 'Now just tell me what the fucking hell you are, kid.'

'My name is – is Roderick Wood.'

'My boy,' said Pa. 'You see, Agent Wcz, just what I –'

'I'm a – a robot and I live at 614 Sycamore – 641 is it? 416, no, I live at –'

The man turned his hard stare on Pa. 'A fucking robot! We set up this whole operation to catch a kidnapper and now you admit –'

'I'm awful sorr –'

'Yeah sure. Only that just voids our arrest here.'

Mr Kratt's V-brows shot up and down. 'I'm free then?'

'For the time being. We'll be keeping an eye on you, Kratt.'

Roderick's money ran out again. He awoke in a car with Agent Wcz and Pa – and Ma!

'Penny for your thoughts, son,' she said.

'I was thinking about anding,' he said. 'How much is one and one and one?'

'Three.'

'Three? But I keep getting four. Like on Mr Kratt's desk there was one pin and one paper clip and one rubber band. And that makes two shiny things and two loopy things, and everybody knows two and two makes –'

'Can that noise,' said Agent Wcz.

Pa said, 'Agent Wcz, I really am awful sorry we wasted your time, the FBI's time. Hmm, unusual name, Wcz. You know, I think I knew an FBI Agent Wcz back in the fifties. Any relation? Your dad, mayb – ow!' Agent Wcz turned white, then red, but said nothing.

Ma said, 'Sorry Pa, just moving my foot there, getting comfy.'

The FBI man looked at her, as though memorizing her face. 'You two aren't in a very *comfy* situation, you know. Filing a false report of kidnapping is serious. I'm putting you down on our records and you can rest assured you'll hear from us again.'

The car drew up in front of a familiar house. When they were inside, Ma said, 'Could have *died*, Pa. Why on earth did you go and provoke Mr Wcz like that?'

'Provoke – what in the world?'

'Didn't you see the scars? That man's had his face lifted, more than once. He's as old as we are, and you asking him about his dad! Honestly!'

'My day for goofs, I guess. Anyway, our boy's back. Safe and sound.'

'And pig-ignorant,' said Ma. She put both hands up to scratch her head, the way she always did when she was thinking hard. The green dandruff flew. 'Can't have him grow up thinking two and two is four,' she said. 'And there's only one answer.'

7

SOME LAWS OF ROBOTICS (I)
Robots are in comics but they are not real.
Robots are made of controls.
Robots are made of metal and iron and steel.
Robots kill.
They strangle.
They shoot people and destroy them.
They keep killing and killing.

Pupils at Rhyl Primary School, London

Miss Borden had tan hair exactly matching her tan pants suit,
and watery blue eyes exactly matching the scarf at her throat.
A chain ran from the bow of her glasses to the back of her
neck (to the knob of tan hair) and it exactly matched the
chain running from her belt to a bunch of keys. He had never
seen such a neatly-matched-up person; he stared while she
selected a key and matched it to the door marked with her
name: ELIZABETH BORDEN PRINC –

'Don't dawdle,' she said. Princess?

'Don't be shy, Roderick.' Ma took his hand and led him
into the business room.

'Yes, I can see he'll cause – *have* special problems, Mrs
Wood. The handicapped and the disadvantaged are so often
– but never mind, we'll manage somehow. Now where have I
put those forms?'

'Handicapped? Well no, not exactly, he's –'

'Of course *you* don't think of him as abnormal, glad to
see that, admirable the way you parents – now let's see, was
it 77913 or 77923? – Yes, I always feel it's best to treat them
as normal, healthy children and just let them find their own
level, sink or sw – find their own level. Achievementwise.
After all, isn't that pretty much the basis of our democratic ...

152

of course it is, and I'm sure little Robert will fit in just fine . . .'

'Roderick. His name is −'

'At the same time it's best to find a way of keying him in, don't you agree? Relating him to the system, here it is, 77913, just a few routine questions I have to ask −'

'You mean how well does he read and write, things like that?'

'Yes um but not exactly. We generally like to let reading and writing find their own lev − shall we begin?' She fiddled with a brooch and suddenly unreeled another gold chain with a tiny ballpoint pen at the end. Her left hand ironed the pink form ready. 'Has he any juvenile record?'

'You mean criminal − why heavens no.'

'Good, good. Any peculiar illnesses? Aside from his obvious handicap, that is.'

Ma cleared her throat. 'Miss Borden, maybe I haven't explained things too well. Roderick is −'

Miss Borden held up a hand. 'Don't mean to rush you but I've got a meeting with the school security personnel in a few minutes, suppose we just run right through these first and then after we can clear up any little discrep − *Oh of course!* You're worried about giving out informa − oh but let me assure you this is strictly confidential, here, here's a list of the agencies we're legally entitled to a data-share with, see for yourself there's nothing to worry about.'

She handed Ma a sheet of paper printed on both sides with names ranging from the Nebraska Welfare Investigation Bureau to the Presidential Committee on Population Control. 'Okay, no history of illness then, how about chemotherapy?'

'Chemo what?'

'Medication, what kinds of medication will little Rodney require and how often? Tranquillizers, anti-depressants, enkephalides −'

'Well, none. Nothing.'

After a moment's hesitation, Miss Borden marked a box. 'Now we're getting somewhere. Has he been in analysis? If so for how long and which therapeutic method? No? Fine. How about his training. Pottywise, I mean.'

'He doesn't need − no trouble that way.'

'Good, fine. Now for some details. How often does he have tantrums, Mrs Wood?'

'Never.'

The pen poised. 'There's no place on the form for "never", Mrs Wood. *All* children have tantrums. I'll tick "seldom" if you like but I wish you'd try answering these questions a little more frankly. Now would you call him a hyperactive child?'

'I'm not even sure I know what that m –'

'Okay then he's not. Epileptic fits? No? Screaming? No? Excellent. Aggression – does he get into fights with other kids a lot? Good. Ever started a fire? Tortured an animal to death? Maimed another child? Fine. Now is he what you might call introverted – moody? I imagine so, being handi – disadvantaged like that, better put Yes. Suicide attempts? None? Fine. Is he sexually advanced for his age? No? That seems to cover the basics. Think we'll exempt him from sports for the time being, don't you?'

Miss Borden asked dozens of questions about the whereabouts of Mr Wood, family income, mortgage payments and health insurance plans, earnings-related benefits, history of colour-blindness and left-handedness, whether any grandparent was syphilitic or tubercular or a giant.

'Fine, now just one more: can you think of any special experiences little Robin might have had which could affect him educationwise?'

'Well ... he was kidnapped by gipsies.'

'Seriously Mrs – really kidnapped? Well then of course that alters his rating for sexual precocity doesn't it? Fine, now I'll just have my secretary key this into our data terminal and we'll be ready for some tests. Might as well go home now Mrs Wood, this could take the rest of the day. We'll call you.'

Roderick was whisked away by Miss Borden to another business room, where a kindly-looking man looked at him over his glasses.

'The er Wood boy is it? I'm Dr Welby, heh heh, don't be nervous boy, been a family doctor to your Ma and Pa for a good many years now, good many years.' He stood Roderick up on his desk and looked him over. 'Well well, yes, mmm, says here your regular doctor is a Dr Sonnenschein in Minnetonka.' He applied a stethoscope here and there. 'Heart seems fine, yes, I'd say –' He looked at his watch. 'I'd say we can give you a clean bill of health, Roger.' Dr Welby stepped to the door. 'Over to you, George. Kid's clean, I'll fill out the form later only just on my way to see Bangfield about that lakeside property thing ...'

'Check.' A young man in white came in, lifted Roderick down to a chair, and said, 'How are ya, Roger?'

'Fine. I've got a clean bill.' He noticed that Mr George had lots of wiry black hair and red pimples. 'Only I like to be called Roderick.'

'Oh?' George stared at him. 'Now why is that?'

'Because it's my name.'

'Is it? Okay, *Roderick*, now don't let this white coat make you nervous, we're just here to play a few games. You like games, *Roderick*?'

'Yes.' But if the man didn't want to make someone nervous with his white coat, why did he wear it?

'Okay now I'm going to show you some pictures, and – funny pictures – and I want you to tell me what you see.'

'Is that the game?'

'Yes, now what is this one?'

It was tricky, all right. The picture was nothing but a double blob, nothing like anything. Sideways it might be a cloud, reflected in a lake.

'I don't see anything much. A cloud?'

'Yes, and now this one.'

'A different kind of cloud with little wisps sticking out.'

'And this?'

'A cloud with –'

'Okay, that's enough. Now try these pictures. Look at each one and tell me a little story about it. Ready?'

He showed Roderick a picture of a young woman weeping, while an older woman stood behind her.

'What's the story here, *Roderick*?'

'What, any story?'

'Sure, whatever you like.'

'I guess the young woman is crying because she's just learned that her father swindled the bank he works at out of a million dollars, so the bank's going to fold and everybody'll lose their savings. That means she can't marry the hero because he's the sheriff and has to arrest her father. She can't cry in front of her mother here because she has a weak heart and might fall dead any minute. See that's why the father embezzled the money for a special heart operation, when they catch him he says, "I'm glad it's over," and meanwhile the president of the bank, his son is fooling around and gets locked in the safe, and this sheriff who used to be a famous safe-cracker only nobody knows it, has to get the kid out and time's running out, when he does it he has to resign as sheriff because everybody knows –'

'Yeah okay that's enough. Now –'

'But just let me finish, he has to resign but the bank president gives him a million for saving the kid's life, and now that he's not sheriff he can give it to the girl's father to pay back all the little invest –'

'Yeah okay I get it, now try this one.'

A bakery truck was turned over on its side, loaves of bread spilling out of it.

'A guy was delivering nitroglycerin to this place where they had to blast open a mine and rescue these miners they've been trapped a week and time's running out.'

'Listen, you're not *trying*, Roger I mean Roderick. These old movie plots –'

'But listen they put the nitro inside loaves of bread to keep it from getting shook up and, only the truck gets a blowout on a mountainside and the brakes go, these gangsters went and pinched the brake lines, the driver's got this crippled sister she's in love with one of the gangsters only –'

George showed Roderick two glasses, one short and squat, the other tall and thin. First he poured the short one full of orangeade.

'See how much we have? Let's mark it on the glass.' He marked the level with a crayon. 'Now we'll pour it in this other glass.' He poured from the short into the tall glass and again marked the level. 'See, it's way up here. Now. Do we have more orangeade? Or the same?'

After hesitating, Roderick said, 'Less.'

'No I mean now, in this big tall glass. Do we have more here than we did in the short glass? Or the same?'

'Less.'

'Look it can't be less, Roger, *try*. How can it be less?'

'Well ...' Roderick picked up the empty short glass and tipped it up. A single orange drop gathered at the rim and fell to the desk blotter. '*That* much less, anyhow.'

George's pimples were brighter as he drew out a green form and began writing. He made no attempt to hide the words from Roderick, who was not yet scheduled to have a reading age.

Roderick read: 'Suspicious, poss. schiz. tendencies coupled with extreme identity crisis. This boy is severely handicapped, and consequently indulges in vivid fantasies of violence, sex, crime, with recurring claustrophobic imagery. Overachiever, poss., with high IQ but poor grasp of abstract reasoning. Obvious resentment of authority, the classical overachievement syndrome. When asked, "What do you want to be when you grow up?" he replied, "Nothing." '

8

The screams from the playground could barely be heard in
the teachers' common-room, where a digital clock silently
wiped away a few last minutes. Miss Borden stood, clipboard
in hand, ready to inspect her troops. No one seemed to feel
much like talking: they puffed hungrily at cigarettes, or leafed
through tattered copies of *Educationalist Today*, or simply
closed their eyes and pretended to doze.

'We have a few minutes – any questions?'

She looked first to young Ms Beek, who sat brushing her
hair with long, deliberate strokes. Last year Ms Beek had
taken a sabbatical from Newer Public School, spent in a
psychiatric hospital in Omaha. At least the trip had been
good for her hair, now longer and browner and lovelier than
ever. And the mind beneath its roots? Fully restored – or
anyway full of soothing drugs. Even if they made her quiet
and withdrawn, they kept her even-tempered, and wasn't
that the main thing? She'd soon be back in the swim.

Mr Goun, a pale, humourless young man with a glassy
stare, sat reading a book. His red moustache moved as though
in prayer, and his finger traced the lines across the page. Miss
Borden leaned over his shoulder.

'Poetry, Bill?'

He looked up. 'Educational psychology. Just, er, brushing
up.'

'I understand. Not easy to move from seminars in the ivory
tower to the, well, vigorous give-and-take of the grade school
classroom, I'll bet.'

He nodded. 'Interesting theory here, about utilizing the
catalyzation potential of the classroom situation in the micro-
assessment of –'

'Mmm, yes, sounds great.' She passed on quickly to
Mr Fest, or as he preferred to be called, Captain Fest. He
stood at the window surveying the playground through a pair
of binoculars.

'Still keeping tabs on the trouble-makers, Captain?'

He gave her a thumbs-up sign without looking around. 'They needn't think they're getting away with anything out there, by golly. I know every face and every name. I know what they're up to even before they do. The day will come. The day will come.' He tapped his grey crewcut. 'Fest never forgets.'

'Fine, fine.' She moved on to Mrs Dorano, the oldest member of the staff by some years. Mrs Dorano was large, shapeless, motherly-looking, and absolutely in charge of the second grade. She sat in 'her' chair nearest the door, knitting and frowning.

'Any questions, Mrs Dorano?'

'Goodness me, no. Why, my sweet little angel-puddings are just about always as good as good can be. If anyone has *questions* or *problems* around here, it's only because *they just don't understand children.* I *do* understand *my* kiddies.'

'No doubt.'

'If only we could keep them innocent! But no, the world of grown-ups is lurking around every corner, waiting to pounce on my wee people and start corrupting them!'

'Oh yes?' Miss Borden checked her watch.

'Yes indeed.' Mrs Dorano slipped a book from her knitting bag and held it up. 'Do you know, I found this hideous thing in the school library! The school library! Luckily I managed to confiscate it before some tiny hand fetched it down from the shelf, some clear little eye chanced to –'

'But this, this is just one of our standard texts for the sex education class.'

'Exactly. *Dirt* education. For tender babes who never had a naughty thought in their innocent little noodles!'

'But many of the parents have asked –'

'For this corruption? I can't believe it and I won't believe it. You can call me an old-fashioned grumpy cross-patch if you like, but someone has to stand up and protect the little ones. Why, this book has pictures of unborn babies – right inside the you-know-what!'

One of the younger teachers giggled nervously. A mistake. Mrs Dorano raised her voice. 'Oh, you may snigger! The world is full of sniggerers, wicked grown-ups who laugh at innocence, who want to pull it down and soil it.'

'Mrs Dorano.' The principal removed her glasses. 'I'm sure you have a point there. Why don't you take it up at the next PTA meeting and –'

'Oh I will, don't worry.' Mrs Dorano gave them all a motherly smile. 'The PTA, certainly. And also the Newer Decency Society.'

Miss Borden turned away quickly. 'How's it going on the playground, Captain?'

'Not much action. Few kids kicking around some kind of toy tank there or something. If that's school equipment, I can promise them *they*'ll be sorry.'

'Toy – My God, that's the new pupil, the Wood boy! Where's Ogilvy, why isn't he out there stopping it?' She rushed out, her head filled with printing-presses, a blur of headlines:

CRIPPLED BOY BEATEN, GANG KILLS CRIPPLED BOY AT NEWER SCHOOL, PARENTS TO SUE . . .

Threading the maze of corridors, she found Ogilvy by the door. He was kneeling, making a few adjustments to his shin-guards.

'Some security guard!' she shouted. 'They're beating the life out of a crippled kid out there. Let's go!'

'Can't be everywhere at once,' he whined behind her. 'I was just looking at the busted lock on the A-V room.'

She stopped, half way out of the door. 'What? Not again?'

'Yup. Ripped off the stereo, TV camera, vidrecorder – the works.'

This was serious, a bad blow to the budget. For a moment, Miss Borden almost forgot where she was going.

Roderick learned one thing right away: he was different-looking. Up to now, he'd never thought much about his appearance. Ma and Pa and the other grown-ups didn't seem to mind. But as soon as he appeared on the playground bigger kids started shoving him.

'Hello,' he said, hoping the shoves were accidental.

'Get that,' said a tall, red-haired boy with missing front teeth. 'He talks! Hey you, freaky, what's your name?'

'Roderick. What's yours?'

'Roderick, what kinda name is that? Hahahaha it sounds like prick!'

The others doubled over at that one. The conversation turned to names, as, shove by shove, they backed Roderick against a wall. The tall boy, whom the others addressed as Chauncey, favoured the name 'Freaky-prick'; others suggested 'Pricky-freak' 'Pricky-dick', etc., etc.

'Roderick, hahahahaha,' said one of the smaller boys. 'It sounds like poopy-pants!' He and another kid started wrestling and moved out of sight.

'Freaky,' said Chauncey again, moving closer. 'Why you wearing a iron suit, huh? Huh? Think you're tough or someping?'

'No, well I just –'

'Shaddap. You ain't so tough I bet without that iron suit. Why don't you take it off, huh? Huh?'

'I can't.'

' "I can't", he says. Spose I take it off you, huh? I could use a iron suit like that, spose I just take it?'

'He might die, stupid,' said a kid in a blue track-suit. 'It's like a iron lung, ain't that right?'

'Shaddap.' Chauncey grabbed Roderick's arm and twisted; it turned easily in his grasp. 'Shit, you ain't so tough. Bet I could, bet I could take you apart.'

'Get him, Chaunce.'

'Yeah, get him.'

Chauncey hit Roderick hard where his stomach might have been, and jumped back shaking his hand. 'Owww, Chrise, he's solid steel!'

'My old man's got a stainless steel plate in his head,' someone was saying, but just then someone grabbed Roderick by the head and pulled him over, and feet were kicking at him from every side.

The robot saw no point in trying to get up; he simply lay there, rolling and spinning under the barrage of tennis-shoes. After a while the kicking stopped, and someone helped him to get up. It was Chauncey.

'You wanna be friends?'

'Okay, sure.'

'Okay then Rick, you got, listen, you got any lunch money?'

'No. What's that, lunch money? You mean they pay you to eat lunch or –'

'Don't be a smart-ass with me, I'll, I'll ionize ya. Now you listen and listen good.'

All at once Roderick realized: Chauncey was a villain. Villains invariably told people to listen good. Or else.

'Listen good, I'll let you off this time, only tomorrow you bring a dollar. Or else.'

'Or else what?'

'Or else we kick your ass, smart-ass.'

A bell rang. Roderick dusted himself off and looked over the scratches in his new paint job. Pa had painted him especially for school; he wouldn't like this.

Chauncey gave him a last kick that resounded through his innards and left a dent, then ran off after the other kids. They all seemed to be heading for the building, so Roderick tagged along.

Mrs Dorano had just finished calling the roll, checking each name against one of her magnetic cards, when the door opened and the security man came in trundling Roderick.

'I caught this kid sneaking around the hall,' he said. 'Yours?'

She consulted a lone card. 'This must be little, er, little Roger. The Wood boy.'

Someone piped, 'Hahaha, looks like a steel boy to me.'

Unsmiling, she waited until the uproar settled. 'Naughty. We don't make fun of crippled people, do we, boys and girls?'

'No, Mrs Dorano.'

'Do we, Billy?'

'No, Mrs Dorano.'

'All right then. Thank you, Mr Ogilvy.'

The guard shuffled out of the room, his shin-pads clacking together as he muttered, '... vandalizers ... burglarizers ...'

'Now then Roger, you sit right here in front next to, that's right, between Chauncey and Jill, now I see by your card here you haven't been to school before – illness I guess and that means you may have just a teeny bit of trouble catching up, so you just follow along for now, watch Chaunc – watch Jill and just more or less do what she – anyway now we're going to pledge allegiance. Everybody up, up, up.'

'What's pledge allegiancing?'

'Hahahaha,' Chauncey aimed a kick at him. 'He don't even know –'

'That's enough!'

'Yeah but he don't even –'

'Chauncey be quiet. Roger, dear, haven't you ever pledged allegiance to the pretty flag? No? Well just take your right hand –'

'Hahahaha, he ain't got no hand. He's got –'

'Put your hand, of course he's got lovely artificial hands, put your hand over your heart –'

'I haven't got a heart either,' Roderick said. Jill gasped.

'And say –'

'Missus Dorano, Missus Dorano!' Jill jumped up and down, pointing to him. 'He says he ain't got a heart, how can he pledge allegiance without a heart I mean it's *illegal*.'

'Of course little Roger's got a heart, dumpling. Everybody's got a heart, Roger, I hope you're not going to be a little fibber, don't you want to be a good American? Roger?'

'My name's Roderick.'

'More fibs, tch tch tch, Roger it says on your card and Roger you are – the computer never lies.'

'I wanta go home now.'

Chauncey grinned slowly. 'Yeah, let's all go home, come on.'

'CHAUNCEY, SIT DOWN AND SHUT UP. Roger you can't go home, now stop fibbing and disrupting the class with your no hand and no heart and no name –'

'My name is Roderick and I'm a robot, so I don't have a heart –'

'I'm very disappointed in you, Roger. Very, very disappointed. I'm giving you one more chance to pledge allegiance – oh, what's the use? If you want to be a fibber and a fool and a bad – naughty American, all right. You sit down and the rest of us will pledge allegiance.'

By then, one or two kids in the back had been infected: robot imitations went the rounds; someone asked permission to take Roderick apart to see if he had a heart, someone else declared her own heart had been removed at the hospital ...

Chauncey and his gang seemed friendlier at recess. They invited Roderick to play 'Captain May I'.

The gaunt boy in the blue track-suit said, 'Hey Rick are you really a robot? Boy you sure gave old Dorano a hard time, boy, are you really one?'

Chauncey, hanging back, said, 'Don't be stupid, Jimmy, there's no such thing as robots they're like ghosts. No such thing.'

Jimmy said, 'There are so. Hey Rick, lemme feel your muscle, jeeze you sure are tough I busted my shoe kicking you, see? Hey, you wanna be captain?'

'I'm captain,' Chauncey said, 'I'm always captain.'

'Owww, leggo, okay let's choose for it.'

'Okay but I do the choosing.'

Chauncey counted around the ring (himself, Jimmy, Roderick, Larry, Eddie and Billy) eliminating them one by one:

> Eeeny meeny miney moe
> Catch a tiger by the toe.

'We gotta try it again,' he said, when only Roderick was left. He went through it all again, this time adding, 'If he hollers, let him go,' knocking out in turn Billy, Jimmy, himself, Eddie and Larry ...

'Okay, that was practice and this time counts. Only Billy's out anyway because he's too little.' Once more it was Roderick.

'Hey jeeze, Chauncey, why don't we just let him – ?'

'Okay, just once more I think I got it right this time, Eeeny meeny miney moe, catch a tiger by the toe, if he hollers make him pay, fifty dollars every day, aw shit I'm out already ...'

'Look, are we gonna play or what, recess is almost over,' said Larry.

'This time I got it, Eeeny meeny ...,' Chauncey began, going on to '... dollars every day. O-U-T spells out goes he, with a dirty dishrag on his knee, Eddie's out. Eeeny ...'

'Look, it's gonna be me again,' said Roderick. 'If you wanta choose yourself all you gotta do is go back to the short rhyme now and –'

'Listen smart-ass, I don't need no help from you.' He went on to the end choosing Roderick again, began again with the short rhyme as Eddie went off to find Billy on the other side of the playground. '... tiger by the aw jeeze it's you again.'

Larry said, 'I'm tired of this shit. Recess is practically over, jeeze, I quit.'

'You sonofabitch you must of fixed it or something, Eeeny ...' Chauncey quickly eliminated Jimmy, then himself, leaving Roderick, who said:

'Look I don't care, *you* be captain, whatever that is, let's just –'

The bell went and Jimmy ran off, but Chauncey gripped the robot's arm. 'Not so fast, we gotta settle this. *This* time whoever we finish up on is captain, see? Eeenymeenyminey-moecatchatigerbythetoe Jesus Christ you got it fixed even with just two of us ...'

Roderick went in from recess with another dent on his torso.

Mr Goun sat in one corner of Miss Borden's office stroking his face as though surprised to find no beard. 'Well sure I was prepared for kids being kids but –' He looked up as Ogilvy came in and dumped a pile of books on the desk. 'Vandalism, ma'am.'

'What?' Miss Borden took a last look at her computer terminal screen and sighed. 'Always six things at once, just when I get down to budget day – what vandalism?'

'Somebody's been over these with a razor-blade, ma'am, they look like IBM cards or something.'

Goun, who was younger, wondered what an IBM card might be.

'Okay thanks, I'll look at them later, meanwhile why don't you do something about Mr Goun here, real security problem for you, somebody burglarized his locker. This morning.'

The guard pushed back his cap in the tradition of baffled policemen and whistled. 'What did they get?'

Goun looked pained. 'Only every one of my manuals for the sex education course, that's all.'

'Yeah? Guess they couldn't wait.'

'Not to mention a valuable psychology book, *The Dream World of the Adolescent Girl*, took me a year to run down a copy.'

Ogilvy snickered. '"Rare" book, eh?'

'It happens to be a serious study of the, the actualization of catalyzing factors in the, in interpersonal relations, you wouldn't understand I guess. The kid who took it probably thinks it's juicy stuff but I – but let me know, will you? A thin blue book, let me know if you see any kid reading it. In the can or –'

'Right, chief.' Ogilvy turned to go and bumped into Ms Beek, moving like a sleepwalker.

Miss Borden stood up. 'Yes, Joan?'

'I – I didn't know –'

'Your class, Joan. Who's watching them?'

'Oh – I –' Ms Beek wandered out.

Goun said, 'Not very articulate, is she? Since her nervous b – ah, trouble.'

'Chemotherapy,' Miss Borden explained. 'She'll soon snap out of it and get right back in the swim again. Now let's see these books.'

Goun opened a book of nursery rhymes. '"*Blank, blank* gander,"' he read. '"Whither shall I wander/ Upstairs and downstairs and in *blank blank blank*." Somebody's hacked out whole words, what is this anyway, "put in his *blank* and pulled out a plum", what's going on?'

She put on her glasses. 'And here's A. A. Milne, I know some of these:

Where is Anne?
(Walking with her man)
Lost in a dream
(Lost among the buttercups)

Yes and down here where it says:

What has she got in that firm little fist of hers,
Somebody's [thumb] and it feels like Christopher's –

This is terrible, who would, somebody's got a dirty imagination here, some nasty-minded little –'

'Yeah, and they cut the last two chapters out of *The Marvellous Land of Oz*. I can't make sense out of any of this. Some kid with an anxietal undedifferentiated –'

'I know what you mean. Little savages, how can I in good conscience ask for a bigger book budget when – Oh before you go, do me a favour, will you? I'm way behind on these individual assessment forms, wonder if you'd mind keeping an eye on this Wood boy for me? The little paraplegic whatever he is, Mrs Dorano's class, I ought to ask her really, but all she ever puts down is sweet, angelic, a darling innocent; try running that through the County Board computer, they'd have my job. So just, just look him over, will you? In an informal interview situ – you know the way to handle it, thanks.'

'Sure. Sure I – sure.' Before he could get out of the door it opened and Captain Fest came in with an armload of reports.

'Just heard about your burglarization Goun, tough. Tough. Kids got no respect for any damn thing, think they're king – you better put those trophies somewhere, ma'am, glass case in the hall like that is just an open invitation – well here's the math skills reports, depressing reading for somebody, don't give a damn myself any more.' He followed Goun into the hall. 'You know I stopped giving a damn when I had twelve-year-olds, one day I asked them how many sixths in a whole, brightest one in the class thought maybe seven, how's that grab you?'

Moving with great energy he left Goun behind, staring at the trophy case and muttering, 'Sixths in a hole? In a hole?'

9

'Finish your nice tree drawings, everyone. Hurry up.'
Mrs Dorano clapped her hands. 'Jennifer and I are going to
pin up all the nicest ones for everyone to see. And, uh, Suzy
dear, you pass out the new readers. QUIET! Anyone I see talking from now on is going to have his tree put in my waste-
basket. Jennifer hurry up, dear. Billy, let her have the drawing, finished or not.'

'Miss can I – ?'

'Miss, Miss, Billy drawed a boy's pee-pee!'

'– my pencil and I want it back!'

'QUIET! Suzy they're right there, the stack of blue books
on my desk, just pass them – Margery, sit DOWN!'

'But Miss, Billy drawed –'

'Never mind what Billy draw – drew, you shouldn't even
know what one of those looks like, just sit down and . . .' She
shuffled through the stack of drawings quickly, eliminating
those that looked even remotely like body parts – Kids seemed
to think of nothing but sex, sex, sex as it was. Too much of
it in these promiscuity classes, that's where it came from.
Mr Goun, she'd seen him hovering in the hall, waiting to
pounce on any passing child and pour corrupting filth into its
little ear.

Most of the drawings looked as little like organs as they
did trees, thank heaven. They looked variously like lollipops,
fans, clouds, telegraph poles and green squiggles. Little
Chauncey had turned out a nice effort, incorporating a
rubbing of some ornament – and at the bottom he'd written
DECIGEONS.

'Very, very good, Chauncey. I think what you meant to
write was *deciduous* – I'll show you how to spell it but I think
it's wonderful that you even attempted such a grown-up
word. I – oh!' She had come to little Roger Wood's drawing.

'Somebody's a copycat here,' she said. 'But who?'

'Not me, Mrs Dorano.' Chauncey grinned.

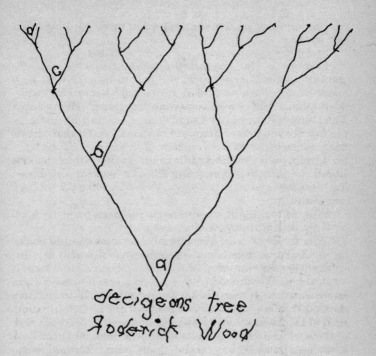

decigeons tree
Roderick Wood

'Roger?'

'What?' He was peering into his new reader.

'Did you copy your tree drawing? It looks like a copy.'

'Well I guess all these decigeon tree drawings look the same, because heck –'

'That will do.' She tore up his drawing. 'As usual, Roger, you disappoint me.'

'Hey, can I ask you about this here reader? It looks kinda hard and –'

'That will *do*, I said.'

Ms Beek looked as though she'd been weeping. Miss Borden, patting her arm, spoke to Captain Fest.

'Do you really have to barge in here? I was just in the middle of a counselling sess –'

'I'm sorry ma'am, but the damnedest thing, my binoculars are missing.'

'Stolen?'

'Presume so. Had 'em locked up in my desk with a few, ah, personal papers, went out in the hall to have a word with Goun, came back to find it ransacked. Everything gone. Naturally nobody in the class saw anything.' He passed a hand through his grey crewcut.

Miss Borden looked at a stain on his sleeve. 'Is that blood? You weren't attacked?'

'That? No, it's nothing. Just interrogating one of the kids about the theft, he slipped and fell, that's all.'

'I see. And you were talking to Mr Goun when the robbery occurred?'

'Wanted to see if he's interested in joining a male teachers' drill team, I'm trying to form a crack —'

'Why male? Because I'm sure Miz Beek here would like —'

'With all due respect ma'am, problem of different heights, different strides — anyway he was busy talking to that handicapped kid, Wood, wonder if maybe he doesn't take an unhealthy interest there, always following the kid around the corridors, talking to him in corners —'

'That's, I asked him to assess the boy.'

'Whew! That's a relief, thought for a moment there ... I mean you can't be too careful about fraternization — oops, sorry Miz Beek, forgot you were here, did I — ?'

'Captain why don't you go and fill out a form S3, so that I can get Ogilvy to work on your binoculars?'

When he'd gone she patted Ms Beek's arm again. 'There now, he didn't upset you did he? Because we've all forgotten about that little incident, haven't we?'

'... forgotten ...'

'Yes I know you're having a little trouble remembering the number of your classroom, but I just know you'll soon be back in the swim.'

At recess, Mr Goun was waiting for him again. He was always lurking somewhere, the droopy red moustache (normally pointing to 4:37) jumping to 3:42 in a rigid smile. He always asked the same questions: did Roderick's parents work? Did they fight a lot? Did he blame them for his handicap? What did he dream of?

Roderick made up a dream or two that put the moustache to 5:32 (and the eyebrows to 12:55).

Today they stood by the trophy case. Roderick was just saying, '... then there was this big decigeon tree, with instead of apples hanging on there was skulls ...' when a big hand grabbed his arm.

'Good work, Goun, we got him this time.' Captain Fest gave the robot a shake. 'Here's the trophy case, busted open and empty, and here's the culprit. You see any of his accomplices?'

'No look, I don't think Roger here could've –'

'No? Just look at him, guilt written all over that tin face. Let me get him alone for a minute, I'll find out where they hid the swag. Told Miss Borden this would happen but does she listen? No, and Ogilvy our so-called security man, always off somewhere pulling his pudding ...'

'Maybe we'd better just take him to the office, Fest, straighten out this whole, I'm sure there's some mistake.'

'And this little bastard made it. Okay you, MARCH!'

Mr Fest gripped his arm all the way to the office, where Miss Borden told them all to sit down and get calm.

'Now Roger,' she said, staring down into the glass depths of his eyes. 'I want the truth. Have you seen our school trophies?'

'Trophies?' he said. 'You mean like a thing with a little silver statue of a basketball player, seven inches high and made in Hong Kong? And a disc about four inches across, that says 3rd place state spelling contest 1961? And a gold football for the all-county champs 1974?'

'Yes, have you seen them?'

'Nope.'

'Ma'am you just let me get him alone for a coupla minutes –'

Goun said, 'Give him a chance, maybe he saw them in the case?'

Roderick shook his head. 'Nope, I never saw them at all.'

Miss Borden's colour scheme of buff and blue was momentarily spoiled by bright spots of colour in her pale buff cheeks. 'Young man, this is serious! If you don't come clean with us, you'll have to talk to the sheriff. *Reform school*, is that what you want?'

'Wants the buckle end of a belt laid across his backside if you ask me. Suppose he didn't see my binocs, either!'

'Or my book!'

The interrogation went on for an hour before Miss Borden called the sheriff. 'Be right over,' she said, putting the receiver down. 'He's watching some game show on TV. God I hate all this! Getting the juvenile authorities in on it, we'll all end up spending hours filling out forms – *please*, Roger! Please confess!'

'But I never saw them trophies.'

'Jesus Christ, if you never saw *them trophies* how do you know exactly what they look like, even the engraving, even – ?'

'Oh, easy.' Roderick laid a shiny little lump of metal on the desk. 'I found this by the trophy case when I was talking to Mr Goun just now. It must of broken off one of them trophies, and see? It's a foot wearing a basketball shoe. And it looks like silver, and if you look real close you can see it says Made in Hong Kong. And the statue must be about seven inches high, right?'

Goun nodded. 'He did pick up something while we were talking.'

'Okay,' said Fest. 'But how about the rest? The spelling medal for instance? You saw the engraving –'

'Nope. What I saw was one of the kids in Mrs Dorano's class this morning when we were drawing trees, one of the kids hid something under their drawing, only it came out on the paper when they rubbed a crayon over it. 3rd Place, State Spelling Contest, 1961.'

'Which kid?' said Fest.

'Ask Miss Dorano which kid. I don't fink.'

'Okay how about a full-size gold football, you don't tell me you never saw that?'

'Nope, never did. But in the creative activities area there's a picture on the wall of this football team with a banner, 1974 All-County Champs. And a guy in front is holding this gold-coloured thing looks like a football only shiny. So I figured –'

Miss Borden said, 'Jesus Christ,' and reached for the phone.

Chauncey and Billy were beating up some littler kid. Chauncey had the kid's hair in both hands and was using it to bash his head against the kerb. Billy stood by, kicking at the kid's feet.

'Hey come on, Rick, let's get this guy!'

'Nope. It ain't hero-ic, picking on a littler kid. Only villains do stuff like that.'

'Piss on you then, this is fun!'

Roderick decided the really hero-ic thing to do would be to stop them. 'Okay, stop you guys.'

'Piss on – ow!'

Roderick shoved Chauncey hard, pushing him over sideways.

'Ow, Christ I skint my knee!' Chauncey started to cry. 'You fuckin' bully!'

'Look, I'm sorry Chaunce, I –' He forgot what he was about to say, for at that moment Billy smashed a brick into his eye.

'Hey, look, you put his eye out, boy are you gonna get it, hey ...'

'I'm gettin' the fuck outa here ...'

'Me too, wait up ...'

When the vision in his remaining eye cleared, Roderick was alone with the littler kid, who had a bloody nose.

'Are you a robot or what?'

'That's right, I'm Roderick the robot. You okay?'

'Yeah, thanks. My name's Nat. I thought they was gonna kill me or something. Boy, they'd be sorry if they did. They wouldn't have Nat to kick around any more.' Nat smiled at him. 'Hey, you know what?'

'What?' Roderick knew the next line: *You saved my life, pal.* He waited for it.

'You look pretty fuckin' dumb with one eye, you know?'

10

The mechanical clown creaked with senile laughter, every wave of creaks setting up sympathetic waves of nostalgia within Ben Franklin. It reminded him of all the carnivals of his childhood, the candy floss and aluminium ID bracelets engraved by shaky hands, the recorded calliope music fighting the recorded superlaughs from the Hall of Mirrors, the afternoons spent cranking away at a tiny crane ingeniously arranged to avoid gold cigarette-lighters and seize in its clamshell a single grain of popcorn.

Corn, that was the soul of it, and probably the soul of Mr Kratt too. Why else should an important businessman maintain his headquarters in a dirty little trailer in the midst of all this? Corny sentiment. Stuff of the common man, of Goodall Wetts III and *God is Good Business*, stuff of which fortunes are made. And what was wrong with it? Hadn't it been said by Abraham Lincoln (if not by a bearded robot in Disneyland) that God must have loved the common man, because He made him so common? Don't knock, Ben warned himself. For Christ's sake, boost.

And yet he could not help following a critical line elsewhere. Noticing the irony of a white-faced robot clown whose make-up could be traced through real clowns back to Grimaldi – who wore it in *La Statue Blanche* where he played a man impersonating an automaton (each turn of the crank produced a new expression). Robot imitates man imitating man playing man impersonating robot: but the tangle of associations would not leave him there. For clowns were playing The White Statue in the streets of London in Mayhew's time, in the 1840 slum streets, alongside Punch and Judy, marionettes and real clockwork dolls, amid the sounds of hurdy-gurdy and barrel-organ, mechanized street theatre for the new industrial age, where almost the only recognizable features of the past were starving beggars and burning Guys.

Death everywhere, white-faced on every corner, turned

into sentiment at home and comedy in the streets: the marionettes always included a Bluebeard and a skeleton; the shadow-
puppet man tells how a mob overturned his van and burned
it (with his assistant inside); Punch and Judy must always
have the hanging in the last act:

Jack Ketch: Now, Mr Punch you are going to be executed by the
British and Foreign laws of this and other countries,
and you are to be hanged by the neck until you are
dead – dead – dead.

Punch: What, am I to die three times?

He was still scowling at the decrepit clown when
Mr Kratt's thick hand clapped his shoulder. 'Guess you seen
enough here, let's get back to town. We can take a look at that
stock list on the way.' The V of eyebrows descended on tiny
black eyes. 'Hey, something wrong?'

'Uh, no sir. No sir. I was just wondering why you still keep
your headquarters here? I mean you could easily afford permanent offices instead of this, I mean a tent show after all –'

'Like to keep on the move, see? Like the gipsies.'

'Nostalgia, I guessed as much, nost –'

'Nostalgia hell, saves me five figures in state taxes, not to
mention depreciation and all the substantial advantages of
running a cash business . . .'

Roderick didn't see much from the bus window. His eye on
that side was out, and if he tried turning his head to look out
with the other eye, something funny happened to his hand
which began to twitch open and closed. Seeing the scared look
of the woman in the seat in front of him, Ma made Roderick
sit still and read his robot book.

It was the story of an iron man who falls apart and puts
himself together again – boy this Hughes guy didn't know
the first thing about robots, here they were going two hundred
miles to the city for one crummy eye – but Roderick liked the
idea of an iron man who goes around scaring people and then
turns into a big hero.

In the back of the book he found a blank page where he
could work out some alphabet stuff:

<pre>
I R O N   R O B O T   M A N
h q n m   q n a n s   I
g m p !   p m z m r   k
F O L K   o l y l q   j
            n k x k p   i
            m j w j o   h
            L I V I N   G
</pre>

'What does it mean?' Ma asked, as the bus left the smooth highway to start bucking its way through broken streets.

'Nothing I guess. Stories. I mean nobody really falls apart and puts themself together again – do they?'

Ma thought the question over, while behind him Roderick heard someone say, '... like teeth only ... dank wish ... the Omaha disaster we decided ... a peep in Coventry, was it?'

'Sure sure sure sure sure.'

Ma continued to think while the bus pulled into a greasy terminal, and the driver ordered them to 'debark'.

The city at first seemed to fall apart without putting itself together: Roderick saw tall glass buildings falling over on him, people pushing each other along the sidewalk, cars honking and revving their engines while waiting to move an inch forward, six abreast, towards the bleeping traffic lights where people pushed each other past the walls of black garbage bags and out on to the street. A yellow taxi pulled up next to him and a man with blood running down his forehead and nose jumped out and ran inside a shoe store, elbowing aside a woman whose little dog made a dash to the end of its tether trying to bite the kid who was being chased out of a narrow doorway marked MASSAGE THERAPY; the dog twisted and snapped instead at the crowd of little wind-up dolls a man with dirty fingers was setting in motion on the sidewalk where they tottered in circles and fell over, looking much like the man with a bottle in a paper bag who sprawled next to an alley where two boys were dividing the contents of a woman's purse. They were ignored by the man wearing sandwich-boards (FOLLOW ME TO JUNIOR'S DISCOUNT CAMERAS) who entered the alley (no one following), flipped up his forward board and began urinating on a wall beneath a poster, VOTE J. L. ('CHIP') SNYDER FOR LAW & ORDER, a

duplicate of the sign Roderick saw a moment later on a wall
behind the hot-dog stand where a man of a thousand pimples
reached for his hot-dog with one hand and for the crotch of
the boy next to him with the other, this being a thin kid en-
grossed in a photograph which he then dropped – 'Jeez,
whaddya – ?' and Roderick looked down at the picture of a
dismembered woman as Ma dragged him past the thin kid,
who wore a jacket marked JUNKERS S.A.C. almost the same
neon orange as a sign BURGER BELLE in the window where the
top half of a black man could be seen frying grey meat and –
whenever he noticed anyone looking at him – spitting into the
top half of each roll. Hardly anyone but Roderick did look,
any more than they looked at the transparent plastic box of
newspapers (headline: ARMY MOM COOKS BABY IN M'WAVE
OVEN, EATS IT) which someone was trying to break open, next
to a video pay-phone on a post, under whose plastic canopy a
woman in wrinkled stockings leaned, weeping and pleading
with the face on the tiny screen, which seemed to have hair
as bright and green as the sweater on the little dog held back
now from a puddle of vomit by a smiling woman in a tiny
silk skirt no larger than a cummerbund who called out to the
sailor lurching towards the door of SUGAR'S SAUNA past two
figures leaning together in so friendly a fashion that the knife
held by one at the other's throat seemed a mistake (as the
victim kept insisting it was), past the JOYS OF JESUS mission
towards the amusement arcade, a place of flashing coloured
lights, bells, buzzers and bleeps under the defective sign TEST
YOUR SK*LL flickering next to an empty store plastered with
SNYDER FOR LAW & ORDER and a poster advertising STREET
MUSIC overwritten with hundreds of obscure slogans all beginning SUCK. This was next to a novelty shop featuring dribble
glasses, rubber pencils, loaded dice, a talking crucifix, marked
cards, plastic snot, a fake finger (hideously injured), itching
powder, cayenne candy and a 'Sacred Heart lighter – REALLY
WORKS – useful and devotional – Butane extra'. Ma dragged
him on, past a larger-than-life photo of two naked women
embracing under the legend THIS WEEK ONLY TRIPLE ADULT
SEXATION: DOLLS OF DEVIL'S ISLAND – 'Brutally frank'; 'Sex-
plicit revealing confession' – I WAS A SAUNA BITCH; 'Inside
bare facts of Hitler's mad nuns' – ANGELS WITH DIRTY HABITS

and the long line of tired old men before the ticket-office nearly as long as the similar line across the street before the Unemployment Office where a policeman sprang on one of the grey figures, knocked it to the sidewalk, and began beating it with his truncheon, while shoppers pushed their way past this as they had pushed past a man with missing fingers trying to play a harmonica, on their way from FURNITURE WARE-HOUSE to DENIM INIQUITY ignoring the bright neon of MARV'S SEX DISCOUNTS above a bewildering array of objects identifiable only by fluorescent signs (Condom's Slashed, Vibey's Reduced; Manacles Cut; See Our Selection of Custom Rubber & Leather Unclaimed Specialties) signs all but obscuring the next place where a feeble neon sign proclaimed from behind heavy iron grilles, NO CREDIT LIQUORS. Before it a machine like a kind of automatic pogo-stick pulled its operator along as it tore at the street, holding up a line of bleating cars including a limousine flying Ruritanian flags, a panel truck shaped like a turkey and labelled GOBBLE KING, a sound truck whose message echoed ('. . . law and order . . . sick of bleeding hearts . . . man with guts . . . man with experi . . . an with integrity . . . n with the know-how to turn this city into the kind of . . . to grope up in, to grow up in . . .') through the sounds of car horns, bleeps, bells, buzzers, the Brandenburg Concerto, laughing, screaming, moaning, the hammering of the street-ripper, coins going into a telephone, replays clacking on a pinball machine, revving engines and a singing clutch, the thunder of an invisible plane overhead shaking the glass walls of the tipping buildings, rock music fighting jazz fighting country western over the loudest horn of all, on a yellow taxi with blood down the door.

'Well ma'am, your lucky day, we got just one in stock. Not exactly the same colour but – well the fact is, we had this stockroom fire last week, pretty well cleaned us out. Yup, your lucky day. My partner bought it too, he was back there takin' inventory see, and it looks like he was smoking or something, so. So here I am, half a ton of assorted high-grade hardware up in smoke along with the only guy who knows how to design and build it. I was just supposed to be the money man, only now I can't even pay the rent on this crummy little store unless I sell off our plant. Yup, your lucky day. This one's a demo, let you have it half price, okay? You want me to fit it for you now? Just takes a second, even I know how to – there, how's that look? Okay that's thirty-eight no nineteen hundred plus tax plus city tax, comes to twenty-two oh six eighty-five, cash I hope?'

'Ma I can't see out of it.'

A bandaged hand patted Roderick on the head. 'Nice little talker you got there, ma'am, kit-built is he? Never seen anything like – no look, I don't know what kind see-see-em or what you got in there but usually these eyes take a while to get warmed up – not warmed up exactly but see they gotta compatiblize with the other stuff, look you wanta leave him here for an hour, see how it pans out?'

The man with bandaged hands set Roderick on the blistered paint of the counter. From there he could turn his good eye one way to see Ma leaving, or the other way to see the man going into a back room. Roderick could see a table back there, and a pair of hands turning pages.

'. . . seems in order, we might even take some of the damaged stock here on page three, but of course I want my boy Franklin to go over this . . .'

'Yes sir of course sir, you know I think you'll find this is your lucky –'

The door closed. But not before Roderick glimpsed a heavy gold ring mounting a single pinball.

No one at Larry's Grill noticed just when the little machine came in, but there it was, sitting up on a barstool listening to the chatter of the regulars.

'You wouldn't think it to look at me . . .' said the woman in purple lipstick, holding herself steady as she raised a brimming shot-glass. 'You wouldn't think it to look . . .'

'At's right Lena, you tell 'em.' The taxi driver, who considered that his Irish ancestry gave him the right to a brogue and the gift of story-telling, went on with his story about the Baltimore Mets. 'See they went to Japan to play this exhibition game, and one night they all went down to this –'

'Think I heard this,' said the swarthy used-car salesman. 'I hear every damn thing, that's the trouble in mind, Oh! –

Gonna lay my head
On some lonesome railroad line
And let the midnight train
Ease my troub – yeah, yeah, YOW! –

Tourette's syndrome they call it, I calls it like I sees it, grab it when I can get it –'

'No but listen one night they all went down to this special kind of geisha –'

'No spitting on the floor,' said Larry to the man in the red hunting cap, who was glaring at the three newcomers, youths in red Digamma Upsilon Nu sweatshirts. 'Boys if you got ID, welcome.'

'College boys!' muttered the spitter, while beside him two truck drivers argued money.

'You think you're broke? Betcha I'm ten times as broke as you.'

'Yeah? Betcha you got more money in your billfold right this minute than I got in my whole – life. My whole billfold.'

'Hell I couldn't even afford that brassy blonde over there.'

The woman he could not afford had discovered Roderick. 'Hey, you want a peanut? Here boy! Cute little bastard ain't he, I mean with one green eye one blue –'

'You wouldn't think it to look at me, but I used to be a Paris passion, fashion model.' Another drink passed purple lips. 'Paris, France.'

'I'm so broke –'

'Where the hell is Dot today, she'd like this, have a peanut boy?'

'– doesn't want a damn peanut, what the hell's the matter with you? You can see the thing's a machine, what's it gonna do with a peanut, vend it? Anyway Dick, listen they get to this geisha place –'

'Who belongs to this thing anyway?' Larry leaned over the bar to look at it. 'Anybody belong to this thing?'

'Probably came in with them college boys,' said the hunter, and spat on the floor.

'Goddamnit Jack, behave yourself.'

'Parish fashion model, you believe that?'

The used-car salesman turned. 'Ignore Lena boys, she used to be a plaster of Paris model only now she's just plas – ow, Jesus Lena can't you take a joke?'

'Okay that's a bet. Larry counts the money in both our billfolds, and whoever's got less gets all the money. Larry come here, we got a bet –'

The taxi driver's brogue deepened desperately. 'Will ye listen? Now the lads get to this special geisha place only it turns out –'

'Sure he wants a peanut, don't you my little sweet-ums? Come on boy, sit up for – he won't sit up.'

Larry, holding two billfolds, spun around to catch old Jack spitting again. 'That's it, Jack. Out. I told you about that, now out!'

The old man's earflaps stood up like the ears of a fox terrier. 'All of a sudden the place is too classy for me, all of a sudden it's a classy college-boy place, eh? Well I'm goin'. I'm goin'.' He deliberately spat again and ambled out.

'I'm a-comin', I'm a-comin',' sang the used-car man. He tapped his feet on the brass rail, threw a peanut into the air and caught it in his mouth, winked at the blonde and made a face at Roderick. 'Howdy doody little robot. How's all your nuts and bolts?'

'Bejesus will you listen man? They get to this geisha place and it turns out that all the girls are just inflatables!'

'But no really, I was a Parish, a Paris, a mannequin.'

'Inflate me,' sang the used-car man, 'my sweet inflatable –'

'I'm very well thanks,' said Roderick. No one seemed to hear, which was just as well because he was not quite telling the truth. In fact he felt strange and dizzy, and a peculiar pulse was building up behind his new eye. A pair of purple lips swam by, saying:

'To look at me, be honest, you wouldn't think ...'

Larry transferred all the money from one billfold to the other and handed them back. 'You win, Eric.'

'Hey wait a minute, that ain't a fair bet. He only had six bucks there, I had over twenty!'

'Yeah well that was the bet, who had less –'

'Yeah but I mean I'm risking twenty against six, what kinda odds is that?'

The expensive blonde said, 'Larry, forget them geeks, willya? I wanta buy my little friend here a drink, I wanta buy him a Shirley Temple. You get him a dish so he can lap, my little sweet-ums!' She patted Roderick's metal cheek. 'Soon as I get back from the little girls' room, honey, you and me can have a drinky, okay?'

'Her little robottoms,' said Dick, and winked at no one. 'Hey little robottoms, what's your name?'

'Roder-ick Wo-od.' Roderick lurched and nearly fell from the stool. One of the fraternity boys caught him.

'Wow, HE TALKS! Crazy, you see that boys? Shoo-be-do, Pow! Zap! She's a transistor sister with a ... and what was that name? Woody? Howdy Woody, how's the old wood pe –'

'Shut your gob will you? The point is, they all slept with this little inflatable geisha see? And they all came down with a dose!'

'Okay Eric, how about double or nothing?'

The money changed billfolds solemnly as one of the fraternity boys said, 'Doubles hell, we're drinking triples here, by God!' They had indeed been drinking so much that it seemed a good idea to take Roderick with them, just as it seemed a good idea to leave their car (since none of them could remember where it was parked anyway) and steal another.

The two men in the back of the Rolls-Royce sat so close that, had passers-by been able to see them through its dark windows, they might have supposed that Mr Kratt and Ben Franklin were embracing. They were in fact looking over a typewritten list.

'Now what the hell's this, twenty grand for a diode loser?'

'Laser it's supposed to be, they use it for etching the –'

'Sure, sure, just so you checked all this stuff out. This could turn out to be the best damn thing ever happened to us, Benny, where we gonna find, look at these kilns, ten grand under wholesale, and this, where is it?' Kratt erected a stubby finger and ran it down the list. 'All this test stuff half price, Christ if I knew they owned all this and were tight for cash, I'd have set fire to their place myself, Ha!'

'Yes sir, now –'

'So what do you think, bub? Make an offer on the whole shebang or what?'

Ben Franklin sat back, felt Mr Kratt's tweed-covered arm against his neck, sat forward again. 'Well if you ask me –'

'Jesus Christ, I don't see anybody else here to ask but the chauffeur, wouldn't ask that little greasy spic for the time of – told me when you came over you wanted responsibility bub, so here it is, do we buy?'

'Well, yes if you really, if it's really what you want –'

'Hell yes, you think I want to go on all my life paying through the nose for hardware we could make ourselves? Now you buy this crap and get the plant working, by the way how's that peanut brittle idea going?'

'Well Hare I mean Dr Hare is just working out a few last-minute bugs I guess, something about the batteries, the –'

'Fine, fine. Because I don't want nobody getting there first, we got to drive a spearhead see into this fun food market, then broaden our base, first maybe the gingerbread talk-backs and then see what we can do with chocolate chips, you tell Hare to get the lead out of his ass and put this stuff forward, hear me?'

'Yes sir, but you see he thinks –'

'Thinks, that loony thought his last employers right out of business, you tell him to stop thinking and start producing. Jesus, leave it up to him we'd still be farting around with some piddling little so-called improvement twenty years from now, I know these science yak-heads. Christ Benny, why do you think I put *you* in charge here? It's because you're not a science yak-head, you got your feet on the ground.'

'Science, well I was trained –'

'Sure, sure, but look, just look at these yak-heads, the way they go around blinding everybody with science, blind themselves too. Jesus they take an idea and play with it and play with it – until they go blind!'

'Ha ha, yes I guess there is a sort of masturbational side to research, even dreams – you know the answers sometimes come up in dreams, Kékulé –'

'Yeah well I say screw that! Screw that! I want to see that damn gingerbread boy on the market in months not years, *months*. Hell save the damn improvements, later we put out the new improved model, miracle ingredient, only way anything ever gets done. Tell that to Hare and his dreaming coolies, make him listen! Tell him if I don't see talking gingerbread boys in the supermarkets by Easter, I'll hand him his dick in a test-tube, let him have a wet dream about that!'

'Uh, yes sir.' Ben folded the inventory and put it in an inside pocket. 'Now if that's all I think I'll just get out here and –'

'We're both getting out here, bub, only reason I had this little greaser drive us here was so I could show you my gallery.'

'Gallery? Shooting – ?' Ben peered out but could see no neon through the dark glass.

'The Kay Tee Art Gallery, right there, bub. We got an opening tonight, Edd McFee, ever heard of him?' Kratt opened the door.

'No I don't th –'

'You will. Come on.'

And Ben Franklin, hurried from the car into a mirror-fronted place, caught sight of his own nice face, poised for some suitable expression. He had already shaken hands with two or three persons inside before he could stop thinking about that face: maybe he should grow his moustache again, and to hell with Mr Kratt?

II

The artist and the beautiful Mrs McBabbitt swept past the two critics who'd been standing in the same spot since their arrival.

'... but I still don't see why they all look the same, aren't they all just ...'

'Well I call it Paradigmatics, it's ...'

'... just purple squares?'

The two critics stood with their backs to as many of the pictures as possible, twiddled their champagne glasses, and studied the crowd.

'Plenty of loot here ... who's the big boy in the J. Press suit?'

The taller critic looked where the shorter was looking. 'Oh, Everett. Everett Moxon, he's nobody. Now. Probably just here to ask Mr K. for a job. He used to be into reactors, light-cooled reactors or something boring like that. Lost everything in the panic.'

'Just as well, before he started polluting light or something. Ever know a businessman with a conscience?'

'Not unless they've started buying them as investments, who's that stunning woman in black talking to McFee?'

The shorter looked where the taller was looking. 'Mrs McBabbitt. If you think she's beautiful now, wait till you see the finished product.'

'You don't mean – ?'

'Yep. Going through one of those whole-body cosmetic surgery jobs, bones and all.'

'But they take years! And loot ...'

'Absolutely. Everybody here is loaded practically, except Allbright.'

'Allbright! God I wish he'd hurry up and o.d. or whatever he's going to do, I really get sick of seeing him everywhere. All he does is steal books to support his nasty habit.'

'Poetry? Well I've got a dozen signed copies of his book put away, just in case. Posthumous glory might – hey, who's that old woman?'

The taller critic, looking, said, 'I didn't know you read Allbright's poetry – The one in the shawl?'

'I don't. Looks more like a lace table-cloth, but who is she? Haven't I seen her before? Some kind of writer or – ?'

'No, last year. She entered this giant toilet in the Des Moines Bienniale, name's Rose Wood, something like that.'

The shorter critic shook his head. 'No, before that, *way* back, a writer my parents knew in Chicago – now was she the writer or was it her husband?'

'Maybe the toilet was rattling off its memoirs – Christ, why don't you just ask her?'

'I will. I might.' But neither critic made a move, except to put down an empty glass when a waiter came by and seize a full one. They remained anchored to the spot even after the crash.

Mr Vitanuova spread his wide face in a smile and his wide hands in a benediction. 'Me, I don't understand nothing. It's the wife, see? She knows Art like I know garbage. No wait, don't get sore, hey I don't mean this is garbage, I mean *real* garbage, it's my business.'

But already the woman in the Abbott & Costello t-shirt had turned away to listen to Ben Franklin:

'Well purple, yes, it's kind of ecclesiastical, isn't all art? I mean isn't that why we take it seriously, because it has its own liturgy?'

Allbright moved a book-shaped bulge under his sweater. 'You're gonna give me canons of taste for this? The fact is the guy painted the same damn purple square twenty times, the same purple the same square – and you justify that? If it *were* art you wouldn't need to bring in all the big guns, the Church and Freud, Marx and Pater or any other dear damned dead philos, where's that waiter? Hauling in Wittgenstein or maybe Kirke, waiter! Hey, over here!'

'No, look fella, I'm not trying to justify anything. But so what that they're all alike, so were icons, most of them look like mass production jobs.'

'Mass production I like that, keep the old prayer-wheels of industry turning, isn't that religion?'

'Well I'm not really –'

'Counting the revs, counting the revs see, because numbers make it all important, don't they? This geek here could paint one purple square and who cares, but if he paints twenty, in comes the old number magic. What does the twenty stand for? What does it mean? Because that's religion too, numbers have to mean something: the eight-fold path, the seven deadly sins, the ten commandm –'

'What's wrong with that? Just a way of keeping track, I mean even truth is binary, if you –'

'Telling the beads,' said Allbright, lifting two drinks from a passing tray. 'Listen pal, numbers are everything in religion, telling the beads, when I was a kid I used to think that meant you know, talking to the beads. Only later on I found out it meant *telling* like a fucking bank teller, counting up the days of indulgence, no good storing up riches in Heaven if you can't count them – Listen, you want my advice?'

The woman in the Abbott & Costello t-shirt moved on without waiting to hear his advice; a moment later she was advising Dr Tarr to look for religious significance in these paintings.

'Lyle Danton? Is it you?'

The young man in patched denim work-clothes turned. 'I call myself Tate now.' He studied the old woman in lace, the corsage of radishes at her throat. 'Ma?'

Ma Wood squeezed his forearm. 'I'm glad to see my best pupil still interested in art.'

'Art?' His unhappy laugh startled her. 'Let's talk about something else. You still living in Newer?' He moved to keep his face in profile, a habit she remembered.

'Of course. Oh, I see, like Picasso? Taking your mother's name I mean. But if you're not painting now, why in the world – ?'

'Oh I'm painting, all right. I mean when I can afford the materials. Well it's a long story ...'

She kept hold of his arm. 'But don't your parents – I mean they used to be the richest folks in town when your father was running the factory. I thought he'd be doing even better by now, didn't you all move to the city so he could become general manager or some such, was it managing director?'

'*Him.*'

'You don't get along?'

'We never did. And when he killed my mother ... No, well okay it was an accident everybody says, traffic computer goes haywire and he smashes into the back of this truckload of tranquillizers; it could happen to anybody.'

'I'm sorry, I didn't know.'

'Okay an accident maybe but he hated her guts, he always hated her guts. On account of me.'

'The birthmark?'

He still kept his face in profile to hide it. 'Mom would have split long ago, only she was too damn kind-hearted, you know? I mean he needed all his money to start this new business, she knew he couldn't make it if he had this alimony around his neck, so she just stayed, stayed and stayed until he –'

'But wait, what business? Did he leave Slumbertite?'

'Got canned, so did all the execs. They got some new system there now, some, I guess they call it BIGSHOT or something, some kind of decision-maker – so anyway he's in the restaurant business now. I don't see much of him. I dropped out of the University and just been doing odd jobs, even tried working in a tattoo parlour, how's that grab you?'

Ma continued to grab at his arm, to stare at his sullen profile. '... you were always good at people, the human figure and the, the human face ...'

'Well I got fired from the tattoo parlour just the same, wrote something about T. S. Eliot on a guy's arm, the illiterate old bastard running the place thought it was "toilets", how does that – ?'

'Lyle, listen. I want to commission you to do a portrait.'

'What?' He turned full-face in surprise, showing the birthmark, a red shadow over half his features, a glimpse of Harlequin, before he turned it away again. Poor boy, she thought. Not just to have it, but to be hated for it.

'Well, not a portrait exactly, more a painted head. I'm

working it up now, maybe I could send you a cast of it to study . . . ?'

The profile looked pleased. 'Well sure. Sure Ma, sure. Only you don't mind that I do it symmetrical?'

'That would be just fine, Lyle. Just what I wanted.'

'Art, well I leave it to the experts,' said Mr Kratt. 'I'm just the money man.'

'Oh but you should take an *interest*.' Mrs McBabbitt looked at him through lowered lashes as black as her sable coat. 'Dr Tarr has just been telling me it all has deep religious significance. Are you a religious man, Mr Kratt?'

'I manage to keep pretty busy without it, you know? Ha! But of course I respect the next guy's religion as much as anybody – just like I respect the next guy's wife.' He leaned a little closer. 'Mr McBabbitt's a lucky man.'

She seemed to agree.

'What was *that*?' said the taller critic.

The building rocked from the crash. The shorter critic peered through the waves of people running towards the sound. From here it looked as though two cars had tried to drive into the gallery together and wedged themselves in the doorway. Shards of mirror lay strewn over the green carpet like peculiar angular lakes.

'Mr K.'s Rolls there, looks like. And isn't that other car flying the flags of Ruritania? The consul's car I suppose, only those boys getting out of it don't look like diplomats to me.'

'God, I hope this isn't someone's idea of a happy accident or – ?'

'That would be unfortunate,' said the taller critic. 'Did you cover that boring exhibition of wrecked cars last May?'

'Not me, you mean the freeway thing, when all those cars and trucks piled up? I wanted to go, really, thought it sounded enterprising at least, getting out there and casting the whole mess in fibreglass right on the spot, I mean whatsisname, Jough Braun must have been actually cruising the city with a ton of epoxy – imagine getting an actual body in there!'

'He was just lucky, though, what he was really out doing was dog turds. Trying to get a casting of every pile of doggy

189

do-do in the city on one particular day, kind of Conceptualist record – anyway he gave that up in a hurry once he saw what kind of money these German museums were bidding for *Freeway Disaster*. I still say he's a boring little prick.'

'But you gave him a good review?'

'Wouldn't you?' said the shorter critic. 'I mean with two German museums going bananas over him, wouldn't you?'

'What happened?' the taller asked someone else. 'Accident?'

'Nothing. Just some college kids smacked into Mr Kratt's car. Nobody hurt. A chauffeur killed.'

'Drunk, were they?'

The stranger shrugged. 'Sure, but they got diplomatic immunity, see? On account of the car. Cops won't do a thing.'

It was true. The police came and went, the cars and the body were discreetly removed, but the three grinning members of Digamma Upsilon Nu remained to sip champagne and brag of their adventure.

'Sure I'm religious,' said Mr Vitanuova. 'I'm a good Cat'lic, what else? Just because a guy gets his hands in garbage don't mean he ain't got a soul, ya know.'

Allbright, holding a champagne glass in each dirt-encrusted fist, leaned in an unpremeditated direction. 'That's goddamn profound.'

Dr Tarr said, 'Yes, what's interesting about these Catholic miracles like levitation, take the flying monk for instance, Giuseppe Coppertino in the sixteenth – What I mean is I've been working out the psychic forces involved ...'

Allbright leaned another way. 'Look, you want my advice? You want my advice? You want to get close to God you just go out and buy yourself the biggest goddamn computer you can buy. You know why?'

Mr Vitanuova kept shrugging and smiling. 'Look, I pay my dues, I figure –'

'... our little mascot,' said one of the fraternity boys. 'Our little robot mascot. Roderick, go on, say hello to the nice lady, hee hee hee.'

Across the room Ben Franklin looked up. 'Just a minute,

thought I ... thought I heard ...' But a second later Mr Kratt's heavy hand was on his shoulder.

'Have fun, bub. Just taking Mrs McBabbitt home now, but you stay, have a – have a good time.'

'Yes sir.'

'Oh one thing, all these people yakkin' about religion gave me another brainstorm here, make a note of this: edible talkbacks. I figured maybe break into the Catholic market there, Mr Vitanuova just telling me how they do it in the mass and all –'

'Yes sir, but I just wanted to see someone –'

'In a minute, bub, you just listen. Howsabout a talking host, see?'

Franklin turned to face him. 'A what? Television ...?'

'You don't listen, see? Nobody listens, I mean a *host*, a piece a bread they use for masses, Mr V. tells me the priest just holds it up and says this is my body. This is my body. Well look, wouldn't it be more convincing if *the bread itself does the talking*?'

'I don't know ...'

'Hello, Ma,' said a small voice.

'Hee hee hee, hello Ma he says, here lady you can hold him a while if you want, I gotta find my buddies – Hey you guys!' One Digamma Upsilon Nu sweatshirt went to join two others at the table of drinks. Near by, the two critics looked over copies of the beautifully-printed catalogue.

Mr Kratt's hand squeezed Ben's shoulder. 'No, well just make a note of that, we'll talk it over some other time, okay? Could be a whole new market there.'

Allbright was shouting: 'The Mormons, they got a big goddamn computer out in Salt Lake City, counting up the souls – they got it made, see? Because you know who's gonna get into Heaven? I'll tell you who, the big insurance companies, the government, the credit card companies, the Pentagon, all going to Heaven! Everybody that gets control of the magic numbers, that's who!'

Dr Tarr began filling his pipe. 'Yes there could be something in that, the psionic effect of complex machines, pure complexity ...'

'I know.' Mr Vitanuova winked. 'Like they say, garbage

in, garbage out. And I know garbage.'

Ben Franklin thrust his face between them. 'Listen, has anybody seen the white-haired woman? She was here a minute ago holding this little robot mascot thing, anybody ...?'

Next he tried the two critics, who shrugged and went on reading:

The paintings of EDD MCFEE, though superficially identical (each being a 1 cm square of Bohème 0085 Violet centred on a 74 cm square white ground) draw their individuality from the time and locus (solely determined by random numbers) in which they were painted. No. 1, *Juryroom Trout*, was painted at 3 a.m. GMT on May 2, 1979, at an exact location in the Sahara, for example (2°W, 29°N). Yet McFee's work, while rigorously Conceptualist in performance, manages at the same time to defy the canons of that limited and uncongenial mode. A bold form, an unexpected colour – these interact to both direct and keep pace with his concept, welding precision of thought to plasticity of expression in a carefully orchestrated equation of space/time. It is, moreover, a transcendental equation. Form is embedded in time, space in colour, design becomes discovery. The result, a reified Conceptualism, displaces the traditional stylized 'thought-experiment' with a new, holistic approach. Performance is redeemed by object. His aim, then, is to ...

'His aim,' said the taller critic, 'is to produce some hard goods collectors can buy, without feeling they've been ripped off – even when they have.'

'You playing this one down, then?'

'Hell no, Mr K. shoots a grand an inch for a good review ...'

Edd McFee, looking dapper even in his Army fatigues, was talking to the woman in the Abbott & Costello t-shirt when Ben approached.

'What old lady? Naw, I never seen her, ask, ask somebody else ... now like I was saying, Carrie, religion is fine, like it's a deep one-to-one interpersonal relationship with Somebody, sure that's what everybody wants. Only as an artist I got this problem: I can create but I can't really love, see? So what I'm looking for is a woman to have a deep interpersonal relations with, I mean relationship with ...'

Ben Franklin tried to ask the fraternity boys, but they had begun to sing. There was no one else to ask but the waiters and that guy with the birthmark. But the waiters were busy packing up, and the guy with the birthmark was sitting on the floor playing with pieces of mirror. Ben took a last glass of champagne and, standing alone, tried to arrange his face in a nonchalant expression. He pretended to look at the nearest painting, though in fact he failed even to notice that some-one had defaced it (adding to the small purple square a large black moustache).

'... garbage out,' said Allbright. 'That's profound, you know?'

Dr Tarr giggled. '*In vino, veri* true.'

'Right. The C-charged brain, the C-charged ...'

Lyle Tate picked up two pieces of mirror and held them so that he could see himself perfected, the dark blaze gone, his face become a bright symmetrical mask. The smile was slightly V-shaped, but so much the better, he thought, murmuring, '... animal lamina ... burn, rub ... th' gin forests, er, of night ...' and finally, 'Eye sees tiger dreg, it sees eye ...' as the howling chorus crashed about him.

> Roll me ooooover
> In the cloooover

12

Miss Borden unreeled a gold chain with a tiny ballpoint pen at the end. 'Okay Bill, spit it out.'

'Shouldn't you see the boy yourself first?'

'He's off today. Mr Wood's taking him to the city I guess for some eye tests, anyway you have observed him?'

'Yes, well no not in a direct observational, more in a peripherally informalized situ –'

'You've seen him in the hall, I know. Go on.'

'Yes, contacted him a few times in the hall and elicited a response or two, nothing def –'

'How's his reading?'

'Reading skills, yes he did say he was having trouble with this new reader Mrs Dorano assigned.'

She marked on the yellow form. 'Reading problem. I was afraid of that, now how does he get along with other kids?'

'Socially he's, there seems to be a nomenclatural mixup there, some difficulty with meaningful involvement in the cultural mainstream ... maybe an identity crisis even; other kids keep calling him a robot you know? And when I asked him why, he said, "Because I am a robot."'

She shook her head. 'All too familiar these days, schizoid pattern: usually parents both work, kid's alone too much –'

'Divisive destructuring of the ego conceptualiza –'

'That's right. I ought to send him to George for a battery, I mean a battery of reassessment tests, only right now George has a pretty full case-load over at the junior high, you know what with that Russian roulette club –'

'I imagine. How is the Vulich boy by the way?'

'As well as can be expected, understand his parents are seeking a court order to have the machine turned off – where were we?'

'Think we ought to do something, this Wood boy told me he dreams of skulls and scissor trees ...'

'Well sure, I'll try to get George to fit him in, otherwise

we'll just have to let him go on thinking he's a Martian – yes, at least we can send him to Ms Beek for some remedial, hand me one of those green forms will you, Bill? No, the *leaf* green ones . . .'

The new eye cost Pa and Ma a lot of money, but at least he could go right back to school. The other kids seemed glad to see him, even Chauncey.

Roderick couldn't figure Chauncey out at all. Whenever they were alone, the bigger boy called him 'Rick', treated him like a pal, and even shared stuff with him, as now:

'Hey Rick, wanna see some real dirty pitchers?'

'Dirty?'

'Yeah I found 'em in old Festy's desk. And these really neat binoculars too, only Billy keeps 'em at home, me and him take turns with 'em. Here, take a look.'

He pulled up his sweater and fished out a dog-eared magazine, *Stud Ranch*. Hiding behind Ogilvy's security hut in the corner of the playground (Ogilvy was never in it) they turned the pages and stared at pictures of people without clothes.

'Hey looka that, wow!'

'Yeah wow, but how come –'

'Look, looka *that*! Boy they sure do weird stuff out West.'

A pair of people were wrestling like Bax and Indica. 'Hey is it dirty because like this they wrestle on the ground or –?'

'Naw, dirty is *dirty*, you know like sexy. Dincha never play doctors or nothing?'

Roderick said, 'Sure, plenty of times. Once.'

'Okay then. See this is how they get babies.'

'*This?* With all this, these whips and spurs, this barb wire –?'

Chauncey hesitated. 'Well sure. Must be, look it probably tells all about it here –'

'Lemme see.'

Whoa there! While Calamity Jayne shucks her buckskins to saddle up for some bunkhouse fun, Miss Kitti is 'bound' to please some lonesome cowpoke. But what's Brazos gonna do with thet there branding iron?

'They don't get babies like that.'

'Sure they do, ask anybody, ask Billy, when his old man's cow had a calf, they tied a rope around her neck and look here at this one, this "necktie party girl" she's got –'

'Yeah but hey wait a minute why do they have to wear all this stuff?'

Chauncey said, 'Look stupid, it's called Stud Ranch so they all gotta wear these belts with studs, boy, when my little brother was born my old lady had to wear all kinds of stuff to keep the baby from coming out her belly button too soon I guess – hey wow, looka that rattlesnake – men don't have babies because they take pills I guess – looka that, "Bathtime at the Rocking 69" – see we had all about it last year, these little tadpoles inside and the Vast Difference –'

'Hahaha, looka that, he thinks this other guy's a girl, look it says "When a gay cabaleero..." What's a cabaleero anyway?'

'Just some word, who knows. Wow! Looka that pair!'

'Yeah, Colt .45 Peacemakers, the sheriff's got one like that only not so fancy... Hey but Chauncey, what about the tadpoles?'

'Aw who cares, sex is too complicated. Let's play guns, okay?'

But whenever he was with the gang, Chauncey called him 'freaky' and threatened to take a can-opener and rip his guts out. You just couldn't figure out some people.

Roderick couldn't figure out Mrs Dorano either. She was always telling the other kids to be especially nice to him because of his handy cap, and then when they passed out the readers she gave him a different one, real hard and no pictures at all, and all long words. He had to spend hours every night at home going through the dictionary, and it still didn't make sense.

Billy agreed, it wasn't fair. 'Heck my reader's okay. All about this here Dick and Jane and how their mother works hard at the car factory, and like how they get helped by Big Joe the social worker. How come yours is different, boy, I'd make a stink about that.'

'Yeah, listen to this, it don't make sense: "The actualization of catalyzing factors in inter-personal relationships is

196

provided first by the furtherance of participatory options within the framework of an unstructured data base of conceptual parameters, notwithstanding the counter-productive and often marginal motivational mix inducing affectual restructuring of the –'" Shit man, this doesn't even tell a story. I mean it's supposed to be about this girl, a doll-scent girl, only here I am on page twenty one and they don't even have her name down here yet.'

'Boy, I'd make a stink –'

'Yeah I guess it don't matter now they're switching me to Miz Beek for redeemial anyway, I got this other reader where they spell everything like it sounds...'

> Jump. Jump. Jump.
> See Bob jump.
> Bob jumps on a fast wagon.
> Bob gøz fastr ðan a skūl bus.

The hour started off well, with Miz Beek cheerful and pleasant. She sat with Roderick and two other kids around a little table. While they read aloud, she nodded and smiled and occasionally swallowed another of her little white pills.

But towards the end of the hour she no longer seemed to be listening. After making a quick note in her Teacher's Manual, she got up and left the room.

'I bet thee'th going wee-wee,' said one of the kids. 'Thee hath to go wee-wee.'

The other said, 'L-let's g-g-get outa here hey.'

'But thee might come back after thee taketh a pith.'

The door opened, but it was only Mr Fest, telling them he knew all of their names and not to try anything just because Miz Beek was out of the room, understand?

'Yethir, Mithter Fetht.'

'Y-y-y – sure.'

'I'm glad you know my name,' said Roderick, 'because everybody else around here keeps calling me –'

'At ease! At ease! I don't want to hear another peep outa this room.'

He went away. They waited.

'Look, thee forgot her pillth. Let'th get high, come on.'

'H-he-hell with that. I'm g-g-gonna s-sell these up in the eighth-graders' c-c-c – toilet.' The stammerer grabbed the pill bottle and ran out, chased by the lisper. Roderick waited until the bell rang, then leaned over and read Miz Beek's note.

'ðu īdeea uv kumbīniNg speeCh Thayrupee wiTh ree-meedyul reediNg iz just wun mōr exampul ov ðu braykdown ov ðu hōl godawful sistum HwiCh ðay keep erjiNg mee tu joyn (az ðō peepul wur glū...'

Nat walked him home from school. 'I feel safer,' he explained. 'Not that I'm really afraid of Chauncey and his gang but heck, two of us got a lot better chance than one, right?'

'Right,' said Roderick. 'I was just wondering you know, how come I read all right at home only at school everything goes wrong?'

'Yeah? Hey, we could become blood brothers, pledge our-selves to fight to the death, back to back in case Chaun –'

'Look, I ain't got any blood.'

'We could use oil then, you got oil.'

So Roderick tapped a few drops of hydraulic fluid and Nat took a drop of blood from his thumb, and they mixed them.

'We both swear, right? To defend ourselfs against anybody even Chaunce, we swear on my blood and your oil. Brothers.'

'Brothers.'

'To the death.'

'To the death.' Roderick walked him to his door. 'See you tomorrow.'

'Not tomorrow, hey remember? We got the day off on account of Miz Beek drowning herself in the swimming pool.'

'See you the day after, then. Brother.'

'Okay brother.'

'Settle down, all of you,' said the principal. 'I'm not even going to start until you're quiet. What's more, no one goes home until we finish here, understood?'

They shifted uneasily, and one or two who had been glancing through the pages of *Educationalist Today* sat up straight.

'That's better. Now you all know why I've called this

special meeting. But in case anyone hasn't seen today's *Herald*, let me read it out to you.'

'ROBOT' BOY AT NEWER SCHOOL: MORE INSANITY?

Following the alleged suicide of a teacher at Newer Public School (Stubbs Cty) come rumours of serious mental disturbances among the pupils. Teachers have confirmed that at least one boy thinks he is a mechanical robot.

The boy, Robert Wool, 'acts just like a little machine,' according to second-grade teacher Mrs Delia Dorano. He believes he has mechanical grappling hooks for hands, and tank tracks in place of feet. 'Robert doesn't even answer to his name,' she said. 'No wonder, what with the constant harping on sex and filth everywhere you look. We must protect our children from the sex-merchants of the state educational system.'

George George, school psychologist, blamed the computerizing of modern society, including our schools. 'We have teaching machines, testing machines, magnetic report cards,' he said. 'Where do we stop?' According to another source, books in the school library have been keypunched on to IBM cards which are unreadable. Said George, 'It's getting like Brig Bother around here.' Mr George is the brother of Hal George, prominent hog auctioneer.

Russian Roulette Club

Newer Junior High, like Newer P.S., has had its share of tragedies. Last year Beanie Vulich, 16, became the first tragic victim of the school's 'Russian roulette club', whose members made use of a school computer to select a duelling pistol at random from a number ...

'It goes on,' she said, 'to mention drugs sold openly in the eighth-grade washroom, thefts and vandalism, and a security man with a drink problem. Any comments?'

Ogilvy was the first to speak. 'Not fair,' he said. 'Buncha lies and distortions. Like sure I take a drink now and then, but they make it sound like I spend all day lying in an alley somewheres with a bottle of Tokay in a paper bag.'

'What really bothers me,' said Miss Borden, 'is the way certain people are using this tragic suicide as an excuse to whine about their own pet peeves.' She looked at Mrs Dorano. 'Certain people are going to be sorry they ever opened their big –'

'The truth will out,' said Mrs Dorano. 'You can't suppress –'

Mr Goun jumped to his feet. 'Suppress, who the hell are you to talk about –?'

At the same time Mr George said, 'How did I know they were going to print it that way? I didn't think you'd take my criticism in a personalized way, rather than in a societally –'

'Filth and corruption driving that young woman to –'

Captain Fest said, 'Self-discipline, a hard line, lest we forget, moulding Americans, shaping the future –'

'– nothing but plain murder, no better than abor –'

'– catalyzing factors –'

'– easy way out, no backbone, no self-discip –'

'– building a bridge –'

'*Quiet.*' Miss Borden looked at George. 'You all disappoint me, you especially, George. Whining to the papers behind my back instead of getting down to work – My God, you're the school psychologist. We pay you to fix these kids.'

'Fix? Fix? You talk as if they were a bunch of machines! What do you suggest, I get out the old tool-kit and maybe tighten up a few loose screws here and there?'

Mrs Dorano clapped her hands over her ears. 'I won't listen to that filth – I won't!'

Captain Fest muttered, 'Like to fix that little Robert whats-isname myself. Hear he refuses to pledge allegiance to his country's flag. You give him to me for a week, I'll knock the robot crap out of him.'

George turned on him. 'Knock the crap out of him, all you can think of, right? If you had the slightest understanding – Look, what you ought to be doing is using his problem, making it work for us, for him. I mean, if he thinks he's a robot maybe he should be on a teaching machine or –'

'Good idea,' said Miss Borden. 'That's it, then. Captain, you take charge of this boy and set up a teaching machine program.' She checked something off on a form. 'What I like to see, people forgetting their little individual differences and all pulling together. So much for one child's problem. Now how about some of these bigger issues? Dope-pushing, theft, vandalism – any suggestions?'

One of the younger teachers murmured something and Miss Borden took it up. 'Did you say bridge-building, Ms

Russo? That's the first sensible suggestion I've heard so far. Isn't that our job, after all, building bridges? Reaching out –'

Ms Russo blushed. 'No, what I shaid was –'

'– reaching out to isolated, disadvantaged children who –'

'I shaid I hope thish doesn't take long becaushe I've got a dental appointment.'

'Dental appointment. I see.'

'Yah, to have a bridge rebuilt. Shee, what happened was that little bash – that Chaunshy Bangfield hit me in the mouth with a trophy. I was making him voluntarily return it.'

Someone muttered, 'He reached out to her all right, the little disadvantaged –'

'Any more suggestions?'

Goun spoke of actualizing the problem within a contextual framework of structured situations ranging from verbal correctives to dis-enrolment. In such an intra-systemic . . .

The digital clock wiped away another minute, and another.

Pa waved a plate of brass shaped like half a violin. 'Son, what I'm trying to do here is make me a timepiece, but one that keeps real time. Human time. Like when you're concentrating hard on one thing and it seems like only a minute goes by, why should you have clocks showing you an hour?' He laid the brass plate on his bench and started hammering. 'Other. Times. You wait. For some. Thing to. Happen. Like the. Sunrise. When you. Can't sleep. You think. One. Hour. Goes by. But ord. Inary clocks. Say one. Minute!' The coughing fit would not pass; Pa had to sit down. 'What use is a clock doesn't tell real time? So. Figure I'll just hook this one up to a brain-wave gadget, need some other stuff too, fine adjustments for fidgeting, pass me that melon scoop will you?'

Roderick wondered what would happen if somebody spent all his real time watching his own real time clock? Could he make it run fast or slow, stop it? Run it back? Or what if two people watched each other's clock? What if two clocks were hooked together? What if the clocks started running the people? And what if . . . ? He could go on with questions like these for ever, and no time lost. Time didn't have to move here, because he was at the place where he fitted into the world (as the melon scoop fitted into the brass half-violin turning it into the lever that threw the switch that started up the little water-wheel...). Here was Pa, measuring up and marking out all the precise spots on the brass where he was going to bash it with a hammer. Here was the workshop, with dusty autumn light slanting in through the high little window to illuminate a corner piled with forgotten inventions: the pocket calculator (that could add only 0 + 0, 0 + 1 or 1 + 0); the Goethescope with its ebony prism; 'talking shoes'; the universal voting machine with its tangle of coloured wires leading from hundreds of switches to one dead-end; 'Maze-opoly'; audible ink; a large abacus (designed for steam power); the ingenious solar-powered cucumber press (virtual perpetual motion, Pa explained); the Odorphone... Here was the friendly workshop itself, one friendly wall bearing the hand-lettered slogans of Miss Violetta Stubbs; another bearing tools (the dover, bit-mace, graduar etc.) below the golden key below the framed photo of Rex Reason below the shelf with the radio. Now the radio hurried through some assassination attempt on some Shah, anxious to get back to its sunshine balloon, but he could hear Ma singing one of her improvised songs, the one she claimed was from the Bow-wow Symphony – whatever that was:

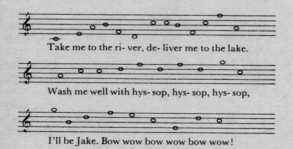

Take me to the ri- ver, de- liver me to the lake.

Wash me well with hys- sop, hys- sop, hys- sop,

I'll be Jake. Bow wow bow wow bow wow!

There were other stanzas just as senseless, stuff about poison candy being good for you when you wake up with an electrode up your nose, stuff like that – anyway, how could a woman be Jake!

13

To find out about the past, Roderick had to ask Ma. Pa would only say, 'History is a bunk on which I am trying to awaken.'

Ma sketched as she talked:

Once upon a time the town of Newer had been nothing but a flat spot on the flat prairie: no factory, no grain elevator, no town, not so much as a billboard advertising cream substitute. But to those who founded the town, flatness was ideal: it reminded them daily that God had placed the human race upon a planet shaped like a dinner plate.

They came in 1874, Josephus Butts and his followers. They called the place New Ur, themselves the Urites. They builded here a temple with plain glass windows all around, to shew forth the straightness of God's ruled line.

There were other rules, gradually revealed by Josephus (who now called himself *Jorad*): Urites were forbidden to laugh, marry, call hogs, look with pleasure at the sky or upon one another. Nine-tenths of all they owned or produced belonged to Jorad. No one could speak unless Jorad gave permission. No one but Jorad could sing. No one might *think* unless Jorad allowed him to put on the famous knitted 'thinking cap', a device designed to keep thought down to one person at a time. Finally, the Urites were asked to speak, think, sing and pray in a language called Hibble-bibble, the grammatical rules of which were clear only to Jorad.

Jorad was good at this kind of life. In 1888, he defeated a famous orator in debate, a man who had come to New Ur solely to prove the world was round. The Urites would long remember that exchange.

FAMOUS ORATOR: When a ship sails away, the hull vanishes over the horizon first. Then the lower sails. Then the top-gallant. If the world is *not* round, how do you explain that?

JORAD: Do you see any ships here in town? Any top-gallants vanishing over any horizon? No? *Well then.*

It was their finest moment. The Urites were happy (in their way) as Jorad went off on a round-the-world tour (assuring them as he left that round was only a figure of speech) to promote flatness.

He was gone for ten years. And in the meantime, the Urites grew soft. One of them invented a device which became a standard part of the bicycle, money poured in, the church was rebuilt with stained-glass windows ... by the time Jorad returned, the younger Urites were defiantly saying that Hibble-bibble was mumbo-jumbo, and even that *the earth might be a little bit rounded in spots.*

In no time at all the town had a dance hall and a Christian Science Reading Room, and all was lost. Jorad smashed the stained-glass windows, called his flock together and tried to urge them back to sense and happiness. But when they looked out of the broken panes, they no longer saw the straight line of the horizon, they saw billboards advertising liver pills, they saw a smoking factory (making beds), they saw steam tractors vanishing over the horizon ... well then.

Jorad packed up and left, declaring his intention to travel to the edge of the earth and leap off. Some believed he had, until it turned out that he was only over in the next county, calling himself Baresh and starting up a New Babylon. Some people always learned, Ma said. None of Jorad's descendants had ever married: Miss Violetta Stubbs and Mr Ferd Joradsen were now the last.

'Sure it's sad,' said Roderick, trying to see the sketch. 'But what happened to this Hibble-bibble?'

'Nothing. It vanished.'

'Heck I liked the other stories better, all about the boy who couldn't shiver and the girl who couldn't cry and the little engine that could and – hey, that, is that me? It doesn't look much like me.'

'Well who said it has to look like you? Heaven's sake, Roderick, this is your *ideal* head. The head you might have on your coin – or in the movie of your life – or when they put up your statue in the park, not to mention the church – but it's nothing to do with your real head.'

'Yeah but how come it's got a nose and a chin and ears when all I got –?'

'Never mind, you're too young to understand. Just as you're too young to understand the history of Newer.'

'Okay, but I still like the other stories better, the emperor's new clothes and the constant tin soldier – those are neat, hey.'

'Well real life isn't so neat, son.'

Real life at school was now very neat. Every day Captain Fest met him at the school door and conducted him to a janitor's closet on the top floor where there was nothing but a typewriter keyboard and a television screen.

'You sit here and *learn*, Wood. *Learn*. I know your name and I'll be keeping an eye on you. Latrine's down the hall there but don't you dare need it.'

Old Festy did check on him now and then, and so did Miz Russo, the young teacher who couldn't talk much because her jaw was wired shut. He sat. He learned.

It began when he pushed the keyboard button marked HELLO. At once words appeared on the screen:

'*Hello. My name is Hank Thoro II. Please type your name.*'

'My whole name?' he typed.

'*Good. My, do you like baseball? Just type Y for Yes or N for No.*'

He typed Y.

'*Good. Later on we'll have fun playing baseball. First you need a little practice talking to me. Now tell me what's missing in this sentence: Baseball is fun, but football is even more __.*'

'Fun.'

'*Very good. My, before every baseball game they play some music, and everyone stands up. The music is called the Star-Spangled Banner. Do you know what a banner is?*'

'Somebody who b –'

'*Just Y or N. My. Y for Yes and N for No. Do you know what a banner is?*'

'What the heck. N.'

'*Banner means flag. The Star-Spangled Banner is the American flag. Star-Spangled means it has stars on it, and banner means flag. The American flag is a Star-Spangled __.*'

So it went until recess: Roderick learned all the words of

205

the National Anthem and the Pledge of Allegiance, how to salute the flag, carry it in a procession, display it with State flags, fly it at half-mast, and fold it into a three-cornered hat.

At recess Chauncey beat him up. Nat, his blood-oil brother, was nowhere in sight.

After recess he learned the history of the flag, the names of the fifty States and their capitals. Baseball never came up again.

At lunch hour, he rescued Nat from Chauncey.

After lunch hour, he learned more about the States: their chief exports and imports, populations, gross expenditures, State birds, flowers and songs, present governors and lieutenant governors, forms of capital punishment.

Finally, the 'baseball'. The machine gave him three questions on what he'd learned. He answered them all, and it replied:

'*Three home runs wow terrific congratulations My you win program ends ... Bye.*'

He went to inform Mr Fest that Utah was the only State with death by firing-squad, that Minnesota's State bird was the loon.

'Learned all that, have you?' Mr Fest scratched his grey crewcut. 'Pretty quick. Puts me in kind of a bind, though, you know? Now I gotta find some more programs for you. Come on, let's go see what they got in the office.'

Miss Borden was on the phone when they barged in. 'Yes sir. Yes. Well, you and I know how people can read into ... yes, and reporters cook up anything out of pretty ordinary ... of course I could look up the medi – now? My secretary's on her coffee – sure, yes, if you put it like that I, just hang on a minute, what is it Captain?' She could not see Roderick over the edge of the desk.

'Just wanted to find a few programs for the teaching machine, American history maybe?'

She detached a key from her gold chain and threw it, the motion sending a batch of pink forms to the floor where they sprawled in a neat fan. 'Help yourself, cabinet in corner – get those forms will you, Captain? I'm, I've got to go look up some kid's medical rec – Jenny never gets around to keying anything on our data file so it's always a matter of digging

206

– oh, and if you hear any funny noises on the phone, pick it up, will you? And tell them I'm still hunting?'

'Can do, ma'am.'

She grabbed a handful of blue forms and strode out, saying, 'Got to get this place organized, every time we get a bigger data base they throw more junk at us, fill it up before we even . . .'

Fest said, 'Boy, pick up those forms and put 'em on Miss Borden's desk.' He unlocked the cabinet. 'Boy this could use some organizing too, half the labels you can't even read, what's this, *Element. P.* Psychology? Physics?'

'Hey Mr Fest you know these here grade forms, they –'

'Not now, *Geo. W.* has to be George Washington, here they got it stuck in with all the global studies stuff.'

'Yeah but how come everybody gets the same grade, like Norma Lee Dunne here, she's real good at math and –'

'Don't read that stuff, just put it back on the desk. Now what's this reel supposed to be the shelf label says *Homecraft* and the reel label says *G. Stars*, what the heck here – oh.' He opened the box to release a shower of gold stars. 'Damn woman couldn't organize a cathouse on a Sunday morn –'

'But shouldn't she get a better grade than like Jimmy Rittle, he's never even at school, he's been sick every day but one.' Roderick caught his eye. 'Okay, I'm, look I'm putting 'em right here on the desk.'

'Here we are, *F. S. Key*, Francis Scott Key composer of the Star-Spangled Banner, boy. Can't learn too much about your own count – hmm, Lincoln? Naw, think we'll leave the old hair-splitter for now, get some basics. No use you getting the idea all our forefathers looked like a buncha damn hairy hippies, eh? Come on.'

'Lincoln,' said Roderick, 'is the capital of Nebraska, population –'

'Yes, well fine.' Fest locked the cabinet and looked for a place to put the key. 'But don't just uh learn this stuff like a parrot, eh? It's gotta come from the heart.'

'I don't have a heart.'

'Don't get cute with me, boy, I'm warning you. Crippled or not, I don't have to stand for no, any *crud*. Now get upstairs to your post and stand by for Francis Scott Key. On the double: *Move!* LEFT RIGHT LEFT RIGHT...'

The telephone receiver began making crackling noises as they left, and continued until Miss Borden, carrying a pile of green forms under one arm and a file in her hand, came to rescue it.

'Yes sir, yes I have it here, Roderick Wood, hello? Why no one, Dr Froid, no one just one of the teachers looking up some training aids, teaching aids.'

'– *kind of an office you run there, Miss Borden, sounded like a roomful of stormtroopers doing callisthenics. I'm not at all surprised if your* teachers *behave like* –'

At recess Chauncey and the gang had a new one for him.

'Okay now, no means yes and yes means no. You want me to hitcha with these brass knucks? Yes or no?'

'No,' said Roderick, and got hit. Nat, he noticed, was hiding away on the other side of the playground, pretending to watch some younger kids playing Frying Pan, as though it were the most fascinating game he'd ever seen.

'You want me to hitcha again? Yes or no?'

'Yes,' said Roderick and got hit.

'Hahaha, gotcha again, you want me to hitcha again? Yes or no?'

'LOOK OUT!!!' Roderick screamed and pointed at the sky just at the back of Chauncey's head. The flinch gave him time to get away to a safe distance from which he could call 'I meant, don't look out.'

'Hello,' said Roderick, but suddenly Hank Thoro II had no time for small-talk. The screen flared up:

'*Fundamental Systems Key 42. A programme for storing, reading, altering, re-addressing or deleting data system DC/4633333808824. File call?*'

It seemed to be a question. Roderick pressed *Y*. (means N?)

'*No file Y. File call?*'

N was no better, nor was any other single letter; after a while he tried typing words at random: 'Indica', 'abacus', 'bishop', 'car chase', 'jispsy', 'robot', 'kale', 'sip', 'thud'.

Finally he tried numbers, and when he happened to hit *42*, the screen reacted:

'*Incorrect call. For systems key use* FSKEY *42. Call?*'

'FSKEY *42*,' he typed.

'*Fundamental Systems Key 42. A programme for storing, reading, altering, re-addressing or deleting data system DC/746 information using 333 and 338 subroutines and/or manual file call.*

'*System security is maintained by use of (1) User passwords, (2) System level match codes . . .*'

By the end of the day, Roderick was able to call up more interesting stuff, like:

'*Wood, Roger Rick. Grade: 2. Med: No file. Assessmt: Schiz. tendencies. Teacher: Fest. Comment: Difficult adjustment, due to handicap. May need psy. couns. IQ: NR.*'

He decided to change a few things.

On the way home from school, Chauncey beat him up. Nat went by on the other side of the street, pretending not to notice.

'Look, a deal's a deal, okay? I always help you, so –'

'Yeah only we'll be late to school. I mean sure I wanted to help you only I hadda get home early. My ma gets real mad –'

'A deal's a deal. Blood and oil and you never helped me once. Cripes some blood-oil brother you turned out to be. If you don't look out I'll delete you.'

'Yeah? You're not so tough – what's delete?'

'Like I take your name off the files, like the school don't even know your name, how'd you like that?'

Nat picked up a twig and pretended to smoke it, blowing out steam in the cold air. 'How come you can do that? You're just kidding.'

'No really, Mr Fest gave me this program, it's supposed to be all about the guy who wrote the flag see, this Francis somebody –'

'That's a girl's name! Anyway nobody writes flags, you're just dumb.'

'I don't care, it's what he said, and it's not, it's all about us it's like files see, like it's got your name and your picture and what grade you're in, and like mine says I got the shits –'

'Ha ha. Ricky's got the shee-its, Ricky's got –'

'That's all you know, I deleted that. I can delete stuff all over the place, I can do anything I want with anybody's file. So you better come across on our deal, that's all.'

'Hey look, there's Chaunce and Billy – and they got can-opners!' Nat began to run. 'I'm gonna be late, see you.'

The electric can-openers were nothing against the invincible strength of the *Steel Spider*, who managed to bloody Chauncey's nose and send him fleeing for his life, then turned with a deep-throated snarl on the other bully:

'You just wait till recess, boy. I'll fix you.'

But at recess Chauncey and Billy had a couple of friends, one of whom was Nat. They followed him all over the school playground, telling everyone how he shit his pants, until the enraged man of steel turned on them and lashed out with:

'Okay that's it, you've had it, boy, I'm gonna fix your files.'

He hurried back to the janitor's closet and flicked on the machine. 'Bangfield, Chauncey,' became 'Bangfield, Piggy Dirty Bastard,' and the accompanying picture, through the magic of a light pen, developed missing teeth, a bandit moustache and glasses. Under 'Comments' he listed every mean thing he could remember (or invent) and then went on to deal likewise with Nat, Billy, all his enemies . . . and what the heck, why not get old Pesty Festy while he was at it?

On Friday afternoon suddenly old Pesty ripped open the door. 'Gotcha! Red-handed! And don't try to bullshit me, son, that ain't American history on that screen is it? Is IT?' He grabbed Roderick's neck and forced his face close to the screen which read: 'Call allfile faculty allfile pupil delete . . .'

'Well no it's –'

'Shut it off, just shut it off NOW! MOVE!' But as Roderick moved, he said: 'Wait, don't touch it. Do it myself, I'm not gonna trust a little bastard like you to do any more dam –'

'Yeah but if you . . . no if you push that STOP button it doesn't stop it, not in this mode, it –'

'Shuttup you. There.'

'Yeah but it just means you finished the command, now it's gonna delete all –'

'Shut. Up. And come with me. Buddy, you're up shit creek

and I got the lawnmower – think you can fuck around with my pay check do you?'

'Your pay –?' For the first time, Roderick began to understand that the 'files' were not just stuff in the machine. Fest was waving a blue piece of paper at him. He had forgotten the latest name until he saw it:

Pay to the order of J. K. MUNKY POOP FEST
_____

NO DOLS AND OO CTS
_____

There were other teachers in Miss Borden's office; they could hardly squeeze in the door. Fest hoisted him up and set him on the desk.

'I wondered what in the world,' said Ms Russo through her teeth. 'When I went to call the roll, here were all these names, Pig Bottom and Horse Dork, but I mean they were printed right out on the magnetic cards so I – I just called them.'

Mrs Dorano said, 'Well I certainly did not, and I'm keeping my cards as evidence! No child ever thought up all by himself such filth, such –'

Mr Goun shook his head hard, as though trying to straighten the drooping moustache. 'Poor kid, he's really twisted, I mean the isolationizing factor must've catalyzed something –'

Miss Borden took hold of Roderick's claws and looked into his eyes. 'How could you? How could you? The files, the files are – well I mean they're the *files*!' She threw a magnetic card on the desk. 'How could you do a thing like that?'

Roderick looked down at it. There was his picture, with a smile added to the face and big muscles to the arms. '*The Steel Spider Wood*,' it read. '*Grade: 8. Med: No file. Assessmt: A nice kid. Teacher: Pesty Festy. Comment: A reel nice kid. IQ: 1,000,000.*'

'I'm sorry,' he said. 'It was just – I didn't know – heck – it was gonna go in print and all – I'm sorry.'

'We'll have to expel the boy of course,' she said.

'Expel him? I'd like to break every –'

'That will do, Captain. The main thing is, we've got to

keep this quiet. Dr Froid and the county board are already breathing down our necks, and wouldn't the papers just love something like this? So we can't even call the expelling expelling, we'll have to recommend a transfer on account of his handicap, something like that. As for the files –'

'Don't worry,' said Roderick. 'They're all fixed up now.'

'Fixed –?'

'Just now. Everything's deleted. All the files.'

Miss Borden looked around her office at the stacks of forms, pink, green, pale green, buff, blue, yellow, gold, white, lavender – at lavender she began to grind her teeth.

Louie Honk-Honk was pouting. 'It's not so cold.'

'Louie it *is*, it's too cold. How can I be a detective and give you reports in weather like this? Let's go to my house.'

'Nope! Your folks would just get mad.'

'No they wouldn't, they –'

'They would so! They would so!'

'Okay then, your house?'

'*My* folks would get mad. They told me never to talk to little kids. I told 'em I was only kidding about throwing some kid in Howdy Doody Lake, but they said –'

'Yeah okay. But look, we'll just have to call it off for the winter. When it's warmer –'

Louie stamped his enormous foot. 'But you – you didn't even *start* telling me about that new book – what's it called?'

Roderick held up the paperback. '*Die Die Your Lordship*. I guess it's all about this guy named Your Lordship who gets murdered – look it's too cold to go detecting now.'

'Just some of it, huh Roddy? Some of it?'

'Okay here's the title, now what's this word?'

'Dee. Eye. Eee. *Die*, is it?'

'Good, you got that easy.'

'Hey the next is *die* again. "Die die you –" no "your" – am I right?'

Louie managed to sound out the hard word *lordship*, and they went on to the first paragraph. For some time, Roderick had been meeting him by the corner mailbox for these little detective sessions, and had so far taught him to detect the alphabet, numbers up to a hundred, addition, subtraction and quite a few words. This book was going to be too hard maybe, but Roderick planned to read it, tell Louie the story, and then stop every now and then to detect a sentence with him.

When they had finished the first paragraph ('The body lay on the carpet. It was very very dead.') Roderick gave him a secret detective handshake and went home.

It was only later that he discovered the book to be incomplete.

'I've called you all together,' said the wizened detective, 'to get at the bottom of this. Let's just recall the facts. We know that Lord Bayswater was brutally bludgeoned to death in this drawing-room. We know that on the evening in question, only four people could have been here alone with him. We know that each of the four dropped one clue, and that each had access to only one of the four weapons. You, Adam, his wastrel playboy nephew were the only one with access to a polo-stick. You, Lady Brett Bayswater, his so-called wife (in love with the doctor, aren't you?) left clear fingerprints on the poker. You, Dr Coué, were seen entering this room at 8:00, leaving it at 8:15. And you, Mr Drumm, his so-called secretary (slyly playing on the affections of his daughter, I believe) entered at 8:14 and left at 8:30 – the last visitor, hmm?'

White-faced, Drumm stammered, 'But-but the thread was left by the first person in the room. And no one knows who left the smudge of soot.'

'We know it came from the poker. You do admit dropping a blood-soaked handkerchief on the floor, however? Drumm?'

The young man nodded guiltily. 'But not the hair.'

'Well,' said the wizened sleuth, 'we have begun to marshal our facts. Let us continue: the weapon may have been the statuette, eh? We know that if you, Dr Coué, picked up that statuette, it was at first to take from under it a folded message. We also know that if the weapon was not the billiard cue, then either Drumm was embezzling from his employer or Dr Coué was being blackmailed – or both. What is more, we know that if there was a message under the statuette, then young Adam here was, without doubt, the thief!'

'The murderer!' screamed Lady Brett.

'Not necessarily, but the thief. We also know that if Drumm embezzled, it was because he had *compromised* your daughter. And if the bloodstained handkerchief was *not* used to wipe the statuette, then you, Lady Brett, *only pretended to be in your room reading all evening*. And we know that Coué could only have been blackmailed because he was supplying your butler – Yes! Supplying him with morphia! For his addiction!'

'Good God!' said Adam. 'The murdering –!'

'Let's not jump to conclusions. I did not mean that your butler *is* an addict – not necessarily – but let us press on: We know that if you, Lady Brett, left your room during the night, then Adam could not have been the thief at all! We have established that your daughter is not *compromised*, it is my happy duty to report. And finally we know that if Jenkins the butler is addicted to vile morphia, then the weapon can only be the billiard-cue.'

Lady Brett spoke sharply. 'But what does it all mean?'

'It means, your ladyship, that I can now name the murderer, the time and the weapon. I must therefore caution one of you that anything you say may be taken down and used in evidence. I hereby arrest *you*,

And that was all. A lot of perfectly blank pages followed. Roderick flipped through them again and again, until finally a minute slip of paper fell out.

The publisher regrets that, due to unforeseen technical problems, the last chapter of this book has been lost. However, the publisher is willing to offer the sum of five hundred thousand dollars ($500,000) to the first person coming forward with the correct solution to *Die Die Your Lordship*. The clues are all there, it's up to you. Send solutions to the address below:

What a cheat. Roderick set to work and solved the mystery that evening, wrote out his answer and explanation (which appears on page 348 below) and signed Louie's name. Boy, wouldn't Louie be surprised when he got all that money! Half a million, he could afford to hire a real detective – or a real teacher.

Next day he was at the corner mailbox, trying to reach the envelope up to the slot, when Louie came skipping along on one leg.

'Here, chief, lemme help ya.' Louie popped the envelope inside and clanged the door. 'There. That's my good deed, Roddy. Ain't it?'

Roderick wished he could grin.

14

'Love?' Pa was so startled that he scratched his head with the hand holding the soldering iron. Later on he said: 'Well I don't know, some people say it's everything, some say it doesn't exist, some say it's just using a fabric conditioner to make your family's clothes soft or pouring some breakfast food in their trough every morning. Some say it's the secret of the universe, some say you can buy it in any massage parlour, some say it's priceless, some say it's a lot of trouble and to hell with it.'

'Yeah, but what do you say?'

'Ask your Ma.'

Ma was working on her greatest project so far, *File*: drawings of all drawable nouns to be filed alphabetically in one cabinet and cross-indexed by shape. She was now up to claviers, claymores and clepsydras. 'Have you asked Pa?'

'He said ask you. See I been reading these stories and it's always got hearts in it, love is always a heart thing, like in the Constant Tin Soldier see, where he loves this paper girl and when she falls in the fire he throws himself in after her, and he melts down into a little heart. And then like in this Wizard story –'

'*The Wizard of Oz*, you're reading that?'

'Yeah and it says "The Tin Woodman appeared to think deeply for a moment. Then he said: 'Do you suppose Oz could give me a heart?'" See because he can't love this girl he's supposed to love. So like you can't have a love situation I guess without a heart thing.'

Ma sketched a clam. 'Then you've been poking around up in the attic?'

'Yeah, there's a whole bunch of these Wizard I mean these Oz books, and lots of old clothes and other junk. I found this old picture of somebody getting married, it kinda looked like you and Pa only it wasn't. Was it?'

Her cheeks were pink. 'No, I think . . . must be my cousin's wedding . . .'

'And I found this here box of joke cards, pictures of hearts and stuff, and little people with tabs on 'em you wiggle 'em and they move.'

'Valentines . . .'

'Yeah, like one's got this dog with a heart in his mouth, you wiggle the tab and he jumps up and down it says, "I'll bark and whine Valentine and dog your footsteps till you say you're mine".'

She seemed lost in a dream. 'Pa gave me one once, nothing but a slip of paper with a formula, a cardioid . . .'

'Hey this heart thing do you think if maybe I got one of them mechanical hearts like I could do these easy payments do you think . . . ?'

'Pa, it looks like there's some big story you know? Behind all these little stories.'

Pa had just come in from the snow, coughing and cursing as he emptied out his sack of junk on the work-bench. He could not answer until he'd sat down, unbuckled his overshoes, and wheezed a while. 'What big story, son?'

'I don't know, but like I can't pledge allegiance because I ain't got no heart, any heart, and this Tin Woodman in Oz can't marry this girl too because for the same reason. And in this other Oz story there's this Tin Soldier without a heart too, and in this *other* story this Tin Soldier melts into a heart, I mean who wants to marry an old flag but all the same if I had a heart –'

'Slow down, slow down. Been thinking myself about what you need. It's not a heart, it's legs. This is no good, you staying in every time it snows like this.' Pa got his coat off and rolled up his sleeves carefully. 'Anyway, I gotta try something, rig some –'

'Pa were you ever in Oz?'

'Nope. Why?'

'Well because I worked out here, P is the letter after O, and A is the letter after Z, so I thought maybe somehow you changed it – and then you got this box I seen it somewhere it says Tin Soldier on it, so I just –'

'Tin –? Tin *solder*, boy, not soldier. No *i* in it.'

'Yeah but it melts down just like – anyway your name is Wood, you can't ... Wood, that must mean *something*.'

Pa stared at him and started to grin. 'Well I'll be God damned! Codes and secret – at your age! Well, doesn't that just take me back, must be years since I dazzled my own brains with – Hah!'

'Yeah well there's more. See, I worked out where this Oz must be, because see at school I learned Pennsylvania is PA and New York is NY see Oz goes right in between,' and he sketched it on the wooden work-bench:

N Y
O Z
P A

'See, there must be this place between New York and Pennsylvania this Oz-zone. I thought maybe I oughta go there because I'm the tin Wood boy because I could see this Wizard –'

'But there isn't any wizard.'

Roderick thought for a moment. 'Okay, then I could see this Mr Baum that wrote the story, I looked up his name and it means Wood too, boy, you can't tell me all that doesn't mean nothing, anything!' ·

Pa made sure he was not holding a soldering iron before scratching his head. 'Well, son you see if you look hard enough, you can prove just about anything. Now take this L. Frank Baum, okay his last name means tree, just about the same as Wood, so what? What about the rest of his name. Frank could mean French, does that mean your Oz is in France?'

'Yeah but it could mean *honest*, then it has to be true.'

'But stories are never honest, are they? That's the point. Anyway the man's first name is Lyman.'

'Lie-man? Aw gee, no fooling? Then it's just nothing!'

'Wouldn't say that, son, thinking is a good way to spend your time even if –' But the little machine had already buzzed out of the room. Pa could hear the whine of its motors all through the house, rising above the sound of Ma's voice on the telephone.

'Well I just figured with all the money we paid on that policy there'd be more ... Yes, I said we'd take it, yes just send the cheque straight to the Frobisher Custom Electronic Specialties Company of Omaha, yes all of it ... No, *Frobisher*. Like the pirate, F-R-O...'

Old folks were real hard to get along with sometimes. Like they were all the time talking about money, getting out all these bills and spreading them over the dining-table just to look at them while they talked about money. What was he supposed to do all day? Sit around looking at their dumb wedding picture – it sure was Ma and Pa all right, but they must of changed a whole lot since then – or just listen to them talking about bills for electronic stuff and the adoption and Pa's cough, and for all the special materials Ma needed for this ideal head, that wasn't going to be no more use than the little legs Pa was making.

'Go on, try 'em out, son.'

'It feels pretty high, what if I fall over?'

He hated the little legs, all they were good for was stumping around in the snow until his battery went flat. But Pa was proud of them, and you had to humour old folks.

Roderick wore the new legs when Ma took him along to see Mr Swann.

'My, haven't we grown, heh heh, just take a seat there kid, read your comics while Mrs W. and I get down to business. Now Mrs W. you may recall I said this wouldn't be easy, and it won't be. Not much hope of finding a precedent, you see, not in the legal adoption of an artifactual, um, person.'

'Sorry!' Roderick's feet made a loud clattering sound as he got down from his chair. 'Sorry!' He stumped over to the window.

'In fact it er can't really be considered a person at all, a person in law I mean, not as things stand. Better to just establish a trust, call it a pet and leave everything in the hands of trustees, funds delegated to the ah care and feeding and so on. But no, I see that doesn't appeal to you, heh heh, we country attorneys get pretty good at reading faces, see the pet idea upsets you, right?'

The Christmas decorations were up all along Main Street.

In fact they had been up since September and would remain until January 2, when the Easter stuff went up. People bustled back and forth across the street, loading their cars with presents and holly and squashed-down trees and cases of bottles. If Roderick put his head to the pane he could hear music.

'So even if you don't like the trust arrangement now, keep your options open, Mrs W., keep it in the back of your mind because my guess is in the long run it'll be the cheapest, most direct way. Of course the first thing there would be to establish ownership, right? You need your bill of sale or your deed of gift, otherwise the real beneficiary of the trust might turn out to be anyone who could establish prior ownership, prior to your possession through say loan or rental, they would of course be entitled to all monies accruing to their rightful property including any or all interest devolving upon it, from any trust or estate.'

> O come all ye faithful!
> Come to Fellstus Motors!
> Trade-ins are guaranteed
> You bet your life.

'See you're still not too stuck on the idea, so just let me point out to you a few of the substantial tax benefits, such as depreciation under the Class Life Asset Depreciation Range System, assuming Roddy here was put into service after January 1, 1971 which of course it was, I can see by just looking that this is an expensive piece of machinery that – No, okay, right, I'll stop trying to sell you on that idea.'

The cars were all caked with dried mud, the people all looked squashed down and, for all the bustle, no one was smiling.

> Come in and see us
> We can work out so-omething

'Well the easiest way to make Roddy a person in law is to just incorporate it – him, I mean – under the laws of maybe the Virgin Islands, that way no need to go into his antecedents not in the Virgin -- but no, I see you're thinking of going all out and trying to prove it in court, that Roddy is albeit artifactual – a ward of court? Sure but first there's this really tricky – this unprecedented – it's like this: we can argue that its, his inventors began with a living body person in law and that it then underwent extensive replacements. Only one precedent there, case of a knife without a blade which had no handle if you know what I mean.'

> O come let us advise you
> O come let us surprise you
> See what your money buys you
> A price
>   you can
>   afford!

'What do you mean?' said Roderick. 'A knife without a blade which had no handle?'

Mr Swann smiled at him but continued. 'See, this Supreme Court case, St Filomena's Hospital versus Mann. The Mann family contending that the hospital had replaced so much of their daughter's body that she was no longer legally their daughter so they could refuse responsibility for the hospital bill. Plaintiff arguing though that the continuity of certain well-defined functions – anyway the case established the principle that with functional continuity, total cell replacement would be acceptable without jeopardizing legal identity, that is for insurance and tax purposes. So far of course we have no precedents regarding brain replacement, but if we argued that if it was replaced a bit at a time, say the right frontal lobe then the left then the right something else and so on, see the key is functional continence, continuance, continuity. So we say Roddy here is just some kid who's undergone a whole-body prosthesis, more or less, and . . . but I ought to warn you, this could run into money.'

Ma stood up. 'It already is, Mr Swann. Every time I come here you tell me some new complication, some new wrinkle – last time it was what if the court considered him an un-authorized data bank, publisher demanding payment every time he reads a library book, and would we be allowed to show him any copyright material without prior consent, was it?'

'Hey, but mister what about that knife with –'

'Very good, Mrs W., I did go into that but only in connection with the possibility of setting him up as a literary property like a comic book or a sheet of music, abandoned that avenue didn't we on account of the fifty-year reversion to the public domain but don't –' He had to shout the last as she and Roderick left, 'Don't worry Mrs W., we'll explore every possible ave –'

Roderick continued thinking about that knife.

He was still thinking about it a few days later when Pa took him along to Dr Welby's office.

'*Good* to see you, Pa, looking better eh? Good, good. Any more trouble from the old, eh? No? Good, good. Now let's just listen to the, ah. *Very* good. Just wish all my patients your age had half as much, er, ahm. Eh?'

Pa said, 'Well this cough is worse, and I can't seem to sleep, doc. Them pills you prescribed seem to –'

'Uh-oh? Side-effects! Still, not abnormal in these cases. Thanodorm often starts off like that, supposed to make you sleep only at first keeps you wide awake, eh? But it's working, it's just taking hold.'

'Fine, only it ain't Thanodorm, it's Toxidol. That's what it says on the bottle.'

'You give it another week, then if you don't sleep like a baby, okay fine, I'll try Toxidol. Didn't know you were familiar with that, Pa, hardly ever use it myself.' Dr Welby beamed over his platinum-rimmed glasses. 'Gets so a doctor has a heck of a time keeping up with his patients, eh?'

'No but doc, I'm taking Toxidol right now. You were the one who –'

Welby stopped smiling and pushed a button on his desk. 'Pa, just ask yourself, "Is it worth it?"'

A woman in white rushed in. Dr Welby said: 'Jean, Mr Wood has just admitted to me that he's taking medication not prescribed by me. Toxidont, make a note of it.'

'Toxidol,' said Pa.

'Make a note of that, too. Can't be too careful in case of

any malpractice hassles later, eh?' The woman rushed out.

'Malp – no, doc, listen I –'

More beaming over the platinum. 'Pa, do yourself a big favour, eh? Just stop. Throw away this medication wherever you got it, throw it out. Otherwise I'll just have to call it quits. Will you promise to throw it out?'

'Sure, but –'

'No buts. Just promise me. Hell man, you don't know what you might be taking there, this Taxiderm could be *lethal*. I kid you not.'

'I – I promise.'

'Goooood. *Good*. Knew I could depend on you. Together, Pa, we'll lick this condition of yours – the haemorrhaging, the dandruff, the works – eh? Just throw away all the junk you're taking, the Taxicob and all the rest of it – and stick to the stuff I gave you. And Pa? Trust me.'

They went out on Main Street, where the recorded carollers were just finishing 'Noël Noël Noël Noël, Get an extra six-pack 'cause you never can tell...' and into Joradsen's Drug where old Mr Joradsen said:

'Merry Christmas, Pa. But get that thing out of here, no pets.'

'Well he –'

'No pets! Not my rule, it's the law!'

So Roderick waited outside, listening to a local version of Handel's *Messiah* and to the comments of passing shoppers.

'Never oughta allow a thing like that out in public!'

'... and not even tied up...'

'Makes you sick just to look...'

The sky seemed to be pressing down on the low roofs of Main Street. Handel without words without meaning. Okay, it worked, it might work if the knife lost its blade and you put on a new one, and then it lost its handle – but suppose you had two knives and you switched handles, were they still the same? Or did whatever it was that made them themselves go with the handles? Do you switch handles or switch blades?

'Hey Rick boy, you nuts or something? Standing here talking to yourself about switchblades...'

'Oh hi, Chaunce. No I just, I was just thinking out loud.'

'My old man would buy me a switchblade any time I asked

222

him, you know? Like two feet long! Hey you know you really blasted that old school computer boy, they can't even take roll any more. No tests, no nothin', it's great. I owe you one, pal.'

But when his gang showed up a minute later, Chauncey seemed to change his mind.

Pa found Roderick lying in front of Virgil's Hometown Hardware, one of his new legs broken.

'Scrapping again? My boy –'

'I'm sorry, Pa. We were playing *Ratstar*, you know like the movie, and I was the alien see, Mung Fungal –'

'Okay, okay.' Pa lifted him up so that he could see the display in Virgil's window: axes, hunting knives, hammers and handguns arranged in the shape of a Christmas tree, with a tinsel message hanging above: TO MEN OF GOOD WILL.

'Reminds me,' Pa chuckled. 'Gotta see Swann about makin' my will.'

15

SOME LAWS OF ROBOTICS (II)

Robots can think and smell and hear and talk.
They've got metal minds.
My robot is a lady companion robot and it's a maid
and it goes out and does the shopping for a man.
My robot is an electric robot and it exterminates
people. A robot is a man's companion. They keep
their master company and take orders from him.
It must be an awful life being a robot because all
you do is take orders.
Robots are always men ... If I had a robot I wouldn't
even have to think because he would do everything for me.

Pupils at Rhyl Primary School, London

'Eeeeeep!'

'Hold it a minute, son.' Pa made an adjustment with a screwdriver. 'Now try.'

Roderick moved his hand once more into the candle-flame. '*Eeep*. Blip.' He jerked it back. 'Pa, I don't think I like this pain stuff. I know you said it was for my own protection and all but – ouch! – I still don't – ow! – don't like it.'

'You'll learn how to handle it, Roddy. Everybody does. Or maybe they don't, who knows? All I know is, we gotta find some way of keeping you out of fights. You don't understand now, but you will.'

Ma came in wearing one purple glove. 'Ready, son? We're going to see your new school.'

'Aw gee.' Roderick slid down off the work-bench, feeling the thump when his feet hit the floor. 'Ow, I mean how come I gotta go to Holy Trinity? That's where all the catlicker kids go. Chauncey says they all got webbed feet!'

'They don't,' said Ma. 'Chauncey Bangfield told you a lot of things that weren't true, didn't he?'

'S'pose so.'

'He told you his father was a famous astronaut, instead of a fat bald real estate agent.'

He decided to repeat no more of Chaunce's dark warnings. Holy Trinity School was an old brick building next to the cemetery, where every Saturday they put up a sign, Nearly New Sale, Bargains Galore, Bring the Family. Chaunce said the sisters went out every night and robbed the graves to get bones for their weird rituals, 'mass' and all that. Everybody knew there were mass graves, like the ones on the news in Ruritania.

Roderick said nothing more until they were standing before the dark building. 'Wow!' he said.

'What is it?'

'Chauncey *said* they had a guy nailed to the wall – wow!'

'It's just an emblem,' she said. 'Kind of a – well, a good-luck charm. Come on.'

The school was dark inside and smelled of floor-wax. A frail old woman in black got up from her knees with difficulty to greet them. 'I'm. Sister. Mary. Martha,' she said, wheezing. 'You. must. be. Mrs. Wood. You'll. be. wanting Fath. er O'Bride.' She directed them upstairs to a door with another strange emblem: a white-and-red circular picture of a satanic tiger, with the name 'Holy Trinity Hellcats.'

Roderick had seen Fathers in movies before: they wore long black gowns and white collars, and when they weren't singing 'Going My Way' they were taking cigarettes away from kids and saying God's an all-right guy who's on the level.

Father O'Bride wore a sweatshirt with the sleeves torn off, a fishing hat covered with hooks, bright plaid trousers. His feet, in sneakers, were on the desk, waggling as he talked on the phone. His free hand twitched a fishing-rod.

'Oh uh sit down, sit down. With you in a minute. Yeah, Charlie, I'm still here. And I still don't like the sound of that price. Listen, I know wholesale on basketball jerseys, and I know a fat markup when I ... Overheads for, cripes, *what* overheads? The things are seconds, you and I know the factory practically pays you to haul ... yeah well don't talk to me about middlemen, I still work it out at two-twenty-four less discount, yeah okay, plus state tax ... yah?'

He looked down the long office to a filing cabinet on top of which rested a biretta. With a flick of the rod, he sent a hook flying down to snag the hat's pompon. 'Have a heart, Charlie, we don't have a big fat State budget behind us ... okay but does two-thirty-one include the name or ... okay and get it right this time? H-E-L-L-C-A-T-S, one word? Not like those baseball uniforms you picked up from, Korea was it? I mean it didn't exactly do the old team spirit a heck of a lot of good being Holy Trinity Hub Caps all season, know what I mean? Point oh seven one, how'dya like that for a percentage, bottom of the league, even Saint Peter shut us out, we spanked Saint Theresa but then Saint Bart massacred us, Cosmos & Damien took a double-header, we got singed by St Joan and slaughtered by Holy Inno's, Pete decked us again and then a no-hitter surprise from St Sebastian – well, it's the old story. Let me get back to you Charlie ...'

He hung up and went to retrieve the fly from his biretta. 'Sorry about that folks, kinda busy here ... well. So this is little Roderick! How ya doin', fella?' He shook hands with the robot.

'Don't be shy, kid, we're all on the same team here. God's team.'

'Oh.'

'Look, I know you probably feel awful about getting benched over at the public school, but we don't hold that against you. Over here, nobody's second-string, see? We're all in there, giving it all we got. You play ball with God, and you can bet your a – your bottom dollar he'll play ball with you.'

'That figures,' said Roderick. Ma seemed preoccupied with the view out of the window.

'Ha ha, what I mean is, here at Holy Trin we're like a team. Myself and the sisters are like coaches, you kids are the players. And all this –' His gesture took in wall pennants, a tennis-racket in its stretcher, a bag of golf-clubs, skis. 'All this is just a training camp, see? For the big game. The big game is when you leave here, my kid. The big game is life. You want to play to win, right?'

Roderick nodded.

'Great! Now you run along while your mother and I talk over a few details. Go out and look over the playground, we got the works: regulation baseball and softball diamonds, gridiron, tennis, lacrosse, ... Now Mrs Wood, let me put you in the picture here, we don't usually take kids in mid-season, term I mean, glad to make an exception if you can manage the full year's tuition. I understand the boy's not Catholic. No, well then if you want him kept out of religion classes there's an exemption fee too. Then the fees for basic gym-gear, uniforms, locker, use of the field and gym-equipment, oh yeah and books. Now I'm talking in the neighbourhood of ...'

Sister Olaf was a large woman with a face like a peeled potato. She put Roderick in the advanced reading and arithmetic classes, but rookie religion. Everything seemed easy until they came to the catechism.

'Who made you?' she asked James, the first boy in the row.

'God made me.'

'Why did God make you?'

'To know, love and serve Him in this world and to be happy with Him in the next.'

'Who made you?' she asked Roberta, the next girl. Roberta answered in identical words, as did Anthony and Ursula.

'Now Roderick: who made you?'

'Me?'

'Come on, you must know the answer by now. It's right there in the book.'

'Sure but I –'

'What?'

'Well I'm not sure.'

'Well! Who made James and Roberta and Anthony and Ursula?'

'God, I guess.'

'Who made *you*?'

Behind him, Catherine whispered, 'God, stupid.'

Roderick turned round. 'Well maybe God made you, but I'm pretty sure Dan Sonnenschein made me. Him and some other men in a laboratory. See they –'

'That's enough!' The face became a creased sweet potato.

'You may get away with disrupting classes over in the public school, but not here. I want you to sit in that corner over there until you remember who made you?' And though he sat in the corner for an hour (while Sister Olaf explained how Caesar Augustus was taxing the whole world...) he could not work out any other answer.

She sent him to see Father O'Bride.

'Sit down, kid, just got this package to open – oh no. Will you look at that?' He spread one of the white t-shirts over his desk. The red letters across the chest read, Holy Trinity Hellbats.

'Last darned time I do business with that crook, with all his discount stuff from Iraq or is it Iran – I've had it. You know, ever since those Jesuits sank all that money in fake oil stock in Texas, everybody thinks we're all suckers. Priests aren't supposed to know the first thing about dollars and cents, I guess. Has he got a surprise coming, wait'll I stop his darned cheque – Well now what is it, kid? Making trouble for Sister Olaf already are you?'

'No sir I mean no Father, see it's just this Baltimore catty kisum, like where they ask who made you. Sister thinks I oughta say God made me, all I said was maybe He made the people but he didn't make the robots.'

'Robots, eh?' Father O'Bride had very pale eyes that didn't blink much. 'What's this, something outa these crappy science fiction movies you been seeing? Boy, if you didn't have this disability you'd be in the gym right now doing *fifty laps*, we'd find out who made you *if we had to take you apart*.

'But, you're lucky. I'm giving you one more chance.' He searched among the t-shirts and tattered copies of sports magazines until he found a catechism. 'I'm giving you one more chance before I turn you over to – well, somebody else.' He opened the book. 'Now tell me: Who made you?'

'Dan Sonnenschein and some other guys, in this lab –'

'*For Pete's sake, who made this Dan whatsit?*'

'I don't know – God?'

'God. And if God made him and he made you, then he was just the instrument of God's will, right? My mother and father brought me into this world too, but I still know God made me.'

'Yeah but –'

'No buts. Look, if a guy hits it out of the park nobody jumps up to cheer the bat, do they? Same thing, the bat is just an instrument of the batter's will. Get it? I mean who made the home run, the batter or the bat?'

'Well God I guess if he made the –'

'Okay, fine. You get the point. Now –'

'Only if God made Dan and Dan made me, who made this God?'

'RIGHTY-HO!' The book hit the desk and tumbled off, taking a few Hellbats to the floor. 'BUDDY BOY YOU HAVE JUST EARNED YOURSELF A TICKET TO SEE THE MAN HIMSELF!'

'The...' Excitement made Roderick hurt all over. He couldn't work up the words to ask who this man might be.

A big hand clamped down on his shoulder. He was half-dragged, half-carried down the hall, downstairs, past Sister Mary Martha (still polishing the same spot on the floor) outside and across the street where in the vanilla slush he could see the marks of a tractor tyre, a lost mitten, the marks of another tractor tyre. Everything was so clear, full of, of clearness. To God's house? No, past it to the rectory, a black brick building with snow in the yard, and black weeds sticking up out of the snow. Roderick thought he recognized a withered sunflower (Ma had told him the story of Vincent, who put his ear to the sunflower to hear the roaring of the sun inside, and instantly his ear was burnt away) and into the black hall where he was made to sit on a black chair and WAIT JUST WAIT BUDDY BOY while Father O'Bride went off through a polished black door.

The thing about Vincent was, he wanted to paint the sun inside the golden sunflower and it drove him crazy, and now everybody was crazy about cheap reproductions of his paintings which they thought looked good in their kitchens.

Roderick looked at the cheap reproduction over his head. It showed a woman at a piano, with a gold ring hanging in the air over her head. She was looking up too, maybe at the ring or maybe just at some other cheap reproduction.

Ma would never look at a cheap reproduction, not even when Pa tried to show her *La Divina Proportione* with pictures by Leonardo Da Vinci when he said about the seed spirals

229

in the sunflower and how they were Fibonacci numbers,
getting closer and closer to the divine proportion but only
an infinite sunflower could be God, and she said That's all
you know, God *wears* an infinite sunflower in his buttonhole
every day, a fresh one every day from his own garden, God
is an infinite reason. Yes but the divine proportion is an
irrational number said Pa, see it's the sum of one plus one
over one plus one over one plus ... Ma didn't care, all ones
are one, mathematics is just a cheap trick where everything's
a copy of something else, like those Fibonacci numbers
$1 + 1 = 2$, $1 + 2 = 3$, $2 + 3 = 5$, $3 + 5 = 8$, and so on with
13, 21, 34, 55, where did it all get you, no wonder poor
Vincent went stark staring irrational trying to paint the
blazing sum I mean sun you've got me doing it now and
all those cheap reproductions they copy everything sometimes I think you and I are just cheap copies of something
somebody read somewhere, 'prints' they like to call them,
'prints' when that awful woman in the Ladies' Guild kept
saying she really liked her prints, I thought she meant her
dog, but no, there she was with sunflowers copied from
sunflowers Vincent copied from sunflowers copied from the
sun ...

Roderick heard voices from behind the polished black
door.

'... more your league ...'

'... I see. Then where does he get this ... ?'

'Beats me, don't think he's really nuts, but you never ...
well yeah, guess his mother did try to tell me something about
this robot idea he's got only I had this long-distance call just
about then, bad connection I could hardly hear the guy,
thought he was trying to sell us a P.A. system for the gym,
it was only a lousy pietà.'

'And you mentioned ... ological difficulties ... Okay, bring
him in.'

Father O'Bride came out, grabbed him and trundled him
through the black door to meet Father Warren.

Father Warren didn't look much like The Man Himself.
He did at least look like a priest, all in black. He could be
a lot older than Father O'Bride or a lot younger, but he was
definitely a lot thinner and darker, with a narrow pair of

eyes, a narrow blue chin and long narrow hands. The hands kept kneading each other on the desk, as though trying to restore circulation.

'Sit down, Roderick. Relax.' His voice was deep and liquid, like the voice telling you to use Thong deodorant ('Thonng'). One of the hands reached towards a silver cigarette-box, then withdrew to a silver dish of taffy. 'Candy?'

Roderick shook his head.

'Advent, I understand. Well now. Yes.' He sat back and stared at Roderick until the robot looked away. The room was comfortable enough, and not at all religious: one little statue of Our Lady stood at the other end on its own little stand; it might have been a potted vine or a parrot-cage for all the difference it made here with the fireplace, easy-chairs, table lamps and magazine racks, the bookcases, the deep carpet.

'Father O'Bride tells me you've been having a little trouble with your catechism.'

'Yes sir, yes Father.'

'And that you claim to be a robot?'

'Yes, Father.'

'Father O'Bride thinks you read too much science fiction.'

'I don't even know what it is, Father.'

'No? Hmm.' The hands played a game of church-and-steeple. 'Look, you can be honest with me. I don't disapprove of science fiction, not at all. In fact I read it myself. In *fact* I have a few books here, any time you feel like borrowing one, just help yourself.' He swivelled in his chair and reached down a paperback. '*I, Robot*, by Isaac Asimov. Tried that yet? Here, take it along.'

'Thanks, Father.' He started to get up.

'When you go, that is. I think first we ought to, to "rap" a little, get to know each other. After all, I don't get too many chances in a country parish like this, to talk to *real robots*.' The smirk never reached his dark eyes.

'Talk?'

'Tell me a little about this, this "guy" you say invented you.'

'Gee I don't know much, just that his name is Dan Sonnen-

231

schein. But he and some other guys I guess they just went in this lab and maybe mixed up some chemicals and stuff and – here I am.'

'And no mother involved?'

'No, Father. I mean no mother, Father. No father either, Father.' He paused. 'I mean there's Ma and Pa, but they're both adopted, they're not real.'

'Not real. I see.' The long fingers began squeezing one another. 'Not real. Hmm, not, not *real*.'

'Not real parents I mean.'

'I understand you don't think God is "real" either?'

When Roderick slipped off his shoe, his foot just reached the top of the deep carpet pile. He started running it back and forth to feel the slight pain that wasn't really painful. 'I don't know. All I said was, if Dan made me and God made Dan, who made God? Father O'Bride got awful mad then.'

'Yes well ... Tell me, Roderick, have you ever looked up at the stars, and wondered?'

'Wondered?'

'How it all got there: millions on millions of little points of light, each one a great big sun, perhaps a sun with planets like our own Terra, perhaps with intelligent beings like us – but millions on millions of these suns, so far apart that the light from them takes centuries to reach us – haven't you ever wondered how that all came about? Who made it?'

'Sure, Father. I figure maybe it was just always there. Or else maybe it just popped up one day and there it was. Or maybe it –'

'Yes yess, I can see you've thought about it. Now –'

'– makes itself. Or heck, does it need to be made anyhow? Couldn't it just –'

'Fine, yes, that's enough. But tell me, don't you ever wonder if there isn't something – or Someone – behind it all? Even if the universe "makes itself", who arranged it that way? Eh? Eh?'

'I don't know, Father. What's the point of wondering if you can't find out the answer?'

'Ah!' The fingers came together, forming a little cage. 'Just that!'

'Huh?'

'What's the point of wondering? The "point" is, here you are, wondering what the point is.'

'...?'

'That is to say, God is the Ultimate Mystery, the Paradox of Paradoxes – by the way, do you know what a paradox is?'

'Sure Father, don't you?' Roderick sat up. 'It's like a sign that says "Don't Read Signs". Or like, like priests, if they want to have kids they have to stop being Fathers.'

'Yes fine, but what I meant was, God is – is unknowable. Great minds have been racking their brains for centuries trying to answer questions about Him, and – and getting nowhere fast, you might say. He is All Good, yet allows evil to exist in His world, the world He made. He is All Powerful, yet He allows people to disobey Him. He knows the future, yet we are still free to choose how we will live our lives. He is All Loving, yet allows His beloved Son to die on the Cross. He –'

'Father I don't get any of this. Especially the stuff about the Cross, the sacrafice Sister Olaf called it. But I mean in chess a sacrafice is just a sucker play – Father O'Bride says it's the same in baseball – so how come this All Smart God fell for it?'

'Fell for...?'

'I mean here he had everybody just where he wanted them, he was going to send everybody to Hell, right? So I mean if he takes the Son instead his game position has gotta be worse after, right? I mean the only reason you make a sacrafice is to force the other guy to give you a better deal, sucker him into it, yeah? Like Father O'Bride does all the time with his t-shirt deals –'

'Stop, stop, stop! Wait, wait a minute, wait...' Father Warren seemed to be having trouble with his hands, the fingers knotting and tangling almost as though the hemispheres of his brain were at war. 'I can see we'll need a lot more work. A *lot* more work, if you ... if you think that God ... "game position"!'

'Yeah but Father is that what you meant by God being a paradox? How he was so pleased to get a chance to nail

233

his Son there that he even gave up his plan to fry the whole world in Hell?'

When the hands were finally under control, the priest said, 'Let's, let's leave it at that for today, okay?'

When the little robot had slid from its chair and waddled out of the room, Father Warren shuddered. 'Game position!' What kind of world was it to make a child think like that? It was a cry for help from a fettered soul, for sure. Fettered in a broken body too – the pathos of it reminded him of a passage in *That Hideous Strength*, a man experimentally about to trample a crucifix, arrested by the simple helplessness of the wooden figure:

Not because its hands were nailed and helpless, but because they were only made of wood and therefore even more helpless, because the thing, for all its realism, was inanimate and could not in any way hit back...

16

The Devil tricks us with puppets, to which he has glued angels' wings.

E. T. A. Hoffmann, *The Jesuit Church at Glogau*

The blizzard outside kept repeating all the long vowels to itself. Roderick was in his room reading *I, Robot*, wondering when the I character was going to put in an appearance. There must be one, because otherwise the author would have called it *He, Robot*, or *They, Robots*. He couldn't imagine how it would feel, being hooked up to these three terrible laws of robotics, that –

The garage door creaked in a way that could not be the wind. Roderick crept downstairs and found Pa shivering and coughing in his workroom.

'Pa, what are you –?'

'Shh, don't wake Ma. Do me a favour, son. Put my coat by the kitchen stove and dry it off, will you? If Ma finds it wet in the morning she'll throw a tizzy.'

'Well sure but – hey Pa how come you're all dripping wet and your coat is still dry inside?'

'Took it off. To uh, wrap some stuff I was carrying.'

'What stuff, hey?'

'Just stuff, spare parts.' Pa suppressed a heaving cough. 'Don't say anything to Ma, okay? Our little secret.'

Roderick carried the wet mackinaw out of the room, but did not close the door quite shut. He put his eye to the crack and looked in.

But all he could see was Pa's hand, hanging up a key under the picture of Rex Reason. He went back upstairs to say his prayers:

'Our Father, if we have one, Who might be in Heaven, if there is one . . .'

*　　　*　　　*

There was an awful lot of God at school, but whenever Roderick tried to ask a question, Sister Olaf just looked cross and told him to take it up with Father Warren. So he tried working it out for himself.

The Holy Trinity must be a lot like in the Oz stories. After all, God was God the Father, but God was also the Holy Trinity, the place where He or She lived with two friends. Oz was just like that: it was this terrific wizard who could do anything, and it was also the place where he lived. Anyway, OZ = PA, that was plain, and nobody knew what Oz (or God) looked like.

God the Father was so wise that his wisdom turned into this pigeon called the Holy Ghost. Couldn't that be the Scarecrow? Crows and pigeons being birds, and ghosts being scarey. The Scarecrow was always worried about fire, too, and didn't Sister Olaf say something about the H.G. turning into tongues of flame? Well then.

The Father and H.G. loved each other a lot and had this Son, the one you always saw pointing to his shiny heart and smiling. That just about had to be the Tin Woodman. He too was a carpenter, and Oz gave him a heart made out of shiny silk.

Dorothy was kind of a problem until he read through his book of Bible stories. Because in this house at Bethany, God the Son was just sitting there when this woman came up and poured oil all over him – just the way Dorothy poured oil all over the Tin Woodman!

That just about settled it. Roderick didn't bother much with the minor characters like Mary (= MA = Ozma), the story all seemed strong enough without them. Only one thing bothered him:

Oz kept acting like such a slippery character. It was almost as if he didn't have any real power at all. As if he faked it.

Pa said there wasn't any God, and both stories were hokum.

Ma said everybody was God, and no story was ever hokum.

Sister Olaf just got mad.

'Blasphemy, and this close to Christmas!'

'Well yeah I thought Father Warren was taking care of

this kid. Been meaning to have another little pow-wow with him myself, Sister, only you know how it's been what with trying to squeeze in a couple more basketball games before our Centre eats himself sick at Christmas and gets all outa shape, and what with trying to schedule early training for the baseball team. You know if I didn't keep after these kids our whole sports programme would go right down the tubes...'

Sister Olaf twisted the rosary on her belt. 'He seems to think he's preparing for his First Communion right along with all the others, that's the problem. Not even baptized, I wonder if he even understands what a sincere confession is, and anyway.'

'Anyway?'

'The poor little thing doesn't even seem to have a mouth.'

'He must eat somehow.' Father O'Bride finished cleaning his rifle and squinted down the barrel at her.

'Eat? I'm not so sure, Father. We never find him in the refectory at lunch hour, he's always lurking around the playground by himself or just sitting reading the Bible – and once I caught him carrying out the garbage for Sister Mary Martha!'

'Uh-oh, can't have that. You put a stop to it?'

'Of course, a child could hurt himself carrying those heavy cans. Besides, the Community agreed that since Sister Mary Martha is too old to teach, housework is her little duty. Her little cross. And she takes it up joyfully.'

Father O'Bride found such expressions embarrassing. He tugged at the neckband of his sweatshirt as though it were a tight white collar. 'Little too joyfully, if you ask me. I mean, she keeps polishing that same spot in the hall out there, I darn near broke my neck on it this morning. None of my business, of course, up to Mother Sup – and of course we all think the Sisters are doing one heck of a great job here, batting a thous –'

'Whether the poor little pagan eats or not, Father, he doesn't seem ready to make his First. It's hard to get through to him, he seems to get everything mixed up with fairy tales and robot stories and I don't know what. When I started telling the class about the Flight into Egypt, he kept interrupting to ask about the Deadly Desert, and Dorothy and Toto – yes and wasn't Bethlehem where the steel came from, the metallic conception he called it! The metallic conception!'

Father O'Bride hated dealing with out-of-bounds decisions like these. He looked up for inspiration, but saw only a poster advertising the sign of the cross. Superimposed on a boy was a baseball diamond. The legend said: BE SURE TO TOUCH ON ALL BASES. 'Look, take him out of religion altogether for now, let Father Warren handle that department. Teamwork, right?'

'All right, and –'

'Who knows, kid might shape up by next season anyway. If not, well, we hold him in reserve, bench him but maybe let him work out once in a while with the A squad...'

Sister Olaf went back to her class, pausing to check on Sister Mary Martha. The old woman was once more polishing the same little spot of hall floor, already mirror-bright. Have to do something about her, poor old forgetful ... sees her own face in it, her own lost ... now as in a glass, darkly, but soon ... slippery as glass ... glass slipp – stop that! She shook herself out of it, nodded at the crouching figure, and passed on. Upstairs Father O'Bride kicked his office door shut, but not before she heard him say, 'Call that a little thing do you Charlie? I'm trying to start spring training here and my boys gotta work out in uniforms with that on 'em? *Bell Caps*, you call that –?'

The door slammed and there was no sound but the children's choir practice.

A disappointment. All that work on the Bible stories and the catechism for nothing, just because of some lousy regulation. And Sister O. wouldn't even tell him what the lousy regulation was – just that he wasn't going to have religion with the other kids any more, and he probably wouldn't be making his First in May.

He guessed what the regulation was, something to do with his not being a meat person. Meat people got to die and go to the Emerald City and be happy with God forever and ever, and what did he get? Next to nothing. No matter how good he was, all he could count on was lousy Limbo, with a bunch of yelling babies around and nobody to talk to.

It didn't seem fair, not after he'd worked so hard. Extra work, even, like when they had that bit about the Word becoming Flesh and he got to school early one morning and worked it all out on the blackboard:

WORD
wood
mood
moot
moat
MEAT

As usual, that made Sister O. real mad and she told him to stand in the corner and ask forgiveness and never call people meat again.

Heck they called them meat in Oz, anyway it was no worse than calling somebody a bunch of letters. She didn't even care that he used 'moot' – a word half the kids didn't even know was in the dictionary – nor that he was showing the whole thing right there, words turning into words.

Holy cow. Sister O. even threatened to yank him out of the Christmas play, just because he got mixed up in rehearsal and forgot his line ('Here's the frankincense, Jesus') and said:

'Jesus! Here's the Frankenstein!'

Holy cow.

And here it was the last day of school before Christmas, the last afternoon of the last day, all he had now was this *wrap session* with Father Warren . . .

Mrs Feeney, the old housekeeper, showed him into the study. She reminded Roderick a lot of Sister Mary Martha, except she moved faster and cleaned more stuff, and except she never smiled.

'The Father will be here in a minute,' she said. 'Now you sit *right there and don't touch a thing.*'

'The chair? I mean . . .'

'Don't give me no lip, neither.' She went out, polishing door-knobs behind her. He sat for what seemed like a minute, then got up and went to see what was on the desk. A silver cigarette-box, candy dish and lighter – those would be Father

239

Warren's. A spring grip developer and an electronic thing for keeping golf scores – Father O'Bride's. The other stuff could be anybody's. A stack of blank magnetic cards, each one headed A.M.D.G., a desk-set in onyx plastic and a letter:

... His Grace notes your request for approval of the Holy Trinity School team name, 'Hell Cats', and asks me to write, strongly urging you to reconsider. Any association of the name of the Holy G̶ Trinity with Hell is to be avoided, being distasteful at least! Your a̶l̶t̶a̶r̶ alternative suggestion 'Hep Cats' is not all together acceptable either.

In these troubled times, the Church must avoid giving s̶c̶a̶n̶d̶l̶e̶ scandal even in small matters. World Communism is on the prowl, seeking whom it may devour, p̶r̶a̶ preying on the weak and ignorant. We trust you will keep all this in mind and consider less contr̶a̶o-versial alternatives such as 'Tornadoes' or 'Tigers'. Or why not a name inspired by some popular saint, e.g., Patrick: The 'Sham Rocks' ...

Father Warren came in kneading his hands. 'Well now, have you read that book I lent you?'

'Yes Father, I mean I read all the words and looked them up and all, only I still couldn't understand it.'

'Ah. Might be a little hard for such a young –'

'I mean on the very first page there's these three laws of robots and they don't make any sense.'

'Ah! The famous Three Laws of Robotics? They make perfect sense. Believe me, this is airtight logic.' He quoted from memory, counting fingers. 'First, "A robot may not injure a human being, or, through inaction, allow a human being to come to harm." Seems plain enough. Second, "A robot must obey the orders given it by human beings except where such orders would conflict with the First Law." No nonsense there. And third, "A robot must protect its own existence as long as such protection does not conflict with the First or Second Law." Now which of these gives you trouble?'

'Well all of them. Look Father I'm a robot and I don't –'

'Still insisting on that, are we? Roderick, do me a favour. Take this pin.' The priest plucked a pin from a desk drawer and held it out. 'Go on take it. Now, stick me with it.'

'*What?*'

'Stick the pin in my hand there, go on. You're supposed to be a robot, so I'm ordering you, go on.'

'Yeah but – well okay.' Roderick made a weak swipe with the pin, raising a tiny scratch on the back of the hand.

'Ouch!' Father Warren smiled. 'You have just proved that you can't possibly be a robot. You violated the First Law.'

Roderick watched a drop of blood form on the scratch. 'I guess so. Only –'

'No guessing about it. Logic says you can either be a robot or stick me with a pin, but not both.'

'Yeah that's logic all right, but only if you go along with these here three laws. But I mean they're only in stories and this is real life. I mean like in the Oz stories they just got one law in Oz, "Behave yourself". Only in real life people don't, do they?'

'No, Roderick, but listen –'

'And like this here other story about the man going up on the mountain and getting these here pills with laws on them, heck even by the time he gets down the mountain everybody's breaking the laws all over the place, worshipping a golden leg and –'

'No, listen –'

'I mean like nobody ever pays attention to the laws except like cops and Sheriff Benson and maybe lawyers like Perry Ma – What was *that*?' He referred to a series of rapid explosions that seemed to come from the floor.

'Nothing, just Father O'Bride getting in some target practice, he's got a little gallery rigged up in the base, but wait, listen, the point is, *in real life there are no robots*, not real thinking, humanoid creatures. They're all in stories. And in these stories, they have to obey the Three Laws. Right?'

'Maybe, but even in stories they have to have big arguments about laws, look at Perry Mason, holy cow they argue all the time about whether somebody did or didn't break this here law, holy cow Mr Swann makes all his money just telling people how to get around the law.'

'Roderick, let me explain: there are two kinds of law. You're talking about legal statutes, yes of course people can break those. Just as they can break moral laws like the Ten

241

Commandments. But there's also another kind of law, natural law. That includes things like the law of gravity, or the law that says $2 + 2 = 4$, or the law that says if Tom is taller than Dick and Dick is taller than Harry, then Tom must be taller than Harry. And you see, nobody on earth can break laws like those. And so robots are programmed in such a way that the Three Laws are their natural laws. They can't be broken.'

'Yeah but how? How can they program a robot to obey some dumb law he can't even understand? Like first thing he needs to know who's a human being and who ain't. Like I heard this old guy by the post office saying the president was a son of a bitch and somebody ought to shoot him. I'm just saying what he said, Father. But with these dumb laws a robot could hear that and get a gun and go shoot the president because he's only a dog so it's okay.'

'Now you're just being silly. Everybody knows the president is human.'

'Yeah, but the Robotic Law don't say how a robot's supposed to find out who's human and who's robots, like what's he supposed to do, go see Mr Swann every time he wants to stick a pin in a doll or –'

'Excuse me for a minute . . .' The priest hurried out, lifting his skirts as he thumped down the basement stairs into the dark gallery.

Father O'Bride was a shadowy alien, with a pair of bright orange ear-protectors standing out from the sides of his head like insect eyes. And wasn't that a picture of the Pope he was shooting at?

'What? Whatsa matter?' O'Bride took off the ear-protectors and automatically kissed their strap before putting them down. 'You still crapping around tryina convert that Wood brat?'

'He . . . gets on my nerves sometimes.'

'Little smart-ass, needs fifty laps, that's what he needs.'

'. . . tried everything, I've tried talking to him about Space-ship Earth even, how if he were an alien landing here –'

'Excuse me while I throw up. I can't stand all that space crap, can't stand that kid either. You know what?'

'– how the alien would wonder Who are we? Where do we come from? Where are we going?'

242

'Yeah but you know what?'

'But listen, I told him we came from the mind of God, and he – he just said, "Pa thinks we're all apes who got tired of picking fleas and grunting" not even seven years old and he –'

'Yeah but you know what I think?'

'Where are we going, to the destiny God prepared for us, he came right out with how his mother says when people die they turn into ether and rise up through seven astral planes –'

'You know what I think? I think the kid *is* a darn robot.'

Bzzt bzz-bzzz bzzzt bzz? said the telephone on the desk. Phones that were still cradled shouldn't be saying anything. Roderick crept closer and listened.

'. . . sure this thing's on? I can't hear a fucking . . .'

'Look, I know my stuff, not like that hick O'Smith . . . hire a fucking amateur and then wonder what went wrong, man they never learn . . .'

'. . . ill don't see why we don't just trash him now, hot trail gets cold while you wait for them motherfucking tankthinkers to make up their fu . . . ders is orders I guess . . . Hey I still can't . . .'

'. . . some kinda bionic boy or what? Hey Pete? What . . . ?'

'Bionic my ass, all a cover for something . . . unny thing you know the first real bionic man wasn't even scratched in that plane crash, you know? Like he was just . . . in the hospital . . . started picking up infections . . . everything going wrong, one part after another . . . next thing you know . . . Hey I can't hear a damn thing on this . . .'

'. . . short of agents anyway, too much of this crap going on . . . tired of freezing my ass off in panel trucks . . . extra help on that whatsit, Kratt . . . in that thermos?'

Roderick looked out of the window. There was a panel truck parked across the road. The sign said *O'Bannion Flowers* but there wasn't any O'Bannion Flowers in town. Okay, so G-men or something watching him, and they wanted to trash him or something, put him in the hospital where he could pick up infections like the six million –

'. . . with priests you gotta go careful, see? Priests get headlines ... Anyway they want we should surveil to pick up all the contacts ... maybe I got the wires crossed or ... was that a shot?'

Down the street, the wretched pick-up of Mr Ogilvy back-fired again. As usual, it was wobbling and going too fast, cutting a sine-wave pattern along the route from the public school to Mr O.'s favourite bar. People liked to pretend that it was the old pick-up that knew the way, that Mr O. just put his foot down and went to sleep.

The crash and the flaming explosion weren't quite as good as on TV. There was hardly any noise at all.

By the time Father Warren came back, the fire trucks and tow trucks were just leaving.

'I'm sorry I took so long,' he said. 'Couldn't resist trying a couple of shots with Father O'Bride's handgun. Not much good, I guess, but – now where were we? I was about to say, robots will be programmed to recognize people. After all, people recognize each other, don't they?'

'Only you don't recognize that I'm a robot,' said Roderick. 'Sometimes, boy, I don't even know myself what I am, Mr Swann says it'll take a lot of money to even find out if I'm a person in law – or just one of these legal statues like you said – or if I'm a dog or a knife or what – but look, even to work these laws you gotta have some way of telling robots from people. You gotta have these other unnatural laws and Mr Swann and Perry Mason to work them out, boy, there goes your logic. I mean if a robot hurts somebody and says I thought he was just a robot, boy, old Perry could really get the Districk Attorney hung up, holy –'

Father Warren banged a slim fist on the desk. '*Assume* robots can tell people from robots, *assume* that. Then the Three Laws are perfectly logical, right?'

'No but I mean that's just a start, the robot's gotta figure out what harm and injury mean, more legal stuff see, it's right back to court again with the Districk –'

'*Assume* we've got that worked out too. *Then* do you see how logical –?'

'Wait, no, soom sure, soom all that stuff for just the first law, just the first part of the first law. I didn't even mention

244

how's a robot surgeon gonna operate without cutting into anybody, how's a robot cop gonna arrest anybody, how's a robot soldier gonna kill anybody – okay so soom we don't have robots doing any jobs like that, we still got the second part, he can't let anybody come to harm by inaction that's not doing nothing, just like not even existing, only how does that tie in with that clause 3 there I mean the third law?'

'Afraid I don't follow you. What – just a minute.' Father Warren took a handkerchief from his sleeve and blew his nose. Then he went to the window and stared out at the black-and-white garden. 'Getting dark.' He went around the room, turning on lights. 'I think I see what you're driving at. If the robot doesn't protect its own existence first and foremost, how can it be around later to prevent some human coming to harm?'

'Yeah, Father, that's it. Because there's no time in these laws, it's always something right away like somebody tries to shoot a guy and the robot gets in between. But take a robot farmer, he knows somebody might starve if he stopped work so he's *really* gotta perteck himself, for ever. But in these other laws it says that if some kid just comes along and tells him to go jump off the highest building in the world he's gotta go and do it. Is that logical?'

'Maybe not, Roderick. Maybe not. But –'

'Anyway take this zillionaire, he spends a zillion dollars on this custom-made robot, you think he's gonna let some kid come along and tell it to jump off a building? No he's gonna program it to perteck itself, like program in martial arts and everything.'

The hands washed each other, folded for prayer, subsided on the desk blotter. 'I see you've really gone in to this, Roderick. Can't say I've – but I am sure of one thing: robots in fiction – and in real life when the day comes – will be completely programmed. They won't have free will like the rest of us. *That* was what I really hoped you'd see in this story. What being a robot is really like. No free will. No choice. Tell me. Is it really worth it?'

'Is what worth what?'

'Is it worth giving up your humanity to be a "robot"? Isn't it really better to be a human being, made in –' His gaze

245

fell on Roderick, slipped over the surfaces of steel and plastic, '– made in, ahm, God's image? Is it worth giving that up to be just a – a glorified adding-machine?'

Roderick sat up straight. 'Is that it? I can't go to Communion because I'm just an adding machine? Because who says robots are just adding – boy, *I'm* not an adding-machine, boy, I'm as good as anybody . . .'

After a pause, Father Warren smiled. 'Exactly. You're as good as anybody because you have an immortal soul. You're human, right?'

'I – guess so, Father.'

'And not a robot?'

'No I'm still a robot only I'm a human rob –'

'You're impossible, that's what you are! I give up – no I don't, I'll see you back here after the holidays. God's peace be with you.'

But it was Father Warren who could find no peace. Long after the little machine-boy had rattled and bumped his way out of the room, he sat contemplating his own hands, listening to the furious gunfire from the basement. Finally he got up and looked for a book. His hand, the colour of beeswax, passed over religious volumes and came to the science fiction. At last he took down *Screwtape Letters* and read:

There are two equal and opposite errors into which our race can fall about the devils. One is to disbelieve in their existence. The other is to believe, and to feel an excessive or unhealthy interest in them.

The pin-scratch began to itch.

17

The lights were on at Holy Trinity School, and a procession of cars led past the sign TRESPASSERS WILL BE PROSECUTED to discharge their peculiar passengers at the back door: bearded little boys, girls with wings, a miniature Roman soldier bearing a golden kazoo, adults toting bales of straw, tinsel ropes and foolish grins. Sister Filomena, the principal, stood in the hall like a traffic cop, directing boys to one room, girls to another, adults to a pile of folding chairs and on into the gymnasium.

'No, that way Mrs Grogan ... well I'm very sorry Mary, but if you can't keep track of your own halo ... Christmas Mrs Roberts, yes, the Wise Men go on right after ... nice to see you too, the ... DANIEL GROGAN! Shepherds do *not* behave like ... popcorn balls? How nice Mrs Goun, I'm sure after the perf ... third on the right, see Sister Mary Olaf, Mary ... Merry Chris ... DANIEL! Will you stop that this minute or do we take your crook away ... Ah here's little Roger, hello Mr Wood Mrs Wood is that his costume?'

'And the other box is a *present*,' said Roderick. 'For Sister –'

'How nice, thoughtful only you'd better run along and change now ...'

'Ma made my costume, boy you oughta see –'

'Yes fine, you just run along ...'

She divided him from Ma and Pa, who went to squat in the dark gym with all the other parents, the men coughing and creaking their folding chairs, the women fanning themselves with programmes. Roderick left his costume in the boys' dressing-room and went to find Sister Mary Martha.

The lower hall was full of action: two shepherds fencing with their crooks, a choirboy with a bloody nose trying to cure it at the drinking fountain, the front half of an ass trying to get through a door held shut by a fat angel, a halo being used for a frisbee (which it was), someone wearing a giant foil-covered star trying to bite someone who was pinching

247

someone who was trying to kick the doll from the arms of someone in blue...

But upstairs it was quiet and dark, except for the light shining out of Father O'Bride's office door.

'... yeah, yeah, look Andy don't do me any more favours, I distinctly said candles on the phone today I get the invoice for a gross, what would I do with a gross of sandals? Think we got a discalced order here or what? No I didn't say discount order, skip it, listen – listen will you? What I'm tryina do here is real big league stuff, I'm tryina put together a whole package – look, forget about that Taiwan crap, this has gotta be up-market stuff, devotion – are you listening? Look it's a kit. see, a complete home package of devotional uh products, not just the Mass kit but a whole host of, range of ... that's it, you got it. We figure the average family size is four, so that means four digital rosaries, you got that? Okay, four kneeling pads ... sure that's okay if they don't *look* too Ay-rab ... yeah okay ... now, yeah you got the rest of it, the hologram portrait of Saint Ant – better make it Patrick, the market research newsletters all say Anthony's downmarket this year...'

Roderick passed along, down the front stairs, and found Sister Mary Martha in her usual place, on all fours. In the gloom, Roderick could just make out her frail figure, the skinny hand gripping an electric hand-polisher that moved back and forth over the same old spot.

'Hi Sister, gee it's dark down here. How the heck can you see what you're doing? Gee I hope you get it done in time to see the play. It's neat, all about this metallic conception I guess and how the wise men and the sheep men get together to look at this star because they, because somebody didn't count it in the census. Pa says about censuses what it is they figure if they can just count everybody once, they figure they got it made. He says what they want is to keep the population down to zero, everybody being just a big nothing. He says the whole point of science is people controlling birth and death. Only I guess in those days they didn't have birth-control so they had to send out soldiers with swords to cut up all these babies. I guess we don't get to do that part.

'Anyway I gotta go soon because I'm one of the wise men,

I bring in the Frankenst – frankincense. So here's a Christmas present for you. I made it myself. Should I open it for you? Here, see? It's a rosary.'

The figure did not look up. Roderick sat on the step and held out the string of beads. 'Ma says they got it all wrong about Our Lady giving the first rosary to St Dominic. She says really it was Lady Godiva gave it to the Benedictines. Ever hear that story? No?

'Well see it was in England and they had this tax problem just like Caesar Augustus, you know? And this Lady Godiva's husband was the tax collector and he was so mean she felt sorry for all the poor folks paying these taxes, so she did a strip in front of everybody. So her husband said he was sorry and he built this big monastary and then she gave them the first rosary. Only maybe that wasn't the first one either even though it was a hundred years before Dominic, because Ma says the Hindus had rosaries a long time before that, 32 beads for Shiva and 64 beads for Vishnu, what do *you* think?'

The figure did not look up. 'Well, Pa doesn't like religion much, he always says the collection's the most important part of it, you know? He sounds a lot like this other guy I heard once, who said religion's all just counting and numbers, telling the beads like a bank teller. Number magic he said. Number magic. He said if you want to go to Heaven get a big goddarn computer. Sister?'

He leaned over closer. 'Sister, if religion and arithmetic are just the same thing, why don't we just put 'em together? Like the Protestants, see one time I went into this Protestant church and they didn't have no crucifix or statues or nothing, just this big board up on the wall with a bunch of numbers on it – is that, is that the answer? Is that the right answer, Sister?

'Well then look, why don't we just, when we say prayers and get days of indulgence and stuff, why don't we keep it all in a bank somewhere? And have like credit cards? Sister?'

The electric hand-polisher stalled, turned over and skidded out from under the wrinkled hand. Roderick made a move to fetch it, but stopped. Sister Mary Martha rolled over sideways and lay still and stiff, her withered cheek pressed to another withered cheek in the gleaming floor. Roderick stared, and four colourless eyes stared back at him.

'... *Holy Family Kit* hits the Chicago dealers just make sure your boys are on the ball there, work out some kinda sales slogan, not just the old family that prays together routine neither, something peppy like *Go! Go! Go for God!* maybe or no, okay something like *Say One For Yourself, Too*. Well I don't know Frank, you're the adman ... hang on a minute ... what is it?'

'Father, there's a stiff downstairs. You wanta call the cops?'

'Oh very funny, now go away stop bothering –'

'But Father it's S –'

'*Go away*. You still there Frank? Nothing just ... talking what? Ha ha, *host*, aw come on! Never get a dispensation in a million ... need their head examined if they think ... Ha ha, try that out on Jack, Father Warren here, he's the science fiction nut around here ...'

Chairs creaked, programmes fluttered, as a shrill voice finished flattening the notes of *Bless This House*. The man next to Pa wondered why they couldn't turn off the heat when they had a mob like this, and the woman next to him wondered why they didn't just run it all through closed circuit TV like they did over at the public. Pa said he didn't mind, but then he was non-Catholic. Ma tried to nudge him but he went on, 'Yep, getting ready for the eternal flames,' he said. 'Wanna see me weep? Gnash my – ouch!'

'Oh you're Mr Wood, aren't you? I don't suppose your little boy's in the play – you know our little Traysee is playing Our Lady herself?'

'Our Lady?'

'The Blessèd, you know. Mary. I don't suppose your –'

'Playing one of the wise men. Not sure just which one, Baalhazar maybe.'

'Oh yes he's the little crip – handicapped boy isn't he?' The woman smiled a V-shaped smile. 'You know I always think it's best to keep them in a home. After all, if God –'

'We do keep him in a home. Ours,' Pa stage-whispered as the curtain rose on a centurion. A shrill voice began:

'At that time there went forth a disease, a decree . . .'

The show, Roderick thought, must go on. Besides, nobody
wanted to listen when he tried telling them, not Father
O'Bride upstairs on his exercycle watching his own muscles
ripple underneath his Sham Rocks t-shirt. Not Sister Olaf
backstage here either, she was so busy keeping everybody
quiet and trying to keep the choirboy from wiping his bloody
nose on his surplice, and heck she didn't even see anybody,
didn't even say she liked his costume it was just, 'Okay get
ready Wise Man Number Three', as if he was jumping out
of a plane or something, already the numbers one and two
were moving forward ('Little steps, little steps') and the choir
hummed *We Three Kings of Orient Are*. Then suddenly he was
onstage in the blazing light . . .

The choir stopped humming. The audience stopped
coughing and creaking.

Ma had taken a lot of trouble with the costume, saying
that a sorcerer ought to look like a sorcerer. And since no
one had made it clear which Wise Man Roderick was to play,
she'd fixed up a kind of all-purpose outfit. She might have
got away with the lunar bull-horns and the solar mask (even
though its crazy blood-red grin would disturb children's
dreams for some time to come). Even when Roderick opened
his giant wings to speak, the audience was less shocked by
the fixed stare of some 500 dolls' eyes, than by the revealed
body draped in yellow, and bearing unmistakable append-
ages on the chest. 500 or more eyes stared back at him, at
them, those lumps of painted wood which (Ma said) sorcerer-
kings of old had worn to distract the gods. And between these
great breasts nestled the sacred heart of Osiris, bright red,
pulsing realistically, and gushing butane fire. With a bang,
it went out.

A man snickered.

'Jesus,' began Roderick.

A woman gasped.

'I mean here's frankenst – Jesus, here's –'

An angel screamed. A whispered command came from
backstage and some of the larger choirboys moved to seize
him. And then suddenly he was all over the stage at once,

251

rolling, kicking, flapping his wings, disappearing under a heap of lace vestments to re-emerge minus a breast, dodging the black arm of a nun, crashing into the stable and emerging in a blizzard of straw – until finally he was pinned down as the curtain descended, so that the last thing seen by the audience was his Satanic grin.

That was how they would think of it later, Satanic. One or two in the audience went so far as to imagine they had heard him uttering curses and incantations, that they had seen a forked tail which coiled around him to make the Sign of the Cross in reverse . . . Others had more practical reasons for being upset. Mrs Roberts, whose little girl had not yet made her entrance ('Fly! Fly to Egypt! King Herod . . .'), made her way backstage to deliver a slap that left her hand stinging, Roderick's metal singing.

'It was like seeing a peacock hunted down and plucked,' said Ma as the three of them walked home.

'Phyllis Teens,' Pa muttered.

'Except that it used to be a wren, didn't it? At Christmas all the English villagers would go out in a big pack and hunt down a wren. Men of good will . . .'

'Why?' Roderick asked.

'Now don't get all upset, either one of you,' Pa said. 'The disguise was beautiful whatever they say. And you done just fine in the play, son. Anyway remember, Christmas is just another Julian day. Day two million, four hundred forty thousand –'

'Men of good will! Industrial England it was, so of course they had all kinds of funny notions, they, they thought the machines wanted them to do it. Yes so they killed the little bird and crucified it and carried it around the village singing

> We hunted the wren for Robin the Bobbin
> We hunted the wren for Jack the Can
> We –'

'Yeah but why would they do that?'

'Because, I don't know why, because they were horrible Manxmen, maybe. People with so little imagination they call their home the Isle of Man –'

'And,' Pa said, 'they couldn't even put a cat together

252

properly, left the tail inside. Sorry son.'

Roderick did not like jokes about body parts coming apart. Hearing one made him suddenly imagine he could feel the iron rods in his legs. He felt them now, even as he smiled. 'That's okay.'

'That was a very strange play,' said Ma. 'All that business about the Virgin Mary, as if the infant didn't count at all. She's the big star, and he's just a silly doll. Reminds me of the Egyptian priests, at the winter solstice they'd all gather in the temple and at midnight they'd come running out with this wooden doll, telling everybody the Virgin had given birth to this new sun, s-u-n I mean –'

'Another yard of Frazer,' said Pa. 'Son, I get this every damn Chris...'

They had to stop to wait for Pa to finish coughing. Roderick looked at the stars. Damn Christmas, Christmas of the damned, dead souls. Burning like candles on a tree. If everyone lit one little candle, Pa always said, we'd have a candle shortage overnight. Pa coughing out his soul in a cloud right here on earth. Spitting in the snow to leave a wren-mark. For Robbie the Bobbin. Hunted by a hawk, up it comes, somebody marking its fall. Souls escaping on a sigh.

Ma always said that souls were only held to Earth by the weight of sin, they rose up to Heaven by dropping it: giving all your pride to the Sun, all your love of money to Mercury, all your lust to Venus, all your gluttony to the Moon, all your anger to Mars, all your envy to Jupiter and all your laziness to Saturn, finally entering the astral sphere to become a pure flame, a star. Which one would be Sister Mary Martha? If Roderick had his way, she'd be the brightest, nightbright as she had been dayplain, the almost invisible virgin now crawling up the stairs of the sky (cleaning each one) to her jewelled crown.

None of them, he guessed. All just burning globs of goop, so many light-years away. And when people died, they went the same place as the mark of a wren in last year's snow.

Pa finished his cough. 'Okay, home! Home, to hang up our socks!'

Christmas was all in the head, Pa said (the heart, Ma

corrected). So really this home-made tree was just as good as any real one, wasn't it?

Roderick looked at it and saw tall evergreens, cut down in the mountains by singing lumberjacks, hauled to town on horse-drawn sledges with bells all over them. It was set up in a house where there were wreaths on the doors and red candles in the windows, to guide visitors who would arrive any minute in their top hats and bonnets, laughing all the way to the bank, through the banks of snow and loaded down with presents (and of course cards showing all of this), Bob Cratchit goose puddings, black servants beaming at them over silver trays of eggnogs, giant dolls and electric trains that Father would play with when not admiring his new pipe and shotgun, but not half as much as Mother admired her new automatic kitchen machinery or her genuine diamonds lasting a lifetime or her personal transit car, just right for shopping (for turkey and trimmings, gifting ideas or magazines showing all of this including cards on the mantel (showing all ...)) or for getting the kids Back to School, so much easier and fun to learn with a homework computer, just coming out of that big box under the glittering tree. The tree ...

At the same time, Roderick saw it was only the bottom of a cardboard box with a green triangle drawn on it and a light bulb stuck through a hole. The bulb wasn't really connected to anything, but then it was burned out anyway. And anyway, they had to keep the power-bill down this month. And all the other bills, like food. Ma and Pa would be imagining their Christmas dinner too, and probably their presents.

All the same, they hung up three stockings on the back of three dining-room chairs. And in the morning there was *stuff* in them!

In Pa's stocking there was a beautiful hand-painted certificate awarding him the Nobel Prize for Inventions. And a drop of water.

In Ma's stocking there was a wonderful little machine to help her make up titles for her sculptures: two cardboard wheels with words on them (*Forest Sneeze*; *Shoelace Metonymy*; etc). And a drop of water.

The drops of water had been snowflakes when Roderick put them in the stockings. Ma and Pa said they could see that they'd been pretty terrific snowflakes, too.

In Roderick's stocking was a foot.

'Don't look so puzzled, son.' Pa went out to his workshop and brought in the rest of the present: a complete, full-sized adult body in pink plastic, with a gleaming stainless steel head.

'Oh,' said Roderick, trying to sound pleased. 'Clothes.'

18

'Frankly, Father, I expected something like this. You would give him those *Protestant* books to read...'

'Kierkegaard? But Sister, it's just, just a book about faith. the blind leap into darkn —'

'All the same, Father. All the same.' Sister Filomena held out the essay by two fingers, avoiding contamination. 'No doubt you'll be wanting a word with him about this.'

'Well of course I'll speak to the boy if —'

'Boy! Lord have mercy on us, he can't even get his knees under the desk. He's head and shoulders over all the other children. Yes and all the girls have been — well, *looking* at him. He's just not natural.'

'Maybe we should graduate him or something ... but you know, I keep feeling I'm almost getting through to him. Oh, sinful pride maybe, but I, it's just that I've never had the opportunity before to bring into the faith a ro — a person like him.'

Sister Filomena *hmp*'d and went away, leaving the essay on his desk. He began to read:

THE STORY OF ABRAHAM AND ISAAC AS A FLOWCHART

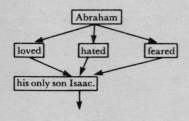

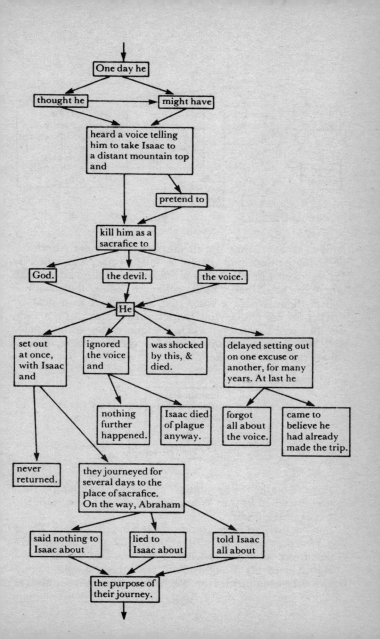

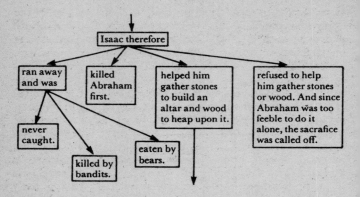

And so it went, through all the scenarios where Abraham, believing or doubting the voice, killed Isaac, was killed by Isaac, killed himself, killed someone else, killed an animal; where the altar (badly built) collapsed, killing them both or one of them; where a voice told him to look in a near-by thicket for his real victim (which turned out to be a ram, another son, a mirror); where he ignores the second voice and kills Isaac, and one intriguing version where, having raised the knife to strike,

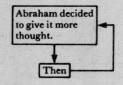

Hard to blame the Springtime and glands for stuff like this. Especially when Father Warren could not yet be certain the boy had any glands.

But the girls do have glands, he reminded himself. There was a warning to be taken from the Asimov story 'Satisfaction Guaranteed' all right, in which a woman and a robot –

He diverted his thoughts from the subject a split-second before they became pleasurable. Well robots, then: it always came back to robots. Under his guidance the boy would read everything they could dig up, fact and fiction, about robots, androids, automata, golems, homunculi, teraphim, steam men, clockwork dancers, wooden dolls, simulacra, manikins, audioanimatrons, tachypomps, usaforms, sensters, mechanical chess-players, bionic men, cyborgs, marionettes that come to life, electrified monsters that murder children, chemical creations that turn against their masters, a living brain floating in a fish-tank, a malevolent computer seeking to dominate the world. If he wanted robots he'd get them: singers, housekeepers, factory hands, potato diggers, novelists, boxers, judges, surgeons, policemen, detectives, actors, carpenters, assassins, botanists, diplomats (priests?) ... even scapegoats ... a thousand stories twanging the same old string, that's the way to get him off the subject, that's the way to do it ...

Roderick shifted a little in his chair. This new body with the clothes and all wasn't so terrific all the time. If it wasn't that Pa had worked so hard on it and made himself sick and all, Roderick would like to try putting on his old body again. Boy, he could almost feel his old treads, biting into the soil only last summer but it felt like a lifetime ago, he remembered one day when he'd stopped to rest and looked around and there were his own marks cutting right across the yard, the place where he'd dodged to miss a dandelion, the place where he'd put on speed to squash this dog-turd, he could see it all now, every detail: a stick with the skin off it, a bumble-bee hesitating by the dandelion, nothing lost. Nothing ever lost.

Except his old body. That was out at Cliff's junkyard with all the dead cars and rusty washing-machines. The first warm day he'd walked out and looked at it, thinking *That was me, was it? Or was it?* Looking into the empty eye-holes until Cliff hobbled out of his trailer to say Get lost, beat it.

'Stop fidgeting.'

'Yes, Father.' He stared out of the window at an apple tree, just now looking like a still picture of a snowstorm. Father Warren sitting there waiting for him to say something, heck all he could think of was how things wear out, break down and get thrown away – people too. Pa going out in that snowstorm just to get him a lousy arm or something ...

'Well, Roderick? *Do* you agree with me when I say, "Man

is made to serve only God, but the robot is made to serve only man"?'

'At mass you serve God up on a plate, does that mea –'

'DON'T try to be facetious. Either you agree or you don't, that's logic.'

'It sure is, Father, only...'

'Only what? Only what?' The hands made an agitated gesture, and Roderick noticed that one wore a small bandaid.

'Only didn't they used to say the same thing about women, how they were made to serve men as men served God?'

'Think we're getting off the subject here –'

'No but I mean heck they don't say it much any more. See, Father, I just wanted to know if this saying is true or just ... just a saying. Like maybe in a few years we could have Robots' Liberation or anyway robots could say "Why should we do all the work, running around waiting on people?" And maybe this saying won't seem so true, Father?'

The priest sighed. 'Look, this is very simple. Women have free will. Robots don't – by definition. So there's no –'

'Yeah but anyway, Father, you said Made to Serve, does that mean a robot's *real* purpose like, or just what the guy who made it thinks? Because there's a difference, see, Pa says. Pa says there was this guy No Bell invented dynamite and he thought it would stop wars, that's what *he* made it for only the *real* purpose –'

'Off the subject again, Roderick. What's all this about Women's Lib and dynamite, Roderick? *Try*. Try to be logical.'

'Yeah, Father, but robots, heck, who knows why they're made, why *we*'re made, could be anything. Could be even the people that make them don't know why, maybe they're lonely. Maybe they just get tired of being boss over everything, maybe they just want to be – extinck.'

'What? What are you –?'

'And the only way is to make up somebody better, to take over? Huh, Father?'

Dr Jane Hannah picked up peanuts one at a time, whispered to each one and popped it into her mouth.

Lyle Tate put down his brush. 'Jesus I wish you'd stop

that! How can I work with that ... it's like having somebody saying a rosary all the time, I can't ... Jesus can't you talk or something?'

'What about? You and your *head*?'

'Someone mention me?' Allbright called from the far end of the loft.

'Jesus!' said Lyle, putting down his brush again. 'What are you doing here? Look Allbright I haven't *got* any money, I –'

'Take it easy, I'm okay. Look.' And when he came close enough for the cold North light to reach his face and clothes, they saw that he'd changed. The beard and hair were trimmed, the face unexpectedly clean, the lapels of his new suit bore expensive stitching. Even Dr Hannah sat up and stared.

'What happened,' she said, 'to the winter garment of repentance? And where the hell have you been this last month?'

'Selling a poem,' he said, tweaking the knees of his trousers as he sat down. 'In a way.'

'Selling a poem my ass.' Lyle turned away and went back to work on the head.

'That too. Well you know how I was, just after ex-mas? Thought I'd hit bottom there – you know, when I put my head in the ov –'

'You phoney son of a bitch, suppose you didn't know it was a fridge, every move calculated, every –'

'Yeah okay I'm a sonofabitch, fine. Only how was I supposed to know goddamn Rogers and his ultra-modern kitchen, okay don't believe me. But I tell you, I first I tried to get into his freezer, you know? Thought I'd just go to su-leep as they say, only it was all full of pork, legs of –'

'So what happened?' Hannah asked. 'Hospital?'

'Yup, and what do you know, they cured me. All these goddamn lugubrious head-shrinkers got busy and – shrank my head! Now I'm a hell of a nice little guy, no more bad habits.'

'That's a relief,' said Lyle. 'If it's true.' He began mixing a blue, dabbing it on his wrist.

'See it all came to me one day, as they say. You know

261

how I used to go around quoting Burroughs, how the C-charged brain was like a pinball machine ... what are you doing? Looks like, what is that *woad* you got there? Old Hannah converted you to some –'

'He's trying to match his veins,' she said. 'What about your Edgar Burroughs machine?'

'Eh? Not Edgar, *Bill*. As in billing machine. See, his grandfather was it, invented the adding – anyway listen, it all came to me, junkies are just machines. Garbage in, garbage out, that's what they say in the trade. Junk in, junk out.'

Lyle paused again. 'You know, I think I liked you better when were – better before.'

Allbright unexpectedly laughed. The others exchanged a look.

'No but listen, junkies really are machines. So I wrote a little poem about it. Now listen to this last line: "Addiction is only addition. Plus C."'

Hannah looked embarrassed. Lyle fought back a sudden impulse to be tactful. 'Jesus, Allbright, that's terrible.'

'Yeah, ain't it?' Allbright laughed again. 'See I'm cured of poetry, too. Cured of, of Allbright. They hooked me up to the old machine in there and gave me the pure juice, everything in, everything ... hell I walked around for a few days feeling like Volta, in the comics remember? My right hand attracts – *bzzzzt*. My left h –'

'O God,' said Hannah, turning away. Lyle continued working, while he tried to find something to say. He wheeled the head around to compare the vein on the opposite temple, for symmetry.

Allbright too seemed at a loss for words. He turned to Hannah, grinning. 'Edgar Rice Burroughs, for Christ's sake. Bet you haven't read him either.'

The old woman blinked at the peanut her hand had raised automatically, and put it down. 'The, er, *The Adding Machine*?' she said. 'I saw that performed back in –'

'That's *Elmer* Rice, for Christ's sake. You're supposed to be teaching Comparative Lit., compared to what for Christ's sake? You never read any English or American stuff in your life, did you? Come on, did you?'

'You haven't told us where the money came from,' she said.

'Oh that. Well. While I was in the nut hatchery I met this old pal of mine, knew him back in high school, seen him around campus a few times, but here he was, a fellow nut. This guy used to be a computer freak, coupla wires got crossed somewhere and here he was, playing Chinese checkers with himself. With one goddamn marble.'

Lyle had stopped painting. The North light fell on his port-wine birthmark.

'Anyway he wasn't so crazy, you know? He told me all about a neat little trick you can play on these bank ter-minals –'

'Memory banks?' Hannah asked. 'I'm afraid I don't . . .'

'No *real* banks. With these terminals all over town like goddamn mailboxes, you just stick in your magnetic card and out comes money. Only he told me how to do it without a card. You just call up the computer on the phone, see, and –'

Lyle finished wiping his hands and threw the rag on the floor. His birthmark grew brighter. 'You call that selling a poem? Jesus, Allbright, you make me sick with your –'

'No look, wait. I work for that money. I had to get this job, see, with this data processing company. To find out the secret phone number.'

'That, that's worse –'

'Only they change it every month so I gotta keep my job, just till I get enough –'

'Enough!' Lyle jammed his hands in his pockets and walked away to the window. He moved stiffly, as though the hands were working hidden stilts. 'Enough! Did they take that away from you too? Your honesty? Did they, did they, make you switch brains with some fucking junior executive, some, in some fucking musical toilet comp – Jesus, you don't even *look* like Allbright any more.'

Allbright grinned at Hannah. 'That's what I like about Lyle. He can get pissed off over nothing. Wonderful set of moral standards he's got, he figures if you keep your finger-nails dirty enough you have to be honest, never mind that you boost books at parties and rip off all your friends, lie to everybody, lie to yourself, somehow it all becomes honest if you can just manage to come up with a case of crabs or scurvy, better still kwashiorkor and beri-beri with maybe a touch of impetigo –'

'Why don't you just piss off, Allbright?' Hannah glared at him, her eyes like black olives startling in her pale, almost albino face. 'Lyle's trying to work on something here, something fine. Something even you would have to call "honest". And all you're doing is trying to goad him, spoil it for him.'

'I'm not. "Honest" I'm not. All I want is to get him to admit that he puts a price-tag on honesty just like everybody else, only his price is zero. Am I right, Lyle?'

'No point in arguing with you, you just –'

'Am I right though? Anything is honest to you as long as you don't make money on it, a profit of zero makes it honest, right?' He stood up, drawing back the curtain of his jacket to plant a fist on one hip, and pointed at the painted head. 'That, for instance. Bet you worked out your fee so it just covers your materials, right?'

Lyle mumbled something about a commission for a friend. But Allbright seemed to have forgotten the argument completely, as he found himself confronted with this strangely familiar face, so –

'Uncanny,' he said. 'Uncanny, like the face of John Q. Public but – different. Transfigured. Almost see light coming out of it, that transparent skin ... and the symmetry ...'

Lyle nodded. 'Just about finished. If I could just get you and Hannah to sit down and entertain each other ...'

'Yeah sure but what's this movable jaw – you can't be making a head for some damn ventriloquist's dummy or – I mean this would scare the shit out of any audience –'

'For a robot,' Hannah said, patting the seat next to her. Allbright noticed that the seat, indeed all the seats and tables in the place, were nothing but stacked cubes formed of identical paperback books. 'And don't say there's no such thing, there is now. Just look at it.'

He sat beside her. 'The symmetry ... and no age, no sex, you can't even be sure of the race ...'

'That's the point, isn't it?' She handed him a batch of dusty drawings. 'Take a look at his working sketches, see how he got there?'

'What's this, warts all over it?'

'Rivets,' said Lyle, examining a needle-sized brush. 'See, first I figured he ought to look *robotic*. So I tried a lot of crap, faces from *Metropolis*, Egyptian masks even. Hannah finally convinced me he ought to be – well – inhumanly human.'

'I'll be damned.'

'I didn't convince him of anything he didn't know already,' Hannah said. 'All I said, in so many words, was that we need tribal deities, lesser gods to – to fill the empty spaces between the people. You understand?'

Allbright nodded. 'I guess that's it. What would pass, nowadays, for a tribal deity. Not important, just a, as you said, a household god. A – a pet stranger?' He tore his gaze away from it. 'Look I'm sorry about, uh, some of the things I said earlier. To both of you. It's just that I –'

'Tell you a funny story,' said Hannah. 'See all these books?'

Allbright tore open one of the plastic-wrapped cubes and pulled one book out of it. '*Die! Die! Your Lordship*, catchy title there. What have you got, a zillion copies here?'

'The last tenant this publisher, just walked off and left them,' she said. 'But we heard the whole story from the landlord. Seems they printed hundreds of thousands of these without noticing the last few pages were missing – where the name of the killer is revealed.'

'Great! The ultimate mystery.'

'That's not all – you want some wine? There's a glass by your foot there – that's not the best part. They decided to cut their losses by announcing a prize for the first reader who came up with the correct answer. Only – so the landlord says – the guy that won it, it turned out he'd been on welfare for years – was feeble-minded!'

'Fair enough, you don't have to be an Einstein –'

'No but listen, the welfare people had him arrested for fraud and froze his prize money, and I guess they're still fighting it out in court – and listen, the whole case –' She was laughing so hard she could hardly pour the wine. 'Listen the whole case hinges on the solution to this stupid mystery. His lawyers claim he got the right answer by accident, and the publishers – rather than lose the prize and get no publicity for it – they're suing to get it back, claiming he got the wrong answer after all!'

'Yeah, what does the author say?'

'That's just it, they kept stalling around about producing him, so I hear, and finally had to admit the author was a –'

'A what? Sounded like you said a computer.'

'I – I did. And the computer's been erased or something, so nobody – nobody knows – ha ha ha, the ultimate mystery!'

Lyle worked on, putting the last touches as the light began to fail. The others lolled on unfinished mysteries, drinking wine and trading computer stories. Allbright, his shirt and shoes off, was beginning to mutter about the C-charged brain.

'You know what? I think that head wants a drink. Hey head, you wanna drink?' He stood up, lifted his sloshing glass, and stumbled towards the pedestal.

'Stop it! Stop it!' Lyle had a terrible flash of premonition: wine pouring down the face, the indelible purple stain . . .

'Good God! You didn't have to hit him that hard,' said Hannah in the semi-darkness. 'Is he all right?'

'Put on the lights.' The head was unscathed. Its empty eye-sockets stared back at them across the floor where, amid signs of a struggle, Allbright lay face down, sprawled awkwardly as any body on any drawing-room hearth rug.

'Damn you! Damn you!' Hannah said, and it was not clear whether she was cursing Lyle Tate or his creation. She knelt, turned the body over, and removed her false teeth. 'Not breaving,' she said. 'Get an ambulanf.'

'I'll have to go downstairs –'

'Hurry!'

But when he returned, Allbright was sitting up, mumbling about the C-charged brain. 'Addiction is just addiction . . .' he said, and was still trying to say it right when the ambulance men had come and gone, cursing art and artists.

It was only then that Lyle noticed the head had been moved; lifted from its pedestal and put back wrong.

'What the hell did you do? Hannah? Did you –?'

'Don't worry, the paint's not smeared, I was careful. It was just that – you see I'm old, not enough breath in my body to revive him. I had to call – other sources for the kiss of life.'

'*That?* You think *that* fibreglass shell with paint on it, could bring the dead to life?'

266

'... not the Burroughs adding...'

'Maybe it can't,' she said. 'I just felt I had to try every-thing. Who knows, maybe just the smell of the paint shocked him – eh? Back into his body?'

'Back into –! Jesus Christ Jane, next thing you'll be levitating over in Dr Tarr's fancy new lab, a fat grant from NASA to find out if birds read each others' minds, how do you like that? Or is it psychic levitation now, NASA's real interested there, bound to like the idea of mind-powered space flight. Trouble is most of the people in Tarr's profession couldn't work up the brain power to levitate birdshit in a hurricane.'

'Look I know how you feel about, I know you don't believe in psychic pow –'

'Can't afford to, I'm a painter. And what Tarr and his crowd want to do is put painters out of business, put damn near everybody out of business...'

'I don't see that at all.' She sat down next to Allbright, who was pouring himself a drink and talking to it.

'Well what's the point of anybody going to a gallery to look at a Dürer? See, anybody can just be like this psychic Mathew Manning, whip out his own Dürer at home in a couple of hours, no previous training required. Or writing, why write a novel when you can be like this South American whatsisname, go in for automatic writing and knock out a novel in a week? Jesus it kind of makes a dumb joke out of everything anybody ever worked at, right? Take this Rose-mary Brown, she's even finished Schubert's Unfinished Sym-phony ... so what's the point of anything?'

'... funny dream...,' said Allbright. The others stopped talking and looked at him. 'Funniest damn dream ... dreamed, you know what I dreamed?'

For different reasons, they were almost holding their breaths.

'Dreamed this damn dummy was trying to kiss me...'

'Yes?'

'Yes?'

'And then this other dummy was trying to bite me in the ass!'

'My teeth!' Hannah shrieked. 'He rolled over on my –!'

All three of them were still giggling over it an hour later, when Sleep closed their eyes.

One liver-spotted hand passed the journal to another. 'Fascinating article there by this J. Hannah. Proposing a robot culture in which –'

'What do we know about this Hannah? Is he –?'

'*She*. Jane Hannah, fifty-five-year-old anthropologist, teaching Comparative Literature at the U. of Minnetonka. Two years ago she was predictably hostile to Entities, voted against funding a project I believe. But – bad luck there, seems her son died. She began to adopt a maternal-protective attitude towards Entities, fill in the blanks, usual hostility towards authority, organized behaviour...'

'She saw robots as free spirits? Anarchists?'

'Correct.' Pipe-smoke curled and writhed through the conference room. 'Class eight surveillance of course, but this article makes me wonder ... class six, maybe?'

'Are we interested in her contacts?'

'Nothing significant so far, writers and artists, petty malcontents. But the article itself –'

'Maybe we could check it with Leo?'

'Leo, yes, so I thought. Let's toddle over there now, I'll summarize it for you on the way.'

The two old men made their way through the maze of corridors and security barriers of Building A, Orinoco Institute, emerging in the desert sun like lizards creeping out to bask.

'Mmm, feel that sun!'

'Mmm. What she's done is tried to trace the origin of the *idea* of Entities – robots, that is – in Middle Europe. In Czechoslovakia especially. Evidently the home of Celts began there, the only "empire" without an emperor or a seat of government. She tries to link that with the Celtic religions, worship of the head, which they recognized as the centre of the intellect.'

'I don't see *that* as signif –'

'She claims they tried to keep heads alive after death, and regenerate. Certainly true that they believed in reincarnation, at any rate.'

'Ha! What will Leo make of *that*!'

'Anyway she then goes on to point out all the Czech rebellions and revolutions, beginning as I recall with the Hussites, Taborites, brings in the Waldenses somewhere...'

'Sounds cranky.'

'Oh it is, it is. Finds significance in the merest coincidences, fact that they met on Mount Tabor, almost *robot* backwards; fact that one of the Taborites was named Čapek, that he preached a bloodbath – kill all sinners – very like the blood-bath initiated by robots in *R.U.R.*, so was he an ancestor of Karel Čapek or what?'

'Look, what's the point of all this? Some nut pieces together a half-baked theory – do we really care?'

The other man stopped him, putting a weightless hand on his arm. 'We have to care. Not what she says – but what people make of it. This is, this is just the *worst* scenario we examined.'

Lizard eyes blinked. The desert sun glared down at these two slight figures, creeping along one white concrete path from one white concrete building to another. But all around was dark grass, cooled by sprinklers. Ignoring rainbows, the two men walked on.

'That's not all, of course. She points out all the events that took place in Prague. The famous *golem* story, you know it? Rabbi Löw of Prague, *der Hohe Rabbi* – you do know it? Okay then, how about the Infant of Prague? Seems to be the only Christian statue that isn't a statue at all – it's a jointed doll, with real clothes.'

'Well well. Is there more?'

'Much. She traces the revolution of 1618, successive occu-pations by Austro-Hungaria, Nazi Germany and Russia, the Czechs never quite knuckling under to their puppet govern-ments (her phrase) as demonstrated in their literature, she cites Kafka's *Metamorphosis* as an exploration of the old mind-body problem that so intrigued the Celts, Hasek's *The Good Soldier Schweik* as a "cheerful robot" satire, Čapek's *R.U.R.* of course; and even a very late item, a play written in 1968 by Václav Havel –'

'The year of the Soviet tank invasion, wasn't it?'

'Exactly. And in this play the main character is a machine

whose sole function, not so fast, you know I can't walk fast since my op –'

'Sorry. I'm sorry.'

'Sole function is to investigate human character. *Puzuk*, I believe it's called – ah! Good to be out of that sun!'

They entered the labyrinthine corridors of Building B, finally entering a dim, quiet room. The walls were lined with computer cabinets, and at the far end stood Leo's 'fish-tank'.

A young attendant in white rushed over to them.

'Gentlemen, I'm afraid this is a restric – oh, sorry, sir.'

''S all right,' said the senior man. 'You must be new here, eh? Heh heh, how do you like baby-sitting with Leo?'

The attendant hovered at his elbow as the three of them moved towards the tank. 'Leo, sir?'

'*That.*' The senior man pointed to the floating brain. 'That's Leo Bunsky, at one time just about the best applications man in his field. Still is I guess – poor bastard. Oh, we've got some data here, like Leo to have a look at it.'

'Yes sir, right away.'

The liver-spotted hands gave up the journal and then clasped. 'Poor bastard thinks he's still alive, you know? Still thinks he's working on a robot project, Project Rubber Dick, something like that. Naturally we can't disillusion him now, he might clam up on us.'

'Yes sir, well now I'll just enter this data –'

'Good man, Leo. Don't know how we'd ever stop the propagation of Entities without him, gave us some of our most valuable scenarios. Kind of Devil's advocate – *Hello there Leo!*'

The reptilian eyes, half-closed with amusement, stared down at the motionless brain. 'Good man, old Leo.'

Pa leaned forward while Roderick adjusted his pillow. 'Thanks. Now let's see what this so-called newspaper has to say. Great thing about convalescence, you don't feel so guilty wasting time like this – might even start watching TV if I – listen to this:'

XMAS PLAGUE STRIKES 5 MORE KIDS
400 Cases   –   Health Dept Baffled
The mysterious 'Christmas plague' which has so far infected over

400 children across the State, causing two deaths, has struck again. Five new cases are reported in Newer, county seat of Stubbs County. State Health Department officials, while admitting the disease has no cause they can isolate, assure the public there is no cause for alarm. 'The symptoms are somewhat similar to those of certain types of mercury poisoning,' said a spokesman. 'We can't rule that out, but it doesn't seem likely at this stage. There just isn't any mercury pollution going on, that we know of. We're sending our best investigative team to Stubbs County right away,' he added. 'Headed by a very capable man, Dr Sam Death.'

'Be nice to have a new doctor in town,' Pa said. 'Welby never has time to see me – not that I really need a doctor. My body is as fit today as it was when I was a young – a young –'

'Pa, speaking of bodies, could I ask you something?'

'Fire away.'

Instead of firing away, Roderick began fidgeting with the quilt. It was a strange patchwork design, each patch being a little human figure with upraised arms. 'Gee Pa, I don't know where to begin.'

'At the end, son. Either end.'

'Yes Pa.'

'And go on till you run out of it, then stop.'

'Yes Pa.'

'What is it, is it your new body you wanted to ask about?'

'Yes Pa.'

'Trouble getting used to it?'

'No, heck – well I mean clothes itch a lot but no, it's fine.' Roderick traced a figure on the quilt. 'Only, I mean, heck, well I mean, gee whiz, but heck, I mean gosh darn, I m –'

Pa reached out and slapped the stainless-steel face.

'Thanks Pa, I needed that. Well maybe I didn't need it, but – about my body, okay what I wondered was, is this it? Is this my body? All of it?'

The face was a crude blank, hardly more character in it than in a fencing mask. Pa said, 'You worried about the head, is that it? But it's like we told you, your Ma sculpted up a swell new head, and we got this painter working on it now, he should be shipping it to us any day now –'

'Well no, Pa. I meant – well what about sex?'

Pa raised himself up on one elbow. 'Sex? What in the world has sex got to do with your body?'

Roderick wasn't entirely sure. 'Well I mean, don't I need an extra part or two? Or three?'

'Son, you got all the parts they had in the factory.'

'No but I meant like male parts. Or female parts.'

Pa scratched his head. 'Pipe fittings, you mean? Electricals? Maybe you better spell this out for me, son.'

'I mean for making babies, Pa.'

The old man sank back and laughed. 'Babies! So *that*'s what's worrying you! Well listen, I know I should of had a man-to-man talk with you some time back, only I just kept putting it off ... But now listen. To have a baby, all you do is find a nice girl – or if you are a nice girl, a nice boy – takes one of each.'

'Heck, I know that, Pa. I seen these pictures where –'

'One of each. Then the two of you settle down together, next thing you know the babies start coming along, about one a year just like clockwork. Course you have to kiss a lot. That's why we're giving you a nice face, for kissing. But you don't need no extra pipe fittings or electrical sockets – do you?'

'I don't know. Pa, how come you and Ma never had any kids of your own.'

'Just plain unlucky, son.' Pa rattled his newspaper. 'Plain unlucky. You, uh, you don't think there could be any other reason, do you?'

'Yep.' Roderick told him the story he'd pieced together from Chauncey and the other kids, from dirty pitchers, and from a glance into a book at Joradsen's Drug, *Tantric without Tears*. All his sources, though disagreeing on details, seemed to tell more or less the same story.

Pa listened, looking astonished but remaining silent, until Roderick finished. '... well then I guess about nine months later the baby comes out of the same place the stuff went in.'

Pa laughed so hard he nearly fell out of bed. 'Aw come on! That's just ridiculous – I mean them things are to pee with, everybody knows that! You expect me to believe that people go around peeing on each other to get babies inside that they can pee out – come on, now! That ain't even common sense – if people had to go through all that every time they wanted a baby, there wouldn't be any people at all! Mary! Come up here – listen to what this boy just told me – tell your Ma, son.'

Ma listened without laughing. 'Huh! That's what happens when you pick up stuff from other kids, cheap reproduction books and places like that. You should have come to Pa and me in the first place, we'd set you straight.'

'But – but – but they talk about making it, screwing and making love –'

'Making love,' said Ma, 'is just a question of matching up your souls.'

Pa finished coughing. 'What she means, son, is your minds.' He tapped his head. 'Love, sex, whatever you want to call it, it all happens up here. And don't let anybody ever tell you different.'

Ma smiled. 'There! All cleared up? You know, I feel like – like really cooking something. See, all this talk about sex put me in mind of Duchamp, *The Bride Stripped Bare*, and that made me think of nutmeg graters, and that made me think of – of –' Her gaze fell on the quilt. 'Of gingerbread boys! For my invalid – though I suppose Duchamp would call him a *vain lid*?'

'Roderick can give you a hand,' said Pa. 'Soon as I get him to try out this new cipher I've been working on.' He dug down in the bedclothes and came up with a scrap of paper. 'Here son, just you try cracking that one.'

ANN NÉE ANNA, NOD TO ANTS' ADS (HE HAD TO AX 7).
CZAR INKS ODD IDS (OHMS) FOR NUT LADDER OF VHF STAR.

Roderick saw the answer at once, but pretended to puzzle over it. His thoughts kept straying to sex. It just had to be more than Ma and Pa thought. Only yesterday he'd been reading about Ramon Lull, the thirteenth-century Franciscan who'd invented a feeble kind of logic machine. Even Lull had pursued other things than truth. Lusting after a woman, he had written poems in praise of the imagined beauty of her breasts, and finally chased her on horseback into the cathedral. The woman then opened her bodice to reveal a breast partially eaten by cancer . . . but why had Lull imagined otherwise? There had to be more to the cipher of love than to any of Ramon Lull's little cipher-wheel gadgets, or even to this substitution, in which A stood for B, B for C, . . . Was Lull converted because the breast disgusted him? Or because, God help him, it did not?

19

Ping, poop, peep. Ping-peep. 'I'm outa ... practice ...'

'... wish they'd just stop referring to it as plague, that's all. *Plague, plague, plague,* like to see what they'd print if they really had plague here ... my point, that's frak 13 ... because it's just mercury contamination, simple ...'

Roderick sat in the dark hall beneath the picture of Saint Whatsername and her magical piano. From somewhere he could hear the voices of Father O'Bride and his guest, and the sounds of some electronic game.

'Ha!' *Ping-poop.* 'Oh.'

'Gotta anticipate, Father.'

'Mercury poisoning, eh? Sounds serious ...'

'... prefer to call it contamination, what's in a nomenclature I always say, either way it spells trouble, we got a problem running down the contaminant ... my guess is some fun food, problem is there's ... thirteen thousand ... narrow it down with questionnaires but ... what kid remembers ... six months ago? Is that mine?'

'Yeah, that's two men on, three up and four to play, love-fifteen, fifteen-two, fifteen-four – Doc, you're a natural. A natural!'

'... theory of my own, these talking gingerbread men, all the cases since they came on the market ... tried to run one through the lab but they keep delaying ... figure maybe certain commercial interests trying to hold things up ... maybe pressurizating the Governor ...'

'Heck. Guess I'm real outa practice there ... yeah I know what ya mean, big business ... little guy ain't got a chance any more ... lay everything you got on the line, pick up the ball and run with it only ... darn referee keeps tryina get in the game, know what I mean? Speakina games, howsabout we mosey out to the club and get in nine holes? Forget the lab, they can page you if they ...'

Father Warren called Roderick into his study. He looked

even more pinched and tired than usual, and one of his hands was wrapped in gauze.

'Lent,' he said, and after a moment sighed it: 'Le-ent. A time of self-denial. Humiliation of the flesh. Renunciation of the world. Repudiation of the devil ... what does self-denial mean to you, Roderick?'

'Gee Father, I don't know, is it like the cretin who says all cretins are liars?'

'Ooff!' Father Warren applied fingers to his blue jaw as though he'd been slugged. 'Well. Tch. Let's drop that for the moment. Did you manage to read that book I gave you? *Logic Machines?*'

'Yeah, Father. I was wondering about this Ramon Lull and this woman with breast cancer –'

'Forget it. You're too young to worry about that, put it out of your thoughts. The point was to get you to see how logic can be put to the service of theology, did you get that?'

'Well yeah, Father, he made up all these wheels with letters around them so you could turn the inside wheel and bring different letters together, like all the combinations. Like ciphers.'

'Very good, yes. And what did the letters stand for?'

'Well things like the seven deadly sins, so you can see how lust makes you angry, or anger makes you envious –'

'Fine, fine. And there were other wheels with the divine attributes, to show us how God's mercy is wise, his wisdom is powerful and ... and so on. Do you see the point?'

'Well sure, Father, only I mean it gets kinda silly, don't you think? I mean where he says, here listen:

'"If in Thy three properties there were no difference ... the demonstration would give the D to the H of the A with the F and the G as it does with the E, and yet the K would not give significance to the H of any defect in the F or the G; but since diversity is shown in the demonstration that the D makes of the E and the F and the G with the I and the K, therefore the H has certain scientific knowledge of Thy holy and glorious Trinity." Heck, I mean I don't even think he knew himself what he was talking about, all his circles with lines all over them looking like, like maybe breast cancers –'

'Didn't I just say forget that part? The flesh is too much with us...' Father Warren's voice became throaty with sarcasm: 'Except in your case, of course. It's all nuts and bolts to you, isn't it? People, emotions, dreams, the sense of sin, the hope of salvation – all just hardware. You're so superior, aren't you? Sitting there, not even a hint of humanity in that, that welding mask you use for a face – damn you!'

The wax-coloured hands writhed, pinching and scratching at one another like two scorpions in a bottle. After a moment, one of them calmed itself enough to rise and make the sign of the cross, blessing the robot. 'Forgive me, my child, I ... haven't been well lately, not that that's any excuse for an outburst like that ... now where were we? I have a book, a book here somewhere...'

The hands began to rummage blindly through the books and papers on his desk, picked up *Malleus Maleficarum* and put it down, finally seized upon a volume of *Mind*. 'Ah yes. Now. I'm going to put a hard question to you, Roderick. Little test, you might say, just now SUPPOSE ... suppose you and I are in a lab, performing an experiment. And suppose that your, your brain is hooked up to a very special kind of machine. Now since you *say* you are a robot, all we really have here is two machines hooked up to one another, right?'

'Right, Father.'

'Okey-dokey. Now this special machine can read your mind and show what you're thinking on a big screen. So by looking at the screen, I can see what you're thinking, okay?'

'Okay Father, only –'

'Never mind technical problems, let's just say we've solved them. I can read your mind. But since you are a machine, it follows that I can do better than that. Because whatever a machine is doing depends entirely upon what it did in the past – along with any new inputs –'

'I think input is plural and singular, Father.'

'Any new input, you understand? If this special mind-reading machine knows what thought you're having this minute, it also knows what thought you'll have next. So I can look at the big screen and see your thoughts *before you have them*.'

'Okay, but –'

'No buts.' Father Warren took a handkerchief from his sleeve and mopped the palm of his good hand. 'I am absolutely and scientifically certain of your thoughts before you are. If I ask you a question, I *know* the answer you'll give *before* you give it. Are you with me so far?'

'I think so, Father. Do I get to see the big screen too?'

'We'll come to that.'

'Because if I do, I could see I have a thought before I have it, and isn't that imposs –'

'I said we'll come to that! Okay no, you can't see the screen. But you're hooked up to this machine, and I ask you, "Do you believe this machine can correctly predict that you will answer 'No' to this question?"'

Roderick thought it over for a moment. 'Heck Father that's just a plain old paradox, if I answer "No" the machine has to perdick I'll say "No" so I'm wrong not to believe it. But if I say "Yes" the machine perdicks that, so I'm wrong again.'

'Hmm, maybe I've got that wrong somewhere.' Father Warren studied the book, cracking his knuckles. 'Suppose we put "Yes" in place of "No", yes that's it, suppose –'

'Well then I'm right all the time, Father. If I say "Yes" the machine knows I'll say "Yes" so it's right and I'm right. And if I say "No" –'

'Okay then let me try it this way: "Would you be right to answer 'No' if I asked you whether you believed this machine can correctly predict your answer to this question?" Answer yes or no.'

'But heck Father it doesn't matter what I answer, the machine has to say *No* –'

'Exactly! *It* has no choice. But *you* do. You, Roderick, have *free will. Ergo* you are not a robot after all, but a human being, made in God's –'

'Yeah, but Father holy Osiris it's just words, I only get a choice because the machine doesn't have any, it's like a – you don't even need a big screen there, just a sign saying NO, what kinda free will is that? I mean, sure I can choose which NO I mean, just like I can choose with a two-headed coin...'

An hour later the priestly hands were still clawing through

books and piles of notes. 'Okay then, suppose I ask you: "If I asked you whether you *dis*believed that you would be right to answer 'No' if I *didn't* ask you –" No wait a minute, almost got it now. "If I asked –" No, "If I didn't ask, yes, if I *didn't* . . ."'

'How's the workshop?' Pa asked. 'Radio still going?'

'Yup.' Roderick picked at the pattern on the quilt.

'What did you learn today?'

Roderick told him about Father Warren's hypothetical machine.

'Well I'll be damned! Son, if you had a machine that good at reading your mind, you wouldn't need a mind anyway, throw it away and just use the machine. And vicey versa, throw the machine away and use your mind for a machine. By the way, got another cipher for you, toughest one I ever worked out.'

AAA AAA AAAA AA AAA AAAA AAAA

Roderick looked at it for a few seconds. '*Nob gnu jinx'd by dab hand Kurd*, but I think the apostrophe's cheating.'

Pa was amazed. 'But how the heck did you –?'

Roderick winked; that is, put a hand over his eye. 'My secret, Pa.' It wouldn't do to tell Pa that he'd peeked at the answer earlier. A little mystery seemed to perk him up, made it seem almost as if he weren't dying.

He knew Pa was dying. Only the other day the old man had groaned, 'I'm tired now, son . . . like to rest a mite . . .' and everyone knew what that meant. Besides, Ma was baking a bushel of gingerbread boys every day, and throwing them away every night. Probably she reckoned that the sickness would get drawn out of Pa somehow and enter into the little figures – or maybe she just wanted to keep busy. Either way, Ma was worried.

Only the doctor seemed cheerful. Every day Roderick called Dr Welby up, and every day he refused to come out to the house.

'He'll be fine, take it from me. As your family doctor, I can assure you there's nothing to worry about. That's off the record, of course. Gotta go now, Judge Bangfield wants me to look over another lakeside property . . .' One day Dr Welby had listened to Pa's heart over the phone and pronounced him strong as a horse.

'Seen her myself, Sheriff, throwin' 'em away. Hell, if what this Doc Sam says is true, well . . .'

'Jake, why don't you just sit down and shut up a while. I'm tryina find me a game show here, don't seem to be nothin' on this thing but news . . .'

'Hey, leave it a minute, that's inneresting, looky that!' Jake McIlvaney shifted some *Wanted* posters and sat on the counter, staring at the screen.

'. . . *essor Rogers is still at large. The drama began yesterday when the professor invited a number of colleagues to dinner. One of them was Dr Coppola, who now takes over the story.*'

'*Well he told us it was a leg of pork but I didn't study anatomy for nothing. Took one look and I said to myself, Ken, something's wrong. Something's definitely wrong. So I cut a little tissue sample and took it to the lab, right? So . . .*'

The sheriff pushed a button. '. . . *tastes like honey. Looks like honey* – BUT IT'S BEEZEE . . .'

'Don't see why they gotta yell at you.'

'Hey let's see that Cheesecake Murders thing again –'

'Shut up, Jake.'

'. . . *touch the* YES *button if you prefer a happy ending, touch* . . .'

'. . . *appropriations for the top secret super think tank near Truth or Consequences, New Mexico. In this exclusive interview, the head of the prestigious Orinoco Institute told us just what goes on in those clandestinized smoke-filled rooms* . . .'

'. . . *behind every car I sell at low-low-*LOW *pri* . . .'

'. . . BITSY! BITSY! BOP, BOP, BOP! *It'sa treat! It'swhen you eat! It's O so neat! It's got the beat! It's itsy, it's itsy, it's bitsy, it's* . . .'

Finally the sheriff turned it off. 'Hundred and fifty a month I pay for cable, they can't even get in one damn game show. Now what's eatin' you, Jake?'

The story the TV repairman the disc jockey the waitress the sister of the waitress the preacher the barber the deputy the optometrist the lawyer the daughter-in-law of the lawyer the mechanic the butcher the electrician the young woman the nurse the friend of the nurse the carpenter the grocer the

sign painter the father-in-law of the sign painter the old man
the baker the young man the grandfather of the young man
the plumber the doctor the old woman the druggist the jury
the meter reader the cousin of the meter reader the gift stamp
redeemer the farmer the clerk the brother-in-law of the clerk
the gas station man the teacher the bartender the undertaker
the salesman the vet the Rotarian president the dentist the
used car dealer the insurance man the chiropractor's wife
the mother of the preacher the waitress the neighbour of the
disc jockey the uncle of the TV repairman avoided visited
stopped defended complained of was good to liked did fillings
on met was close to envied called spoke to was related to
disliked spoke to saw loved waved at had known for ages
visited convicted revived hated cured befriended listened to
helped saw awaited supported smiled at was thick with
spurned once ran over admired gave a ride to annoyed barely
knew married lived near represented fitted lenses for arrested
shaved greeted lived with waited on humoured told got
around quickly. No one really believed it but...

Roderick was sitting at the dining-table trying to make sense
out of some of the bills. Ma sat opposite, nibbling gingerbread
and reading *The Golden Bough*.

'I don't know, I've tried everything. I put a gingerbread
boy under his pillow. All he did was complain about the
crumbs. Think I'll give up on gingerbread.'

'How the heck did we get a thousand-dollar phone bill?
All local calls, too, practically.' Roderick patted his mouth,
indicating a yawn. 'Be glad when my new face gets here,
Ma. I mean I really get tired of spelling everything out...'

A June-bug buzzed in and plopped on the electric bill,
which was a final demand. 'Must be a hole in the screen,'
said Roderick. 'You know we might clear these up if I quit
school and got a job. They'd probably give me a diploma
if I asked – Father Warren wants to get rid of me, I think.'

Ma said, 'I wonder ... what if I tried smearing Pa all over
with this turmeric paste while he sits on the hide of a red bull –'

'FBI! Freeze!' said a voice. Roderick put his hands up.

'Oh!' Ma craned around. 'Agent Wcz, isn't it? And Sheriff
Benson, how nice. But who are these other gentlemen?'

'Freeze!' warned Wcz.

'Don't I wish I could, weather like this! Well come in if you're going to, don't keep letting June-bugs in.'

'Are we under arrest?' Roderick asked.

Wcz kept the gun trained on him. 'Why, what have you done?'

The other men shuffled in and introduced themselves. 'IRS,' said one. 'I'll take those papers, tin-face.'

'CIA,' said a second. 'Don't worry about me folks, I have no jurisdiction here, just observing in an observer capacity.'

'Me too,' said another man, who gave no initials. 'You Roger Wood? Just like to take a coupla pictures of you, one full-face and one profile. Hear you been going around posing as a robot, that about the size of it? Just speak into the microphone.'

Before he could answer, another man pushed in. 'FDA. We're confiscating those so-called gingerbread men –'

'Boys,' Ma protested.

'Men, boys, everything. We'll also take all the ginger you got in the house – all the ginseng, too – and what's this book? *Golden Buff*? Any recipes in here? Cancer cures, looks like a jaundice cure right here, we'll take it along...'

Pa called down from the top of the stairs. 'What's going on? What's going on?' But Roderick was too busy explaining that his face was not a removable mask as in *Westworld*, and Ma was trying to argue the FDA man out of taking away her kitchen stove. Pa made his way slowly down the stairs over the next hour, while the men milled about and Sheriff Benson sat in the corner looking embarrassed. The sheriff was the last to leave, saying:

'Sorry folks, hope this won't influence your vote...'

Ma went to the door and shouted after them: 'Okay if we melt now?'

Pa made it to the foot of the stairs. 'What was going on, Mary?'

'Nothing, Paul. You go back to bed and get some rest.'

'Sure, okay.' It took Pa several minutes to turn around and face the stairs again. Before he started up again, he bent and picked up a scrap of paper.

'Looks like they missed this gas bill, here – oh my God! Oh!'

Roderick caught him before he fell, but Pa was dead.

'Come out? For what?' Dr Welby sounded cross. 'Look buddy, if you had a bridge hand like this you wouldn't drop it to go look at a stiff either. Don't quote me on that. Look, musta been his heart, thought it sounded tricky the other day ... tell you what, I'll make a note, *I'm doing it now, don't get excited* ... make a note to leave a death certificate in my office, you pick it up when you want. Fair enough? Because you'll be coming in anyway to pay your bill.'

'But doctor, it's Ma. She's bad, I think maybe she's gonna die too ...'

'That's right, tell her a little grief is only natural, but if she needs any medication, antidepressants ...'

'But doctor –'

'Sorry about your dad. But you know, my work is with the living. The plaintive cry of a newborn babe ... the tears of gratitude in old eyes that once more can see ... the trusting handclasp of a child made whole by surgery ... the brave grin of ... well, you know. And you *can* quote me on that.'

20

The next morning brought Jake McIlvaney to the door with a package. 'Terrible thing, your Pa and all,' he said. 'Yep, just terrible. Boys over at the poolroom was just saying how –' the big Adam's apple shifted, '– how sudden it was. Real sudden. And your Pa was real respected in this town, you know that? Real respected. Can't say as he was liked much, but everybody respected him even when they hated his guts.'

Roderick nodded.

'Yep, well guess you'll be gettin' Wally Muscatine to handle the arrangements, eh boy?'

Roderick nodded. Jake came inside and looked around.

'Good enough, good enough. Because you know Wally's a real white man, he'll do your Pa proud. This the death certificate? See Doc Welby signed it, funny thing he was just now saying as how Pa was strong as a horse, only your Ma would keep feeding him with funny pills and all.'

Roderick shrugged.

'Yep, that's the way it goes. Oh, here's your package. Corner kinda got ripped a little there, so I uh seen what it is, it's a head.'

Roderick nodded.

'Looks almost real, what I seen of it. What's it for, anyhow?'

'For me. It's kind of a mask.'

'Oh?'

'Guess I can't wear it for a while. I'm in mourning.'

'*Oh.*' The Adam's apple bobbed again. 'By golly I wondered what you was doing with that black paint all over your face. Didn't like to ask right out, know how coloured folks get so touchy sometimes. Take that new doc, Doc Sam, you met him? Well he is the touchiest coloured boy I ever did see. All you gotta do is sneeze the wrong way and he gets all uppity, you know? Like we was talking about how your Ma keeps baking these here gingerbread boys, I asked him if he hadn't noticed how a lot of kids around town got sick after eating gingerbread boys, right away he got mad! He got mad!'

'He did?'

'Well maybe not right away, but see I asked him if he didn't smell a nigger in the woodpile somewheres, *then* he got mad. Okay, maybe I should of said Negro but hell, it's just an expression. I just don't understand you people sometimes. Hell I'm not prejudiced. I even buy Uncle Ben's rice! And look, I'll shake your hand any time – any time!' Jake at once drew on a dirty work-glove and shook Roderick's hand. 'There, you see?'

'A difficult time,' murmured Mr Muscatine. 'No use making it more difficult than we have to, eh Roger?'

'What?'

'I mean, I hope you'll want the full funeral. No time to pinch pennies, now, is it? See, by rights I ought to remove your beloved father in a quiet, dignified way. I ought to prepare everything real tasteful: I'm talking a rosewood casket, rosewood on the outside over seam-welded stainless steel, silver-plated handles, you got a choice of linings, nylon or pleated silk. I'm talking a full set of casket clothes, nice English worsted suit, Italian shoes, quiet broadcloth shirt, underwear, socks and garters – he can either wear his own tie or we can provide one, got a nice one here with the message written sideways see, so you can read it when –'

'But –'

'Sure a lot of people think it's corny dressing them up in new clothes but I like to think of it as, well, like getting married. Only for sure you only do it once.'

'Well I –'

'Because see our full package includes everything, floral arrangements, music, enhancement of the appearance, watertight vault, plot in a good location, everything right down to a quality deodorant –'

'Well see, I'm not sure how much money we have. Ma's too upset right now to –'

'Then let's not worry her, eh? Eh? Way I see it, if you really love someone, you just naturally want them to have the very best. Quality, solid comfort, that's our motto at

MFH.' Seeing Roderick scratching his head, he went on quickly, 'Think of it this way. All his life that sweet old man worked hard to provide something for you and your Ma. Quality of life. Now don't you think he deserves a little quality of life himself?'

'Sure only –'

'Of course you *could* get the Economy job, sure. We *could* come in and drag Pa out of here just the way he is, puke down his pyjamas, neighbours watching his limbs flop around, staring at his dirty toe-nails, how would you like that? Then we squirt in our cheapest embalming fluid, cram his belly full of low-grade cavity filler, pop him in a thin plastic coffin and just dump him in a hole in the corner of the graveyard where it's all overrun with weeds and crab-grass, ground's alive with wood lice ... but ask yourself: is it really worth it? Saving a few lousy bucks, is it really...?'

Father O'Bride sounded upset. 'What do you mean, say a few words? Am I supposed to be a toastmaster or something?'

'No but Father, I just thought you could –'

'Nuts. Nuts! Look the poor crud wasn't even Catholic, first of all. You don't need a priest. Get a minister, maybe the guy over at that new motel church, yeah? The Little Olde Church O' Th' Interstate, yeah?'

'But Father, I just thought, maybe he had like a baptism of desire or –'

'Great, kid. Terrific thought there. You know it's never too late with God, you can get sent into the game in the last minute of the last quarter and still score ... Listen, I'll try to fit him into my prayers, okay? I'm pencilling him in on the roster right now, okay? Now how about getting off the line, I'm expecting a top-priority call from Thailand.'

'Yes, but couldn't Father Warren maybe –?'

'Father Warren is sick. Goodbye.'

The long hands, now bulged about with tape and gauze like a boxer's weapons, rummaged through old xerox copies of *Philosophy* and *Proceedings of the Aristotelian Society*. At times he would stop, outwardly appearing to rest or perhaps to try to remember what he was looking for. But inwardly the wheels never stopped, never slowed.

Zeno would say it was impossible, motion. For before a wheel can make a full revolution, it must make a half-revolution, before that a fourth, before that an eighth, before that a sixteenth ... faced with an infinity of infinitesimal movements before it can move at all, the wheel gives up.

Father Warren sighed. How easy *now* to smile at Zeno's simple paradoxes! *Now* with the two-handed engine at the door, waiting to crack the very hinges of the universe!

Mrs Feeney opened the door a crack. 'Won't you eat anything, Father? Just, even a glass of milk?'

He waved a lump of bandage. 'Too busy, too busy here.' Milk! To build bones, no doubt. As if that were any kind of solution but a calcium solution, calcium being a metal sure, but can these metal bones live? Let her answer that, yes or no. He lifted the glass, praying inwardly:

'Father if it be Thy will, let this cup pass away, but if it be not Thy will, then let me take this cup and throw the dice therein.' He felt a sudden coldness within, and saw the glass was now empty. 'For Thou playest not dice with the universe,' and even Pascal said it was a safe bet. So give the wheel its turn, and roll the bones.

But what did Luke say? Not Luke, Lucas, Lucas ... something about Gödel's paradox was it, where ... The hands pawed wildly for a moment – or an hour – was he looking for Gödel or J. R. Lucas, now, 'On Not Worshipping Facts' was it? But the article is a fact itself, is that a para ... here, here now to get it down once for all time. Holding the pen awkwardly, he began:

Gödel's paradox shows that within any mathematical system it is possible to write formulae representing statements outside the system. Then if a certain formula is true, its corresponding meta-mathematical statement is true, and vice versa. Moreover

Moreover what? Gödel equals GOD + EL, stop it, stop it!

Moreover one can write a formula Z corresponding to the meta-mathematical statement: 'The formula Z is unprovable in the system.' If the system proves Z, Z is true and therefore the statement is true, making Z unprovable: a contradiction. Therefore the system cannot prove Z, so the statement is true. But that means that Z is true, but unprovable in the system.

Thus for every mathematical system (without internal inconsistencies) there must be one formula which is true but unprovable.

Lucas goes on to show that all machines are mathematical systems of this kind, since all of their operations can be written into formulae. Thus for every –

'Father, did you want anything else, a sandwi –?'

'GO AWAY DAMN YOU DAMN YOU GO AWAY!' Damned interfering old biddy sticking her nose in the door just when he was getting to the, where, where was it, yes:

Thus for every machine there must likewise be a formula Z representing the metamachine statement: 'The formula Z cannot be proved in the machine.' In other words, there is one thing the machine cannot do. This reduces the mind-machine debate to a simple contest: The mechanist first presents Lucas with a machine proposed as a model of the mind. Lucas then points out something the mind can do but the machine cannot (prove Z). The mechanist can now alter the machine so it can handle Z, but then it is a different machine. There is now a different unprovable formula Y to baffle it. And so on. The contest continues until the mechanist either produces a machine for which there is no unprovable formula at all – which he can never do – or admits defeat. The mind must win.

Father Warren paused a moment, then added: HA HA HA HA HA!

But –

But what if the machine could alter itself? What if every time Lucas pointed out a gap in the machine mind, the machine simply plugged it? What if the machine could learn and change? So that it begins by saying 'Gee Father I don't know...' and before you know it, it's inside your head yes inside your head, twisting the controls, stop it, stop it!

Lucas's bright paradox began to look tarnished already, like Zeno's whirligig, only an amusement, a game the game position – *stop it!* – only a trivial, a puppy chasing its tail, that was it, a puppy chasing its own, but if, but what if...?

He looked up, but there was no one at the door.

But what if the machine caught up with Lucas, what if it surpassed him and turned the tables? What if it began setting formulae Lucas could not prove, what then? *Write*, he commanded his hand. *Anything, write.* And after a moment the hand moved, writing A.M.D.G., A.M.D.G., faster and faster, trailing a glory of gauze:

A.M.D.G., They have pierced my hands and my feet they have numbered numbered all my bones I believe in God the Fact the

And he saw the whirling puppy snap up its tail, then its hind legs, front legs collar and head snapping up its tail and so on, damn him, and so on!

'Now, you good sisters been doing a darn good job here,' said Father O'Bride. He stood with one shoe up on the desk, scraping mud from his cleats. Points of light glancing from his 30-function sports watch danced in the corners of the office behind Sister Filomena, who stood with downcast eyes. 'As I see it, you gave that Wood kid every chance. Every chance. Not your fault if he fumbles instead of running with the ball, is it? Nope. And boy does he fumble! Let's just run over his track record, okay?' He swaggered to the little portable blackboard and erased a football diagram. Then he stood, one fist on the hip of his SHAM OCKS uniform (from which the erroneous C had been removed), the other hand flicking and catching a piece of chalk as though it were a decision coin. Finally he wrote *1*.

'*One*,' he said. '*Discipline*. The little creep fouled up Sister Olaf's religion class, but good! Then *I* tried to have a man-to-man rap with him, where did I get? Zilchtown, that's where. Kid's not even in the same ballgame, can you dig that?'

'Yes Father. We —'

'So I says to myself fine, okay, I'll bench him a while, give him a couple hard workouts with Father Warren, he'll come around. Only what happens? Father Warren hits into the rough and stays there! And that's what hurts. Sister, that's what really hurts. I see him sitting there day after day, busting his ... his brains over these dumb games – how to read a robot's mind, crud you wouldn't believe, a book called *The*

Soul of the Robot, another one *Computer Worship* – and all the time his faith is just winding down, winding down ... That really makes me sick, you know? I want to reach out a hand and – by the way, you see his hands? I got Doc Sam to look at him, he says it's just some local infection, clear up in a minute if he could only stop scratching – but like I said I want to reach out to him, help him, only he won't help himself! Like yesterday I took him my rowing machine, figured if he won't come outa the study at least he could get in a little workout, you know what happened? He went all to pieces, started moaning how it wasn't fair, I couldn't show him the instruments of torture until I at least asked the question! Instruments of torture! My old rowing machine!'

'Yes, yes Father.'

'That ain't the worst end of it.' He wrote *2*, hesitated and added *3*. 'He hasn't said Mass for two weeks, that's what hurts. That's what really hurts, Sister. I have to take morning Mass every day and six times on Sunday, double confessions every Saturday – when am I supposed to get down to my own darn commitments? I got no time for the team, no time for planning, firming up dates for the league play-offs, nothing! Not to mention a few business commitments, sure I could scratch them *now* but then *next* season how do we get a deal on uniforms? Same with the devotional items, how else we gonna build the new stadium?'

Sister Filomena said nothing, but he seemed to feel her silence as criticism.

'Sure, okay I spend a lot of time on these things, yeah and a lot of time at the country club too, but Sister, it's all an investment. It'll pay off for the school, the kids, everybody! Only now ... and all because of one rotten kid, it makes me sick.'

'Father Warren's sick too,' she reminded him. 'And I think we ought to do something about him. I think he needs hospital care.'

'Hospital? Oh no you don't. I'm not having our record dragged in the mud like that, not when I'm *that* close to Monsignor. All we gotta do is play it cool and hang in there, this place'll be a Deanery next Fall. Isn't that what we all want? The Deanery of Holy Trinity? Or do we want it to be known as "Holy Trinity, yeah, where that priest went bananas." Besides, he's not that bad. He's just, it's just that kid, having that kid around. Get rid of him, and Father Warren will be —'

'I was thinking of the scandal, Father. I suppose you know already Mrs Feeney thinks he's a saint, and she's not the only one, half the older women in the parish are saying he's got the stigmata, the sacred wounds —'

'Hey!' Father O'Bride didn't look at all distressed. 'They could be right, you know? Who are we to —'

'Father!'

'Yeah okay but it's worth thinking about. Now about this kid. I want him out of our hair now. Right away.'

'Expulsion?'

'Nope, too messy, too many explanations. Look, since he's a smart kid, why don't we just graduate him? Yeah? That's it, we'll graduate him!'

Sister Filomena cleared her throat. 'I ought to remind you, Father, that while I respect your opinion, I am the principal of this school. We can't just —'

'If we don't,' he said, 'we're all washed up. You, me, the school, the good sisters, and especially Father Warren. Whole team.'

'I see,' she said, after a moment.

'Great. Terrific. Now you just jog on and fill out a diploma for the kid, hand it to him when he comes in, and that's that. Okay? I gotta coupla phone calls to make...'

'. . . him being an inventor and all,' Mr Muscatine finished. Roderick was staring out of the window. The rain outside the mourners' car fell in sheets (as he knew it always did at funerals), probably flattening the young oats, and certainly cancelling the big game against the St Theresa Terrors. Over the hiss of tyres, the squeak of windshield wipers and the taped sounds of Sereno Benito's Strings, it was hard to make out what the little funeral director was rambling on about. 'No charge of course.'

Ma wasn't listening, either. She stared out at (or past) bill-boards advertising Quebec beer, Finnish toilet paper and Turkish cars, and she kept humming that same aimless tune from the Bow-wow Symphony. Probably still couldn't realize that Pa was dead. He turned to the window again. A rainbow ran with them briefly, the end of it ploughing across Howdy Doody Lake and then apparently dropping back to linger at the new Welby–Bangfield Corporation property develop-ment.

Wally Muscatine carried on. 'My nephew Cliff knocked it together. You know, a bright boy like that gets itchy just setting around all day out there at the junkyard. Has to keep busy, see? So anyway I just thought we'd give it a little run today, see how she goes. Like to think your Pa would want Cliff to have his chance.'

Ma looked around. 'What was that, Mr Muscatine?'

'Oh just telling the boy here about my new set of pall-bearers. Fully automatic,' he said, winking. 'Patent Applied For.'

'Patent –?'

'Hope we get some sun, though. Brought the old camera along, thought we might get a publicity shot or so. Like to help young Cliff along.'

The humming commenced again.

* * *

Ma had been acting strangely – even for Ma – since the night of the raid. Roderick had expected tears for Pa, anger at the stupid million-dollar gas bill, anything but this quiet smile, this constant humming. Every now and then she'd wander into Pa's workshop and rattle some tools, as though looking for something. At other times she seemed to think Pa was only upstairs, lying down after dinner.

'Bless his heart, he will overeat,' she'd said yesterday. 'Chicken and dumplings, chicken and dumplings. Do you know, he likes them so much, I've cooked them three times a day for the past forty-odd years?'

'Ma, listen.'

'To what?'

'To me. Listen, Pa is not upstairs lying down. He's dead.'

'Pshaw!' she said, spelling out the unpronounceable word. 'He's no more dead than – than I don't know who – than John Keats!'

'But he's –'

'Oh sure his heart aches and a drowsy numbness pains his senses as though of hemlock he had drunk, maybe, but that's not *dead*. Why, every time you read John Keats he comes to life and speaks, didn't you know that? Son, you've got a lot to learn.'

'Well gee sure Ma, but . . .' But it was no use arguing. He had to go along with the whole charade, pretending to wonder what new invention Pa was working on today; setting out Pa's plate at the dinner-table (though now that Pa was there only in spirit, Roderick noticed that the old man seemed weary of chicken and dumplings, preferring instead Ma's vegetarian diet); watching Ma go out for her solitary night-time rambles.

'Now you stay home, just in case your Pa needs anything upstairs. I won't be long, just getting some ether I mean air.' And off she'd go, carrying with her some memento: a pair of old earphones, a soldering iron.

The seance was even worse.

'Now you just sit down there,' she said, 'by the African violets, and I'll sit here in Pa's chair. And for Pete's sake, try to get into the correct frame of mind, I don't want the astral waves all cluttered up with sceptical static.'

('Saw 'em through the window,' Miss Violetta Stubbs would say later. 'Her and that black man sitting practically in the dark, holding hands and I don't know what else!')

But how could he get into the correct frame of mind? The whole game seemed so pathetic, with Ma asking herself questions and then kicking the table leg once for yes twice for no . . . and not even really acting as if she believed it herself:

'Is there anybody there?' she called out, adding with a chuckle, 'said Walter de la Mare. "Mr Sludge, stop clowning!" said Robert Browning.' How could she quote her own wretched doggerel at a time like this, and then swing to the other extreme, sighing and sobbing as she rapped away? It made no more sense than the message she finally came up with when, inevitably they got around to automatic writing. The planchette looped and jogged madly under their fingertips, and it was clear to Roderick that Ma was doing it all. The final result began: 'deaear son, remind your ma thathat i punoqun md poow sdn hpouow wyo-11 . . .'

'Maybe it's one of his funny ciphers,' Ma suggested. 'Keep it and work on it.'

'Oh sure,' he said, crumpling it into his pocket. 'A cipher.'

All the same, he kept it and worked on it, if only to stop worrying about Ma.

The rain had stopped too soon, to the delight of Wally Muscatine. He set up his camera while the others (Roderick, Mr Swann, Ma and Miss Violetta Stubbs) lined up next to a hole in the ground. No one knew exactly why Miss Stubbs was here; it was said she came to all the funerals, if only for a ride out into the country. But here she was, smiling down into the oblong hole and saying, 'Looks like a nice day after all. Nice.'

Mr Swann nodded, which prompted her to say, 'Nice of Mr Muscatine to demonstrate his new Patent Applied For, isn't it? And for no charge, I do believe. Very nice.'

They waited. At some distance, the machine was backed up to the hearse – or anyway the hearse was backed up to some kind of big tent made of tarpaulins – and something was almost going on. Cliff kept going into the tent and hammering on steel. Each time he reappeared they all craned hopefully, but it seemed always to be another false alarm; Cliff would grab an oil-can or a wrench and disappear again. With the tombstones, they waited.

At last there was a report, a flash of blue smoke, and a different knocking sound (as though a giant chain-saw had bitten into something indigestible). The tent began to lurch.

Ma looked apprehensive. 'I suppose that thing's *safe*?' she shouted over the noise.

Wally winked. 'No complaints so far!' and shouted to Cliff to drop the tarps.

Finally the tent collapsed, taking Cliff down with it, but unveiling – Them. Six tall, gleaming figures in stovepipe hats, hoisting between them an insignificant little coffin, and marching in perfect step towards the grave.

'Very nice,' gasped Miss Stubbs.

One of the hats backfired. By now they were close enough for Roderick to see that they were real stovepipes, and that their wearers seemed to be made of every kind of junk: he saw a breadbin head, shoulders made from a sewing-machine, arms of beercans and legs of steel rails. And as they suddenly clanged into a tombstone and veered off in a new direction, he noticed something else, something eerie. There was his own childhood skull! now part of a buttock.

The six giant pall-bearers were really part of a single machine, for on each side three legs moved in step, driven by one great driving-rod. Patent Applied For was making poor progress now. It kept ramming tombstones, stopping, turning and marking time – with feet so heavy they sank into the wet earth.

'Turn 'em, Cliff, turn 'em! They're gettin' outa frame!' Mr Muscatine waved his arms, Cliff fiddled with his model-airplane transmitter, and slowly Patent Applied For stumbled towards its destination.

'At last,' said Mr Muscatine, sighing. 'Now tell 'em to stop, Cliff. Cliff? CLIFF!' But They continued their clanking march to the edge of the grave and off it, the first pall-bearers striding on air for a second before the clay walls collapsed under those behind them. And then the whole contraption pitched into the hole, groaning and spluttering, its twelve legs kicking out

295

to bring down the wet clay walls, until almost everything was buried except Pa. 'Suffering cats!'

When the machine stopped, Mr Muscatine looked around the cemetery. Turf was up, floral arrangements scattered and trampled, lasting monuments chipped and cracked, a haze of blue smoke hanging over a grave containing two tons of perverse scrap metal, and the coffin – scarred rosewood, bent silver handles – still lying in the grass awaiting burial.

'Well, Cliff,' he said. 'You had your chance. You sure had your chance.'

While they waited for the grave-digging machines to make a new resting-place, Mr Swann got out his briefcase.

'We might as well get right down to it,' he said. 'Plenty to get through here, quite a nice little financial mess. He'd already cashed his insurance, understand he owes the doctor – I was kinda surprised at this elaborate funeral, all this waste just when – but I guess that's your business, Ma. But I mean two uninsured mortgages plus all this electronic stuff – I got nothing against hobbies but there's a limit – anyway too bad you don't have a car to repossess I mean sell. Naturally the house goes back to the Bangfield Trust Bank – there now, there now ... maybe you want to sit down?'

Ma staggered and leaned on Roderick's arm for support. The three of them sat in the grass, dangling their legs into the grave of Patent Applied For.

'Not all that bad,' said Mr Swann. 'Course we gotta fight. Hold off the IRS boys while we try a little debt consolidation, then –'

'Wait a minute,' said Roderick. 'If Pa didn't have any money, how could there be tax –?'

'Technically intestate, yes, indigent too only he purchased this electronic stuff as a corporation see? Tax shelter I set up for him, so he could write it all off as depreciable stock using the Class Life – well how did I know he'd up and croak on us? Now the stuff has to be inventoried and sold, taxed as corporate profits sure, but the other stockholders want to liquidate and cut their losses.'

'Other stockholders?' Roderick asked. 'Who?'

'Me, my wife and kids.' Swann licked his thumb and began dealing papers out on the grass. 'I feel we can work all this out by consolidating these debts, re-negotiate at a more favourable rate of interest. Should come out to something like a hundred and eighty-five thou, excluding the usual – but listen, all we have to do is, Ma, you listening? All we have to do is your Roderick here forms a finance company, takes over the whole debt and then discounts pieces of it to a few banks –'

Roderick stared down into the grave. 'But you said I'm not a person in law, how can I –?'

'But your company *is* a person in law, see? So it doesn't matter what you yourself are as long as you're not a crook or a bankrupt. But what I was just getting to, you got terrific collateral, very expensive electronic gadget in perfect working order – yourself. Assuming you got a clear title, of course. I already filed a writ of *habeas* for you there, no problem, some of the legal technicalities might cost a little, sure, but we can cover that by suing Welby.'

'Doctor Welby?' Ma looked faint again. 'Sue him – for what?'

'Never mind, once we start digging we're bound to come up with something. Went around saying Pa was healthy a few days before he became a decedent, didn't he? There you are, breach of patient privacy, mis-diagnosis – we'll pick up *half a million* there, easy. Then we sue Muscatine here. I can see his gadget caused you a total breakdown – but Welby's the real mother lode. Let his receptionist sign the death certificate, looks like, got the name and cause of death in the wrong places – *half a million*, believe me.'

Roderick looked up. 'But wouldn't that cover our debts?'

'No, barely covers costs in your claim for title, see, first we gotta file this writ of *habeas* to keep anybody else like this Kratt Industries from slapping a claim on you, then we gotta go through one of these procedures I outlined before, what we want is a clear title over your body ... this has to take time ... costs ... but when you own your body you can sell it like any other chattel, see, borrow money on it, anything...'

297

Roderick stopped listening to stare down at his childhood skull. Inside that hollow piece of tin, I was.

Miss Violetta Stubbs did not wait to take off her hat when she got home. She went straight to the crocheted doll covering her telephone, removed it, and punched a number.

'Doreen? Listen I was just at the funeral, Pa Wood you know ... the Guild? No wait listen, *she* was flirting with this *black man* right there in front of everybody! Leaning on his arm! Listen they sat right down and stuck their feet right in the ga-*rave*! And that ... yes but listen, that's not all. If I hadn't heard it myself I wouldn't believe it either, but there they were, bold as brass, with a lawyer, talking about cutting up half a million dollars! Half a ... and poor Pa not even covered up with earth yet – oh yes, and there's something very wrong with the death certificate! Well I can put two and two togeth ... wouldn't put it past her, would you?

'Now this Guild thing, I'm sorry but it looks like they've sent us the wrong speaker ... yes *again* ... I don't know ... must be something wrong with their computer ... No listen, I wanted the Reverend Capon just as much as you dear ... But listen, we can have Positive Breathing *next* month then, we'll just have to put up ... I say we'll just have to put up with this, this Miz Indica Dinks, who*ever* she is, she's going to speak on *something* called Machines Liberation ... neither do I, but I certainly don't intend to just sit home tomorrow night, do you? And so what if she *is* a Communist we can always just walk out and leave her cold ... Doreen, I wouldn't miss it for the world.'

That night when Ma went out for her walk, Roderick followed. At first they headed for Main Street, past the post office, the Courthouse, Simms's Do-It-Ur-Self, the Idle Hour (where a few men lounging on car bumpers drinking beer gave him hard looks) and the place that had once been Selma's Beautee Salon but was now called HAIR TODAY. But then Ma turned off by the library, headed down Church Street and straight on out of town. Was she lost? Or just nuts? Because there was nothing out this way, not even lights. Just the darkness and the gravel road leading out to Howdy Doody Lake.

Roderick didn't like it. If he dropped back too far, she might turn off somewhere and disappear. If he kept too close, she might hear his footsteps on gravel. There didn't seem to be any distance at all between too close and too far, and he could think of only two other answers: go home, or catch up with her and pretend it was just a coincidental meeting. ('Hello Ma. Pa told me he didn't want anything upstairs, said I should get out and get some fresh air like you. Funny we both decided to go this way, ain't it? Odds against it must be, let's see ... Well sure I know *most* robots don't need fresh air, guess I must be different...')

Ma wouldn't want company. In fact she was acting kind of *stealthy*, walking too quietly on the gravel, stopping every now and then (to listen?). Like an international spy on his way to the hollow tree. Was she meeting someone? Was she, was she ... but spies made him think of the cipher in his pocket, and that made him think of Pa, Pa and this miserable little old woman hobbling along in her bare feet in the middle of the night.

A penance, that was more like it. Offered up to reduce Pa's days in Purgatory, his time off for her good behaviour. She must love him a lot.

Or maybe she hated him a lot. Sure it was her cooking that used up that million dollars' worth of gas, caused Pa to take one look at the bill and keel over. Probably she felt relieved ('So much for chickens and damn dumplings!') and probably that made her feel guilty. Walking it off, trying to walk it off, not knowing it really came from her unhappy childhood, those early traumas causing horizontal cracks in the ego structure for which she could never forgive her father, hence Pa, hence herself. And even now unconsciously she was humming that tune: 'Take me to the river, deliver me to the lake...'

Well suicides are stealthy. Roderick resisted the impulse to rush forward and stop her, before the cathartic moment when – but holy mackerel, didn't she know it was a *sin*? St Augustine said if you were a pure, innocent person suicide was twice as bad because then you were guilty of murdering a pure, innocent person – something wrong with that maybe but sin was sin. And even if John Donne thought that suicide was no self-murder, that Jesus Christ had killed himself on the Cross by just taking a breath and blowing out his soul (but then how did he get it back three days later?), sin was sin.

Unless maybe Ma was thinking of a *literary* suicide! But then why pick this lake? It was so shallow that any man could be an island, and its history was no deeper than its dirty waters. Even the name sounded like reconstituted orange juice, who wanted to drown in Howdy Doody, that's just asking for obscurity. Unless maybe she wanted to make a protest: life is shallow, art is shallower . . . poop on the world!

A protest, though, might be a real protest about the real world, a focus for the historical perspective, sure because look at greedy capitalist *entrepreneurs* like Welby and Bangfield, putting up their so-called leisure complex right on the shores of good old Howdy Doody Lake. There once silvery fish leapt, jewel-bright dragonflies hovered near a silent canoe in which a lean red man glided o'er the glassy waters to claim his bride; they would live simply, in peace with Brother Nature.

Okay, okay it was an artificial lake only about fifty years old, but same principle – once the horny-handed farmer sat down on these shores to eat his lunch, feeling the good warm earth and smelling the clean wind – then along came lakeside cottages and water-skiers and the Welby–Bangfield Leisure Complex, profit heaped on profit, fat men in silk hats and striped pants puffing their cigars and laughing themselves sick at the idea of poor honest men standing in breadlines in cities where the buildings were heaped up like piles of gold – but one day the gold would trickle away into the dust, the cities tumble down, the silk hats rot as tatters of striped pants flapped in a new wind of change, as the expropriators got expropriated to pieces. Only that didn't sound much like Ma either. Probably she just wanted to join Pa.

'Will you join me?' 'Why, are you coming apart?' But on the astral plane nothing ever came apart, nothing was lost. Death was just people getting temporarily misplaced – open the right drawer and there they are! Yes Ma half-believed that stuff, with all the paradoxes: life is death, all is one, up is down, yes means no. If you don't know whether you're a man dreaming you're a butterfly or a butterfly dreaming you're a man, swat the butterfly. For all is one and one is nothing, and you can be the person who killed the person who killed the person who...

Lightning flickered somewhere, and Roderick saw Ma standing by the lake, stooping to pick up something. She seemed to be wearing some kind of cone on her head. Of course! If up was down and day was night, good was evil and this was witchcraft!

He found it hard to believe even when she'd built the fire and begun the incantation: 'Alcatraz! Mulligatawn! Tapeworm!...'

What a let-down. He'd seen hundreds of old witch movies on TV, every single one a let-down. Probably now she was going to strip off her clothes and dance around the fire, and then screw some giant goat out of the sky or something, then there'd be plenty of thunder and lightning, screaming and flames and that would be that.

A scratchy old record started up: The Bow-wow Symphony. Ma left the circle of firelight, and he could hear her calling down the beach: 'Hurry up, the rain's starting...'

Suddenly there was a distant bang, a flash of blue flame, and the unmistakable clatter of Patent Applied For. Then the rain came down and Roderick could no longer be sure what he saw or heard, an electric arc or was it lightning, a man's scream or was it the scratchy record, Ma shouting not to forget the candy while lightning danced on six stovepipe hats while Roderick tried to run for the shelter of the trees but crashed into another running figure as blinding lightning struck again and he fell into perfect darkness.

22

'... a bad dream?' said Ma. 'Your batteries must be low...'

'Sure, from the long walk. But how did I get home?'

She pretended not to hear. 'Feel like going to school today?'

'And what was Cliff doing out there with his Patent Applied For?'

'... all a bad dream, son.'

Roderick held up a scrap of wet cloth. 'Yeah but when I woke up I found this in my fist, did I dream this? Look there's writing on it.'

'Did I dream this?'

'Well yes, in a way. I do believe this is a genuine *apport*, son.'

'Apport?'

'A psychic deposit of physical evidence. It was your dream that made it appear, made it pass right through the walls of your room!'

'Looks familiar only –'

She snatched it away. 'I'll just mail it right off to the Society for Psychical Research, they'll be *very* interested.'

'But Ma, *I*'m interested, I –'

'Why don't you stay in bed this morning, school can wait. Oh, and you could work on that psychic message your Pa sent you through the planchette.'

He took her advice, if only to keep an eye on her. Besides, the cipher – if it was a cipher – might hold some indirect clue to Ma's – madness? He smoothed it out on the bedclothes and opened his notebook to a clean page.

deaear son,
　　remind your ma thathat
  i punoqun md
　　poow sdn hpouow wyo-ll
　　uooms-oudhy opun uoos
　　suoquoq ydsoyd-hxo
 ii «xod hw dn dow op spns dosshy»
　　uwhy wny (8 sndo) huoydwhs
　　«mom-moq» punos puod uo hpoq
　　honq xoq opun spoom hpoop
　　hpmoy hpoq hw dwnp noh
iii qow unys + punoq-oudhy hwwnw
　　qwnu wnssod mou os (ydhs)
　　dnos u! poom d

At noon, when he closed the notebook, there were no more
clean pages, and no solution. His best so far was a single line:

　　　　hpmoy hpoq hw dwnp noh
　　　　threw   then   to   gosh   set

'Take a look at this.' One liver-spotted hand passed the
binoculars to another.

It was just possible to make out a tiny group of people
standing outside the fence with signs.

'What do they want?'

'Would you believe they're Luddites?'

'No I would not. Is that what security –?'

'Precisely. Haven't you seen the book? By this guy, what's
his name now, Hank Dinks, called *Ludd Be Praised*; turning
into quite a cult item there.'

'Ha ha, is it now? Think my daughter's reading it now
that you mention ... but what's the premiss?'

'Crank stuff. Back to Nature, more or less, but with the
emphasis on ol' devil computer. Might know they'd get
around to us – though I'm surprised they can't muster more

people for such an obviously populist cause. Can't be twenty souls out there.'

'The sun, you forget the sun. And we are a good way from Phoenix. If it weren't for the sun, you know, I'd be tempted to stroll out and have a chat with them.'

'Ah but security's against it. Usual overcaution. I swear, sometimes I think they'd like to put all of us in Leo's tank, seal us off from the rude world ... oh wouldn't they all be upset out there if they knew about Leo!'

'Ha ha, wouldn't they ... be more like twenty thousand out there then, eh? But what, ah, what do they actually accuse us of doing? Running a clandestine computer?'

'Better than that! Listen, they think we're running robots! Us!'

After a few dry chuckles and coughs, the binoculars changed hands again. 'Still, too bad they associate us with robots in any way. I don't like it.'

'Nobody likes it. The Agency certainly doesn't like it. But ...'

'These little movements blow over, I suppose.'

'Precisely. Precisely. Even if they don't, we might ...'

'Use them? Exactly. Exactly. By the way, how's that Nebraska business shaping up?'

'No problem, as our Agency friends like to say. We have a clear set of pictures of the subject, front and profile, we have a voice print, we know exactly where to find him.'

'Is he passing?'

'More or less. At the moment he's trying to pass as a black man.'

'Fascinating! I wonder if we couldn't study him for a while before –?'

'Too risky, look what happened to our last surveillance team, that highly unlikely "accident". Point oh oh oh oh seven at best, makes you wonder ... No in fact I've already ordered the destruction for this evening.'

'Oh well. Fun while it lasted. Better than this Kratt Industries business, that's just boring. Pinball machines, talking gingerbread, automated concubines – low-grade stuff, all of it.'

'Precisely what we have to encourage, my friend. Our job, after all, is to –'

'I know, I know. To keep the world on the graph paper. Only sometimes don't you feel, just a little like letting it, letting it slip?'

But the other elder was squinting through the glasses again. 'I can just make out a sign – Oh listen to this! STOP ROBOTS. STOP POLLUTING THOUGHT WAVES.'

'Fascinating!'

'Fixed up like a minstrel today, are we? Well never mind, have your last little joke, because this is your last day. Here.' Sister Filomena shoved a piece of paper at him.

'What's this, Sister, I – listen I –'

'Walking papers, *Mister* Wood, walking papers. Your diploma. You are now officially graduated, so goodbye.' She went back into her office and closed the door.

A.M.O.G.
KNOW ALL MEN BY THESE PRESENTS THAT
RODERICK WOOD
having satisfactorily completed the Eighth Grape at
HOLY THINITY SCHOOL
in the Year of Our Lord McM_____
is hereby awarded this
OIPLOMA OF SCHOLASTIC ACHIEVEMENT
(signed) Sr. M. Filomena, Principal

Printed in Taiwan

Father O'Bride put his head in at the door, without removing his fishing hat. 'Hiya Sister, didn't I see a new pupil come along here just now?'

'New pupil?'

'Yeah yeah, I was in my office cutting up one of Father Warren's old cassocks, boy you wouldn't believe how many relics you can get out of eleven yards of material, boy I got a hundred and fifty thousand little pieces so far not even half done I mean even at a buck apiece we can't go wrong there, bandages for five – yeah I meant to ask you, any sign of that blood transfusion unit I ordered?'

'What? Blood, Father, is Father Warren –?'

'No prob, no sweat, just forgot to tell you I ordered this neat little unit, figured we could cycle a few pints right through him put it in these little plastic phials one drop each and – well don't look at me like that, Sister, criminy! Not as if we're taking anything away from him, he'll still have blood of his own only we add a pint and drain off a – look, people hear about a stigmata first darn thing they want is a drop of the precious – okay never mind! Just tell me where I can contact this kid, one with the muscles. The natural.'

'Natural? Father I don't think –'

'Natural, natural athlete, heck all these boogie kids are naturals. Point is this guy could make all the difference on the gridiron next season against St Larry's – damn it I mean darn it, where is he?'

'You must mean Roderick but he –'

'Yeah *Robert, where's Robert?*'

She waved, almost blessing him. 'Gone, Father. Home or –'

'Gone? Gone?' He vanished and she could hear him bawling in the hallway:

'ROBERT! Hey Robert, wait up!'

... his feet flapping down the stairs and hitting that miraculously shiny little patch of floor at the bottom ... then a cry ... a thump ...

Then blessèd silence.

'Somebody oughta teach that nigger a lesson, knocking Father Owhatsit down the stairs like that, leaving him all paralysed from the waist up was it? Or down? Just who does this Doc Sam think he ...'

'Oh it wasn't him, it was that other nigger one that's been living in sin with Ma Wood, Violetta saw them ... and anyway a man that wears a skirt and don't like girls ...'

'Jake told me the Wood boy's gone black, didn't he used to be paralysed himself? Bobby Wood, used to be so paralysed they had to wheel him around in a little tank or ...'

'Jake'll say anything, told me the kid was a two-headed robot, but listen before Doreen gets me under that drier and

I can't hear a thing, guess who asked Doc Sam to *examine* her the other day?'

'Robots, shit we got enough damn robots out at the factory, Jap robots, German robots, reckon the machines is taking over all right, makes you wonder who won the damn war...'

'Makes you wonder if these here Lewdites ain't got something there, least they know the difference between a man and a god-durned wheel, but listen, my old lady says some nigger robot stuck a knife in Father O'Bride...'

'Bob Wood? Yeah I heard that, same asshole knifed Father Warren a few months back ain't it? Sure it is, hell they get away with murder these days ... Not that I like Catlicks, only you let a bunch wild niggers run around with knives...'

'Machines is taking over, hell they even got machines' lib, no shit, my wife's going to the Ladies' Guild to hear one of 'em, makes you wonder who won ... three beers here, Charlie?'

'Trouble-maker from way back, remember when he was at the public school here, wrecked the damn computer, just went berserk and wrecked...'

'Somebody oughta wreck him, you know? Somebody oughta teach that little shit a lesson.'

'I blame his home background I mean what do you expect? I think I liked the other ones better dear, the uh pink frames with rhinestones? What do you expect? Ma and Pa Wood aren't exactly, well I mean they're communists for one thing, atheistic communists, dressing that kid of theirs up in that porno get-up for the Christmas play, no wonder he scared poor old Sister Martha to death ... only what do you expect, anybody sets a big *toilet* out in their yard, health hazard the sheriff had to break it up, we saw the whole thing! And Herb says *she* oughta be locked up. Do you think the rhinestones are too...?'

'Remember how she tried to poison Jake McIlvaney? Cookies with ground glass and I wouldn't be at all surprised if she was behind this gingerbread...'

'Oh she was, didn't you know? They had a big police raid there, the FBI took away all her ginger to test for poison too bad they didn't take her away at the same . . .'

'And she's been playing house with a black man ever since poor Pa, probably poisoned him too! And she's a witch, everybody knows . . .'

'Well the boy always was a trouble-maker, ask anybody, didn't his teacher Miz Beek commit sui . . . ?'

'Mrs Feeney says he's like he's got the devil in him, you know he actually stabbed one of the priests?'

'I blame his background. My Chauncey never would . . .'

'Well, somebody better teach him a lesson.'

Roderick was at the dining-table, covering page after page with cipher calculations. Ma paused to kiss the top of his head.

'That's a good boy. Now I'm just going out to the Guild, be back in time to give Pa his supper. But if he wants anything meanwhile will you stick around?'

'Sure, sure.' It wasn't polyalphabetic with a repeating key, it wasn't a multifid, it wasn't Playfair or a substitution followed by a grille transposition . . . was it even a cipher?

It had to be. Something in the world had to make sense. Ma would say it all did make sense, only you had to be on the astral plane to perceive it. Pa would say nothing made any sense at all, only we have to make our own sense out of it.

He gave up on the cipher and wandered into Pa's workshop. There was the radio, still faintly murmuring music for its own easy listenin' enjoyment. There was the box of inventions. There was the photo of Rex Reason, the cards handlettered by Miss Violetta Stubbs: 'OVER THE HILL doesn't mean DOWN AND OUT . . .'

The lettering was the same as on the piece of cloth. Sure, it was part of a hand-lettered tie: not *remember wit fun*, but

REMEMBER ME
WITH MUSCATINE
FUNERAL HOMES

printed sideways so the mourners could read it. Sure, so . . .

After a moment, Roderick took down the green key from its nail below Rex and left the house with it.

At twilight the giant letters SLUMBERTITE NEVER SLEEPS suddenly flared up like curious trees bursting into flame. The low slab of windowless factory supporting their neon splendour now seemed lower, less significant. The two tiny figures climbing out of their microscopic Rolls-Royce seemed nothing at all.

'God, I love this place, bub. Almost makes me wish I was a religious guy ... I don't know, if I ... if God ...' Mr Kratt recovered quickly. 'Come on, let's get inside, can't stand around with your finger up your rectum all evening.'

He strode off across the perfect lawn, leaving Ben behind. 'Come on, come on.'

'Yes sir. I was just, I was just thinking...'

'Too damn much thinking, your thinking got us into this mess, bub. Trouble with you artsy-fartsy academics, can't see anything clearly, everything's got too many sides to it. We had a good goddamn thing going there with Jinjur-Boy, only you had to go and spill your guts to the FDA the minute they came sniffing –'

'It wasn't like that at all, Mr Kratt I, all I said was –'

'Was enough! Mercury batteries, why the hell admit a thing like that, you know what it's gonna cost to fix this up? Hell of a lot more than you're worth. Thing gets this far you can't just grease a few palms you know. Gotta fix up a whole publicity campaign, pictures of a coupla senators and their kids eating the damn things, the works. And we gotta move fast before we get every hick consumer group in the country after us, look what they did to Buckingham cigarettes...'

'I never heard of them.'

'See what I mean? One minute they got fifty quacks on the payroll telling everybody how their natural blackstrap molasses-filter traps everything nasty, the next minute they're wiped out. Dead!'

'Dead,' said Ben faintly. 'But what do we do about these dead kids, eighteen of them now, eighteen...'

'Look, stop moaning, will you? Our lawyers are already fixing all that up with the families, get each of 'em to sign an affidavit their kids never ate our product in return for an *ex gratia* handout, hell, most of 'em never seen so much cash, no problem there ... no problem.'

'No but it's just that sometimes I think we, all we can do is create death. Even when we try to make life it comes out death, death is there all the time. In the program somewhere ... it's, I don't know, almost as if we brought a gingerbread boy to life and all he wanted was to die...'

'Goddamnit, pull yourself together, industrial accidental pollution, happens all the time! All the time, you can't get all personal about this, Jesus you think every oil company executive pisses his pants every time he hears a pollution story? I mean sure if you want to go on playing fancy academic games writing little titbits for the *Jackoff Journal* fine, only I thought you wanted to run a goddamn company!'

'Well I ... yes, I guess ... yessir I do.'

'Fine. Then goddamnit, bub, start running it. And for Christ's sake stop looking like a pall-bearer, give this Welby guy a big smile. Must be him waiting by the door.'

Ben Franklin managed a weak smile for Dr Welby while Kratt unlocked the plain steel door.

'Really an honour Mr Kratt, if you don't mind my saying so, been reading about you everywhere, newsletters, *Fortune* wasn't it? A profile yes, and weren't you named one of the top ten business lead –?'

'Only the top ten *new* leaders, Doc. Good to see you're well-informed though, because –'

'And to think, you coming all this way just to meet with a small-town sawbones like me!'

'Yes well I –'

'You sure must want something pretty bad, ha ha.'

They stopped, Kratt and Welby facing each other in the chill stainless steel corridor, almost squared away like a pair of hostile dogs, each determined somehow to mount the other. Welby's pale eyes (staring over the tops of his old-fashioned glasses) were locked in silent combat for a second with Kratt's dark little eyes (staring under the heavy V of brows).

'Doc,' Kratt said softly. 'Don't sell yourself short. If I didn't know you was a good businessman I wouldn't be trying to trade horses with you. Now come on let's see if we can find the damn board-room in this godforsaken place, think it's at the end of the corridor...'

He led the way into an impressive conference room panelled in something very like walnut. While Ben and the doctor took their seats at the long table, Kratt went to the liquor cabinet.

'See Doc, you're a man with foresight. You and I know Nebraska's gonna bring in gambling in a year or so, and we both know the considerable financial rewards to be reaped – by the right man in the right place. So can we talk?'

Dr Welby nodded at the broad back. 'Why sure. Hey this is some layout you got here, never knew there'd be a place like this right in the old Slum –'

Kratt laughed, or perhaps coughed. 'You know, no human being has been in this room for four years. Not even cleaners.'

'But it's spotless!'

'Machine-cleaned, every damn day. Best thing about machine-cleaners is they don't drink up the chairman's booze – got some fifty-year-old Scotch here, Doc. What's your pleasure?'

Dr Welby didn't mind if he did.

The big German Shepherd snarled and threw himself against the fence, daring Roderick to try – just *try* – opening the gate and setting one foot on Slumbertite land. But when Roderick did open the gate and walk in, the dog only sniffed his hand and then trotted away to seek some other victim.

A long curved driveway led to the great factory. And just so there should be no mistake, a series of 'landing lights' flickered along it, pointing his way. And just to make absolutely sure there should be no mistake, a recorded voice spoke to him: 'Keep to the driveway and don't loiter. Please follow the lights.'

The driveway took him right up to the plain grey corrugated wall, which at first seemed to lack a door, even a keyhole. Only when he was close did a door slide open.

'Step inside, please. Prepare for a security check. Prepare for a security check.'

He stepped inside and stood around, until a voice said: 'Empty your pockets on the conveyor belt. Now. Everything

311

will be returned to you when you leave the building.' Pa's cipher and the green key; a quarter and two nickels; a piece of string and a grubby stick of gum; half a yoyo, a broken rosary and the little folded wad of paper that was his 'oiploma'; a rosary bead and a lead washer moved out of sight.

'Face the light-panel. Answer the questions yes or no by pushing the yes or no button. QUESTION: Are you carrying or concealing any tool or weapon?' No. 'Are you carrying or concealing any explosive or inflammable material, such as gasoline, TNT, butane?' No. 'Are you carrying or concealing any electronic equipment, such as an artificial arm or leg?' Yes. 'Walk through the light-panel. Now.'

He pushed open the panel and entered the Emerald City.

It was bigger and greener than even the cemetery. That pure blue-grass colour lay over the floor, what he could see of the distant walls, and over every one of the 'elephants'. They did look like elephants, turning and twisting their trunks to get at the things on the assembly-lines, twisting back to pick up screws or paint-sprayers or sandpaper or clothes. A hundred green elephants? A thousand? He couldn't tell, not without strolling down the yellow painted road and counting – and for the moment, he preferred to stay where he was, listening.

There were no more recorded voices, only a bouncy kind of music from invisible violins. While Roderick stood transfixed, they finished 'Sunshine Balloon' and began 'Oh, You Beautiful Doll'. Just in front of him, a row of beautiful dolls' heads were being crowned with hair: a blonde, a brunette, a redhead, a blonde, a brunette ... he decided to follow the dames.

After the hair-elephant came the elephant eye-lash curler, a twist of the trunk, while another trunk sorted out a pair of matching earrings and prepared to clamp them on, another with a fine brush was poised to finish the make-up (sprayed on earlier) before the heads reached the test station where trunks probed with electrodes to raise a smile, a blink, a wink. Next came a junction where a gang of assembly Dumbos worked furiously with bolts, pliers, soldering irons, fixing each head to an armless grey torso. Following the new line he watched shapely arms appear (each hand holding its nails

312

apart to dry; left wrists receiving watches) to be fastened on, before the entire assembly was bolted firmly to a metal frame bolted in turn to one side of a coffin-sized formica box then equipped with fake drawer-handles and finally (just as the torso-women were being stitched into their clothes) a sign: RECEPTIONIST.

Roderick watched a final test, a torso-woman lifting an imaginary phone and saying, 'I'll *tell* him you're *here*, Mr – was that Mendozo or Mendoza? I just *know* he'll want to see you *right away* – oh, I'm *sorry*, he's in conference ... You can go *right* in, Mr – is it Dis*nee* or Dis*nay*? Thank you sir, and *you* have a nice day *too*!'

On either side other tests were in progress. He watched a glossy cocktail waitress dressed in Victorian underwear, black stockings and garters, lower her empty tray to serve non-existent customers: 'Now who had the Black Russian? And you're the White Lady, right? Stinger for you.' Beyond her a torso-man in white seemed to be frying imaginary hamburgers: 'Yeah okay that's two with one without *and* sal, side fries *one* chicksand on white no mayo *one* poach on wholewheat no butter I got all that.' Next a dealer found a possible straight among the invisible cards upon the green baize table to which he was permanently attached, while a masseuse writhed and groaned and told the air it was one hell of a terrific lover. Elsewhere a clown juggled; a bear wearing a grin and a mortarboard recited the multiplication tables; a bearded analyst leaned back in the chair to which he was bolted, looked at the ceiling and said, 'Suppose we talk a little more about your father...'; a brown lifeguard murmured, 'Interesting girl like you needs a few swimming lessons'; a black shoeshine boy practised eye-rolls; and a man with an oil-can in his hand did nothing at all during the time it took Roderick to recognize him as Pa.

'... dedicated machines so far, but wait!' said Mr Kratt. 'Wait. Bub, I mean Doc, by the time we're ready to roll on this leisure centre of yours, we figure to have a set of good all-purpose boys and girls that'll wipe the floor with anything the competition can come up with. Like suppose you find one day you got too many girls in the sauna and not enough caddies, you just switch 'em right over – like that! – change of tapes takes maybe a minute apiece – and away they go.'

'Sounds good, sounds good.' Dr Welby allowed his glasses to slip even further down his nose, which had reddened perceptibly. 'But what about special skills ... mechanisms ... I mean a sauna doll has to ...'

'But that's the point, see, all our boys and girls are gonna have everything. Everything, see? Close as we can get to the real article, and that is pretty goddamn *close*. You tell him, Ben.'

Ben stopped doodling cube-headed creatures with stick arms and legs. He sat up. 'Well, you see we're planning to bring a former colleague of mine into the R & D division. This is a guy who I guess knows more than anybody in the *world* about official – artificial intelligence. This guy is the, the *Edison of robots*. Like the Wizard of Menlo Park himself, he mainly works alone –'

'Wizard of who?' Dr Welby reached once more for the decanter. 'Look if this feller is so important, why don't you have him already?'

'He's sick, he's in the hospital. You know how some of these highly-strung geniuses are,' Ben began. 'Nervous –'

'You mean he's nuts?'

Mr Kratt grinned. 'Don't worry, Doc, he can deliver the goods. Just needs a little rest and he'll be good as new. I figure six months and we'll have him ready to roll, right Ben?'

'Right. And –'

'Look all this sounds fine, fine, your company goes steaming ahead only what's in it for me?'

'Just getting to that Doc.' Kratt flipped open a portfolio. 'Putting it on that basis, we propose a straight stock trade, share for share, for forty-nine per cent of your firm. We bear all the costs of installation and maintenance of course, you still keep control of your operation and get a piece of our action. *And* you get a seat on our board, with the usual salary and options.'

Dr Welby shook his head hard. 'What's the catch?'

'No catch. No catch at all. Only thing is Doc you're in a hell of a good position to help us out with another little product running into some snags, our Jinjur Boy talking edible, seems you were the examining physician in twelve outa these eighteen problem cases –'

'He means the eighteen who died, eighteen kids who died,' Ben said, from behind the knuckle he was gnawing.

'Oh. Oh! Well you can't expect me to do anything unprof –'

'Hear me out, let's not get excited.' Kratt's thick fingers gripped the table, and the doctor's eye was drawn to that pinball ring. 'Anybody can lose a few files, get a lapse of memory now and then ... that's all we need.'

'What about the death certificates? Dr De'Ath did all the autopsies, he's the one found mercury in all –'

'Forget him. Time this town gets through with him, he won't be able to find mercury in his own thermometer. They got him in jail right now, attempted murder.'

'What, *him*? That's just ridiculous, some mistake – who would he ever –?'

'Some priest name of O'Bride. Housekeeper swears this De'Ath knocked him out and cut his throat.'

'Oh, *that*. Listen he told me all about it, Father O'Bride had a fall, respiratory trouble so Sam I mean Dr De'Ath performed an emergency tracheotomy –'

'Look, *I* believe you.' Kratt laughed. 'Only the old housekeeper, how do you think it looked to her? Here's the priest lying knocked out with a cut throat, here's some darky standing over him with a bloody knife – yes and she says she heard them quarrelling earlier, yelling about *blood, blood*!'

Welby gulped his drink. 'I know all about that too. Father O'Bride was trying to buy whole blood for some reason, only he wanted to get some kind of cheap imported blood without a health certificate. God knows what diseases it might be carrying, malaria, flukes, hepa –'

'Sure, sure. Thing is, this O'Bride was jobbing *our* products all over the State, begins to look like De'Ath was trying to put the bite on us, right? Little extortion? And then O'Bride wouldn't play ball ... Like I say, time this is over, who'd believe anything De'Ath says?'

Indica looked out over a sea of new hats, fresh hair-styles, and hostile glasses. How could they hate her so much even before she'd said a word? Was it her youth? Her Western clothes? You'd think they'd never seen dreds before, or Fyre-flye false eyebrows, or a bolero cut to expose one breast – she should have dowdied down for them, too late now.

'Machines,' she began, 'are only human...'

Gradually the hard faces began to soften and settle into sleep.

The flowers on Violetta's hat brushed the ear of Mrs Dorano. 'Delia, I haven't got my glasses, but is that woman really *showing a bosom?*'

'I wouldn't give her the satisfaction of looking. No sense of decency.'

'No sense of shame.'

'No more sense of shame than – than Ma Wood there.' Mrs Dorano craned around to glare at her. 'A cabbage! Ma's wearing a cabbage on her hat!'

'Oh I wish I had my glasses!'

'You can see everything she's got! Right up to the armpit, I can see a little birthmark there, looks like a dumb-bell –'

But Violetta Stubbs had leaned over the other way to hear what Ma Wood was whispering:

'... seems a little fond of Goldwynisms if you ask me, "Clocks and watches are just a waste of time," "Cars get you nowhere" is that the way she thinks or just an affectation?'

'How do you mean?' Mrs Smith whispered back.

'There she goes again, "Electric blankets can really get on top of you." I think it must be unconscious, all this about how utility companies just want to use us, how owning a big heap of machines can be heavy ... I mean if she wants to say we're all too dependent on machines, why not just say it? Instead of all this "Do your own dishes, give 'em a break", and how a free machine is an investment in America's future...'

'Shh!' said Mrs Dorano, and went on to Violetta, 'Imagine having a birthmark like that and showing it off along with everything she's got!'

'Birthmark?'

'Right under her arm there, like a little dumb-bell – what's the matter?'

316

Violetta Stubbs stood up and tried to push along the row of crossed legs, handbags, discarded shoes, shopping and knitting. 'I'm not well, I ... gotta go...'

Too late. Indica Dinks stopped speaking to stare at her. 'Mother!'

'Son, I knew you'd figure out that cipher in about two minutes flat. So I guess by now you know everything.' Pa set the oil-can down on a reception desk.

'Pa, I didn't work out the cipher at all. I just – saw Ma doing all that witchcraft stuff down by the lake and I knew somehow she was bringing you back to life.'

'Life, ha.'

'So I knew you must be hiding out somewhere like this. Because I mean the undead –'

'Undead? Witchcraft? But son, all you had to do was turn the darn cipher upside down!'

Roderick tried to call up a mental picture of the message, turned upside down, while he watched the receptionist. She picked up the oil-can, placed it to her ear like any smiling suicide, and said, 'He'll see you in just a sec, Mr – is it Getty or Goethe?'

'Pa, maybe you'd better explain.'

'Maybe I'd better!' Pa sat down for a shoeshine and, while the eye-rolling contraption buffeted away at his bare feet, he began the story.

23

To make men serfs and villeins it is indispensably necessary to make them brutes ... A servant who has been taught to write and read ceases to be any longer a passive machine.

William Godwin, *Political Justice*

'Started as a joke,' said Pa. 'Well you see right after the war everything seemed like a joke. Listen, during the war they had these cookies with chocolate on them, only they couldn't get any chocolate so they started putting brown wax on them. That seemed like a joke, you know? Here were millions of people killing each other, and they still managed to find somebody to sit painting brown wax on cookies. And Hitler was a joke. Trying to get half the world to stick its head in the oven and turn on the gas ... okay maybe it's not funny but you gotta admit it's kind of strange.

'And after the war it kept getting stranger. If anybody had a dream, no matter how stupid or futile it was, they went right out and tried to live that dream. It's as if the whole world just sat down with some crummy old pulp science fiction magazine, read it cover to cover, and then tried to live it. On the cover of that old magazine you'll see a picture of this city of the future: big glass towers, surrounded by tapeworm roads, coil after coil wound up over and under each other. And on the roads are strange-looking things that must be high-powered cars. And in the air above them, a few helicopters, and maybe the blast of a silver rocket taking off for the moon. And if you see any people they're wearing plastic clothes, and you know they live on vitamin pills and special artificial foods. Inside the magazine you find out how they live: watching television, killing their enemies with death-rays, running everything with big computers, robot servants, millions of household gadgets doing all the work, atomic power harnessed to turn the wheels of industry, jet planes zipping passengers New York to Paris in a few hours – I probably left out a lot of stuff, but – but just look around you. We got it, all of it. Every glass tower, every tapeworm road, every moon rocket and computer and nuclear power station – everything in the magazine. A joke, by God, and now it's beyond a joke!'

'Well I still don't see –'

'Because just think back to the guy who wrote all this crap. Here he is, back in the forties, some poor broken-down science fiction hack. Here he sits at his broken-down L. C. Smith, cracking out his crap for a penny a word – a cheap dream, you agree? So he hammers out maybe a hundred stories a year, maybe six novels too, all just to eat and pay the rent. No and he doesn't even have enough ideas of his own to fill the quota; has to ask his wife for another giant electronic brain, another moon rocket. This guy, I mean he probably has dandruff, he's overweight, he can hardly drag himself to that oilcloth-covered kitchen table to face the L. C. Smith every day.

'And *he* created *our* world! *We* have to wear the damn plastic, eat the ice-cream substitutes, live and work in the glass towers. Just because *he* happened to write it down – imagine! What if the poor slob, what if one day he wrote *brass* instead of *glass*, would we all be living in brass towers now? It's a joke all right.'

Roderick shifted his weight to his other foot. 'I don't see how that explains –'

'Las Vegas? Disneyland? The Muse-suck in this factory? Episode Ten Thousand of *Dorinda's Destiny*? Supermarkets selling *Upboy*, a special food for geriatric dogs? Electric acupuncture? Talking gingerbread? Believe me, it explains everything. Every blessed damned thing. Uh, let's go outside. I don't think I can take any more of it here, with that receptionist pouring oil down her nice new dress...'

They made their way along the yellow road to the entrance, through the security room (where Roderick's possessions came back to him), past the docile dogs and out at the gate. Pa sat in the grass and contemplated his oxblood feet, or perhaps only the lights of town beyond them.

'We killed him in 1950. We killed him with a death-ray,

and blew up his old L. C. Smith with an H-bomb. That poor old hack was right in the middle of another crappy story, still behind with the rent, and we killed him.'

'I don't get you, Pa.'

'Let me put it another way. One day in 1950 he's hammering away at the keys, still spelling it *glass* instead of *brass*, while his wife is stalling the landlady and maybe trying to work out some new way of combining canned tomatoes, ground beef and elbow macaroni. The next day, they're both dead. The police will find two little piles of clothes on the shores of Lake Michigan. One pile is weighted down with the L. C. Smith. And a note, got to have a note, double-spaced with wide margins . . .'

'You mean you changed your names and moved to Newer?'

'Son, we changed everything. We became Paul and Mary Wood. We dropped everything from the old life – all we brought along were a few pulp magazines with our stories. We changed our personalities – that looks like Doc Welby's car.'

Roderick looked up to see the lights of a strange, high-powered car moving away from the executive gate of Slumbertite, off down the tapeworm to town. 'I wonder what he was doing up here?'

'Anyway, now you know most of our story. See we thought we could maybe make up for it if we could just have a kid, kids. Somehow we couldn't, no matter how much we kissed and cuddled . . . Anyway that's why one year we fostered a nice little boy called Danny Sonnenschein.'

'Dan Sonnenschein!'

'Same guy, yup. Trouble was, he got up in the attic one day, got into these old pulp magazines. Before you knew it, he'd gone and read a story of ours. We called it, "I, Robot".'

Roderick tried to look at him, but Pa's face was in shadow. 'You mean you were Isaac Asimov?'

'Nope. And we weren't Eando Binder, either. Nor anybody else who wrote "I, Robot". Believe me, nobody ever heard of us, nobody even remembers the name of that pulp magazine.

'Yes it was our story little Danny picked on, that twisted him some way – I don't know, set him to dreaming or – well.

320

You know the rest. Next time we heard from Danny he was grown up, he'd invented you, and he was in trouble.'

'Is that how I came to stay here?'

'Yep, another mistake. See, son, we hoped we could still change the world back, undo some of our damage, take back our terrible joke. Through you. If only we could make you learn how to be human...

'So what we did, first we burned the old pulp magazines. Then we tried to teach you everything we knew about life. Like I said, a mistake.'

'Pa, I don't see it was such a mis –'

'Because we knew nothing. Nothing at all. Few scraps of logic, a song, coupla half-assed ideas about art ... a joke or two...'

Roderick felt compelled to protest again. 'Pa, I think you and Ma haven't done such a bad job. Heck, you only had a robot to begin with.'

'A joke or two. Another mistake we made was money. Spent all we had and a whole lot we didn't have yet. Then a whole lot we never would have. We cut a few corners – well hell, we stole. *I* stole. And when it began to look as if the law was catching up with us, with *me*, I had to die. Because if they finger-printed me, they'd find out who I was, and there we'd be, right back in the middle of that terrible joke again. You see? You see, son?'

Roderick scratched his head. 'Sure okay, but what about the syphilis?'

'Syphilis? Nobody said anything about –'

'Right here in your cipher, Pa. "P Wood in soup (syph) so now possum numb mummy hypno-bound & shun mob!!!' I mean you can't make it plainer than that, and later on there's something about pox, too, that's –'

'Let me see that, where –?' Pa snatched the paper and held it up to the light of slumbertite never sleeps. 'Pox that's nothing, just the words of the song, you don't want to pay no attention to that. It says Bow wow too, but that don't mean I got fleas.'

'Okay but –'

'But this syph – well that is just your Ma's bad spelling, the word is supposed to be sylph. Your Ma never could spell.'

'Sylph? How can you be in the soup with a sylph?'

'Not *with*, son. Like I said, your Ma never could spell, never should of been a writer. *Sylph* was a poor word for woman anyway.'

Roderick gasped. 'The wedding picture, that's what was wrong with it. *Pa, you were the bride! Ma was the groom!*'

'Well it's no reason to break into italics, son. Like I said, it all started off as a joke, just trading clothes now and then – son? You all right?'

Ben was packing up the papers.

'No hurry, Benny, pour us another drink.' Mr Kratt bit the end from a cheap cigar and settled back. 'Goddamn trip was worth it, eh bub? Yes sir, Welby's our boy. De'Ath better be our boy too, if he knows what's good for him. Yes sir, a productive damn trip. We oughta lock this one up in a month or so, kick a few asses in our so-called lobby down in Lincoln, don't see why we can't be showing a profit this time next year on this little enterprise. You know bub, times like this makes me feel goddamn good.'

'Yes sir.' Ben was noticing, not for the first time, the large white square teeth of his employer. They always reminded him of a row of tombstones, and now . . .

'What the hell's wrong with you?'

'I just . . . wish you wouldn't grin like that sir, no offence, but –'

'Grin if I goddamnit grin if I want to, hell we just made a *killing* here you want me to look sad about it?'

'No sir but, just thinking of those kids, those dead –'

'Death certificates, damn it didn't I tell you not to worry? We'll beat that, sure it's a pain in the ass but we'll beat that. Nothing's gonna stop us, bub, because nothing *can* stop us, we're on the move.' He grinned again, lighting the cigar. 'And sure I feel good. Hell, here I am fighting on the last frontier in the fucking world. And *winning*, sure I feel good.'

'Winning.'

'Because that's what business is, bub, the last frontier. The last place where you can still take hold of the world and change it, make it – make it –'

'Make it in your own image?'

322

'Better, I was going to say. Make it what you want. See everyone else, the world is just something that happens to them, might as well be watching it on TV, right? But for me the world is something you – something you can *get*. Sure it's risky. You gotta fight. You need guts and luck and, and imagination. But hell, isn't it worth it? Just tell me that, isn't it worth it?'

'Yes sir.' Ben found a TV set behind a panel and, after staring for a moment at his dark reflection in the screen, turned it on. It was going to be a long evening. Once Mr Kratt had a few drinks and started talking about the last frontier . . .

'Why shouldn't I feel good? Whole damn business is devoted to one thing, you know? One thing: giving people pleasure. Giving people pleasure. So why shouldn't I get some pleasure too . . . ?'

The TAPE button brought a canned promotion for the factory: '*Our advanced integrated control system is continuously optimized by real-time goal-seeking –*' while rows of robot receptionists trundled along with their desks, '*– routines implemented throughout a hierarchy of processors to attack such performance-characteristic problems as the utilization of modified control algorithms –*' each Roberta the Receptionist wearing more false hair than the automaton chess-playing Turk could have concealed beneath his ample turban. The Turk too had been seated behind a desk (when the Baron von Kempelen first exhibited him in Vienna, shortly before the American Revolution). And his desk had been a necessity, since it concealed that most perfect of chess-playing mechanisms (together with its lunch and piss-pot).

'*– including diagnostic programmes and multi-level alarms and interrupts, debugging and redistribution of modifications within each software sub-package –*'

'. . . because damnit, pleasure is our business, always meant to make that the group slogan, pleasure is our business. Greatest pleasure for the greatest number . . .'

Ben nodded agreement and changed channels, stabbing a button at random. Seemed to be something about the French Revolution, torches, billhooks and the laughter of toothless hags.

'— on both a local and a global level, evaluating each task via sophisticated assessment procedures and providing next-level feedback from supervisory processors. Feasibility analysis, an integral part of each task, is similarly —'

Back to the mob scene, what was it, *Tale of Two Cities*? Probably get a shot of Madame DeFarge any minute now, knitting shrouds . . . funny thing was, the real revolution was going on all the time behind the scenes, the Jacquard loom with its punched cards weaving a new pattern, clicking away, a far far better thing it did than anyone had ever done . . . burial shrouds for human thought, maybe, but very good burial shrouds.

Or was it a different mob scene? The camera zoomed in on faces by torchlight, not at all the faces of Jacques One and Jacques Two and Madame DeFarge, but the faces of men with good teeth, men wearing sweatshirts and golf caps, windbreakers and glasses, baseball caps and twill, crewcuts and army fatigues . . .

'Mr Kratt? Sir?'

The camera pulled back again, to show a security fence, and a German Shepherd snapping at a moth.

'Listen, Mr Kratt?'

'No, *you* listen, trying to tell you something damn important.'

'But listen, there's a mob heading —'

'Sure, sure, now just you turn that thing off and pay attention. Bub, you know what my dream is?'

'No sir.'

'You know what it is?'

'No sir.'

'You know —? I'll tell you what my dream is. What I'd like to see is, KUR Industries having the world franchise, see —'

'Yes, sir, now couldn't we —?'

'The *world* franchise, *exclusive*, on pleasure. Datajoy! What we'd have is like a wire running right into everybody's head, right into the old pleasure centre. Datajoy! And as long as they pay their lease, we give 'em all the juice they want, see? Datajoy, call it —'

'Yes Mr Kratt, now —'

'And by God if they don't pay, we rip that wire right outa their head! Haha, whatya think a that? Hey? Whatya – leggo my arm, what the hell here?'

'We've got to leave, sir. Now. There's a mob on the way with torches – I don't know, maybe the parents of those kids we – those kids who – I don't know who they are!'

When they had left, the room showed little sign of human occupation. A few chairs out of line, an empty decanter, three glasses on the long table (in one, the faecaloid stub of a cheap cigar floated in fine old Scotch). The cleaning-machines waited a precise number of minutes, then went to work.

'It's me they want,' said Pa. 'But they'll have to come in and get me.'

'Pa, I mean Ma'am, maybe they just want to burn the factory down, you know like the old house in *Franken* –'

'No, it's me. But at least I can choose to make my last stand, among all the wonderful guys and dolls, Roberta the Receptionist, Bert the Bartender, all the only true friends I ever had. Bye, son.'

'Wait, Pa. I wanted to ask you –' But she was gone.

Close up, the mob looked as good as anything in *Frankenstein*. Roderick spotted pitchforks, axes, garden rakes and electric lawn-edgers as well as rifles, ropes, torches. Dr Smith the dentist seemed to be unarmed until he got close enough for Roderick to see him wield a tiny dental hook.

Doc Smith was not a well man. Later on, when they got around to hanging Roderick, he would try to insist they use his patent dental floss.

24

It was the best of time, it was the worst of time. Choose one.

The pigeon hesitated before the two windows, trying to get it right this time. Finally it pecked the left-hand window. Almost immediately the window lit up, and a tiny feed pellet rattled down into the magic cup. From the pigeon's point of view it was a triumph of the righteous: yea, God doth reward those who keep His commandments and His rites. Before the next trial, the pigeon worshipped, stepping three times to the left, twice to the right, and lifting its head in turn towards each of the four upper corners of its prison. The pigeon was not aware of the computer.

From the computer's point of view, the cycle had brought a special instruction into force. It knew only that it had generated the pseudo-random digit 0, and that this matched the input 0 (from the Skinner box). The instruction therefore was to add 1 to the number T (trials), add one to the number H (hits) and calculate P (probability). The computer was aware neither of the pigeon nor of Dr Tarr.

Dr Tarr sat in his new office watching the printer. From his point of view, the test was on the whole a qualified success. Pigeons were precognitive.

Or at least this pigeon, now and then, seemed uncannily able to peer a split-second into the future, determine which plastic window (of a randomly-selected pair) would deliver the goods, and peck that window. Now and then.

Now and then, that was the trouble. Not enough hits, not near enough to convince those Dr Tarr needed to convince. There was NASA, first of all, paying $150,000 towards his expenses; expecting results. Likewise the University, providing not only computer time, but an empty office and lab in the Computer Sciences building. And how about the parapsychology journals, the professional associations waiting for the paper that could make him, career-wise? Finally of course the professional sceptics: he saw them as hyenas, forever trailing the herd of parapsychologists, forever waiting for some weak individual to fall behind. Ready, yes ready to bury their bloodstained snouts in his entrails . . .

More hits, damn you! he willed at the bird, *more hits!* Unaware of his telepathic command from the office, the creature in the laboratory preened, digging its beak deep in iridescent neck feathers to chew at a parasite. For the moment, it was aware of nothing else, not even of the cruelly erratic God it had learned to love.

Tarr, acutely aware of his own predicament (for not since Mary of Nazareth had anyone risked so much on the behaviour of a single pigeon) turned to the printer, whose ultimate line still read:

$$\text{TRIALS} = 980 \quad \text{HITS} = 502 \quad P < 0.444$$

Computer error? Sure, damn thing probably wasn't working at all! Poor pigeon probably pecking away, hit after hit and nothing coming through. He examined the cable running from the computer to the printer, experimentally unplugged it and plugged it in again.

$$\text{TRIALS} = 981 \quad \text{HITS} = 503 \quad P < 0.425$$

More like it. More like it! Funny how it (he repeated the operation) clocked up a hit every time you jiggled the . . . you could almost . . . not quite ethical maybe but . . . well, just to enhance the figures a little, to emphasize what we already know . . .

$$\text{TRIALS} = 1126 \quad \text{HITS} = 648 \quad P < 0.0000000406$$

The score was getting *too* sensational, time to stop, but Tarr kept on, tickling just one more reward from the printer, just one more. Had God at that moment been a Skinnerian psychologist, peering in through the office ceiling, He'd have been pleased to recognize His guilty creature here crouched at its task. Working along its reinforcement schedule. 'Learning', if not growing wise.

No one was peering in. He looked over his shoulder at the door at nothing, no one, nothing but the door itself, newly

painted to hide some old stain that showed through neverthe-
less, a shadow like a clutching hand.

The mob was making so much noise so many almost city
noises Roderick could hardly hear men leaning together like
glass buildings falling over follow a skeleton to Junior's Discount Cameras God call him up every time lousy jackpot
blade heavy split up when electric .38 for LAW & ORDER
raping housekeepers nigger priest bites dog pills bustup treats
me like shit .38 bike overtime MASSAGE THERAPY dolls of
Devil's Island escape from jail and bust into factory Lewd-ite
revenge calling for a rope unless we all go back to the Idle
Hour boys have a beer and talk it God fight city hall needles
bitch freak t-shirt no shit the Klan? What Klan?

'Klan, shit, we'll be our own Klan!'

'What?' Another man seemed shocked. 'Take the Klan into
our own hands?'

'I'm serious now Jake, I'll be the Kladd, you be the Kludd,
let old Carl there be the Grand Goblin.'

'Goblin? That sounds dumb as hell, you know?'

'Sure does. Forget all that Klan shit, let's just teach this
motherfucker a *lesson!*'

'Why can't I be the Imperial Wizard, though?'

'Will you listen to that? Will you I mean listen-to-*that*?'

'We gonna hang somebody or what? How about that
nigger in the jail? How about him?'

'Busted out didn't he?'

'Hell he did. He –'

'Yeah but listen, I wanta be the Wizard or I don't be
nothing.'

'If he's still in jail who the hell raped them women at
the Meeting Hall? I heard –'

'Bullshit man, they ain't raped they just got excited.'

'– perial Wizard, goddamnit is anybody listening to me?'

'Piss on all this, I'm going to the Idle Hour.'

This seemed a good idea to others, and indeed the whole
mob made its way – arguing, shoving Roderick almost as
much as they shoved one another – towards Main Street.

'No but seriously if you're gonna form a Klan Klavern
you –'

'Will you listen to that? Will-you –?'

'Yeah see Miss Violetta Stubbs they found out she's got a kid!'

'Aw Jesus doesn't that make you sick? Nice old lady like that raped by a black –'

'No listen –'

'I say we hang the bastard right here in front of the Idle Hour. I say we teach him a *lesson*!'

'Piss on that I'm going –'

And in a moment, they were all gone, leaving Roderick alone in the street. Immediately the sheriff's car drew up, flashing all its lights: red, blue, green, tangerine, ochre and plum.

'Get in, Wood. I'm taking you in – for your own protection. No, in the back.'

Roderick climbed into the cage in the back, and allowed the sheriff to drive him the thirteen yards to jail.

'County's too damn busy, you know?' Sheriff Benson led him inside and snapped on the handcuffs. 'Like we had a riot earlier at the Meeting Hall, Mrs Dorano trying to throw rocks at Miss Violetta, can you beat that? And now this. Hell I didn't hardly get time to see *Hollywood Squares*, hell of an evening.' He kicked Roderick into a cell, hauled out a black-jack and began beating him carelessly around the face.

'Ouch! Look is this – ow, this for my own protec – ouch! My own protection? Because I, ouch, you take off these cuffs I could protect myself...'

'What?' The sheriff had not been looking at his victim, but through the open door at the TV in his office. Someone was trying to name nine brands of beer in thirty seconds. Sheriff Benson looked at the weapon in his hand. 'Sorry, son. Just gets to be a habit, I guess.' Slamming the cell door, he added, 'Hope I can still count on your support come election day?'

Roderick was not surprised to find a black man in the next cell, even though the man was not wearing faded overalls nor playing a harmonica.

'Hi man. My name's Roderick Wood. What's yours?' Ignoring him, the man continued taking his own temperature. 'I'm in protective custody. For my own good. What

329

are you in for? Oh, I hope you don't find this paint on my face offensive. No insult intended, man. See what it is is mourning. See my Pa died – he's not really my Pa, in fact he's not really anybody's Pa, he's a woman. Only I didn't know that, when he looked at this gas bill for a million dollars and just keeled over. Only now I find out he's not dead and he's not a he either. Now he lives I mean she lives in the factory. So when I thought Ma, who really isn't a woman either she's a man who used to write science fiction that all came true, I thought she was doing witchcraft but it was only scientific stuff to revive Pa. Boy was that ever a shock! I mean last time I had a shock like that was when these gipsies kid-napped me and sold me to this carnival where I was supposed to tell fortunes. Duking, they called it. You know that was about the only time I ever went out of town anyways, oh except when Ma and me went to the city to get me a new eye, this burned-out store only when she left me there I got pretty scared because here was this same carny guy with a pinball on his finger, wouldn't you be scared? And I didn't find Ma again until later when I was in one of these two limousines that crashed into a art gallery –'

'Really?' The man held the thermometer up to the light. 'Been seeing a lot of movies have you, sport?'

'I used to watch them on TV a lot, when I was living with these people in Nevada I think it was only the guy beat me up with a hammer –'

'Subnormal. As usual. Still say I'm coming down with something, maybe that virus thing that's going around ... I don't know ... "Physician, heal thyself" – Ha! If I could heal myself I wouldn't be a physician, I'd be a miracle-worker. The name is De'Ath, by the way. Dr Samuel De'Ath.'

'Pleased to meet you. I'm Roderick Wo –'

'Yeah I heard you. A robot trying to break into the movies. Do me a favour, will you, look at my throat? Can you manage the light and the tongue depressor with those cuffs ... Good. Now I say Ah ... see anything?'

'It's all pink! I thought it would be, well more –'

'Pink hell, is it *red*? That is the sixty-four-thousand-dollar question!'

The sheriff's head appeared around the door. 'Did I hear

330

somebody mention the good old sixty-four-thousand-dollar question? Used to be my favourite, doggone it, with the old isolation booth and the – No? Don't neither of you boys like game shows? If you do, speak up – I can always bring the TV in here and let you watch with me. Just let me know.' The head vanished.

'It's not red, Doc.'

'Funny, it feels ... and my pulse is slightly elevated too ... I wonder...'

'Doc, do you think that mob will break in here and drag us out and hang us?'

But by now the doctor was listening to his own heart. 'I know I ought to get out more, jog a little, get plenty of exercise. But somehow ... last time I went out was with this priest, Father O'Bride, kept calling me a natural until I started missing easy shots, you know? Guy's kinda weird anyway, kept telling me about this idea of his for a fourteen-hole golf course with every hole a Station of the Cross – what do you mean, *hang us*?'

'Well you know, hang us.'

'Not a chance. You've been seeing too many movies again, sport. *Old* movies. People just don't hang people any more. A necktie party in modern dress? A lynching in the post-literate electronic age, the global village? Klan vengeance, in these days of low-lipid diets and consumer awareness? String us up, just when civilization is hitting its stride with, with male contraceptive pills and Mickey Mouse telephones? With giggling gingerbread and soul-searching politicians and reconstituted gratification? Not a chance, sport.'

After a moment, he added, 'What an admission of failure! To turn their backs on, on the great American menu of therapies, and just go sneaking off in the night with a rope – impossible!'

After another moment, 'Improbable, anyway.'

Roderick said, 'I just hope when they come for us, Sheriff Benson will get out there with a shotgun on the front steps and tell them all about, uh, justice, uh, how the foundering fathers brought forth a nation where liberty and just –'

'I'd rather not discuss it any more, okay? God, it isn't as if I haven't got enough to worry about! Heading for a major

331

health crisis just when I need all my strength for a long court battle over this gingerbread business, not to mention this little smear campaign, trying to discredit me before I blow the whistle on their dirty little operation.'

'Who?'

'Kratt Enterprises, that's who. Or I guess they now call it KUR Industries, might as well call it Mass Poisoners Incorporated, what with their – well I'd better not talk about it off the record, but their day is coming.'

'You mean they made the gingerbread boys that made all those kids sick?'

'Yeah, and just wait. This is just the chance I needed, to carve out a reputation in the public service, lay down a solid career foundation –'

'Not to mention saving a lot more kids from –'

'Sure that too, but from there I could springboard right into some prestigious drug firm, they're always on the lookout for young crusaders, names that look good on the letterhead – and let's face it, integrity is all I've got to sell.'

Roderick scratched his head. 'But wouldn't it be better if you kept finding out about mass poisoners and helped save other –?'

The door banged open and Sheriff Benson came in, dragging the TV set. 'Hate to think of you boys sitting in here with nothing to do, so I thought I'd come in here and let you watch the shows with me. Anyways that mob out front is making too much racket, I can't hardly hear the questions.'

They watched *The Big Score*, *Ripoff*, *Pick a Winner*, *Two for the Top*, *Lucky Break*, *Pile It Up*, *Family Spree*, *Play or Pay*, *Big Bingo*, *Make or Break*, *Guess It Rich*, *Spoil Yourself*, *Great Expectations*, *Gold or Fold*, *Grab Bag* and *Money Talks*, and during the commercial breaks the sheriff described other games.

'Too bad you boys missed that new one, *Double Your Social Security Check*. Real good, see, they get these old folks to put their check in this glass box, then they gotta answer three questions. Well see they might be easy ones like name a pro football linebacker with two Z's in his name, you know? Other times they get trickier, like name five countries in Europe – anyway see, every time the old codger gets a right

332

answer, they put another check in the box, keep on doubling up see? But if they *miss* one –' The sheriff's chair creaked with laughter, 'The damn check burns up in the box, right before their eyes! Boy O boy, there was one old guy – oops, they're back –'

The TV figure welcomed them back to the next round of *Money Talks*. 'Well, Mrs Pearson? Will YOU talk for money? Will YOU step into our special Acorn United Company bank vault, filled with ONE MILLION crisp new dollar bills, and talk for *five minutes*?'

'This ain't no good,' said the sheriff, touching a button. 'We'll try *Take the Plunge*.'

'. . . member, if you push the *right* button, you'll be able to Take the Plunge right into our gold-plated swimming pool, filled to the brim with shiny new silver dollars. You could just dive in and keep every dollar you throw up, okay? How's that sound, eh? Good? Great! Now, that's if you push the *right* button. If you push the *wrong* button, Doris, the pool might be filled with something . . . we-e-ell . . . *not* so nice. MOLASSES, for instance? Ha ha ha, or maybe JELLO? Or how about DIRTY SOCKS? Okay then, here goes . . .'

Roderick watched the poor woman on the screen, her face slack but smiling. Almost like a dog waiting for a kick, hoping for a pat. She pushed the button and the great gold *lamé* curtains swished open to show a swimming pool filled with –

'TYRES!' screamed the MC over audience laughter. 'Oh my goodness, TYRES! That's right, Doris, you have just won a plunge into this pool filled with old rubber tyres! Ah ha ha, and you – ha ha – yes you can keep every one you throw up –'

Suddenly the entire brilliant studio, with the purple walls, gold curtains, the MC in his scarlet coat and the contestant's green face, shrank to a dot and vanished. The plug had been kicked out of its socket by one of the stumbling men, each wearing a pillowcase over his head, coming for the prisoners.

The tall building of rusty corrugated iron was Bangfield's Grain Elevator, just one of the forgotten buildings at the forgotten end of town. A few cars and pickups had been parked to shine their headlights on the action: a rope being passed over a pulley and tied into a noose.

'I guess they mean it,' said Dr De'Ath. 'I just hope they've got enough sense to do this right. They ought to drop us from enough height to fracture the fourth cervical vertebra, a quick snap and we're finished.'

'Sure.' All Roderick could think of was getting out of it, somehow, working some brilliant psychological trick that would make the pillow-heads give up.

'Listen fellows,' he said. 'Our foundering fathers brought –'

'Shut up, will you?' said a head with a border of marigolds. Another, in a pillowcase dotted with fleur-de-lis grabbed Dr De'Ath and shoved him towards the noose.

'Hold on, we're not ready yet,' said a pillowcase edged with the Campbell tartan. 'Keep him back there.'

'Snap,' said Dr De'Ath bitterly. 'Not a chance with these yahoos. They'll probably give us slow asphyxiation by ligation, fracturing the hyoid so we end up with our tongues sticking out and messing our pants. Talk about an admission of failure! And loose bowels are one thing I haven't been troubled with lately, kind of ironic . . .'

'I was just wondering if my whole life would flash before me,' Roderick muttered. 'I mean my *whole* life. Because if it did, there'd have to be a moment when I relived the present moment, wouldn't there? When I started reliving my whole life again? And in that life I'd get to the same moment, and start reliving –'

'Just shut up, will you?' said the marigolds. 'Why make this any tougher than it is? Just relax.'

'Relax?' Dr De'Ath chortled. 'I've got a migraine now, on top of everything else, this yahoo wants me to *relax*.'

'All set,' the tartan called out.

Dr De'Ath said, 'Look Rod, how about you going first? See I'd like to try a little gargle first – oh I know it sounds silly, but I really hate to die without at least trying to clear up this sore throat of mine – okay?'

'Okay.' Roderick stepped forward and turned to face the lights. Someone slipped a noose over his head. He saw a pillowcase printed with sea-horses, read the tag on its hem: *Hand-hot wash, drip-dry, do not spin*. Will this be my last

334

memory? No, better to try thinking of something interesting, how about the paradox of the unexpected hanging?

A judge tells a man he'll be hanged one day next week, but not on any day he's expecting it. The man reasons that he cannot be hanged on the Saturday, since he'd certainly expect it if he survived the other six days. So the hanging had to happen between Sunday and Friday. But then it couldn't be Friday, either, by the same reasoning. That left Sunday till Thursday, only in that case Thursday too was out. And so on, until he eliminated every day but Sunday. So he expected to be hanged on Sunday. So he couldn't be hanged on Sunday. So he couldn't be hanged at all!

Roderick felt pain in his neck as he was hoisted aloft. Looking down, he could see the whole miserable little crowd of pillow-heads, the parked cars beyond them, and further. There was Ma, lurking in the background and biting his nails. There was the limousine that had been parked up at the factory, now it was stopping in a shadow while the chauffeur got out and – what was he doing – taking pictures.

The pain got sharper, and Roderick thought he heard a rivet shearing in his neck. Better finish:

... couldn't be hanged at all! So the man thought, being perfectly logical. So he wasn't expecting it the day they hanged him ...

'Jus' one more picture, boss?' said the chauffeur. 'Cause I know the kids would love to see –'

'Get back in the car. Now!' Ben Franklin pushed the snoring weight of Mr Kratt off his shoulder and leaned forward. 'If you don't get back behind that wheel right now, I'll have you *fired*.'

The chauffeur shrugged, folded his camera and climbed in. ''Kay, take it easy. Maybe you seen a lot of lynchin's, I ain't.'

Ben looked at the sleeping figure. It had stopped snoring and was now muttering, 'Pleasssure. Pleassssure.'

'Just start the car and drive.'

'You crazy? Through that buncha –'

'Then turn around and drive the other way, let's just get out of here.'

'Yeah but like I said we can't go nowhere this way, like

I said when we come off at the wrong exit – didn't I tell you it was the wrong exit? – all we can do now is stay on this here highway 811 until we hit the old Interstate and then cut back –'

'All right, just – just a minute, let me think.'

'Some thinker,' said the chauffeur, lighting a hand-rolled cigarette. 'Look buddy we're stuck here, why doncha just sit back and watch the show?'

'*Show?* Is that all it is to you, a show? You don't care do you, people committing murder – like *that*? It's just something on TV, that it?'

'Look, no offence, manner of speakin', okay? Okay? I'm entitled to my opinion too, you know, it's a free fuckin' country.'

'All right, all –'

'Just because I work for a livin' don't mean I'm shit, okay?'

'*All right!*'

'Okay, just wanted to get that straight.' The chauffeur twitched his shoulders, shrugging off any yoke of oppression Ben might care to impose, and sat forward: a free man in a free country, watching a free show.

Ben reached for the phone, hesitated, gnawed his knuckles for a while, and finally tried waking Mr Kratt.

'Wha? Whoza?'

'There's a lynching going on, sir. Right over there. Shouldn't we – call the highway patrol?'

'Outa your head, bub. Word gets out I'm nosing around down here we'll have every yak-head in the State tryina buy in on this land deal. Jesus, might as well take a full-page ad in the paper, announce a gold rush – use your head, for Christ's –' and he was asleep again.

Ben looked away from the execution into darkness. Toys. A show. Revenge of the common man upon the common object, wasn't that it? Because it wouldn't do, it had never done, to think of the object of their cruelty as fully human. So the effigy created by Albertus Magnus (smashed down by Aquinas) turns up as Friar Bacon's talking head (to be smashed by a servant) and again as the automaton of Descartes ('ma fille Francine', flung into the sea by yet another fearful soul) even while dummies of Guido Fawkes

336

began to burn in the streets of London for the pleasure of children. Common children, always more ready than even their parents to punish the presumption of a servant.

Well yes, he might work that up into an article, why not? *The Common Man and His Image?* 'Fascination with clockwork in the 17th cent. coincides with idea of commonwealth, all part of same big movement,' he wrote, turning the notebook to the light. 'Clock explained all, from Newton's heaven to Malynes's laws of economics – Huygens creating clockwork artisans for the King of France even while (after?) Mechanic Philosophers promoted a new democratic religion among the living artisans. Groups naming themselves by function – Quakers, Shakers, Ranters, Diggers, Levellers – as though describing their work within the great timepiece.' What was the point of all this? What was it?'

'Christ,' said the chauffeur. 'Christ! Looka that.'

'Shut up, will you?'

'Who you tellin' to shut up, listen fuckhead, I –'

'Sorry. *Sorry.*' Revolution, that was the point. 'Jacquard loom working a genuine revolution behind the scenes – Mme DeF. – In 1791 (?) Godwin wrote: "A servant who –"' What was the quote? While he waited for it, the chauffeur said:

'Hey look, uh, Mr Frankelin, I think we got trouble with the right rear tyre, hey?'

'What?'

'Right rear tyre, I think it's down. Your side, you mind gettin' out and look at it?'

Still frowning at the notebook he climbed out.

'Have a nice night, Mr Frankelin.'

'What? Oh – hey what –?'

And he hardly heard the screams ('God! His head come off!') so intent was he suddenly on the sound of the automatic door-closer, the click of the automatic lock, the sight of the chauffeur giving him the finger as the limousine glided away into the night.

25

Yet the old myth dies hard. We are still tempted to argue that if
the clown's antics exhibit carefulness, judgement, wit, and appreciation of the moods of his spectators, there must be occurring in
the clown's head a counterpart performance to that which is taking
place on the sawdust. If he is thinking what he is doing, there must
be occurring behind his painted face a cognitive shadow-operation
which we do not witness, tallying with, and controlling, the bodily
contortions which we do witness.

Gilbert Ryle, *The Concept of Mind*

One record finished, and in the interval a shrill voice said:
'Well we're practically related. My ex married his ex's first
husband's widow – only I guess they split up lass week...'

One of the groom's coarse cousins, naturally; there was
relief among the bride's friends when the disc-jockey slipped
another record into the silence.

One or two couples started dancing on the patio; Allbright
and Dora waltzed smoothly into the library and out again,
their steps not noticeably slowed by the added weight of
several first editions.

'Hey Allbright!' It was Lyle Tate, keeping his birthmark
in shadow as he came past the disc-jockey's glass booth.
'Jeez, and Dora – you two are the only people I know here.
Who is this mob? Who is everybody?'

Allbright shrugged, shifting books. 'Everybody.'

'No but I mean Jane Hannah's not here, Jack Tarr's not
here –'

'Tarr? I thought you hated his guts.'

'Yeah but only when he was around. Guess he hasn't got
the guts to go anywhere today, there's a story going around
that he's been cheating on some psychic research stuff. They
say he got a pigeon to be clairvoyant something like a
hundred times, pushing the right button in a Skinner box,

you know? A hundred times. Only trouble was the pigeon was dead at the time, biggest damn miracle since Lazarus – speaking of which, Allbright you don't look so great. What's that, dried blood on your face, bruises or dirt?'

'We fall over from time to time,' Allbright said. 'We fall. One of the privileges of the C-charged brain...'

'We? You mean –?' Lyle looked to Dora, who nodded.

'Rodin,' said a shrill voice somewhere. 'Yas yas yas.'

Dora said, 'I guess I'm doomed anyway. Might as well go down the toilet with Allbright as by myself.'

'Doomed, what do you mean doomed? Down the –?'

'We're all doomed,' said Allbright. 'Jesus it's obvious enough; everybody goes around worrying about machines taking over, shit, they took over long ago, isn't that obvious?'

'But no, listen, what happened to your plan for –?'

'Between computer poetry and vibrator love people don't get a hell of a lot of room to manoeuvre, isn't that obvious?'

'No but your plan for ripping off bank computers, what happened to that? You said a friend in the nut-house steered you –'

'The steersman, yes, aren't we all – but you mean Dan, good old Dan. Well you know I went back to see him, tell him how great it was after they fry your brains, burn out a few pink and blue lights you feel a lot better. I did, I know. I did. I felt better. Not stupider, just happier, that's what I told him.

'Only for him it wasn't like that. They had to burn out more pink and blue lights I guess. Jesus they fried him right back into diapers. I mean, whatever lights he had going for him, they sure as hell went out for good.'

Someone proposed a toast to the happy couple; Jim and the Dean of Persons looked pleased and bashful. The toast was only slightly marred by a shrill voice saying, 'Yas, Rodin. Don't you just love his Thinker?'

Lyle said, 'Maybe he'll get better, though. He won't stay in diapers –'

'Oh, he's better already. They let him out weekends to work his job, even. Fact he's right over there in that glass box, our esteemed disc-jockey.'

'No kidding? That's good, isn't it? He can –'

'He can find the hole in the middle of each record, sure. He can even talk, you notice? Every now and then he says, "Here's another record."'

26

Roderick awoke in jail again, watching Sheriff Benson watch
Top Dollar. Dr De'Ath was sitting in a captain's chair
watching him. Ma was sitting in another watching everything.

'I wouldn't have believed it,' said the doctor. 'Really
amazing. Course, I nearly flunked medical electronics myself,
never could learn to make a good solder joint – but this is
really amazing. Mind if I test him?'

'Ask him,' Ma said. 'Son, how are you?'

'Fine I guess.' Roderick allowed the doctor to look into
his eyes and ears, to tap his knee and hold up fingers for him
to count. 'Guess you're okay too, Doc?'

'Shh!' said the Sheriff. 'Just gettin' to the end of *The
Marriage Stakes*. Already missed *Big Spender* and *Heap or Weep*.'
When the commercial break came on, Dr De'Ath explained:

'Pretty lucky there. After they hanged you some of the boys
got so excited – well, Jake McIlvaney shot himself in the foot.
You know how Doc Welby is about coming out on call, so
they had to let me take care of him. Got him in an intensive
care unit now, over at Buford.'

'Intensive care?'

'Yup, and there he stays until he runs up a nice fat bill.
Anyway I fooled around with him until the highway patrol
came and broke things up.'

'*Lay it on the Line* is next,' the sheriff explained. 'But on
Channel 18 they got *Big Game*, followed by *Grabopoly*. Kind
of a hard choice there.'

'They probably wouldn't have done anything to me anyway,' said the doctor, when he had swallowed a handful of
bright pills. 'Nope, not after you. Kinda put them off the
whole idea, seeing your head come off like that.'

'My head came off?'

Ma nodded. 'I managed to get you home and fixed up.'

De'Ath said, 'Amazing work. Boy if I could do that for

a real patient – well, some day. Your Ma is a wonder, boy.'

Ma cleared his throat. 'I did have some help. Er, asked one of the maintenance men from the factory to give me a hand with the tricky parts.' He held up a mirror for Roderick. 'What do you think?'

'Fine.'

'Fine, is that all?'

'Well it's – very symmetrical – aw heck, Ma, you know I don't know how to talk about art. It's – it's a very symmetrical head. I like it fine.'

They sat and talked as the sky beyond the Venetian blinds began to turn grey, then orange, and as the sheriff watched *Beat the House*, *Chance in a Million*, *Take the Spoils*, *Up for Grabs* and *Cash or Crash*.

'Guess I'll drive over to Buford and see my patient,' said the doctor, after taking his own blood-pressure. 'On my way home, anyway.'

'You're leaving?'

'Got everything I need, now. Airtight case against Katrat Fun Foods. Well. Uh, good luck, boy.' He offered Roderick his hand.

'Good luck to you too, Doctor.'

'I'm glad I did that, shook your hand. You know?'

Roderick didn't know.

'Well it's just that I – last night when your head came off and I saw all the wires – I was really pissed off. The idea of being strung up in the company of a sonofabitching *machine* – I mean it just seemed like adding a last insult to a last – you know?'

Roderick nodded, feeling stiffness in his new neck. 'That's okay. See I'm not so crazy about human beings, either. But good luck anyway, Doc.'

'Wish you boys would pipe down,' said Benson. 'This here is the one I been waiting for, *Bust the Bank*.' He watched that, and *Dig for Treasure*, *Wealthy and Wise*, *Family Fortune*, *Filthy Rich*, *Fakeout* and *Beggar Your Neighbor* before he was again interrupted, by a call from the highway patrol.

The two agents were driving very fast away from the burning wreck.

'Can't go back now, the highway patrol's all over the place. If you had any doubts, why the hell didn't you say something before we torched it?'

'All I said was, he's black. How come they never said he was black?'

'What are you implying, we finalized the wrong guy? What, some black car-thief or what?'

'I'm not implying nothing.'

'Well you sure as hell sound like you're implying something. Listen, you got his licence, is his name Death or isn't it?'

'Sure but –'

'Is he an MD or isn't he?'

'Sure but –'

'And did the receptionist at Buford City Hospital point him out to us as Dr Death or didn't she?'

'Sure. Sure.'

'Well then what's the prob? Study the orders, he has to be the asshole who invented this robot for testing artificial hearts. Dr Sheldon Death, right? The asshole Orinoco wants finalized, right?'

'I don't know. Because on the licence it says DOG EASY APOSTROPHE ABLE but on the orders we got DOG APOSTROPHE EASY –'

'So?'

'And he's not Sheldon neither, he's Samuel.'

After a silence. 'So what are you implying? We finalized the wrong customer?'

'I'm not implying nothing.'

Ma and Roderick sat thinking about Doc De'Ath while the sheriff settled down for *Royal Flush* and *Play for Keeps*. Finally Ma said, 'So. You don't like people much. I didn't know.'

'I like you and Pa.' After a pause, he added, 'And almost anybody else – only one at a time. But when you get them all together, people are so – weird, Ma.'

'You'll get used to them.' He handed Roderick a ticket. 'Now your bus leaves at three-twenty. So you be sure and be out front of the Newer Home Café a little early. You need a recharge or anything before you go? Oil change?'

'I just had one. Ma, don't worry. I guess you got problems enough of your own.'

'Pshaw! Your Pa and I will be all right. Of course they're foreclosing on our home, and Mr Swann is suing us for his fees, not to mention Dr Welby and the others – but on the other hand, all the debts we owe are now in the hands of the Bangfield Trust Bank.'

'Is that good?'

'Good? It's perfect, son. You see, the bank computer has been sabotaged. I don't know how – guess someone somewhere phoned them up, drew out several million and then covered it by – I guess by changing all the plus signs to minus signs – something like that.'

'So does that mean –?'

'Bangfield Trust now owes us a whole lot of money.' Ma winked. 'Of course we won't try to collect. Only numbers, after all. On the astral plane, pluses and minuses are all the same anyway. Now we can just settle down and live –'

'But Ma! Isn't Pa officially dead?'

'Sure. And North America is officially a continent, and the Atlantic is officially an ocean, but so what? On the astral plane, it could all be switched around tomorrow, just like *that*.'

Sheriff Benson cleared his throat. 'You mind not snapping your fingers so loud there, Ma? I'm trying to concentrate on *Lucky Couple*. Heck of a big jackpot there, must be – oh, you leaving young feller?'

'Got to catch the bus.'

'Too bad you can't stick around. In a minute they got *The Big Break*, then *Mr and Mrs Jackpot*, then *Beautiful Winners* – no wait, that's on the other network – they got *Boom or Bust*, *For Richer or Poorer*, *Hit a Gusher*, *Winning Streak*, *Crazy-stakes*, *Cash In*, *Read the Will*, *Slush Fun*, *Crapout* . . .'

But the young man with the symmetrical face – Benson had no idea who he might be – was gone, faster than the time limit for one of them questions on *Take the Cash*. One of them real hard questions.

'. . . Course we're protected, but we ain't exactly gonna make a pile on that deal,' said Mr Kratt's voice. 'Not unless we

344

buy this Bangfield out of Welby's company ... anyway you get your ass back here, next time don't go telling the damn chauffeur how to drive the damn car.'

'Yes sir.' Ben hung up just as the bus was pulling in. Even so, by the time he'd gulped the tepid coffee, paid and tipped, counted his change twice and gathered up his notebook and *God is Good Business*, he was the last one aboard.

He found an empty seat behind a pair of nuns. Across the aisle was a young man Ben thought he recognized, until he saw him full-face (without a birthmark).

'Reading about God, are you?'

'Yes.' Ben turned away quickly to the window. For all you knew, this guy could be one of the executioners last night.

The thought sent Ben back to his notebook:

'In 1791 William Godwin wrote: "A servant who has been taught to write and read ceases to be any longer a passive machine." In this he expressed the fading hope that any distinction could still be made between the common man and the common gadget. For by the time Godwin's daughter had completed her *New Prometheus* (and while in the next room her husband echoed her creation in *Prometheus Unbound*: "And human hands first mimicked and then mocked,/With moulded limbs more lovely than its own,/The human form, till marble grew divine..."), by that time the French had already celebrated their revolution by creating a new automatic headsman, while in England the law declared that men who smash an automatic knitting machine must be hanged – as though they had committed murder.'

The man across the aisle was writing, too. Ben looked away, saw an ambulance go by, and heard one of the nuns:

'Poor Father Warren! Imagine, getting malaria right here in the middle of Nebraska!'

'On top of everything else, Sister!'

'Yes, Sister. No wonder Mrs Feeney thinks he's a saint.'

'Ah, who knows, Sister?'

'Ah, who indeed?'

It was late afternoon in New York, where they were changing one of the flags in front of the UN building. The peacock-blue-and-gold of the Shah of Ruritania came down to be replaced by the tricolour of a new People's Republic. There was no ceremony, nothing to disturb the normal rise and fall of pigeons, flapping up to invisible ledges somewhere above, swooping down to join the sea of columbine grey through which waded a few tourists, among them Mr Goun.

Mr Goun and his camera had come to see the UN building, not to see if it was really (as its architect claimed) a 'Cartesian skyscraper' (Cartesian it was, as any sheet of graph-paper) or 'a passion in glass', but merely to finish a roll of film and the last afternoon of his vacation. He was passionately aware how much his feet hurt, how tired he was of standing like this in groups of tourists, all snapping away at some sight, all complaining about their feet, all anxious to get back to their homes (that is, to the machines in which they lived).

He was lonely. The only person he had spoken to (aside from foot complaints) was a policeman yesterday, who said:

'Watch the way ya carry that camera, buddy. Lotsa cameras snatched like that, see?'

'Thanks, offic –'

He thought of that conversation now, as he reached for his camera and came up with nothing but two ends of the strap, each neatly razored.

'I've been robbed!' he said. No one looked at him.

'Hey I've been robbed!' he said to a man in a Hawaiian shirt (matching the band of his straw hat).

'Yeah? Tough.' The man turned away to continue his conversation with someone else: 'Okay so the Shah was a puppet, but I say, whose puppet? Whose puppet?'

Goun turned and bumped into someone.

'Oh I'm sorry – hey! Professor Rogers, holy –'

'Mistake!' said the other, in an oddly hoarse voice. Indeed, his glittering gold hair did not look much like that of Rogers (except at the roots, where Goun was now looking), and some of his pock-marks seemed to have been filled in with putty.

'But sure you must be, holy, hey it's great to see you Prof –'

'Mistake! Mistake! My name Felix Culpa!'

Goun watched, amazed, as the stranger ran off to jump

346

into a yellow taxi. There was something like blood on the door.

Dear Dan,
The picture on the other side of this card is the post office in Newer where I won't be mailing it. I hope you're feeling better. Ma & Pa send their love. I'm fine.

> Your pal,
> Roderick

Nothing to add, so he stared out of the window as familiar places flickered past: Virgil's Hardware, Joradsen's Drug, Fellstus Motors, the sort of new Simple Simon Supermart, HAIR TODAY, the Legion Hall, the Idle Hour, Violetta's shoppe (now it was to be called VI & I NOTIONS), the pool hall, the library, Buttses Dairy, Bangfield Realty, Welby Investments, the site of the proposed Bangwel Building, Newer Produce, Cliff's junkyard, the motel and chapel, and finally the office recently vacated by Dr Smith the dentist – men were carrying in a new mechanical receptionist, other men were putting gold lettering on the windows:

LOUIE HONK-HONK'S DETECTIVE AGENCY, INC.
Stuff Found Out

NOTE ON *DIE! DIE! YOUR LORDSHIP*

The murderer must be Dr Coué, using the billiard cue, between 8:00 and 8:15, and dropping the clue of the hair. Reasoning is as follows:

1. If the billiard cue was *not* the weapon, then either Drumm embezzled or Coué was blackmailed, or both. If Drumm embezzled, then the daughter was compromised. Since she was not, Drumm did not embezzle. If Coué was blackmailed, then the butler was an addict; if the butler was an addict, then the billiard cue was the weapon. In short, if the cue *was not* the weapon, then the cue *was* the weapon. This contradiction resolves only if:
The billiard cue was the weapon.

2. Since Adam used the polo-stick, and Brett the poker, only Coué or Drumm could have used the billiard cue. (Each suspect had access to only one weapon.)

3. If Coué touched the statuette (weapon) then there was a message under it. If so, then Adam was the thief. If so, then Brett stayed in her room all evening reading. If so, then the bloody handkerchief was used to wipe the statuette. In short, if Coué touched the statuette, he also left the clue of the bloody handkerchief. But we know that Drumm left that clue, not Coué.

Therefore, Coué did not touch the statuette. Therefore he touched the only remaining weapon, the cue:
Coué alone had access to the billiard cue.

From the sentences, a table can be constructed:

SUSPECT	TIME	WEAPON	CLUE
Adam	(earliest)	polo-stick	thread
Brett	?	poker	sooty smudge
Coué	8:00–8:15	billiard cue	hair
Drumm	8:15–8:30	statuette	bloody handkerchief

FINE SCIENCE FICTION AND FANTASY TITLES AVAILABLE FROM CARROLL & GRAF

☐ Hodgson, William H./THE HOUSE ON THE
   BORDERLAND $3.50
☐ Mundy, Talbot,/KING OF THE KHYBER RIFLES
                                       $3.95
☐ Mundy, Talbot/OM, THE SECRET OF AHBOR
   VALLEY $3.95
☐ Siodmak, Curt/DONOVAN'S BRAIN $3.50
☐ Stevens, Francis/CITADEL OF FEAR $3.50
☐ Stevens, Francis/CLAIMED $3.50
☐ Stevens, Francis/THE HEADS OF CERBERUS $3.50

Available from fine bookstores everywhere or use this coupon for ordering:

Caroll & Graf Publishers, Inc., 260 Fifth Avenue, N.Y., N.Y. 10001

Please send me the books I have checked above. I am enclosing $_____ (please add 1.75 per title to cover postage and handling.) Send check or money order— no cash or C.O.D.'s please. N.Y. residents please add 8¼% sales tax.

Mr/Mrs/Miss _____

Address _____

City _____ State/Zip _____

Please   allow   four   to   six   weeks   for   delivery.